Wayward Wulves
Beware

To Nick,
An explorer extraordinaire
& fellow traveller to
applecrans.
Very Warmest Wishes
L N Passmore
april 21, 2018

Wayward Wulves Beware

Eye of the Wulf Series

L. N. Passmore

Star Tunnel Press

ISBN: 1545423091
ISBN 13: 9781545423097
Library of Congress Control Number: 2017907264
CreateSpace Independent Publishing Platform
North Charleston, South Carolina

Published by Star Tunnel Press
Book Cover Illustration by John Patrick

For Dan: More than the integrity and wisdom that define your character, your heart is special.

Table of Contents

Visit www.lnpassmore.com to see a full color map and b/w printable map.

One

Sky-Wulf sees all.

The stars sang their light upon Lisnafaer as gale winds carried a lone wulf's howl across the frozen land. He cried two names: "Anell. Akir."

Akir's spine stiffened. The high wulf choked down a response. Rib-sucking hunger had focused his attention on finding prey; an intruder wulf made a difficult hunt dangerous. He sniffed the gust that lashed the fur on his back, checking for scents and calculating the weather. Winter's icy grip continued through a starving time of relentless snows. Layer upon silent layer had killed off all but the strongest quarry. When Akir's pack grumbled each time a deer or fox escaped their jaws, he told them, "The life of a wulf. Eat snow." Doing the same, he shared their pain.

An unknown wulf's howl near their territory at Lac Lundi meant Akir couldn't long dismiss a deadly challenge to his command. More troublesome, he questioned how it knew his name—and his mate's.

Anell also heard. She joined him. Beaded snow covered her gold coat and mane with the gloss of copper hairs. She shook the snow from her head, showering Akir, and then touched her black nose to his. "Akir. What?"

The two high wulves' steaming breaths evaporated the snowflakes that escaped their hot tongues. Their ears turned, directed toward the last call. As they stared into each other's amber eyes, unsounded questions played back and forth: *Who? Where? Keeper wulf? Answer?*

Akir's black-rimmed eyes shone within a mask, white below and tawny above, reaching from snout's tip to the top of his head and black-tipped ears. His fur, the color of the curling bark of the downy birch along the river banks, bristled. He bared his fangs. That cue taken, Anell joined her mate in a warning howl, guttural and shrill. The rest of the pack joined in from the nearby site of a stripped, half-buried deer carcass.

The interloper called again, this time his urgent cry closer. "Anell. Akir."

Ordering silence, Akir turned back to Anell. *Bold rival or rude fool?*

Anell's sister Feela came to stand beside her: two golden wulves, Anell light, Feela dark. Her russet and auburn markings mirrored Anell's, especially around her soulful eyes. Feela yelped in a tone not at all threatening, welcoming in fact. Akir's black-streaked, soot grey sister Birk struck Feela's ribs before clamping a jaw full of dangerous teeth over Feela's golden brown snout. Birk took care not to draw blood but stifled any further sound from Feela. Having proved her dominance, Birk looked to Akir for approval. He ignored his sister. Feela's flecked tail drooped, but her eyes, focused on Anell, remained defiant.

The strange wulf cried their names a third time. The high wulves debated: *Threat? Warning?*

Akir's tail thrashed, but his rumbling gut urged pursuing food, not a fight. "Forget him. We need to find deer."

Birk's head bobbed.

Feela licked her bruised lips and stared at her sister. *We can't ignore a wulf who may be a keeper—and Birk always agrees with Akir.*

Anell turned to Akir. "But if it's a keeper wulf with lore needful to know, we must answer."

Akir breathed deeply, pulling a hundred scents from the night air. Searching the spring sky, he judged the month of the Ash tree to be about half gone. Soon light and dark would share the day as equals; then, eating the dark, light would grow in strength. Winter's stranglehold must soon fail. His mind made up, Akir ordered the pack's immediate trek north.

"We leave Lac Lundi. Deer head north toward the waters of Lac Alina and I seek deer."

More determined than a scavenging raven, the lone wulf had sought Anell and Akir for five days and nights. Close by the western bank of River Melvalina and at least a half day's run from Lac Lundi, he picked up signs of their pack. Though his spirit remained keen, his tired body rebelled. He needed help. He shook snow and ice balls from his thick ivory fur. In cover of the flurry he transformed, fur changing to bare skin, four legs to two. Standing erect, the former wulf beat his slender-fingered hands upon newly formed arms. After stretching, he let out a piercing whistle . . . and waited. A raw bellow announced a prime stag, panting clouds of frozen breath; the hunter leapt upon his back, his pursuit renewed. Snow muffled the sound of the stag's hooves, a stag carrying a naked rider whose blue skin bore images of wulves. Impervious to the cold, the tattooed Faer One, his white hair streaming in the wind, implored the stag to hurry.

Ten leagues away, the retreating wulves heard the whistle and answering roar. The junior wulves' mouths watered. They turned toward the east. Birk nipped at their tails. "Whatever you think you heard, the cry of a hawk, an owl on the hunt, move on!"

Eight determined wulves pushed north, single file: Akir, Anell, and senior wulves in front, the juniors in the rear. They broke their way through snow drifts spreading like a vast frozen sea.

The shape-shifting Faer One hugged the well muscled neck of the stag and whispered in his ear. As if the very wulves they chased were hot on his tail, the stag raced at a much swifter pace than his rider in faerwulf body had managed after days on the hunt. With each leap they lifted ever higher into the night sky. When the stars twinkled through the stag's royal rack, it seemed a celestial tree hung with lights.

Where wind had whipped away snow from pine-topped undergrowth, the wulves' scent lingered. The stag's body trembled, but the Faer One's knees pressed its sides, urging greater speed. At last the blue rider relaxed and called a halt to the stag's labors. He laid a warm hand on his quivering shoulder. "Accept my thanks, hot-blooded stag. You saved me running many a mile on this bitter chill night. My task demands all my strength and wits." He looked up to the wulf-star, his guide for so many miles. "Go in peace, loyal friend, and may you find your way safely home to your herd."

The Faer One dismounted with a handspring into a high, twisting vault over the antlers, changing back to wulf in mid air. His heart raced. He felt the light of the wulf-star wash over him in waves, singing in his inner ear. He listened and gave thanks. His nose twitched. He knew he was close to the pack.

▲ ▲ ▲

Dawning light crested Mount Enion, most northern of the Wulf Jaw Mountains, and turned the crystal coated snow to smoking gold. The air hummed with invisible currents, like the pursuing wulf's breath, a specter cast upon the wind. Akir had felt it along his spine ever since the pack left Lac Lundi. In the eerie morning mists, pale amber and rose, that haunted Lac Alina, Akir exercised caution. Insisting that he alone seek the intruder wulf, the high wulf had to be fierce with Anell. "Keep safe with the pack. When I return, we'll hunt."

Akir's intuition guided him as he worked his way through the crevices and around the tumble of boulders left after the glaciers' retreat that created the Ice Cliffs of Ice-North. He saw deer tracks in the snow between the slender trunks of hawthorn trees that shot up wherever they could get a root hold. The deer had stripped their bark and departed, perhaps two days ago. He remembered being hungry enough to eat bark. Now that Anell was carrying new life again, he must find food. The thought of Anell warmed him.

"Akir, I bid you halt." That voice, the same that had called Akir's name, came from somewhere above him.

Akir froze. A massive granite outcropping, shaped like a rough-hewn wedge, loomed twenty-five feet over him. Striated rock, covered with ice-coated moss, glowed green in the morning light.

Akir berated himself: *stupid, careless.* He needed no bodiless voice from the sky to tell him not to move. Straining to find the concealed threat, to get a whiff on the wind, Akir bristled. His peaked ears turned in hopeless expectation of sound. His tail, held out but not high, displayed controlled aggression. He ordered, "Show yourself! Your name?"

From the cover of ivy-entangled scrub the ivory wulf, a good twenty pounds heavier than Akir, advanced to the boulder's rim. He gazed down. His fur standing on end, tail pointed to the sky, ears spiked forward, he exposed his teeth but remained mute. Silence compelled Akir to look up. The gaze of Akir's amber eyes locked with that of his pursuer's green eyes.

Akir crouched slightly; his eyes narrowed. *Green! A hide-changing Faer One?*

Two strong wills grappled.

The ivory wulf answered, "I could claim many names." He allowed his black lips to reveal the slightest hint of mirth. "Perhaps on a safer day I'll share one with you. Now you need only know I am but a herald, sent to warn Akir and Anell—"

Akir grunted, pleased to hear his name first.

Hearing that Akir had appreciated the appeal to his vanity, the unnamed wulf shared the cause of his pursuit. "Akir, your Lady and you face danger. I bring not keeper lore but counsel from the sky."

Akir lifted his head to the heavens.

The wulf scowled. "Look not to Silver Gealach by night, nor Gold Grian by day. Sky-Wulf, the wulf-star, calls. I am sent to high wulf Akir. Invite me to stand before you. We must share level ground. I may not speak these tidings aloud to blight the innocent air."

Such an appeal caught Akir off guard. He longed to attack, but his strong will held this blood-fueled urge in check. The heavier wulf had the advantage of high ground. Akir was no fool; he dropped his tail. It didn't matter that Birk would have laughed in his face had she seen; he could sense Anell's warning. "Be wise for the sake of the pack."

The green-eyed ivory wulf, glowing like an iridescent pearl in the light, half crouched; his front legs hugged the rock's ledge. Never wavering in his gaze, he urged, "Akir, bid me stand before you."

Anell called.

The ears of Akir's adversary turned toward the sound. His eyes intensified their gaze at the bemused Akir.

Akir thought of their unborn cubs. His body shook. "Come."

The wulf leapt down, landing five feet from Akir.

Backing up, Akir curled his lips to expose red gums and glistening white fangs. Up close, Akir watched the noble wulf's sleek coat ripple as he breathed.

The ridge up his snout drew Akir's gaze to the white lashed green eyes that seemed to envelope him in their gaze.

Akir's tail flailed in halfhearted beats that dwindled to a stop.

"Akir, lend me your ear."

Akir held his breath and then nodded.

The wulf moved forward, mere inches with each step, straining against advancing too sharply and causing calamity.

His snout passed Akir's wet lips then brushed his twitching ears. "Sky-Wulf warns, 'Have a care for Alba's heirs.'"

"Heirs?" Akir's brow wrinkled. "Anell is Auld Alba's heir."

"Aye, heirs. Ye two have mated, have ye not?"

Akir's nostrils flared. "No concern of yours, messenger wulf."

"True. . . ." The wulf's shoulder muscles rippled. "I am sent by those far greater than I. More there is to Sky-Wulf's words:

'On fateful night bright shooting star
With two tails blazing ice and fire,
When Alba's heir in lawful tryst conceives,
Brings omen from the Otherworld afar.
Fire and ice conspire to warn of auld beasts dire
Before they come and cause all Lisnafaer to grieve.
Have a care for Alba's heirs: the two, the fated pair.'"

⋏ ⋏ ⋏

Sky-Wulf's herald shook his head. "I bring this warning from on high of what the wulf-star saw beneath his eye. Elder called to elder; far underground the wyrm heard. Lisnafaer trembled. The wyrm, he who hoards songs auld and new, made known Sky-Wulf's song. Take heed, Akir."

Avoiding the deadly marrow of the message, Akir chomped on the bone. "Who? Who greater sends green-eyed wulf to accost Akir?"

"Och, have you not heard? Thick-headed, proud wulf—ponder with whom Light Wyrm keeps counsel. Though his realm be deep and dark, he has friends in high places, highest of the Faer Ones. I go in peace, Akir. Sky-Wulf never lies."

He bounded away.

Akir nodded. "Aye, but Faer Ones may, Faer Ones whose hide may change—but not their eyes. Green-eyed wulf, if we meet again—no matter the shape—I'll remember your scent."

Two

New Cubs, New Cares

One great singer: Faer Ones. One greater: wulves.
One great hunter: ravens. One greater: wulves.
One great killer: cutters. None greater.

All winter the Faer Ones sang for the Return of Light. As if determined to hold on to a last stronghold in the sky, the snow defied fledging grasses inching their way up the mountains to Lac Alina. By Oak Month when wulves give birth, the pack welcomed patches of spring green in the melting snow—soon, better hunts and new cubs.

South of Alina, a land of forested rolling hills and lush glens, they pursued the cries of a red deer in distress. The heavy scent of blood and sweat quickened the pack's pace, but drawing closer to their first meal in a week, they paused, wary of a metallic scent. Creeping forward, they discovered a hind very much alive, but unable to flee. Terrified, she thrashed and bleated, showing the whites of her eyes. The iron teeth of a trap held a mangled leg.

Hunger overcame their horror at the detestable device that crippled the hind. They fell upon the creature and ripped her to pieces. All her pain ceased. Akir warned, "Don't tarry to feed. Trap setters may be lurking. Watch for ambush."

They fled north, hauling portions of the former hind, including her un-born calf, the trap in tow. Ravens that had not stayed behind to devour the discarded remnants followed like kites tethered on short strings.

▲ ▲ ▲

Near their den in the mountains north of shimmering Lac Alina, all eyes of the pack focused on Anell. They panted, wet mouths dripping, their heads turning left and right as she wore a path in the snow. With clenched jaws the pack waited for her to give birth. Pine boughs laden with a fresh coating of white canopied the brown scrub and rock shelter where she paced. Light drained from the sky. Eager to hunt, the pack pawed the ground. They awaited Akir's signal.

Anell stopped pacing. She stood rigid but alert.

Sniffing in all directions, the pack detected no danger, but the scent of impending birth, drew their gaze to Anell.

True enough, the cubs-to-be, as yet safe from ice and snow, made known to Anell their time had come. She sought her mate. "Akir, bring me a fat haunch to crunch after the work of the deep den passes. That and your safe return will cheer my heart."

Akir shook his head. He barked, short and fierce. "I stay with you, Anell. I have a right to greet the new ones."

Gathered apart from the bickering high wulves, the pack agitated the snow. The seniors, tails busy, trampled a large outer circle while the ju-niors, their tails hanging discretely down, turned in tight circles within. Akir and Anell glared at each other. The pack froze. Akir growled but lowered his tail.

Her time running out, Anell insisted, "Go. I need food more than your shadow at the den's mouth." Her gaze softened before she cautioned, "Beware the pesky ravens that darken the sky, driving away the warm days that should sweeten Oak Month. They will be on your tails, hungry as ever. 'Feed us! Feed us!' they'll cry."

Left alone, Anell brought forth Kalar and Sonsie, bound for gloom or glory she knew not. Fear and hope battled for supremacy in her heart. She kept her sons snug in their den away from the bite of wind-driven sleet. Lulled by her heartbeats for weeks, they suckled and slept while Anell, starved enough to eat rocks, longed to laugh in the light and chase prey-mates at night.

The pack welcomed the cubs with grateful hearts, thinking them future hunters like any other newly born addition to the pack. Their sire and dam exchanged worried gazes. One of the faerie Lords in wulf guise had hunted them down in the bleak end of winter. His words kept Akir and Anell awake. Not even Auld Dunoon had lore to explain what he meant. Akir snapped whenever any of the pack mentioned Faer Ones.

Ever eager to stretch and run into the outer world, Kalar and Sonsie, their eyes barely open, poked each other and their patient dam. Each time they scrambled towards the light, like bears to honey, Anell nabbed their wagging tails and dragged them back into the wulf-scented dark. Dirt tumbled upon their heads. No nattering ravens would pounce and count the small number of her litter or pluck their fur. Her hot breath swaddled them. "Be not so eager for the world outside with all its wild wonders and woes. Stay and eat while your meal is free and you are strangers to the hunger that burns."

When Feela brought food, Anell confided, "Who can tell cubs anything?" She listened for the Faer Ones' songs and consoled herself with visions of chasing fat deer or running down a shaggy goat distracted by daffodils swarming like bees over the glens.

▲ ▲ ▲

In the month of Holly near the time of the solstice, a few weeks after their birth, Kalar and Sonsie escaped the den. In their new world of light they nosed uncoiling ferns that hid purple and white violets and snatched juicy black ants crawling everywhere. They pestered Akir and Anell to let them roam free but gained only a confined patch for their romps. The smell of spring mud oozing between their toes competed with the biting tang of torn grass and the crazy sweetness of wildflowers. Kalar scuttled along the stream that flowed by the mouth of the den but yearned to break through the natural fence of pines, birch, and thickets of scrub willow that protected the den. Sonsie ran in all directions, seeking the source of the Faer Ones' melodies that haunted his dreams. He watched the ravens soar across the meadow, over the trees and nearby hills, through the morning mists, and on to the high snow covered mountains farther north. He longed to follow, tried to run fast on his stubby legs and leap into the air. As always, he landed with a thud and the sound of laughter from the others, mostly Kalar if he was close by.

The wary pack complained of strange scents, curious sounds, and glimpses of shadowy movements not far from their camp, something other than the scurrilous ravens that rarely gave the wulves any peace. The always fretful adults tightened their guard on the new cubs. While Kalar and Sonsie played with pine cones or scampered after bugs, Akir studied his sons, so different: one dark, one light; one full of spunk, one clever but dreamy.

"Have a care" echoed in his mind. Discovery of the loathsome trap turned vague suspicions into active fear. Proof of trespass with deadly intent, even miles from Anell and their cubs, chilled his blood. Counting on the water kelpies to dispose of the iron-manacled bone, he had cast it in a nearby deep pool. He brooded over who had set it. Not the ravens. Only cutters and Faer Ones had the clever long-toed paws they called "hands." Without doubt, the faerie Lords irked him, but he agreed with Anell—Faer Ones would never harm the very wulf allies they had sworn to protect.

The rest of the pack attempted to make the rambunctious cubs stay close to the den, but oblivious to danger, Kalar and Sonsie nudged their noses, inch by inch, beyond every sticking place. Without fail they heard, "You have much to learn, wayward wulves!"

Undeterred, Kalar scrambled along forbidden trails. Feela lost sleep trying to manage him. "Stop at that rock by the broken pine. . . . Come back . . . now! And don't you shake your face at me!"

Akir threatened to send fierce Birk after Kalar.

Sonsie's eager ears captured enticing, wind-borne music. Anell said, "It's nothing, Sonsie, just the leaves. Come back, now. Take the stick." Her flame-tinged gold coat shone in the light of day. She looked to Feela and cocked her head. *What am I to do? No prey-companion laid that trap; what if. . . ?*

Feela nodded. *Best keep Akir and Birk happy. Get back to the hunt. I'll stay close to the wee ones.*

When the cubs drew in great gulps of air that carried the faintest suggestion of cutter smoke, they muttered, "Smoke? Where?"

"No," Feela said, "the bears are walking. Their hot breaths melt the snow." Her nostrils dilated. She glanced uneasily to the east.

"Where? Where?" demanded Kalar and Sonsie, each keen to see the monster, all hair and claw, not cutter but standing on two legs.

Kalar leaned into the wind. "I will bite him!"

When the junior wulves, two years older than their brothers, were not routing hares nearby or running deer far afield, they chased after Kalar, who remained deaf to warning howls to return to the den. If he outran Birk, his bright eyes beamed. Brindled grey Beag, a joyful senior hunter no matter the prey, often ran him down for the sheer fun of it. Every time he found Kalar, he gave the miscreant a quick swat and added, "Let this be the last, Kalar! You keep us from the hunt—or don't you like to eat?"

Kalar grew like the wayside thistle, all gangly legged. When Feela lugged him home, cat-like, his four paws dangling askew in the air, wulf grins broke into knowing laughter. He twisted and bared needle teeth, braving their worst. No clout or menacing snap ever checked his attempts to elude his exasperated caretakers. More than once his sable coat caused even Anell to mistake him for a black bear cub scurrying through the greening underbrush.

Feela cautioned, "Keeper wulves call from the Wulf Jaw to warn of two-legged cutters sneaking within Lisnafaer's borders."

Birk sneered in disbelief. "Wulves scare away any blade-wielding cutters who dare enter faer lands. You fear what cannot be, nursemaid Feela, useless all last year." Her grey-flecked snout twisted into a feral smile. "Their howls drive the flighty deer to huddle in deep forests where we take our pick."

Akir turned to face the pack. His glossy, hunt-honed body radiated power. Leaning into his determined stride, he pushed between grey Birk and amber

Feela. He nodded agreement with Birk. "The Wulf Jaw Mountains and wulves keep cutters away from Lisnafaer. We never fail our trust."

Feela drew a ragged breath. She lowered her head and curled her golden, black-flecked tail under her belly but dared to challenge Akir and Birk. "Our far-flung kin send warning: cutters grow desperate in the lands beyond Wulf Jaw . . . and we did find a trap."

Three

BITING OFF MORE THAN HE CAN CHEW

Faer Ones: Lords of the Green. Light Wyrm: Lord of the Deep.

E ver since the summer solstice in Holly Month, the light of Gold Grian
dwindled by minutes each day. Such was Light of Day's power that even
now, a month later in Hazel Month, her glow illumined the wooded hills
around the den far into the night. The pack yawned and stretched. Eager to
drive out the last pangs of the long winter, they prepared to chase down a good
meal. They hooted and howled then raced about, stealing sticks and discarded
bones from one another.

The leaping cubs begged first Akir then Anell to let them go hunting with
the pack. Not persuaded by hearing, "No!" they pestered Beag and finally
Feela. Both shook their heads and reminded them their dam and sire had said
"No!" Kalar settled in a sulk under a clump of wild thyme. Sonsie batted the
jawbone of a hare with his nose, picked up what he thought was the sound
of Faer Ones singing not far away, and attempted to push the jaw in that
direction—only to have Birk land on his head. She rolled him over, pressed
his white belly with her big grey paw, and declared, "We go. You stay—or I'll
bite off that nose of yours so you'll never again go chasing bones—or songs!"

Sonsie slunk back to the den, sighed and curled up, but he didn't sleep or lower his head.

About an hour after Grian retired to her island bower, Akir led the pack on a hunt, leaving the two youngest alone with stern warning to stay put. Full-faced Silver Gealach, Light of Night, had just begun to rise. Twilight embraced the land. For several hours Sonsie watched Gealach's light wash over the den site. All the trees and shrubs and especially the rocks seemed to grow taller and fuller, casting crooked shadows in the dead of night. When Gealach's face shone at its fullest, Sonsie could no longer endure being kept from what he was certain beckoned him in the streaming light. He belly-crawled in the direction Akir had led his pack. Equally restless, Kalar bristled. If he had to remain at the outgrown whelping den, so did Sonsie.

Kalar tracked his missing brother with a determination that would have gladdened his sire's heart. Sure enough, Kalar spied Sonsie as he slipped beneath an elderberry bush then scooted along the trail, happily humming one of his infuriating tunes. Overjoyed, Kalar ran to attack. On legs long for one his age, he leapt over the bush. With his paws stretched wide, he fell upon his brother but only grappled Sonsie's tail. "Stop that dratted racket!"

Sonsie yelped. His racing heart pumped iced blood through his body. With eyes wild and angry, he turned to look for Birk. After breathing in Kalar's scent, he expelled a relieved breath. He stuck out his wet, red tongue. "Kalar! Get off!"

Kalar barked. "You get home!"

They fought, first the one then the other on top, their legs and paws flailing so awkwardly that they resembled furry tumbleweeds. They both attempted to bite the object of their cub-sized wrath, but their frenzy merely filled their snouts and mouths with muddy grass. By the time they stopped, they found themselves back at the den.

Kalar glared at Sonsie. Through a huffing that caused his chest to burn, he tried to roar; out came a few angry squeaks.

"We're . . . supposed . . . to stay . . . here! Don't . . . you . . . ever listen?"

"I listen. To everything!"

"Ha! I won't stay . . . here alone, Sonsie! You stay here. Like Birk said." He paused to take a breath. "I'm making a new den . . . just for me—not you!" His rant over, Kalar turned his tail to Sonsie's face. He made great show of striding off on a mission, strutting around the massive, fallen tree trunk that provided shelter to their den site.

On Kalar marched. He ventured far beyond their fixed boundaries, ignoring Sonsie's call to return. "I would take you with me. If I thought you'd come."

Gealach cast her glamour over the countryside. Kalar headed straight for a gnarled oak. Confronted by immense, twining roots that wove around its base, he stopped. Under Gealach's light the swaying branches cast flickering shadows. The roots appeared to writhe.

Sonsie followed the sound of digging. Peering from beneath a tangle of green scrub and fern, he saw earth fly through the air and land behind Kalar, thud upon thud adding to the pile. He crept up from behind to watch his crazed brother dig like an angry badger. He listened, amazed, as Kalar gnashed his teeth, as if gnawing on an imagined bone of countless injuries, and muttered dark thoughts about being left with a "magpie like Sonsie . . . unfair . . . I can outhunt Feela, at least."

Sonsie's nose twitched. *I could be a hungry bear or a curly-tusked boar for all he knows.* He tried to decide whether to laugh or shake his head in dismay at the target of Kalar's waving tail.

Some earth flew directly behind Kalar, barely missing Sonsie; the rest of the loosened dirt and rocks fell into a hole he had never made.

The opening exuded a strange odor. Sonsie grumbled. Kalar kept on, getting the same results. Finally Sonsie growled, "Kalar, stop!"

Kalar paused just long enough to whip his gaze in Sonsie's direction. In a face worthy of Birk he cried, "I don't need you." He started to dig again then turned to face Sonsie. "I don't want you—not anywhere—but most of all, not near me!"

His sudden backward movement tumbled him into the hole. His legs thrashed as he fell several feet into darkness lit by an eerie glow off to his left. Debris showered his head and back. He swiped his tail back and forth and shook.

From above Sonsie called, "Kalar!Areyouhurt? What'sthatsmell? Watchout!"
"Sonsie! Go Away!"
"Get out of there, Kalar, before—"
Too late! Some beast twice the size of Akir, maybe bigger, undulated toward Sonsie's rash brother who lay trapped. The creature's scales reflected Gealach's shining face as an iridescent, silvery light within the confined gloom. The wyrm slithered nearer, ever nearer, enveloping Kalar in the scent of primeval earth.

Kalar refused to budge, but his nose curled. He coughed. Sonsie could hear Kalar's heart pounding as fast as his own. What they saw—a legless dragon, glowing white and silver flecked—amazed their young eyes. This wyrm had no wings, but atop his triangular head sat glistening, curved ram horns.

Kalar's ears lay back against his head. His eyes widened. His lips pulled back to expose tiny teeth. With all his heart Kalar wanted to attack, if only to rid himself of the detested panic this creature inspired. Kalar willed his ears forward. He attempted a feeble growl over parched throat and dry tongue. The ram-horned wyrm reared, fixing his baleful glare on Kalar. A slender black tongue issued from the wyrm's mouth. It tested the air between them, all the while fixing his glittering eyes on Kalar's.

Enraged at this affront, Kalar rose to attack.

"No!" Sonsie screamed, jumping into the pit. He pressed against Kalar so tightly that they looked like a two-headed wulf.

The bright wyrm coiled, leaned forward, and reared again.

Sonsie burst into song. He let all the spectral images that had teased his brain day and night live through his tongue. His young voice filled the pit and lifted into the night. What he sang made no sense to the wulves, but the entranced serpent relaxed his tightly wound spine and swayed.

Kalar charged. All his longing and frustration fueled his leap, right at the wyrm. He clamped his jaws on the cold, reptilian body and shook his head with all his might. The strangled snarl of a frenzied but overmatched wulf reverberated within the hollow. Sonsie gaped in horror.

The halting of song on top of the physical attack served one terrible purpose. The wyrm's attention snapped to the invaders of his domain. Gathering strength, he tossed Kalar in the air; his horned head butted him smartly. Kalar thudded against the earth wall. Sonsie froze, torn between wanting to defend Kalar and needing to acknowledge the wyrm's astonishing splendor. He voiced that beauty in a heartbreaking melody—to remarkable effect.

Light Wyrm raised his head and glided left and right, back and forth, until he came to rest before Sonsie and stared at him, head lowered and prodigious jaws cracked wide. His black tongue slid forth to an alarming length.

A sulfurous vapor assaulted Sonsie's nose. His throat closed.

The wyrm's tail smacked Sonsie. He gasped a breath.

"Ah, little wulves, so bold, so foolish. Break into my hideaway. Offer no token of good will." His black-slit oval eyes glared at Kalar. "And bite me!"

He slithered ever closer. "To kill ye. . . ." The wyrm paused, his tongue flicking in and out between curved fangs. "A waste . . . if ye be the Ones? Little one . . . more than black? Little one . . . more than white? What be the truth of ye, tiny beasts of hide and hair? I shall taste ye."

Sonsie backed up until he bumped against the wall where Kalar stood, awestruck. Side by side they faced this strange creature who spoke to them of tasting. They trembled but dug their nails into the ground. The wyrm crept closer. The aroma of countless scent-markings fallen deep within the moist earth assailed their wet noses.

Sonsie sneezed. *Stag?*

Kalar's snout wrinkled. *How stag? This shining thing is no red deer!*

The wyrm smiled. His forked tongue stretched toward the brothers. It slid over their noses and lips. With eyes closed in a seeming dream, he hummed to himself. The brothers ceased breathing. Never in their short lives had they encountered such a beast. Certainly none of the pack had warned of a black-tongued, ram-horned wyrm shining white like Gealach. Yet the fantastic creature loomed before them, way too close for comfort.

"I kiss your eyes, black boar wulf. I kiss your ears, white apple wulf." Once again the tongue flicked and then gently slid over Kalar's eyes, Sonsie's ears.

"Ye both must leave. Do not come back. In future times, as ye are running with your pack or chasing the faer singers of the forest, should ye come upon any of my cousins, do them no harm, as I have done none to ye. Keep on your paths, mighty hunter, gallant singer; no doubt we shall meet again. Now go, before I recall how hungry I get when attacked and think that wulf cub is my favorite meal."

The wyrm herded the cubs with his ram-horned head. He lifted them out of the hole. Once their paws grasped the curling roots of the ancient oak, they clambered for dear life and raced for the very den site they had been told not to leave.

Having taken good measure of Anell's new pups, the wyrm disappeared into the bowels of the earth before they had cleared the coiling roots. He brooded over the unexpected guests: brother wulves. The highest of the high wulves' sons. White and black. Something deeper . . . and hidden? Light Wyrm's ancient mind debated if they could be the ones of whom Sky-Wulf had sent warning. The curious wyrm curled into a wallow, rested his ram-horned head upon a pile of rubble, and ransacked his treasure trove of memories. All night the wyrm's black tongue, highlighted by the glow radiating from his coiled body, disturbed the air.

Gealach shone directly above the gnarled old oak, its leafy crown showing green in contrast to the black and grey leaves below and those of neighboring trees. As she declined to the west, the light dimmed so that only the keenest eyes could see. By the time a wooly caterpillar could crawl to the oak's tip, Grian had already begun to rise. Mingling their light, Gealach and Grian held the world in a silver-gold net.

A pile of winter-dropped leaves near the oak rustled. Two huge eyes emerged from the mound. They belonged to the tree's guardian ghillie dhu, a Solas Faer One who resided in the sprawling birch thicket that nearly surrounded the oak. Clothed in leaves and moss, he seemed invisible to most, except to those who tended the trees and all that lived in their shelter. He saw much but said little. The ghillie dhu blinked and rubbed his eyes, pondering the disturbance to his night's sleep. New wulf cubs usually meant good gossip to pass along to a Greenguard. He shook his head. *But this? Anell and Akir's cubs . . . and the White One Who Crawls! Must find the Greenguard.*

The dull thwack of metal hitting wood distracted it. *Cutter axes? On this side of Wulf Jaw Mountains?* He shuddered.

Sneaking away from behind a nearby rock, a creature that looked like a hedgehog rolled in the direction Kalar and Sonsie had taken. It picked up their scent in the weeds along the trail and sucked the leaves upon which the cubs had left invisible pieces of themselves. Foam, tasting just like Kalar and Sonsie, overflowed a whiskered mouth. A tongue reached from below a little black button snout to lick quivering lips. Having done so, the urchin transformed into its usual Dorcha Faer bogey shape. Coarse and shaggy matted hair sprouted in patches from blotched skin crusted with scabs. The small bogey hobbled along on clawed hands and feet to follow the unwary cubs, intent on getting home to their den before the pack.

Four

Songs and Secrets

To find food, follow the scent. To learn secrets, follow the raven.

That same night late in month of the Hazel, Anell joined the pack for the first time since Kalar and Sonsie's birth. Engrossed with finding elusive prey-mates, she and Akir let their sons drop from thought like lost tufts of winter hair. Near dawn of the morning after the cubs' fateful escapade, while Faer Ones sang and the wulves hunted, three of Raven Lord Dooleye's eager spies flew south of Lac Alina. They spotted Akir and his pack, just leaving the cover of rhododendrons and willow scrub to make their way through a lush mix of waving ferns and grasses.

Moving closer to the wulves, the sky-scavengers viewed the packs' heaving ribs and empty jaws. They looked for any prey the pack had missed. Then they recognized Anell—hunting with the pack.

One said, "Their cubs must be back at the den, alone!"

The second said, "Lord Dooleye could have warned of perils for unguarded cubs."

The third answered, "Yet what proud wulves seeks advice from ravens?"

They swooped near enough to count the wulves' whiskers. The weary pack plowed single file through wet grasses. Sharp leaves upon thick green stems, heavy with tan seed heads, whipped their legs and caught on the wulves' draggling winter fur. The squawking ravens swooped across their path.

One laughed. "Akir will suck muck-caked paws this day."

The second said, "Hungry cubs will cry for food."

The third cautioned, "Hungry wulves, hungry ravens!"

Akir leapt. His flaring tan ruff accentuated his black-rimmed eyes. "Again! Come to steal the last bite from a wulf's mouth. Scunner ravens!" He spat. "Try eating mud."

A tease before turning back, the ravens flew beyond his gaze, honed to a deadly resolve.

Feela cried, "False-hearted ravens!"

Anell added, "They laugh, but no mirth; they cry, but no tears!" The sisters' golden bodies shook.

The dry-mouthed wulves licked their lips. Eager to return to the den with enough prey to restore the fat lost through the harsh winter, they shrugged off their tormenters' return, grimly amused that no food denied the robber-ravens even one bone to fight over.

In the first glimmers of morning light the laughing ravens turned again and flew straight to the den nestled in the folds of tree shaded hills, well hidden from all—except those who command the sky. Dead silent and keen-eyed, they scanned the terrain until their hearts raced at an unexpected sight—the cubs dashing home—shadowed by a shambling bogey!

▲ ▲ ▲

Once safely at the den, Kalar pulled his muzzle into an ugly scowl. "Never speak of this, Sonsie."

Sonsie swallowed a big lump of pain. "Trust me, Kalar."

The bogey wriggled under a tangle of vines. Its rough tongue searched for a few more specks of the wulf-spiced froth. "Nae, nonnie, nonnie, not me, not me, wayward cubs."

Silent laughter convulsed its scabrous body, but as a trio of shadows crossed over, it locked stark-stiff, knees grasped to chest, to transform into the semblance of a hedgehog.

Daring to look up, the bogey saw three ravens settle into the towering grandfather oak that gave them cover and full view of Anell's den. The bogey put its ear to the ground. Sibilant chanting made its head buzz. Quivering, the bogey muttered. "Busy night, this. Eeny meeny miny mum. . . . More to come . . . more to come."

▲ ▲ ▲

T he ravens' triumphant black eyes reflected dawn's light. Two cubs! Only two! Black and white. The ravens kept mute. In addition to the cubs' mewling for food, they heard the ground sing, no, some song arising from the ground, somewhere near the massive roots of the tree. Then they sniffed something that skewed their tail feathers. *What's this? What's this?* They fidgeted, nearly driven mad with desire to screech. Snippets of unfamiliar song floated on the air that carried the fermented lava scent of Light Wyrm. Near Anell and Akir's pack!

"To Raven Lord!" Swift as thought they flew south to their roost in Wulf Paw Forest.

▲ ▲ ▲

D ooleye's curiosity blazed. No raven can abide wulves with secrets—especially cub secrets. If those secrets included Light Wyrm . . . ? In all of Lisnafaer, Dooleye knew of no greater hoarder of secrets than the ram-horned dragon. He had to know why the wyrm lurked underground so near Akir's pack and sang about "cats-fire" and "woes-dire."

From dawn to dusk he stirred the smoldering coals that fired his cunning brain. A blanket of grey clouds blew in from the coast. Leaves rustled in the roost. The ravens flew scavenger sorties, but Dooleye's iron claws held his perch in a death grip. He scratched his black head against a low lying branch. What did "troubles doubled" mean? He searched his memory for an auld tale: apples . . . apple thief . . . wulves. . . . Wulves! Anell, heir of Auld Alba the apple thief? Anell and Akir . . . or . . . their *two* cubs? Grian's light flashed from the western sea and turned the under clouds to flame.

Dooleye screeched as if flying to battle. He soared from his roost to see for himself. In his wake followed the three spies: Bumflebeak, Grouser, and Dooleye's cousin Knackerclaw. Maneuvering in a tight aerial cartwheel, Dooleye turned upon his pursuers and sent them back to Wulf Paw Forest. On this starless night he alone claimed this quest.

An ebon streak in the fiery clouds, he flew to the ancient oak. In the last dregs of light Dooleye could make out the two wulf cubs, embracing in a curled fuzz ball, grey under the night sky. All well and good, but he detected no sign of the wyrm, neither by song nor by scent. He dug his claws into the bark, arousing the sleeping tree, none too happy at having his slumber interrupted.

"Wisdom-Shield, where is Light Wyrm?"

"Gone!"

Under low clouds Dooleye flew south, straight to another of the wyrm's lairs near Lac Lundi. The relentless bird's hunch paid off. The wyrm's strong scent pulled him down from a sky as dark as his feathers. Settling in a tall silver birch near several shorter whispering aspens, Dooleye folded his glossy wings under his tail. Silently he watched—and listened. Upon the blackest hour of the night when Raven Lord became invisible, the wyrm rewarded him with what he had come to hear.

Laughing, in spite of the chill that gripped his heart, he took to the sky, savoring the notion of gloating before Akir, not now, oh no, but some glad-some day when he could turn this nugget to his advantage. Dooleye whipped the wind with his shining wings and caught a glimpse of Great Grian the Gold, just rising in the east over Wulf Jaw Mountains. Unable to stifle the urge to tell her what he had learned, he cracked his polished black beak and greeted Grian, as yet unaware of the menace threatening her world for which she gladly shed her light.

⋏ ⋏ ⋏

"'Stones for faerblack hunter, bones for faerwhite singer,
Snails for terror dire, tails for cats-bane fire,
Beans for green, beware the ever-never seen,
Light for white, beware the kiss that bites,
Huzzah for songs that hold back endless night
When troubles doubled unleash foul appetite. . . .'"

⋏ ⋏ ⋏

Raven Lords with secrets—wulf secrets—is another thing ravens cannot abide. In flight over Lac Alina far away from their Lord, Knackerclaw, Grouser, and Bumflebeak gossiped, trying to crack a tough nut. Dooleye slept, one eye open, with cats and cubs on his brain, but what had cats to do with wulves—deer-friends, deer-foes? Grouser said to forget the deer and find out why wulf cubs, why now? Beside him, Bumflebeak held that Dooleye worried about rats on a wire or cats afire. From above Knackerclaw merely chuckled. "Wulves don't burn cats; that's cutter work, foul work for grim deed—"

"And thereby shakes a tail," Bumflebeak cut in.

They heard a cackle. "Forget not what Dooleye mutters in the dead of night: 'fire and cats, cutters mad, green burnt. . . .' Knackerclaw shrieked. 'And Dire Ones returned.'"

Grouser shot him a look of pure malice. He confided to the companion at his side, "Never! The Faer Ones hold the Dire captive."

"For now!" croaked Knackerclaw, calling down to his double shadow.

Five

Who is Master of the Hunt?

Let a raven pick your bones—expect to choke.

The next day a heavy downpour accompanied the dawn, quite usual for the last days of Hazel Month. The pack out on a hunt hardly noticed, but Kalar hated getting soaked. If he stayed outside the den, he got wetter. If he scrunched inside, he carried the wet with him into the mud of his own making. He growled, irritated beyond endurance at being stuck with auld blatherskite Sonsie, especially after his own blunder almost got them killed.

He couldn't shake off the water fast enough or find dry shelter. Thoroughly miserable, he began to howl, only to choke on the water.

Sonsie laughed, curled his tongue to the rain, and drank his fill.

Kalar squirmed. "Sonsie, shut up!"

The skies cleared just as the bedraggled pack returned to camp. All rejoiced over the good hunt—at last—all but Kalar and Sonsie who nursed their terrible secret. The wind picked up, carrying a sweet fragrance through the silver birches. Two of the junior wulves called it wild cherry smoke, but the rest of the pack declared they sensed no hint of the cutters who pursued their strange ways east of the Wulf Jaw Mountains. High in the pines and oaks a haunting tune seemed to flow from branch to branch and broke into merry song as if all the leaves had turned to skylarks.

Sonsie shook the last drops from his fur. Such melodious trees, certainly a sign that Faer Ones were near, captivated his attention. So far he had not seen any, but he had seen the bright white, long-fanged serpent with the wrong head. Sonsie trembled, ecstatic—and afraid. Could the shining white wyrm be a Faer One?

"Sonsie," called one of his elders.

"Sonsie." This second voice seemed like an eagle's cry from beyond the horizon.

"Sonsie!" Birk barked. "Come here to eat. Now!"

Feela watched Sonsie. Alert to the allure of the enticing sensations that lingered after the passage of the Faer Ones, like dream creatures, she feared the call of their delicious melodies would increase their hold upon his soul. Her sharp nudges to Sonsie's furred rump often failed to make him mind. She made her way around Birk and gave him a powerful smack. "Better me than your sire," she said.

Birk snarled but, being too hungry to bother with the cubs' nursemaid, passed on the opportunity to harass Feela.

After the drenching rain, the day continued hot and steamy. The wulves had gorged on their catch and now lay mingled in sleepy clusters, grooming themselves. Content, they rested in the shade of the rhododendrons and birches, trees much favored by the Faer Ones. Two juniors, Karlon, a prankish male with black, grey-flushed fur, and sharp-eyed Mundee, a female with pale gold-dusted black and brown coat, nestled against a fallen timber covered in moss. Its exposed roots helped to hide the den. Its white trunk reached across the rocky stream about twenty-five yards from the den. Sweet-faced Ro, their den mate, had plopped herself at the edge of the riotous wildflower meadow that separated the rocks and water by the den and the higher, treed ground.

A breeze blowing across Lac Alina north to the den site brought a welcome coolness and picked up the fragrance of the bluebells and foxglove in full bloom. The pack roused enough to discuss the fast-growing cubs, off by themselves tumbling over each other as they attempted to catch field mice and voles. Upon concluding that Kalar was hopeless, the pack turned their attention to Sonsie.

Their full bellies encouraged the junior wulves to join in. Karlon ventured, "Sonsie never openly defies us. He merely wanders off the well-marked paths."

Ro joined her brother and sister. She was a pale cream all over except her face, distinctly white, until just below her eyes. The hairs from the eyes to the tip of her ears produced a mask in a subtle mix of gold and beige. Even when she scowled she somehow looked pleased. The rest of the pack knew to watch for occasional temper flares. Ro shook her head. "Wanders off? He's gone like the hare when the eagle's shadow swoops down the glen." She laughed, but her eyes remained defiant. "I will no longer chase this troublesome gnat."

"Och, you will!" Birk snapped. "Your duty, now that Anell has rejoined the hunt. We need her with Akir, leading with Beag and—"

"And you, fleet-running Birk, yes we know who's mad to lead this pack," Karlon broke in.

"Swallow your tongue, bent-tailed Karlon, or I'll give you another scar over your other eye!" Birk glared, her fangs bared and snout wrinkled. Her close set eyes accentuated her sharp snout.

Eager to prevent a tussle, Mundee, the most even-tempered of the three juniors, ventured, "Isn't Sonsie growing into a fine howler for a wee mite?"

"Och! A daffin wanderer, Sonsie, squeaking and yelping on and on." Beag grinned. "And on! Easy to find. Birk, be glad for good kills and full bellies. Soon we'll move the pack; good trails mean good order."

Feela quickly added, "Sonsie's such a lovely color, like foam on shining water. Have you noticed? When light beams stream aslant the land and cast rock shadows, they cling to him like fog."

Birk sneered. "What drivel! And where are the whelps, Feela?"

Feela bristled, thought better of it, tucked her tail before Birk, but pointed her nose toward the den. "Right over there where I left. . . ."

Kalar and Sonsie were nowhere in sight.

As if lightening-struck, Anell dashed to the den, sniffed, and ran off through the bracken.

Akir joined her in grim-jawed pursuit. Birk took the opportunity to bite Feela's haunch. Only then did Birk lead the rest of the pack to join Akir and Anell's howls to call home the cubs.

Feela chewed her tail then wailed a lament that rose from her heart's depth. Hours later, it seemed to her, they heard a great commotion. Akir arrived first, carrying and shaking Kalar whose tail wagged like a willow branch. Not far behind them came Anell, her jaws clamped firmly on Sonsie's ruff.

Their full mouths prevented them from voicing the fire in their eyes. They spat out their sons who rolled, their tails well tucked, into the junior wulves who leapt in the air and howled. Akir and Anell pivoted and reared in time to confront a sight that set the entire pack yelping in angry snarls.

Beating wings churned the air. Raven Lord Dooleye dropped from the sky. In his claws a creature changed from a screeching hedgehog with spikes flared to a snorting pig-muzzled bogey. Behind them a phalanx of ravens flew like a battle banner of death. The frenzied pack's spittle burnt the grass. Their snarls nearly drowned the ravens' cries. Dooleye's honed talons ripped the throat and gut of the bogey then tossed its carcass to Knackerclaw. The wulves and ravens long debated whether a merciful Raven Lord kept the bogey from being torn asunder by the maddened wulves—or, as the wulves claimed, he took advantage of Akir's fear for his sons to mock the high wulf before his pack. When Knackerclaw and his blood-beaked gang hopped close to Akir then danced away, their jig more irritating than their taunts, what else could they think?

Kalar and Sonsie nestled between Karlon, Mundee, and Ro. All shook, their indignation battling fear.

Dooleye flew upward until he seemed a speck in the sky.

Knackerclaw strutted up to Akir. "From his flights far and wide our Lord brings back a teaser from the wyrm, he who rules the crevices and caverns deep of Lisnafaer. Know you his riddle, High . . . Wulf . . . Akir?"

Akir glared. Ravens had a unique talent for calling his name and sneering, turning his honor into insult. The air smoked—the danger palpable.

"No?" jeered Lord Dooleye, having plummeted two hundred feet before landing nearly on top of Akir's nose. "Allow me to share Light Wyrm's poser:

▲ ▲ ▲

'Two there be who run by two; both by four when a horse will do.
One there be who changes shape; the blade of the other few escape!
Solas or Dorcha it matters not; all be caught in the gruesome plot.
Worse by far the auld brutes grim, the venomous tail, the jaws blood-rimmed.
Cats afire to no avail, unless ye hear Alba's heirs wail.
Faerblack, faerwhite these brothers must be, before, alas, auld dule ye dree.'"

▲ ▲ ▲

Dooleye's scouts surrounded him. Bumflebeak coughed. "Shape-shifting Faer Ones. Chancy!"

Grouser spat. "Hewers and hackers. Deadly!"

Knackerclaw puffed his breast. "Caw! Their leavings, by ambush dark or battlefield red, feed many a hungry raven—"

"But who," interrupted Lord Dooleye, "dare call back dire grief to suffer?"

Raven Lord signaled his cohorts. With a mighty whoosh they left the bewildered wulves who chomped at tail feathers wagging in merry derision.

"Hungry wulves, hungry cutters," Bumflebeak cried.

"Wary Faer Ones," Grouser called.

"Ravening Dire Ones," Knackerclaw added and nodded to his cousin.

Intending to have the last word, Raven Lord turned and glided down to Akir before he led his flock into the clouds. "So, sire of wayward sons, who is master of the hunt?"

Six

Who Watches the Cubs?

It takes a pack to run deer—long may they thrive.
It takes a pack to raise cubs—long may they live.

Kalar and Sonsie pressed their bellies into the moist earth but held their heads high, their ears twisting left and right. They watched Akir alternately pace and run all around the den site, treading down weeds and wildflowers alike. Suffering Akir's anger proved worse than facing the wyrm. They winced at his howls, punctuated with wet-toothed snarls. His fangs, double pronged, sharp and curved, needed no venom to kill. When his wrath died down, Akir called the pack. They assembled before him in a semi-circle, like the seven Wulf Jaw Mountains that guard the eastern borders of the Faer Ones' realm.

Kalar and Sonsie tried to follow Feela, but she burdened them with threats vivid enough to make Akir's teeth seem no more than pine needles. Her loving eyes softened her harshness, a sign not lost on the cubs. They watched her slink up to the agitated pack; all glared at her, even Anell. Unseen, Kalar and Sonsie crept to the fallen birch to hide within the exposed roots. Their wide-eyed gazes followed Feela. Her sigh chaffed their ears. She shook her head and looked wistfully toward the fragrant glens within the rolling hills to the west.

Akir led a pack howl, so severe it made Kalar and Sonsie cringe. Feela hurried to join the group and add her voice, but when she got to the assembled wulves, Akir commanded the raging cries cease. Feela tucked her tail under her lowered body and placed her head on the ground before the high wulf.

Sonsie felt sick. He crawled forward under cover of the rocks.

Akir refused to acknowledge Feela's presence. Birk bared her teeth and started a growl that sounded like churning gravel.

A flicker of remorse prompted Kalar to creep to his brother's side.

Anell cut Birk short. "Akir!" she cried.

He barked at his mate but forced Birk to back away. After a glance at Anell, he confronted Feela. "How did my sons escape your watch? Why did they have to be rescued from a bogey! By Dooleye?"

The cubs stared at each other. *What bogey?*

They climbed the rocks to get a better view of the whole pack.

"Kalar and Sonsie. . . ." She raised her head. Seeing Akir's grim expression, she calmly lowered her gaze but could not stifle her racing heart. "More bold . . . more. . . ." She coughed, clearing her throat. She dared to look up; confusion flickered in her eyes. "More ferlie than any of our cubs, living or dead, ever were. Restless. . . ." She paused to collect her thoughts. "Kalar's scrabbling paws . . . Sonsie's dreaming head. They make escapes like lucky hares finding a hole." She tucked her muzzle between her front paws on the ground.

Anell's eyes narrowed. "Any other bogies or dangers?"

Akir raised his tail and fixed his stare upon the nursemaid. Feela remained silent. He started to pull a low growl from his gut.

"There's always danger for the young," Feela muttered, head down.

The cubs strained to hear.

Akir's breath raced hot and dry. "Any two-legged cutters and their blades? Or worse— any meddlesome Faer Ones spying and singing their dratted songs?"

Sonsie's tail wagged dangerously. Kalar whacked his head against Sonsie's.

"No." Feela looked for the cubs back at the den mouth, but they were gone. Her heart thudded so that the cubs, hiding way too close to their irate sire, could hear. She raised her head to Akir. "Just prey bigger and faster than—"

"So, Feela," interrupted Anell, "are you not up to the task?" She stared directly at Feela. "Only two . . . alive . . . after all, at this birthing."

With an effort Feela kept her haunches on the ground, but her tail whipped back and forth. "I am. When they won't stay by the den, I wear my paws nearly to the bone chasing them. But I am only one. Kalar is going to get his too long nose in a too short badger hole. He'll be the worse for it."

The flies swarmed, playing games, whispering nasty secrets in the wulves' ears.

Akir snorted. He lashed his tail and bit at the flies. "Serve him right. See what he's made of. Sooner he learns the better."

"True." Anell spoke for Feela.

"True," Feela agreed, "tears and tatters heal. I can nurse a cub wounded by a cranky fox or pine martin. It's Sonsie who shadows my heart."

Akir barked. "Sonsie sits on his rump staring into the air like a stone stump. It's not Sonsie shadows that grind my bones. Lords of Light! So the Faer Ones call themselves." Peering all around, he growled. "Faer songs, faer shadows—night and day—annoying prey with their Grand Trooping Rades, always—"

Anell interrupted. "Aye. Perhaps a stone Sonsie is no bad thing when . . . will-o'-the-wisps haunt the woods."

Akir snarled then named the favored members of the pack: "Anell! Birk! Beag! Karlon, Mundee, Ro!"

Kalar and Sonsie watched Feela being forced to the outer rim of the newly formed muster. She planted her paws firmly but at a distance, near the fallen birch. Hardly daring to breathe, they witnessed her discovery of their paw marks leading to the tumble of rocks by the den behind Akir and the pack. All the golden hairs along her spine stood on end. When she stared at the two trouble makers, Sonsie stifled a nervous yelp.

Akir drew their attention. "Our cubs take on the big snout and the long legs." He scowled. "All must attend them, but let them roam Wulf Paw to learn its secrets and the ways of our prey-mates. Keep them away from the Faer Ones: the Solas Court and Greenguard, the Dorcha Host and Nightguard." He sneezed, sounding as if he were coughing up sick grass.

Anell's withers twitched.

Their noses quivering and mouths dripping, the cubs concentrated on their sire.

He sniffed the air. "The wulf must share the night with Dorcha-Faers who prowl Lisnafaer at dark, they say to "keep order." But I like not bogies and others of their ilk. They interfere with lawful hunts. Spook prey. Put hunters off the scent. The one Dooleye caught was up to no good."

He howled three staccato bursts. "The Solas-Faers who love the light care more for their prancing, caterwauling tours than they do for the trees they claim to guard.

"Both our new sons," Akir continued, "are prized prey. Let the Faerdark steal cutter cubs. Not Kalar and Sonsie. Watch well. We must keep them safe from bear and mountain cat, aye—" Kalar and Sonsie wriggled happily to hear Akir's unexpected praise and care for their safety, but they dislodged stones that tumbled down the rocks. They halted and held their breaths. Happily for them, Akir frowned at Mundee and Ro. After the junior wulves heard the noise in Akir's throat, they stopped scratching. The cubs breathed a subdued sigh.

Akir paced, grinding his paws into the grass as if he were stamping out noxious ground beetles. Flashing a second glower at Mundee and Ro, Akir continued. "We must keep Kalar and Sonsie safe from Dorcha-Faers *and* Solas-Faers whose wily songs lure the foolish."

He continued to pace. "I want hunters, both cubs, not just Kalar. They hunt prey-mates. Not faerlight song! Where Sonsie goes Kalar may follow."

Sonsie's ears perked.

Akir's snout wrinkled into a dreadful grimace. "Born of Auld Alba's heir, they risk ruin should they meet strange prey from the sky with tails of fire and ice."

The bewildered pack looked at Akir as if he had eaten the warty red-capped sick mushroom.

Expecting the sky to fall upon their heads that moment, Kalar glared at Sonsie.

The breeze whispered itself out to leave behind the late afternoon heat and the distinct hum of bees gorging on nectar. Flies searched for any dead flesh the wulves may have dropped.

Akir nudged Anell. She trembled. She pretended to bite a fly. "So, heart's rest, you take the faerwulf's warning to heart." She laid her head over Akir's shoulder and stared at Feela whose tucked tail nearly reached her lowered head.

Sonsie nosed his brother. "Faerwulf? What warning?"

Akir broke away and pivoted, tail and ears erect, ruff raised. "Aye! Are they not my sons? Kalar bodes to become a great hunter. Sonsie . . . a keeper. But let him stray beyond lore of trails and prey, Alba's blood will doom him, Kalar too."

Puzzled, Sonsie stared at Anell who turned toward Feela. As if Anell were at his side, Sonsie heard her thought, *No doom to me.*

Looking up, Feela nodded.

ᐱ ᐱ ᐱ

Birk moved forward, positioning herself beside her brother. The beige and black hairs that surrounded Akir's amber eyes emphasized his keen intellect. Birk's grey eyes showed mere cunning in less defined coloring, a gradual white to grey-flecked hairs from the tip of her long snout to her close set eyes. She curled her lip to Anell but quickly looked down.

Akir sneezed, as if to clear his snout of a worrisome flea. "I sense spies on unwary wulves, young and auld." His tail lashed. "If Faer Ones—we do our own watching of the cubs!"

His ears turned, catching a faint metallic ringing. No song of larks or faeries, this sound no four-legged being, no winged creatures of Lisnafaer ever made. "If cutters—beware their traps. We move from the den. Soon."

He turned to direct his eyes up to the rocks. "You two. Come down. Now!"

As if snake-bit, the cubs leapt up. Akir's slit-eyed gaze pulled the clambering Kalar down the rocks. Just as Kalar moved, the sound of whistling many miles to the east distracted Sonsie. It worked its way into his inner ear, awaking one of the dream melodies that haunted his night. His tail flailed, almost out of control. He yipped, broke into a high pitched howl, and took off over the rocky mound to the east, heedless that his eager heart invited calamity. Kalar turned and followed, stretching into a cub-sized lope.

Chasing them and gaining on both, Feela dashed to get ahead of their mad run. Outmatched by their surprisingly swift caretaker, the cubs ran smack into her wide open jaws. By the time she had them on their backs with one of her paws pinning each of their exposed bellies, the pack caught up to them. They all circled Feela and the once again disgraced cubs.

"Good work, Feela," Anell said.

Akir grunted. After his breathing settled, he rasped, "Get up!"

The wulves made their way back to the den site with Anell and Akir in front of the cubs and Feela, Beag, and Birk right behind, followed by the juniors.

Akir and Anell kept a strangled silence all the way to their encampment. Kalar and Sonsie must be punished. They both agreed. No comment necessary. They couldn't forget the last time they heard a whistle.

The procession clambered down the rocks, past the fallen birch, and stopped at the mouth of the cubs' outgrown den.

Akir ordered them to enter the hole. "Stay there until—if ever—I call you to leave. You are too big to fit back in your dam, but not too big to return to the green womb of your birth. To make certain you stay, Birk will sit at the opening. Just try to escape! Birk, keep guard."

Feela lowered and shook her head.

Seven

UNINVITED GUESTS

Solas-Faers, sky-kin, hide the sky under green.

N one of the wulves noticed at first. They scratched, dug, and gnawed, as wulves will do on a hot summer day. The only breeze for miles around came from their tails beating the tall spear grasses or fanning away flies. No wind blew through the green birch leaves; no airstream carried scents or sounds north over Lac Alina or down from the nearby hills, some still adorned with patches of snow. The burn that flowed by the den slowed to a melodious purr, blending into the pleasant buzz from the nearby meadow. Soothing murmurs enveloped the dozing pack, pressed upon their nodding heads, and weighed down their eyelids. Lulled to sleep in the sonorous heat of Vine Month, they breathed in slow, undulating rhythms, like swells on the open sea.

Sonsie lay curled on his side within Feela's outstretched legs, his head resting on her right forepaw. Both faced the mounded rocks that he and Kalar had so recently used to spy upon their elders. Kalar had flopped on his belly near Birk, but not near enough to arouse her ire. Sonsie fought sleep. He closed his eye nearest to Feela's paw but kept the other open. At least he tried to keep it open; he couldn't be certain if he dreamt the large she wulf or saw her before him, sleek and alive. Either way, she climbed the rocks and peered over the precipice to view the slumbering pack.

To Sonsie she seemed a wonder, vivid white against the green leaf background. Her black-rimmed eyes, shaded by white lashes that highlighted their mysterious beauty, mirrored the green all around her. Under Grian's full light at her highest in the azure sky, the wulf's coat shone, as if dusted with diamond or silver so lustrous it created the illusion of Gealach come to earth to walk the green glens in broad daylight. The pack's resonant drone melded into a wulf-hummed tune, a whispered lullaby for all, high wulves to cubs, all blissfully asleep.

The white interloper took the measure of each one, paying particular attention to the cubs. She sang of clear, well-lit nights and happy hunts; of flower-strewn meadows, croaking frogs, and slow-footed hares; of gallant deer that make all wulves rejoice to be wulf. She sang herself away before the night breezes could ruffle their fur and tickle their noses, alerting them to a stranger in their land. She smiled and bade them a silent farewell. Through his open eye, Sonsie watched her disappear, as if the rocks had split and swallowed her whole. He fell into a stupor. Visions of frogs and hares, cavorting through the dancing feet of a deer herd on the run, advanced straight toward him. His heart raced, yet he slept, bound to the earth as if by the weight of a thousand rocks.

▲ ▲ ▲

Akir and Beag intensified their search for an elusive presence in the hills that joined Wulf Paw to Faerswell Forest and the mountains uniting South and North Wulf Paw. Tree limbs clattered. Twigs and brush crackled. Akir had even gotten a whiff of something from the Black Woods of Tara-Ardra carried north to his domain, but they never hunted down anything to sink their teeth into. The rest of the pack took turns guarding the cubs, who begged daily to join any hunt—no matter the prey.

Birk and Mundee thought they had glimpsed something queerie close by, neither bear nor mountain goat; they couldn't be sure. A scent, at times wulf, other times some kind of horned one, enticed them to hot pursuit, but they found no tracks to name or follow. Burdened with the lingering sensation of being followed, the pack pondered the danger each time they returned to camp. Daily they left scent markings one upon two upon three and let loose their fiercest warning howls. No other pack returned call in greeting or challenge.

"Curious," Mundee said. "It seems we are alone."

Ro looked around. "Then why do I feel crowded?"

🔺 🔺 🔺

While returning to the den site a week after what Akir called "Dooleye's insult," the pack debated what stalked them. Some agreed woodland Faer Ones, maybe the Greenguard, or Auld Lord Green Himself wanted to herd the deer.

Newly released from disgrace, Feela objected, "Not at all. She's the one, by Auld Alba's apples! And she's watching us, watching the cubs."

"Who?" yelped Beag. His grey brindled hide crept; his shining black nose and grey whiskers twitched.

"Lady Light whose woods these are."

"Paugh!" Akir spat. "The woods belong to us and the deer . . . and the rest."

Karlon cocked his head toward Akir. Provoking the high wulf might guarantee another scar; even so Karlon urged, "The rest?"

"Aye . . . the rest." Akir barked. "The Covenant Cohorts. The rest!" His tail thrashed.

Feela exhaled a long sigh. "You have forgotten the Faer Ones and the others who look Faer yet are not."

Anell clamped her teeth over her sister's jaw, not like a boar to spear and grind, not like Birk, but warning enough for immediate silence.

Karlon laughed to himself.

Birk shot a withering look at the two sisters then directed attention to the cubs. "Why would Lady Light watch Kalar and Sonsie?"

Akir opened his jaws in a tremendous cry and lashed his tail. The rest joined in one after the other; their howls tumbled from the skies into abrupt, absolute silence. From a distance at home camp Ro and the hungry brothers answered, Ro first. Then came Kalar's cry, full and deep, followed by Sonsie's sweet, pure notes.

Akir paced and pawed the ground. "Why did a bogey track our cubs?"

⊼ ⊼ ⊼

As soon as the pack returned, Kalar and Sonsie scurried to greet them, mobbing any who seemed likely to cough up prey into their hungry mouths.

Akir's eyes narrowed. "Och! My sons. Fine cubs, true, but bright-eyed faces don't protect fools." He bared his teeth, directing his stern gaze at Anell. "I dislike that Faer Ones lure more than the strange, two-legged cutters into the woods. Should the Lords of Light entice Sonsie away—"

A familiar sound interrupted Akir. From the direction of Wisdom-Shield came a rustling of leaves and the scent of old growth forest. Making slow progress, dropping leaves as he came, the ghillie dhu approached the pack and nodded. He stopped about five yards from the senior wulves, standing guard in a ring around the cubs, and nodded. More leaves fell. He straightened to his entire four feet height and cleared his throat, sounding like twigs clattering in the wind. He had a pleasant if gnarled face that featured kindly grey eyes and a large mouth much given to smiling. The ghillie dhu loved his tree.

Akir had no quarrel with tree companions, especially Wisdom-Shield's. Proud to protect this venerable tree, Akir barked a cautious welcome. Even though he gave ghillie dhus grudging approval, one never knew what these shy Faer Ones would do.

The ghillie dhu removed his acorn covered cap and nodded. "High Wulf Akir, I bring friends, a tree friend and a healer to all that dwell in the green." Making such a long speech exhausted the ghillie dhu. He made a crickety chirping sound and beckoned in the direction of Wisdom-Shield.

Two Greenguard stepped from behind the shelter of the immense oak. Dressed in green, the blue-skinned Faer Ones nodded and held out their sky blue palms. Leaving the shade of the oak behind, they stepped into full light of day; the wulves saw the tall male's face tanned a deeper blue than the female's.

Akir's tail rose. His whole body bristled. He sniffed for the scent he would never forget.

The male wore a green tunic, hood down, and tights woven in a pattern that so imitated pine boughs that he looked like a walking fir. He doffed his green cap with the eagle feather cockade. White blonde hair formed an aura around his fine-boned face. "Greenguard Lanark-Kyle, at your service."

The female wore tights and a sleeveless tunic over a silk blouse with flowing sleeves, all in varied shades of green. A short cape of the same weave as her companion's garb, its hood down as well, draped rakishly from her left shoulder. A starsilver clasp fastened it at her pale blue throat. She took off her simple blue bonnet, tossed her rose-gold hair, and said, "Greenguard Iova-Rhu, at your service. We bring greetings from Lady Light and all the Faer Ones of Lisnafaer."

"Aye," Lanark-Kyle continued, "we congratulate Akir and Anell on the birth of their two fine sons."

Akir's tail shot straight up. His ears pointed forward, but as yet he had not bared his teeth. Although this Faer One was not the faerwulf who had destroyed his peace forever, that didn't stop Akir's growls, rumbling like a rock slide.

Upon hearing the Greenguard mention them, Kalar and Sonsie crawled forward until they poked through the barrier of wulf bodies. Wide-eyed, the Faer Ones gazed at the cubs.

Akir snapped, baring his teeth. Birk and Beag sat upon Kalar and Sonsie so hard that the air whooshed from their lungs.

As if stalking a timid deer, Akir moved toward these uninvited guests in his domain. Their scent of huckleberry and wild iris filled his quivering nose. He gave no sign that he approved of their total outward stillness. Upon hearing their rapidly pumping hearts, he squelched a triumphant cry. *Proves they have one.* "Leave my sons alone, Greenguard. They are our concern, not yours."

Lanark-Kyle lowered one knee to the ground but kept his back straight, his eyes focused forward but below the tip of Akir's nose. "Yes, High Wulf Akir, your care . . . but ours as well. It takes all the forest Cohorts to raise the young to health and happiness."

Anell came to her mate's side. Birk and Beag rose so as to release their squirming captives with warning to keep silent if they valued their lives. Anell and Feela remained calm, but the senior wulves' hackles flared; their tails stood erect. The bright-eyed cubs drooled.

Iova-Rhu knelt before Anell who looked deeply into Iova-Rhu's faergreen eyes. Anell winked.

Iova-Rhu took a deep breath then said, "High Wulf Anell, dam of two fine sons, shun not our offer of respect and protection. The forest rustles with murmurs of some unknown threat. We seek naught but good for all your pack—and your new sons." She reached into her tunic and withdrew some object. "Take this as token of the Lady's goodwill."

In her palm rested an apple, green-flecked red and gold, just as fresh as if it had been picked that day. Anell luxuriated in its sweet-tart aroma. Her mouth watered.

In an instant Akir's sharp-toothed jaws snatched the apple from Iova-Rhu's hand, an act both ferocious and delicate. He tossed it up and away in a great arc toward Wisdom-Shield. No one breathed. Kalar buried his head under his paws, but Sonsie kept his gaze on the apple. The rest of the pack froze in place, all looking at Akir, except Feela, who unsuccessfully sought the eyes of Anell.

Akir looked to the shocked Greenguards. "We can't eat good will. We don't eat apples."

From a mound of rustling dried leaves, twigs, and downed branches, the ghillie dhu's brown, bark-skinned arm reached out. His twiggy fingers grasped the apple that swiftly disappeared into the tangled undergrowth.

Eight

What Harm One Little Apple?

Keep the Covenant. Revere the apple.

Lanark-Kyle and Iova-Rhu knew better than to pull the tail of wood wroth Akir. Claiming the need to return home, they bowed and took their leave. They headed east, back toward Flower Dale and Lac Morna.

Akir clenched his jaws against any apology or even one word of thanks to Lady Light.

Told to get behind the birch and to stay there, Kalar and Sonsie retreated to the familiar shelter of the fallen tree.

Anell climbed a nearby hill to watch the emissaries of Lady Light disappear under a canopy of tall pines, their many twisted boughs covered in summer blue-green needles. Far-reaching oak limbs wove themselves through the pines into a living thatch. Their deep green leaves flashed like emeralds in the late afternoon light. Anell turned her gaze west and caught a glimpse of Beag and Birk who hustled Karlon, Mundee, and Ro away from their peevish high wulves. She watched as they scouted a familiar trail that led to the far shore of Lac Alina and become lost to sight under swaying oak and birch boughs.

Following the promptings of her heart, Anell looked southwest toward a sea she could neither smell nor see. In that direction a tartan of greens from near black to bright yellow-green covered a succession of glens and ridges broken by grassy meadows, marshes, and snow capped peaks above the timberlines. Here and there rivers like silver snakes glinted in the light. Wildlife too numerous to count followed wooded trails or took to the air and waterways. All sought their own favored prey-companions to change into new life, all to live on in new bodies.

About one-hundred yards below Anell Akir paced back and forth. She ignored him. He called her name. Disdaining to answer, she turned to watch two owls, a golden female and a silver male, silently circle in large, lazy sweeps too early for a night hunt. Like the wulves, they seemed merely to be scouting the lay of the land. They could keep that up for hours and spot a mouse from at least a mile.

▲ ▲ ▲

Kalar and Sonsie's rumbling bellies reminded them they hadn't eaten since late morning before the arrival of the Greenguard. Considering their sire's dangerous mood, they dare not beg for food. Kalar plopped his head upon his front paws and huffed his frustration at the Faer Ones for spoiling the day. Sonsie tried to remember what they had said, how they looked and smelled, but the shining image of the Greenguard's gift to Anell stuck like a cocklebur in his way too curious mind.

"Kalar, the Greenguard have gone. Now is our chance to get the apple!"

Kalar rose to peer over the rough bark of the fallen birch. "Aye! No Wait! I don't see our sire. Where is he?"

"Not by Wisdom-Shield. Come on, Kalar. We can get it for our dam. Hide it in the den."

Kalar could not stop his wagging tail. "Let's go!"

The two-and-a-half month old cubs belly-crawled toward Wisdom-Shield, imitating their elders' hunting stealth. The apple's spicy-clean scent, like wild rose on a windy day after showers, drew them on. About five feet from the ghillie dhu's mound they heard leaves rustling. They reared back, but their ears and noses strained for any clues as to what they faced.

The ghillie dhu peeked out from the debris and tossed them the apple. "Here, Anell's cubs."

They stared at it, big as Akir's huge paw, a deep red, blushed with golden green on one side and on the other a mix of gold and red, as if the red were washing away from the gold just as someone picked it. Its smooth, hard surface shone in the afternoon light. The top center dipped into its core in streaks of red and gold-flecked green to a rougher surface from which a brown stem stood erect. A tuft of tiny brown spikes left behind when the blossom dropped off emerged from the center of the little well at the bottom.

Sonsie scooped it up in his mouth. In his heart he meant to take it back to the den before Akir discovered them. But one little nip released the apple's full sweetness, more than equal to its heady aroma. Intoxicated, he bit the apple in two, making the skin snap and crackle. His teeth sank into the firm flesh. Juice, a jolting sweet tartness like honey coated pine boughs, filled his mouth. He tasted sunlight and air and cold mountain water after they pass through a pine forest. Never had his tongue been so happy.

One half fell to the ground. As if it were the liver of a fine stag, Kalar leapt upon the morsel with the five-pointed star at the center. The brothers devoured it. They licked their lips, their greedy tongues searching for any last drop of that sweet-tart goodness to prolong their joy. That's when they saw the tiny brown seeds. Their wet red tongues lapped them up.

Once again, Akir called to Anell.

Kalar stared at Sonsie who gulped and said, "Never speak of this, Kalar"

Bound by yet another secret, they made their way back to the den. They tried to copy Birk's strut but looked more like egg-stealing weasels.

Akir tried again, using the cry of a wulf with a broken leg. Quitting her hilltop lookout, Anell sauntered more than ran to his side. She touched her nose to his then laid her head over his ruff. Akir had the good sense to abide in silence. Anell's sad eyes had been rebuke enough to alert Akir to his offense, a fact that rankled him as much as the intrusive Greenguard.

⋏ ⋏ ⋏

Later that afternoon Iova-Rhu and Lanark-Kyle perched in a tall pine, grooming their gold and silver feathers. They had sought seclusion in a stand that sheltered a clear pond many miles from Akir and the den he protected. Wavering images of gnarly-limbed pines, green and burnt umber, obscured by intermittent batches of clouds, floated on its surface, a twin sky rippling in a breeze that bent the water reeds.

The silver owl watched a golden-ringed dragonfly bob on one of the green stalks. Taking flight, the owl circled the pond and landed at its bank. He turned his flat wide-eyed head back and forth then pulled his beak into a wide yawn. Assuming his usual greenguard shape, Lanark-Kyle fluffed his feathers which turned into his familiar green garments. He managed a rueful smile and called to the gold owl, "That meeting could have gone better."

Iova-Rhu flew to his side in a graceful, golden glide. She blinked, fluttered her wings, and transformed into his greenguard friend, once again dressed in green. She shushed him with a wave of her hand.

He persisted, "Of course Akir is wary for his sons, but the Lady's apple! To insult the Lady?"

"Who controls a wulf? Done cannae be undone. The ghillie dhu will safeguard the apple. The cubs must be watched, but not by us and not today. We needs must confer with Master Arklevent. Let the wulves tend to themselves. The cubs are fine."

"I'm not so sure."

The tall Greenguard adjusted her cape and settled her bonnet on her rosegold hair.

Clutching his feathered cap to his chest, Lanark-Kyle implored her, "Ever since Arklevent first sent me to scout this pack, they have made a home in my heart, I confess. The cubs are bigger each time I return. Their coats have changed—faerblack and faerwhite; you must have discerned this for yourself, brief though the view was . . . before Akir went mad.

"About the ghillie dhu—something's afoot. I need your help, healer and confidante of all wildlife."

His strained voice caught her attention. "The ghillie dhu is ill? True, we did not see him in our hasty retreat."

"No, not ill. Perhaps . . . barmy."

"Forester, ghillie dhus are shy but never harebrained. So what causes these sighs and worried frown?"

Lanark-Kyle pushed his near-white hair off his forehead. The smile he intended faded from his lips. "Just before I returned to Mount Enion, the ghillie dhu told me . . . the cubs had stumbled into a hole. Just when Light Wyrm slept under the roots of Wisdom-Shield."

Iova-Rhu gasped. "By the Light! This far north? And the cubs?"

"'Lifted up on his great ram-horned head,' that's what the ghillie dhu said." Lanark-Kyle twisted his cap, bending his proud eagle feather.

"Who knows? Master Arklevent, of course." She nodded, confident she was correct.

Lanark-Lyle groaned. "I didn't tell him."

Iova-Rhu's eyes shut as she clamped her hands over her lips. After taking several deep breaths, she opened her troubled eyes and scrutinized her companion's miserable face. She poked his chest with a not so healing finger. "Not tell him? You are the barmy one! Why not?"

"I didn't believe him. The wyrm doesn't bother with wulves. Deer Lord and his deer, aye, but—"

Iova-Rhu poked him again. "Perhaps Arklevent sent you to learn the ways of those with no roots, wulves and others who share the green, consider that, tree friend. The ghillie dhu confided in you. Ghillie dhus never lie. You failed to speak the truth. We best carry our tidings to Master Arklevent—soon."

What she read in his faergreen eyes gentled her speech. She grasped his ice-cold hand. "My heart yearns for Lac Morna. Azaleas are bursting with blooms. Let us discuss this on our way to the fat and juicy blackberries, begging to be picked. Come."

She tugged at his sleeve. "Yes, my friend? Tell me about these wulves as we wend our way home. You talk. I'll keep one ear open to the forest gossip."

⋏ ⋏ ⋏

The next afternoon tree frogs and crickets vied with one another to disrupt the peace of the sheltering pines Iova-Rhu so loved. All the way back to

Flower Dale Lanark-Kyle told her every detail about the "grand pack, the best of the blessed Apple Coast, may it remain forever hidden."

By the time they entered southern Wulf Paw Forest with ancient evergreens to rival the pines of Boar Bristle Forest, he spoke of Anell's ancestor Alba and his theft of the Faer Ones' blessed apples, "an audacious exploit on behalf of all wulves, so the auld tales go."

They crossed River Melvalina into Faerswell Forest. He chuckled and confided to his companion, "I have missed the antics of the far-straying pack of Auld Alba, the apple thief."

"How so?" Her attention strayed to the squirrels passing gossip and nuts overhead.

"I usually tend the Lady's apples at Avalach Crossing. For ages before Akir became high wulf, this pack roamed the coast, true sea-wulves. In the last several seasons, Akir forbids his pack to roam the forests and cliffs sheltering the apples."

"Aye, ferlie the bonny apples, marvelous and sweet. No wonder Avalach Crossing a favorite haunt of Lady Light and her court." She twisted a strand of golden hair.

"They should return. The deer grow fat and lazy and, it may be, just a little dull." He removed his feathered cap, ran his fingers through his hair, and smacked the cap against his thigh. He scowled.

Iova-Rhu's faergreen eyes glinted. "You know nothing of the deer, forester. Ask Aden-Cree. Though you would lie at ease in the apple groves, dreaming summer lasts forever, best to safeguard your part in the Balance Green and I mine." With a teasing smile she whisked the cap from his hands and nestled it on his head. "Now be still."

Not to be turned from his passion, he recounted one theft after another: faer apples, wulf songs and faer songs, stolen back and forth in rapid succession. As he pictured Auld Alba stuffing his belly with apples, he laughed, holding his sides, but never stopped talking until Iova-Rhu placed her slender blue hand over his mouth. "Forbear, forester. Enough!"

"But it's more than Kalar's faerblack and Sonsie's faerwhite fur; did you not see the whisper of a glow that seems to hover about their heads like they've been touched?" Lanark-Kyle's brow wrinkled. "I marvel that the pack suffers them to live."

"No! And even if they had this aura, the wulves have no gift to discern such a ferlie light."

"Ah, but the Dorcha, abroad just when the cubs are most alone, they do."

Nine

In mountain, forest, glen: Faer Ones mind the wulf.

Master of the Green Arklevent scowled, darkening his deeply tanned blue face and defeating his half-hearted attempt at a smile. He dressed simply: a traveling cloak patterned with interwoven oak and holly leaves, a dappled green tunic, and forest green tights. A lowered, knot-embroidered hood revealed his gold hair held secure under a silver circlet of deer and wulf in full chase. His favorite walking boots, the color of deep woods moss, caressed his feet on a day he chose not to ride. The meeting of the Greenguard demanded no frills, no fine silk attire with silver trim such as he might wear for the Faer Ones' Grand Rades. Like all Guards, he carried a silver hunting horn upon his braided belt.

During warm mid month of the Vine he usually looked forward to returning to Lac Morna and Faerswell Oaks, the very heart of verdant Faerswell Forest. In this season of long light he had counted on solitude to commune with his tree friends, known many hundreds of years since his youth. The abundant bluebells and waving ferns that surrounded Lac Morna and her mist-shrouded isles never failed to delight him—until now. From Lisnafaer's starry heights Sky-Wulf's cryptic warning had awakened the slumbering wyrm, coiled within the deepest chamber of his underground lair. Word came to Faer Home within the halls of Mount Enion. Arklevent knew Lady Light had dispatched a special emissary, as was meet and right, to Anell and Akir. All seemed passing fair, but he could not ignore unsettling rumors. In cries that rattled inside Arklevent's eardrum like a bag pipe badly tuned and ill-played, Lord Dooleye nattered about a wulf pack. "Fallen apples out of apple thief." The last thing he wanted to hear.

He walked down a canopied pathway to a natural stone circle formed from river rocks untouched by chisel and hammer. Oaks, other companion trees, and lush shrubbery embraced the circle and between the stones filled gaps the size of a stout horse from nose to tail. Within the open center the fragrance of clover blended with daisy to entice butterflies and bees.

In his last few moments alone Arklevent looked up to Lightning-Eater, an imposing guardian oak that anchored the living wood and stone ring. His hand ran over twisted bark, stopping to caress rough furrows, the marks of the guardian's undying quest to follow Grian's bright face. He waited for Lightning-Eater to speak. No deep-throated words of wisdom answered his greeting. Arklevent sighed. "So be it." He gave his friend an affectionate pat.

From the canopied portal to the circle, he viewed all the milling Guard who could be spared. Booted and dressed in rustic green, they also bore silver horns and deer skin sporrans that carried necessities for their life in the wild. He focused on those who had entered the Greenguard when a slimmer Lightning-Eater stood only twenty feet tall, a far cry from the present strong-limbed giant.

Rosslyn-Tir: tall even for a Faer One, his white-gold hair and fair blue face shining in Grian's light. He had come from scouting the Covenant Lands east and north of Boar Bristle Forest on his way home from the borders beyond the northern Wulf Jaw Range.

Aden-Cree: mistress of the deer, wearing faer-dressed deer hides, a gift from White Stag in appreciation of her care for his herds.

Barras-Garve: famous for his sweet tooth, sucking on a honey stick, as expected. Beside him stood his cousin Brodie-Gare, who always wore an eagle feather in his bonnet. The boisterous duo's ginger hair shone as if fire framed their laughing faces.

Master Arklevent signed for all to be seated. Some took to the lichen-covered rocks. The rest reclined upon their traveling cloaks spread on the ground. He looked for but could not find Iova-Rhu and Lanark-Kyle.

Buying time, he indulged their chatter until they murmured into silence. Knowing the health of the trees or the number of woodland bairns did little to dispel the notion that some unvoiced disquiet yearned to be set free. Arklevent reached up and grasped a branch, allowing some ants to run over his hand. Eager for good tidings to cheer this day, he gazed west over Aden-Cree's head to the trail he knew the latecomers must take. Disappointed, he called for food and drink. Before it arrived, the last two Greenguard emerged from a fern bower to join their comrades.

Arklevent beamed. "Ah, well met, Lanark-Kyle. And Iova-Rhu, how lovely." She wore a simple cream tunic that covered her green riding breeches. Strands of her hair like curling honeysuckle escaped the woven grasses and delicate meadowsweet that bound her brow.

Lanark-Kyle, wearing a serviceable plaid weskit, but adorned with silver buttons, attempted to move off to the side, but Arklevent took Iova-Rhu's hand to pull her forward as his other hand clapped Lanark-Kyle's shoulder. "Come, come. Sit with us. We shall share water from the Healing Well and honeyed apple cakes, enough for even you, Barras-Garve."

Laughter rippled through the companions. Their spirits lifted by Arklevent's blessing, the company relaxed. They licked the warm honey from their finger tips.

Too soon their leader rose. He turned everyone's attention to whatever lurked in the shadows of their hearts. The look he gave them quickened the pulse in every throat. "If one can believe the ravens' prattle, Lisnafaer bears watching for . . . now what did auld Dooleye drop like a chestnut in my ear?" He tugged his right earlobe. "Ah, yes, 'mischief, murder, and marvels.' Now, my Guardians, what do ye suppose he meant?"

He stared at Lanark-Kyle and Iova-Rhu. "What report of the pack that has the ravens pulling their whiskers?"

Lanark-Kyle sought the eye of Iova-Rhu. She smiled. "A brave pack, good neighbors to all in the forest."

"So might a ring of toad stools be. What else?" Arklevent's mouth grew taut.

Lanark-Kyle felt the perplexed gazes of all searching their faces. He rose and paced. "They are a small band but powerful. They make good the Change."

"So, too, a pack of mountain cats taking down the agile goat. What else?" Barras-Garve said before Arklevent had a chance to speak.

The two friends looked to one another. Lanark-Kyle tugged at the buttons on his weskit. "Lately Akir finds reason to avoid the Apple Coast. He and Anell hotly debate where and when to move the pack. He would go deeper into Boar Bristle, yet his lady harkens for the apples."

Master Arklevent nodded. "As if boars and apples will keep safe the sons of Alba's heir!" He strode towards the two Guardians, his mottled traveling cloak swaying. "And yet the ravens pluck their tails! Their clamor fills the heavens." He glared. "What do ravens see that ye do not?"

Lanark-Kyle closed his eyes, touched the bridge of his nose, and muttered, "We did not see . . . ." He looked up and stopped. Arklevent shook his head.

Iova-Rhu frowned. "We sense something, em, very special about the two new cubs. As to keeping Kalar and Sonsie safe from ravens—"

"Did I say ravens?" Arklevent's piercing gaze highlighted the sharpness of his voice.

Iova-Rhu looked to her partner, who said nothing, and then out to the trail they had taken to this urgent Gathering of the Green. Overhead as the topmost boughs swayed in the warm breeze, flickering light and shadow chased back and forth. Through the foliage they heard the cries of a passing skein of wild geese fade into the distance.

Arklevent broke the silence. "Tell us more of this 'sense' and these young wulves." He paced between a sturdy oak to his right, where stood the ever more rigid Iova-Rhu and Lanark-Kyle, and a rock to his left. The other Guardians shied away.

Unable to move back and loath to move forward, let alone to allow the slightest twitch of one muscle, Lanark-Kyle and his loyal friend remained wide-eyed and mute.

Arklevent arched his unruly eyebrows. "I see ye both are reluctant to slip the jess; let your hawk fly."

They breathed deeply, filling their lungs with woods-scented air.

Rosslyn-Tir prompted, "Some mark, do ye see, some strange curl of the tail, a bent ear?"

In answer, Iova-Rhu merely dared to exhale. Lanark-Kyle cleared his throat. Followed sharply by Iova-Rhu, he began. "Kalar is most black, most definitely blackest of black—"

"So black that—"

"Well, in fact, green—"

"Aye, so very, very green it's—"

"Black!" Lanark-Kyle concluded.

Lord Arklevent gestured with a stiff forefinger. "Do . . . ye . . . suggest?" His brows knotted. He summoned his breath from deep within. "That this wulf is *Royal Green?*"

Iova-Rhu nodded. "Now that you say it, Master Arklevent, that certainly explains—"

Lanark-Kyle blurted, "Sonsie is *faerwhite* and has *green* eyes." Before his nerve failed him he pressed on. "They seem both way back—and new—like the past come to life now, like unto wulves of auld whose bones carry new hide."

Unable to contain himself, Brodie-Gare's laughed. "Your eyes deceive ye, mates. Trick of the light, nothing more." His smile vanished when he caught sight of Master Arklevent's glare.

His face a storm of emotion, Arklevent stifled additional comments. "Your tale of wulves, faerblack and faerwhite, *and* faergreen eyes, hinting they could be Auld Ones or the banished—"

"No! No!" the alarmed Guardians exclaimed together.

"—will do as a faer's tale for the young. Your cohorts here know better. I will have the truth. Now!"

"What mean you?" Lanark-Kyle forced his gaze to meet Arklevent's.

Just then, Lightning-Eater shook from the depths of his roots to his uppermost boughs. Several Guardians felt the tremor. Awestruck, the company fell silent. A mighty rumble issued from the heart of the ancient oak. "Ask Wisdom-Shield."

Master Arklevent pivoted. "Were I to do so, auld friend, what would the grand warder reveal?"

The Greenguard maintained stark silence amidst the jabber of wildlife going about their daily tasks. Lightning-Eater, taking his time, finally issued one final directive. "Blundering wulves and burning cats. Ask the two who watch the wulves."

One of Arklevent's hands gripped his belted silver horn; the other balled into a fist at his hip. "Wulves and cats? The two? Yes . . . the *two*."

He faced Lanark-Kyle and Iova-Rhu. His earlier scowl turned dangerous. "Masters of delay and evasion! What have ye not told me?"

Lanark-Kyle sighed. Two thoroughly miserable Guardians stood stiffly before Master Arklevent. The smoldering fire of his gaze convinced Lanark-Kyle to let his words tumble. "We saw them not with our own eyes. The local ghillie dhu told me. He said they had dealings with the ram-horned wyrm. Kalar fell in his lair. Sonsie leapt in after him. He heard faer song in wulf voice. That much he knows for certain."

Iova-Rhu raised her shoulders, gathering her courage. "Tell him the rest." Her voice steadily diminishing, she nearly fainted. "The ghillie dhu told you for some reason."

Keeping a straight face, Lanark-Kyle swallowed—more than once. "They came out alive . . . lifted on the ram horns. A marvel, that is! He believes Light Wyrm did more; what, he is unable to say—or won't—something ferlie."

"By the Light!" Master Arklevent's outstretched hand trembled as he pointed to the Guardians. "Why was I not informed at once? Why this ludicrous tale about the color of their fur, topped off with eye color . . . and . . . not . . . one . . . word . . . of . . . Faerwald?"

"The color of their fur and of Sonsie's eyes—most true, we swear." Both Guardians nodded vigorously. "We did not, in truth, see Faer—"

"In truth, whatever ye saw or saw not, ye did not speak, and for all your vows to safeguard the Green and all its creatures, Anell's young get caught in an encounter fraught with peril."

"Yes, my Lord," they replied in unison, their heads bowed, shoulders slumped.

Arklevent pursued a darker thought. "What know ye of cats and the wyrm?"

Bewildered, the mortified Guardians shook their heads. "Nothing."

The silence deepened. Conjuring a mental image of the rash young wulves, Arklevent considered the two penitents. He scowled. All children, he thought; it matters not that two are Greenguard and two are wulf. Faerblack? Faerwhite? Long distant sons of Auld Alba. No wonder. Alba's blood—potent? Aye, but . . . a curse?

He allowed the faintest hint of a sad smile. His firm hands, gentle in the touching, lifted Iova-Rhu and Lanark-Kyle's faces.

"What of the rest of the pack? Why not kill such ferlie-touched ones?"

"We think they see and see not, my Lord."

"Any reports of harmed cats?"

"None, my Lord," Lanark-Kyle managed to whisper, dread clouding his face.

"Ah."

Lanark-Kyle breathed easier. "They seem well guarded, my Lord. Kalar's gallant heart yearns for the hunt. Already he begs to join his elders, fearing the ravens will pick the bones of a fine deer and leave not one bite for him."

Arklevent's green eyes flashed, whether with mirth or foreboding, only a wulf could discern.

"And his brother gulps in even the faintest echo of faer song like it's his last breath," added Iova-Rhu, happy to have survived Arklevent's ire.

Arklevent pondered their words. As he rubbed his brow, his ring glinted in the light. "Overhearing faer songs in the Green is one thing. But to have the Power in song? Och!" He waved his hand, dismissing the possibility.

"Just so!" Lanark-Kyle urged. "Master Arklevent, the ghillie dhu says he repeats faer songs well enough to be mistaken for a Faer One, as if he . . . em, had studied in our halls."

"I see." Arklevent sat. His deep silence seemed to pull all sound from the air.

Then the wind through the oak boughs picked up force; leaves, sliding against one another by the thousands, rustled and flapped. The Guardians stood immobile; the steady thrumming of crickets and croaking of tree frogs enveloped them. They awaited any signal that the interview was over.

At last the master of the Green stood, his face composed, his eyes seeming to watch visions invisible to his audience. He said, "Hunter and singer: boar wulf and apple wulf, born of boar wulf and apple wulf, challenge enough. But *faerblack* and *faerwhite—faergreen* eyes to boot! Lanark-Kyle, continue your close and careful watch."

He turned to the others whose undisguised gaping mouths belied their usual composure. "Our friends' reluctant confession accounts for the ravens' squawking of 'mischief'—or is it 'marvels?' No matter, all bad. As to 'murder,' what say the Greenguard? Say it be no worse."

One weathered Guard mentioned the yet unknown source of two-legged tracks. Rosslyn-Tir nodded. Ever cautious, he spoke as if he had viewed Lisnafaer and lands beyond from atop Mount Barra. He told of a steadily growing migration from the east, stopped by Mounts Barra and Dreich. Some refugees, cutters proper he feared, not the people of the Green Way, settled at the threshold to Lisnafaer. Others skirted the Wulf Jaw and continued north. All signs—hacking and digging, tearing and burning—suggested cutter.

Another Guard demanded to know what sort of burning, by bolt or by hand.

Rosslyn-Tir shook his head. "Cutter hands work their mischief to clear the trees."

Arklevent's lithe body stiffened. "What is planted to replace murdered trees?"

"Nothing. So far, the trees that escape fire make crude shelters for cutters and their broken beasts . . . and fences—"

"Beasts? Confined? By cutters?" Barras-Garve's fist crashed on the nearby rock, narrowly missing a wood spider skittering for cover. Several brows raised in unison at this unaccustomed force betraying the usual calm of a seasoned forester.

Some railed against the grave affront of cutter fences used to divide neighbors and confine beasts. No one could explain why cutters slew trees and profaned the Covenant.

Master Arklevent directed them to the more important question. "Has this vile desecration breached any Covenant Lands?"

Rosslynn-Tir's sad countenance offered little hope. "Not yet."

Aden-Cree, fresh from her patrol of Lisnafaer's borders, leapt upon a stone bench and raised her arms toward the group. She testified to having seen cutters push beyond the lands of the people south of the Wulf Jaw, attempting to pass between the Gloomy Deeps and Murky Caves to Eagle Claw Forest.

"Ah, the wide valley between Cadman and Dreich, of course!" Brodie-Gare cried. "Are they blind to the danger, what with Lone Grumli and the Dorcha-Faers?"

The cousins' lively discussion veered into a heated debate as to the threat of giants and Dorcha, what the Dorcha must be up to, and why they were "sneaking and creeping," according to Brodie-Gare, well past Grian's rising. Barras-Garve insisted that the Dorcha, expected to maintain order in the night when Grian and most Solas-Faers sleep, were "roiled up about some fangle-dangle thing or other!"

Many remained thankful that the Dorcha and the giant Lone Grumli watched their borders. Others weren't too sure.

Aden-Cree blew on her silver horn. In the immediate silence that followed all eyes turned toward her. She argued that any threat by giant or Dorcha amounted to "a midgie cloud, a mere irritation." Her face flushed lavender. "If ye have eyes, ye see that cutters, pushing through faer friends' lands at our borders, menace all Covenant Cohorts. I blame the cutter chiefs, no longer fathers unto their children but tyrants, driving them from their homes to the sea. Most move around the Wulf Jaw Mountains to the south, as well as north."

Directing her remark to Rosslyn-Tir with a nod, she warned, "More will come, a great horde, against the Wulf Jaw."

Unable to contain himself, Brodie-Gare began to pace and wave his cap. "Lisnafaer beckons, a haven to the lost and miserable."

Rosslyn-Tir agreed. Now warmed to his task, he told of a desperate madness looming on the borders. "Red jacketed soldiers, not Dorcha, drive into our friends' lands, chop huge swaths of trees, and make roads the width of several wagons abreast. Slash and burn is their way to care for the Green. The border wulves cry warnings to beware of cutter traps. Traps! Bad enough their blades, but these abominations recall dire days. A desert seems to be the wild dream of the cutters." He strangled a cry.

"So," Arklevent cut in, his voice dark with mounting anger. "It seems Lanark-Kyle is not the only forester to eke out vital knowledge like a cut deer dying one bloody drop at a time. Tell me, Rosslyn-Tir, this ruin, is it confined to those lands immediate to Wulf Jaw?"

Rosslyn-Tir bowed his head. "Yes, my Lord."

"Look to it." Brodie-Gare poked his cousin's chest. "They seek to make Lisnafaer their own!"

Master Arklevent raised his right hand, the one wearing the great silver ring entwined with oak and holly. "The cutter advance must never get near rivers Doakie and Lavina. See to the land west of Mount Ansgar. Once the sickness crosses the Doakie, or worse, Rona, the apples are in peril."

Aden-Cree's eyes glared under knotted brows. "Lord Green must know of this treachery. I have a special concern for his far-ranging deer who roam the Green at will."

Relieved to enter the discussion with some reason to hope, Lanark-Kyle reported a thriving Green with deer happily growing fat. His Lordship had been seen in the blinking of an eye all over Lisnafaer, and their friends on the Apple Coast affirmed that the hunt continued as usual.

They waited

The late afternoon light shifted from tree to tree, flashing gold through green leaves. Arklevent finally raised one hand in blessing. "Be diligent, Guardians. Ye all have cares anew. Keep me informed, especially if ye should see Lord Green, for surely his deep-earth companion has told him of these cubs . . . and other portents, I fear."

Ten

Time to Move, Time to Run

Heed signs, live. Heed not, die.

Freyen Scanlon lived on the southern edge of Boar Bristle Forest near enough to the Black Woods of Tara Ardra and Eagle Claw Forests to be disputed territory. He gave shelter, if little else, to his brother Earm, Earm's sickly wife, and their child. Freyen sat hunched upon a stool in the doorway of his hangnail house filled with tension and bitterness—not that the three he kept in his grip dare complain. His calloused hands turned a hand-sized whetstone, caressed its rough surface and stroked each side with his broken-nailed thumbs.

On an oiled cloth at his side lay several hunting knives, their blades now keen and bright. He boasted he could describe every creature he had ever gutted and skinned and how they tasted, roasted or raw. He reached to run his scarred hand over the knives, fingering their tips. "Makes no difference to auld Nick and Slash and Digger, do it?" He picked up Hack, a felling ax, crossed his right leg over left, and shifted his weight from the numb right buttock to the left. Pulling at a crick in his neck, he pondered the ax blade. Patience, he thought, a man needs patience with blades. "Never took a grinding wheel to my beauties, now have I?"

Pain streaked up his left leg and attacked his hip. He leapt up, cursing the sciatica that aggravated an already bad case of gout, but took care to hold on to the stone and Hack. He yelled for Earm's wife to bring him beer. In the silence he scratched his balding head with the stone, finally recalling "Grub," as he called her, had crawled back to bed at mid morning, about the time he had finished sharpening Slash.

Pocketing the stone, he trudged into the kitchen. He laid Hack aside, his fingers lingering on the handle, and poured himself a mug of beer from the keg sitting by the water pump. He downed the warm brew, sucked his mustache through crooked brown teeth, and wiped his chin and mouth with his dirty red sleeve. "Now that your master has wet his whistle, Hack my friend, let's fix you to break the legs of those pines down by the creek, eh?"

He laughed and clutched his ax in a death grip. "Someday, Hack, I'll put you to better use, and it won't be to break her legs." He laughed all the way back out the door he had never bothered to close. His sister-in-law hated flies.

He sat down with both feet on the ground, taking care not to knock his gouty big toe, and laid the ax handle across his thighs so that the butt pointed to his crotch and the blade his knees.

He took the whetstone from his pocket and spat at the blade, spewing specks of meat that had been stuck in his teeth since breakfast. The stone slid over the nicked seven inch blade with the tenderness of a lover's tongue on a bared throat. "Let's put a shine on, what d' y' say, Hack?"

⋏ ⋏ ⋏

Anell called Kalar and Sonsie to her side. "My sons, Grian is nearly settled in for the night and Gealach is awakening. All must hunt tonight. Prey-mates grow scarce."

The cubs danced, bumping into each other, and yipped in high squeaks. "Let us go. Let us go!"

Anell looked at them as if they had coughed up pine weevils. "Are you mad? You must bide in safety close by this fallen timber and running water.

Drink at need, aye, but stay on the shore. Keep your paws on the shining rocks. Do not go near the deep pool."

They cocked their heads and waved their tails. Their large eyes shone. "Why?"

"I said so." She pondered something bothersome about Sonsie who blinked under her scrutiny. Unable to detect what bothered her, she said, "Be here when we get back."

She nuzzled them and hummed a wee tune to cheer them. She slid her tongue over their noses, gave them a stern look, and then bounded after her mate, carrying her misgivings in her heart.

The brothers fixed their gazes at the water then took a furtive glance toward the distant oak. They shook their furry spines and plopped on the ground where Anell had left them. For the time being they lay still, content to curl their tails over their snouts and peer cautiously through the long hairs.

▲ ▲ ▲

The pack emerged from the woods to take up an easy, steady pace for several hours, stopping briefly to test the wind for scent of likely prey. Their hunt turned successful in the deep dark before dawn. They got a whiff of lush grasses and deer. Their mouths watering, the pack followed the scent to where starlight on this clear night disclosed the silhouettes of the deer huddled in a black glen.

Facing the downwind, the pack sniffed out an elderly hind without calf. By the time the herd had cleared the glen, she fell to their running attack. Akir and Anell fed first. Giving thanks for the deer she changed to wulf, Anell filled her belly with chunks of liver and entrails, leaving the tough yet good red meat to Akir. This time she kept all for herself and let the others carry food to her cubs.

After she withdrew to Akir's side, the rest of the pack took turns changing the hind to wulf. Dawning light slowly revealed blood on torn and trampled grasses. Karlon and Mundee had nearly finished their night's meal. Her body fed, Anell lay at ease, grooming herself and Akir, but her attention turned to her sons.

"We must go home. Akir, turn the pack."

"I don't like to feast and run. Stay here beside me, Anell. After the least of us has eaten, we return and feed the cubs."

Anell stood and sniffed the early morning air. Turning toward home, she watched a black cloud flying low and fast in their direction. Not a cloud. Ravens. Diving toward them. Anell's heart raced. "Hurry, Feela," she called. "Tear what you need; leave the rest to the ravens. We must go!"

Her tail thrashed against Akir who looked up. He roared his disgust. "Dooleye! Fly on, winged doomster. No bloody bones for you—all for my cubs."

The Raven Lord brought the flock to rest in the nearby tree tops. "Cubs no more. Wulf sire, wulf sire, flit away home; your den is all crumbled; your cubs are all gone!"

Anell howled. "Lead—or I will."

Akir turned the pack. With Anell beside him they raced back to the den.

They approached the site in clear morning light. Anell and Akir called their cubs. They heard a thrashing in the water, not near the den. The pack hastened to the water's edge about twenty-five yards downstream. There an urchin bounced up and down, snorting from his pig snout. The spikes of his coat stood up like an overgrown thistle. Even worse, from the dark pool stretched forth two long arms at the end of which long-nailed, bony hands grabbed at Kalar and Sonsie, attempting to drag them under the water.

The cubs planted their paws in the swift stream that flowed over their backs. They bit at the hideous hands. Each time one of them clawed their fur, the cubs shook and barked with all their might, choking on the water. The urchin laughed through gurgling phlegm.

Anell, Feela, and Birk surrounded Kalar and Sonsie. Akir and Beag attacked the creature with the long arms, heedless of becoming its next victim. The combined efforts of all the adults released the cubs from its grasp. Now that the pack had returned in high wrath, the urchin adopted the guise of a hairy black rat. Having done his worst by luring the incautious brothers to a watery doom, he slunk away in the commotion, swishing his long tail in the grasses.

Anell and the other senior females ushered the cubs to the den, not crushed after all, leaving them in the care of Ro and Mundee. Taking Karlon with them, Anell, Feela, and Birk joined Akir and Beag. The five of them dragged the spindly limbed crab-spider creature out of the water, the source of its power, and shredded its body. They peed upon every scrap of bone, scale, and shattered red carapace they could find, but not one speck of the bogey-beast did they change into wulf. They buried all the broken bits and peed upon the ground.

Overjoyed that his sons were not missing or worse, Akir ordered that Kalar and Sonsie be fed immediately. That day, however, none of the wulves curled into their usual nap. The cubs were too excited, the others, laughing Ro included, too worried.

⋏ ⋏ ⋏

That evening at gloaming Akir led the entire pack along the shores of Lac Alina to the eastern banks where it joined the River Melvalina, the one that flowed between the Wulf Paw and Faerswell Forests. The wood vetch and wintergreen in late Vine Month had burst into full bloom. Akir disdained local flowers. He urged speed, only stopping to test the air, full of competing odors, most of which he distrusted.

He motioned Beag to his side and growled low. "Smoke or some other foul breath?"

"Nothing but the marsh gasses belching in the air, Akir. All is well."

"I sense the passing of Greenguards, heading home, I hope. But what lurks behind?"

Akir and Anell drove the pack who took turns carrying Kalar and Sonsie. Squint-eyed, they wriggled, their ears turning this way and that. Mundee and Ro spat them to the ground and swatted their rumps.

"Just you settle down, both of you," Ro said.

"Hard enough to race the ravens, worse to carry two fat cubs," Mundee added.

Pushing between the junior wulves, Birk glared at the cubs. "With such bad manners."

On the last part of the journey they bounced like milkweed pods in the wind. Finally the pack stopped several leagues south of Lac Alina within the Wulf Paw side of River Melvalina.

Sonsie whispered to his brother, "Feeling a little woozy?" Kalar's dripping mouth left a trail in the dust. He refused to answer.

Heedful of the fray at their last den, the pack sought a safe place to hide Kalar and Sonsie when the adults hunted. At last Anell and Feela found a grove of ferns and rhododendron. The wind had blown their crimson blossoms over water-washed rocks by a nearby burn. After Feela remarked at their beauty, Birk's tongue cut as sharply as any blade. "Looks like bloody rocks to me."

Akir liked the surrounding stone in the midst of willow scrub backed by thick pine and alder sentinels. Beag and Birk explored the burn for tell tale signs of foul water creatures apt to attack foolish or unwary cubs. They found none. The pack romped, happy to find a place where trees came right down to both banks of the water, and beyond, wildflower meadows led to sheltering hills.

"Good," Akir said. "Good," Anell answered.

The pack foraged all through South Wulf Paw Forest. Frequently they scouted Raven Wood to the west and Boar Bristle Forest to the east. Time and again, Akir made them head south toward Lac Ardra and then east, attempting to penetrate Boar Bristle. Just as often, Anell argued for hunting around Lac Tara nearer to the coast.

They returned to their gathering spot covered with aromas of places Kalar yearned to see: the beaver dam on River Melvalina, the salt licks Faer Ones put out in the Deer Rack Mountains, and the shining mink slides beside the waterfall that marked the beginning of Boar Bristle.

After feeding the cubs, the pack gathered for the daily nap. Kalar and Sonsie knew not to expect a romp right after eating yet remained hopeful that each night they, too, would be asked to join the hunt. Before sleep, the adults passed gossip from the trail back and forth. The cubs listened, avid for any detail.

Anell recalled bygone days of her youth and the land leading to the sea-kissed southern coast. "I long to smell again the summer-warmed pine of Avalach Forest, and ha! chase the deer through the Pass of the Piper. Someday, we must run through the spearmint crowding the new green grasses of River Avalach. When nothing else comes to mouth, Avalach fishing is always good." She sighed with closed eyes.

Akir huffed. "Too many Faer Ones. Bad as ravens."

Anell and Feela hinted of someday taking Kalar and Sonsie to these places, even Lac Lavina. There great eagles crowded the skies and harried young boar who came to drink the cold water.

"Us too," Mundee cried. "Take us all to Wulf Tongue Pass." She flashed a wulfish grin but shivered nonetheless.

Karlon reared on his hind legs and pawed the air. "Yes, the Wulf Tongue. We want to climb the crags overlooking the sea like you did."

Kalar asked, "Sea?"

Feela coughed. "Great water beyond the wooded mountains that brought the Ice-North raiders, long banished. Go to sleep."

The cubs wrestled, repeating "Ice-North raiders" over and over, until Feela fell upon them, weighing them down with what felt like a boulder of fur and bones.

"Hush, foolish cubs. Better you call the worst of the Dorcha than even one of the icy hearted raiders with a long-tongued blade hungry for blood—wulf blood!

Eleven

New Wulves, Auld Names

A smart wulf learns all the names for Lisnafaer.

During Kalar and Sonsie's first summer the packs' thick winter coats had turned sleek. Their run-tested muscles, firm but supple, assured good hunting that proved the wisdom of the new gathering site. They were fit and happy. The cubs grew from playful fur balls to young wulves. When Sonsie gazed at Gealach each night and bathed in her light, his silver-tinged coat turned to alabaster. He often escaped his teachers only to amble home in a dreamy state. Akir knocked him head over tail more than once. Kalar's ebony fur rivaled the sheen of any raven's wing. He pounced on anything, including rocks and logs, and crashed into the spiteful whin.

Each time Karlon and Mundee pulled out the prickly spines from his paws they repeated, "Lift those huge paws, Kalar. Bushes don't move. Leap!"

The active hunters, busy flushing and chasing prey-mates, told the cubs to enjoy their new home, a safe haven where soon plump berries would drop into their mouths.

The indignant brothers groaned. "Berries!"

As the pack left to hunt each night, Kalar and Sonsie cried out, "We're ready!"

The adults merely shook their heads. "Stay here. Watch. Don't come out for bear, badger, or bogey-beast."

⅄ ⅄ ⅄

Stuffed to bursting from feasting on one of the pack's fresh kills, Dooleye and his kin often followed them home. They filled the tree tops. Under cover of the flush green leaves they preened their black feathers and spied. Raven Lord watched the cubs. He bided his time. The day after a hunt that pleased Akir, Kalar and Sonsie pestered grey, battle-scarred Karlon to delay his afternoon nap. They wanted to know about some tree they had heard the pack call "Lord Green." Dooleye hopped down to a lower branch.

Karlon yawned and stretched. Lord Green wasn't a tree, he explained, but he that is nowhere and everywhere, Lord of the Green. When Beag added Deer Lord and said he had other names, Sonsie asked if everything had so many names. That started Kalar chewing his paw. Beag praised Sonsie for paying attention.

Kalar glared. "Shut up, Sonsie."

Her nap ruined, Anell barked. "You have many names to learn. Go to sleep."

But Sonsie wanted to know the Faer Ones' name for Wulf Run. Karlon looked to Akir who slowly opened and closed one eye. Curling around a patch of light, Karlon said, "Faer Ones call it Lisnafaer, so named by Lady Light, High Faer One."

Kalar lunged at the ravens that depressed the flowering rowan boughs just out of reach of his snapping jaws.

Knackerclaw called down coyly, like a weasel choking, "All know 'Lisnafaer,' even a fool of a hare. Awk! Young wulves, what does it mean?"

Sonsie joined his brother in one bound. With tail and ears high he proudly cried, "Faer Haven." His smug look withered as the entire tree erupted in feathered laughter.

Dooleye croaked like a bug-a-boo caught in a cutter trap. "Too easy little cricket—and *wrong*." He plumped his glossy feathers. "What big ears you have, Sonsie, so full of the Faer Ones' nonsense cast upon the wind! You'll lose your head!" The clatter of raven laughter fell upon Sonsie's eager face.

Akir barked. "Silence, you maggot-teeming death-token, or the next time you scavenge one of my kills, you'll leave a wing if not your fly-spawned head behind!"

A whirl of a hundred black wings disturbed the early summer day; fifty voices cawed in retreating defiance. As if a storm cloud had vanished, leaving a refreshed sky, the wulves blinked into the light. Only the panting of the angry pack broke the silence.

All looked to Akir, but none more ardently than his two youngest sons. They cried together, "We know the names. Let us hunt!"

Their bright eyes widened. Their impatient souls threatened to leap from their aching throats. Gasping, Anell crossed between her mate and her sons. "You shall not cause jangle and wrangle to the pack—and yourselves—worse than any insult of the raven."

Anell circled the brothers, herding them, increasing the space between them and their sire. She climbed upon a nearby rock, worn smooth in mountain storms. In the light her copper hairs shone like a fiery cloud. She started a howl that all joined.

Still, Sonsie heard nothing new, no new names, just a howl to make the pack stand side by side, proud wulves hunting to stay alive, loving the pure joy of the run.

Looking up he asked, "What else?"

"Nothing else, my son."

"That's not what I hear."

"What?"

"Nothing."

⋏ ⋏ ⋏

Anell called Feela. "Come with me to the beaver dam." By the time they reached the pool above the dam, Anell's silence and clenched jaws warned Feela that something was amiss, something that Anell kept fast. When the clatter of chirping birds and rustling leaves whirled about them, Anell faced Feela. "Tell me, tell me now."

"What?"

"You know what. Sonsie! I demand to know the truth. You're his caretaker. Don't tell me you haven't seen his eyes—"

Feela barked. "Not here! Let us hunt vole along the way to those clump of rowan near the gorse thicket."

Anell scrutinized Feela's face. They covered the half mile in silence. Along the way they scanned the sky and trees for hiding ravens. Satisfied they could not be overheard, they entered the shelter of the rowans thick with berries. Anell demanded, "Why haven't you told me of his eyes? They're *green*."

Feela's brow wrinkled, making her look almost old. "I wasn't sure; he's so young. Gealach has turned her face only three times since the cubs were born, still with their cub teeth and all—"

"Feela. Cease. I saw them myself. Who else suspects he's a faereye?"

"None. I've kept my suspicions to myself, not finding the safe time to tell you, only sure after I smothered their foolish calling of the raiders."

"Feela, faergreen could mean keeper. But surely . . . not another Dunoon." She stomped around her sister. Anell's waving tail matched Feela's distressed pants. "But with his dreamy-headed pursuit of faer song." Anell turned and retraced her steps. "What if he's an apple-eye?"

Anell halted, a relief to Feela, but then she became rigid. "Akir! He'll grind rocks if he suspects Sonsie is headed to the Gates of Song, bad enough to accept another keeper in the pack." Her tail drooped. "Oh, Feela!"

Feela drew near her sister. "Whatever you do, now that you know, you must tell Akir, high wulf to high wulf. He swallowed Sky-Wulf's bitter gall. After last season's deaths, no blame to you, he'll break his back protecting these sons, star-touched or not. Akir's not the worry, gruff but true to Greenlaw. It's Birk."

"Birk!" Anell bit at the air. "More boar wulf than her brother. By Alba's Apples, she'll make Sonsie's life a misery."

Feela stared into Anell's eyes; the familiar amber had shaded into hazel. Feela coughed, began to speak, and stopped. Anell, nerves rubbing raw, demanded that Feela loosen her tongue.

"It's not only Sonsie, may Lady Light bless him. Delay your midday rest. If you notice how Grian's beams brush their fur, you'll see what I suspect. Sonsie, faerwhite, no surprise. Kalar . . . faerblack, though so far, I swear, he passes for just another midnight wulf."

Anell reared back. *Royal Green*?

Feela nodded.

"Alas, my sons. How could this be true? If true, if Kalar, if Sonsie. They're lost to me."

"Anell, tell Akir of the eyes. No more. The rest will show itself in Greenlaw's ripe time."

"I'll deal with Akir and hope for the best . . . if you will take on Birk and the pack."

"Your desires are my deeds."

Treading lightly in the meadow grasses, they headed back to the gathering site in silence. Just before they came to the willow scrub, Anell said, "My thanks, Feela."

⋏ ⋏ ⋏

The next day Akir rallied the senior wulves to scout for deer, but Anell told Beag and Birk to stay by the pack and get them ready to hunt that night. After their return, Akir would lead them to sure success. She tugged on Akir to join her in a romp through the woods. "Today, just you and me, Akir!"

Biding her time, Feela gathered the three junior wulves to teach the cubs secrets for getting food from the nearby stream yet avoiding any encounters with water-bogies. Sonsie watched the water swirl over the giant pebbles that lined the banks. He listened to the babble and tried making sense of it. He laughed whenever the minnows swam between his toes and fancied pouncing on the small fry that hid in the grasses at the water's edge, the bogey long forgotten. Kalar scorned fishing even though his teachers insisted catching a trout rivaled capturing the furred prey-mates.

Ro shook her head. "They have much to learn."

Late in the day, Feela chided them. She asked Beag and Birk what should be done with such poor learners. Birk thought it would be good to make them to sit and watch their warm up games. The junior wulves, eager to be free of the cubs, agreed. Feela said, "Your desires are my deeds."

🝞 🝞 🝞

While Sonsie lazed and let the mountain breezes carry hints of song, Kalar's muscles strained, barely containing his urge to bolt. He clawed the grass and batted his tail.

In close formation the leaping pack assessed the growing cubs. The juniors doubted they'd ever please Akir and complained about their little weasel tricks, sneaking out of sight, playing games with the light. The seniors laughed about cubs always having fidgets.

Karlon dropped a wild cherry stick. "When Gealach hides her face, Kalar fades from sight, like Dorcha."

The pack turned to stared at the youngest wulves in their care.

"Karlon!" Feela barked. "Take back that name! No wulf ever verted to Dorcha!" She captured the wet stick and stomped it under her thick-nailed front paws.

The pack halted. They saw Kalar and Sonsie staring back as if they had been condemned to the Gloomy Deeps far to the south in the shadow of Mount Ansgar.

Mundee could no longer bear the silence; she smacked her lips. "Someday Kalar will run down the swiftest stag. When he comes into his own, we will eat our fill."

Beag grunted. "Och, he has the discipline of a hare."

"At least he tries to hunt, unlike his howling mist-eyed brother!" Birk said. The pack stared at Sonsie who wagged his tail.

Feela risked a challenge. "You praise the strong hunter, but we need more than steaming livers and dripping bones to live."

Birk snickered. "Say you, Feela, nursemaid."

Feela lowered her tail but only lowered her head to lift the stick and offer it to Birk, who merely sniffed.

Dropping the stick at Birk's feet, Feela dared to add, "On the hunt we cry out warnings, signal directions."

"True," Beag said, silencing Birk. "Say on, Feela."

"We also hide deer haunches against days when hunger bites our bellies and scorches our tongues."

Ro coughed. "True." Her eyes barely concealed anticipated amusement. "Go on." She stole a look at Birk.

"We must know the trails, safe or deadly, the weather signs, where the prey hides.

Keepers know more. They save auld lore of our sky-kissing crags and green glens. A keeper is no bad wulf." Feela's bold eye held them all.

A sneer wrinkled Birk's black lips. "And silly Sonsie is such a one?"

Beag attempted to a new tack. "A day may come . . . when deer grow scarce and darkness threatens all who dwell in Wulf Run. Then we will welcome another keeper—even if he eats more than he catches and sings more than he sleeps."

Ro chuckled. "Sleep? With Sonsie near—or far?"

They all sneezed in laughter, breaking the tension, except Birk who said one keeper was one too many. As they circled about, the cubs studied their every move.

Birk huffed. "Why Sonsie?"

Feela jumped on the question. "When Sonsie listens, the gold hairs lining his inner ears dance, alive to silent song. He follows voices others in our pack hear not. Yet never has he gone astray."

"Feela, such twaddle." Karlon chuckled. "A blind bat could follow the trail you leave.

Sonsie is a pest, not a keeper."

Feela pushed her face into Karlon's. "No bat, blind or not, but . . . his eyes." She pulled back, hesitated, and licked her lips.

"What about his eyes?" Karlon stood his ground.

"Em." She snorted and looked over their heads and then to her feet. "I suspect they're turning."

"All wulf eyes turn. Not so soon, I grant you," Ro said.

Feela answered in a voice so low that the grasses seemed to call out more loudly than she, "Green."

"Feela!" they all shouted.

Every head turned to stare at the cubs.

Mundee objected, "He's too young."

They all turned round and round, agitated yet curious, their ears turning this way and that.

⋏ ⋏ ⋏

The rattled cubs knew their elders debated something that seemed to relate to them, but they couldn't hear distinctly enough to satisfy their curiosity.

Sonsie nudged Kalar. "Why do they stare at us?"

Kalar moved aside. "Something about you."

Sonsie turned his tail toward the pack. "Why?"

"How should I know? Ask your precious Faer Ones."

⋏ ⋏ ⋏

The pack resumed their huddle.

Before Ro could finish, "But what if—" Karlon snapped, "Don't be daft."

Birk snarled. "Feela should teach Sonsie to hunt, not examine the hair in his ears or the color of his eyes."

Beag grimaced, deep in thought. Unfazed by Birk, he turned to Feela. "Truly, if we have a faereye, you should have told Anell. Having a throwback who even hints of Auld Alba in our pack? I don't know."

"You know Akir curls his tongue at mixing with Faer Ones!" Birk added.

Feela's eyes narrowed. "She knows."

Birk bared her teeth and glared steadily at Feela. Refusing to back down, Feela appealed to the others. "Death lurks on the trails we take. Fell winds carry the ring of cutter axes past the Wulf Jaw. You all, weary from long hunts, find signs that demand wulf-hearted courage."

The pack burst into a grumbling scuffle, much butting of heads against each other's flanks, punctuated with short yowls and waving tails.

Alarmed, Sonsie and Kalar scrunched together.

Feela stood aside, tail down. She waited for them to settle. At the first second of silence she urged, "We can teach them movement of the herds or where the sweetest water spills from the green earth. But if deer 'grow scarce,' Beag's 'darkness' may hide Dorcha—Dorcha stalking wulves. A keeper equal to that darkness needs more training than we can give."

Feela paused and, nodding to Beag and Karlon, gathered her pack mates closer. She avoided looking directly in Birk's eyes.

Karlon's brow knotted. "Dorcha don't hunt wulves!"

"Not yet." Feela's ears drew back; her troubled eyes narrowed. "The water-bogey—just a fluke? Why Sky-Wulf's warning?"

"And you think Sonsie—" began Mundee, only to have Ro cut her off, "will save us?"

Beag snorted, annoyed. "Stop this idle chatter. Prepare to chase the deer. Akir expects ready hunters." He looked over at the cubs. "As to Kalar and Sonsie, only their training matters. Good hunting makes safe wulves with full bellies. Mundee sees clearly; one day Kalar may bring down a great stag." He tossed a fat pinecone to Birk.

She raced to the end of the meadow and pivoted, daring the others to follow. Over her head butterflies and grasshoppers collided in a frenzied blur.

Mundee loped half the distance to Birk and stopped. Karlon looked from Mundee to Birk. He joined Mundee. The hoppers settled in thick grasses; the butterflies headed for cover in nearby trees.

Karlon shook his head and took one step toward Birk. "A wulf who sings whatever he hears—or thinks he hears—might as well be a magpie." He bit a stick and carried it to Birk.

Birk swallowed a juice-spitting hopper and smiled, but her gaze remained harsh.

"Go get the cubs!"

Twelve

Sonsie Forces the Issue

Seek if you dare all the names in Lisnafaer.
How many deer dance in the light?
How many apples stole Auld Alba at night?

S onsie should have followed Beag's lead in leaping over the rotting pine, toppled ages ago in a mountain storm. Instead, the hum of the tree frogs overcame him. One moment he stood snout deep in the meadow leading to a ring of pine that circled a grassy mound. A heartbeat later Sonsie found himself in a strange land. The bright light of day had shifted to twilight.

Like a fading echo in a dim memory, he heard Birk's raspy call, "Sonsie! Sonsie! I know you're near; I smell you."

He shook his head, afraid to move, afraid to answer.

She called again, more faint this time but just as angry. "If I come get you, I'll make you sorry!"

Desperate to get his bearings in the subdued light, Sonsie let Birk's growls wash over his determined silence. His nose quivered, alive to the aroma of heather magnified a hundredfold. His ears turned to a sweet sound carried on the fragrant air. He ran toward the sound.

Light flickered then flashed. Sonsie's solar plexus throbbed. His paws, still on the run, touched down in the familiar meadow. Spotting Feela nearby in the waving grasses, he howled a few melodic notes that turned into song.

⋏ ⋏ ⋏

"Green land for the running, blue sky for the leaping,
Wulf Paw partners, wulf and deer,
Wulf, deer, and Faers, thriving as one,
Blessed Green, Lisnafaer."

⋏ ⋏ ⋏

"Sonsie!" Feela shook her head.
Catching the warning in her voice, he dropped to the ground and closed his paws over his snout.

"Where did you hear that song?"

"On the air. Woven by the wind through the high, bendy boughs. In the night when the rest of you stalk prey-companions." He stared, wide-eyed, wanting to smile yet hesitant.

A grim-jawed Birk loomed over Sonsie and his caretaker. "Oh really? You little mag—"

"He sings common truth, what any wulf or prey-mate knows," Feela broke in.

Birk turned on her. Her black lips curled to expose long, white teeth. She raked Feela's snout and nipped her withers. "What true-hearted wulf speaks as if his brain had sopped in honey? Karlon is right." She snarled. "You deal in foolishness. Perhaps we need a new nursemaid."

Feela lowered her rear and tucked her tail, yet resisted her tormentor. "By all means, Birk, sure you have the patience to teach the cubs all they need to know."

Just before Anell and Akir returned, Feela took Sonsie away from the pack. "Sonsie, keep your songs and how you heard them to yourself, above all when Akir and Birk draw near."

▲ ▲ ▲

Anell took a good look at Akir as they loped along one of their favorite trails east through high grasses toward water. She risked a leap into dangerous waters. "If Sonsie seeks keeper lore, what harm, if he's meant to be a keeper? Remember Auld Dunoon? It's an honor to have a keep—"

"No, Anell." Akir jerked to a stop and stood taut, as if scouting King Stag. "First a keeper, then a makar, then, worst of all, drudge-dog to those meddlesome Faer Ones. We are hunters!"

He roared. After the flurry of the startled the birds, the forest ceased its chatter.

Breaking the silence that enclosed them, Anell chided, "No deer within an eagle's flight heard that."

Akir snarled, thinking to end all discussion. "My sons will be hunters!"

Anell stood firm, her eyes bright. "Our sons must hunt what best suits their nature, like Auld Alba."

Akir pawed the ground. He raised his tail a fraction higher than Anell's. "We are hunters. Not thieves."

Anell echoed him, "Aye, hunters. . . ."

She laid her head across Akir's ruff and breathed into his ear. "'Thieves' make right the Balance. Greenlaw: we steal the life of the deer; deer steal the life of the trees. Greenlaw thieves give back what they steal. Faer Ones steal light from the heavens and feed it to the Green. All eat. Alba gave more than he took. All sing. Some better than others."

Akir shook her off. "What tick has burrowed into your brain?"

Anell persisted. "Your son is a faereye."

Shock fired Akir's every nerve. "Which son?"

"Sonsie."

Determined to play the stone, Akir moved not one muscle, not one hair. He stared at Anell.

"Yes, Akir, Sonsie, one of Alba's heirs."

"And Kalar?"

"Och, have no fear. Kalar's eyes are fine. He will make a great hunter, maybe a boar wulf."

Akir howled as if he had witnessed the escape of a prime stag after long chase.

"Akir, you are high wulf, a true boar wulf. But the Green and the dark harbor more than deer and boar. Sonsie will also be a fine hunter. Heir of Kark, as you teach Kalar, don't neglect Sonsie. Teach him to hunt what he, and no other, must hunt. The eye of Sky-Wulf watches."

▲ ▲ ▲

A new day witnessed an unrepentant Sonsie who chased the stick with Kalar, the juniors, and Feela. The four best hunters feigned disinterest, but from the cover of the high bracken they followed every move. Sonsie bolted, spun around, then, eyes wary, hunkered down and calculated the turns of his rivals. He easily wrestled the wet stick from the jaws of the junior wulves and matched each of Kalar's chases and recoveries. Tugging bravely, he yanked it from him and ran. Kalar pursued; his hot breath escaped burning lungs.

Sonsie turned. The tang of Kalar's mouth clung to the stick; Sonsie spat it out. Each wulf in the pack had a different taste, some salty, some more sweet, and Kalar like a hot rock dug from a dry creek bed.

"Take your . . . auld stick . . . salamander mouth." Sonsie hissed, his breath coming in gasps.

Kalar stopped, eyes wide.

After the game ended, Sonsie asked Feela, "Do the Faer Ones chase the dancing, dauntless deer?"

"What might a sprout of a wulf such as you know of deer, 'dancing' or 'dauntless'?" She shook her head.

"Oh, I hear things," he assured her.

"Well, hear this—the 'dancing' deer are as dangerous as they are 'dauntless.'"

Mundee clucked her tongue. "What could you possibly hear with all the caterwauling you do?"

"I do what I'm told." He bit at a fly. "You all go away. We wait alone for once-eaten prey." He shook his head, spraying saliva on Kalar's paws. "I am left with Kalar, silly for every cracking twig in the forest."

Kalar leapt upon his brother. They somersaulted over and under, paws flailing, teeth biting. Each attempted to summon the fiercest snarl yet heard in Wulf Paw Forest.

▲ ▲ ▲

The senior wulves watched, their eager eyes focused on the brothers.

Beag nodded approval. "Our Sonsie, not the wholehearted hunter like his brother, holds his own in a fight."

"A stick is no stag," Akir said. "We have many trails to cover before hunger slinks into the dawn after a good hunt. Wait and see."

Anell called her growing cubs, "Stop tearing and tumbling, my sons. Tell us more, woeful Sonsie, of what you hear when we leave you so much alone in the company of your hasty brother."

Sonsie's ears tipped forward; he scurried to her, wagging his tail. After a low howl, he sang, full-throated.

▲ ▲ ▲

"In blessed Green, Lisnafaer,
Wulf and deer, equal and strong,
Cantering cohorts, Covenant partners.
Gallant the Noble Three:
Glad and free the song of the strong-jawed wulf.
Swift and pure the dance of the light-hoofed deer.

Bright and true the light of the green-eyed Faers.
Wulf, deer, and Faer Ones, thriving as one,
Lords of Light, rejoice."

▲ ▲ ▲

F or ages, it seemed to Sonsie, Anell eyed her panting son in silence.
Sick dread fused with sweet pride nearly overcame her. How far would his
faergreen eyes take him? She glanced at her mate.

He yawned. "Another faer song? No good to hunters."

Sonsie almost yelped in pitiful imitation of a mewling pup, but a blister-
ing look from Anell clamped his jaws shut.

"They got the part of the 'strong-jawed wulf' right," Akir added before he
strutted away. Anell gulped air as if she had just emerged from a deep pool. She
turned to the rest of the pack, witnesses to Akir's curt dismissal of Sonsie. "We
hear nothing untrue, nothing cut or spoiled. Any wulf with many seasons on the
hunt would know the same. If he knows it now, rather than later, I find no fault."

"Och! Can he bring down the prey-companion at need?" Birk said.

"Leave it. I find no fault."

Birk withdrew to the shade of the nearest clump of gorse bushes, but
glowered as she turned around three times before hitting the ground.

▲ ▲ ▲

K alar and Sonsie so hated the dull summer routine of eating, sleeping,
playing—and waiting alone—that they harassed their elders beyond all
caution to let them run past the near hills.

Kalar demanded answers. "What else? No more trails to take? I won't stay
here until my teeth fall out. I'm sick of these sticks. Show me the deer. Let me
bite him! When do I hunt?"

The eyes of the silent adults beamed approval. They sniffed the wind.

Sonsie refused to leave unpicked the bones of his passion. "No more names? Who makes the names? Who makes the songs? Where do they come from? I'm sick of these sticks. When do I hunt?"

The eyes turned cold.

Sonsie's unexpected appeal to hunt arrested Kalar's helter-skelter pursuit of voles and hares. Once stopped, he grew curious himself.

"Yes," he said, "tell us the names of the places where you 'grab the red deer by the throat and melt the grasses with hot blood.' I hear you talk. Why are the deer and the mountain cat and goat 'too dangerous' for us? You don't let us hunt anything good. You don't say when we can hunt anything good. Tell us where."

Affection for his hunt-mad brother swelled Sonsie's heart.

Feela sighed.

▲ ▲ ▲

On the way back to the gathering site from the teeming hunting grounds that stretched along Lac Alina and River Melvalina the high wulves debated changing its location. Anell wanted to draw the pack through Raven Wood to cross River Tara, move on to cross Avalach, and then head south. Akir insisted they turn southeast from the shores of Lac Lundi, head to Lac Ardra, and scout the boundaries of Boar Bristle Forest.

Unmoved, Anell faced south.

Ro scratched her creamy white fur and hit Karlon's rump with her tail. "Here we go again!"

"Hush, don't you see Akir is out of sorts?"

Akir bridled. "I say boar, not apples."

Anell claimed their sons would be safer near the apples.

Akir scoffed at the idea of hunters hiding in apple groves. "They say they want to hunt; let them hunt proper prey-mates."

In answer to Anell's chilling silence he finally granted that some names would be good for young future hunters to know, "whatever they hunt."

She turned and lightly brushed his nose with hers then consented to circle Lac Ardra on their return home. She nuzzled him. "Heart's rest, how good to be at your side, here . . . or far away at the sea where the apples make glad the bees. There the Faer Ones turn light to love."

▲ ▲ ▲

The pack awoke from their meat-drugged naps. After a long stretching and yawning, Anell called Kalar and Sonsie before her. As if a lightning bolt had streaked through the ground, the pack jumped, fully alert. Eyes narrowed, they stared at Anell.

She mounted her favorite rock to look down at her sons' handsome faces. The crickets hummed in the warm grass.

"You have asked," she began, "for the names our wulf keepers—" She shook off Akir's warning stare. "Sing what all hunters must know."

Sonsie crept forward, his wet mouth open.

Birk struck him. She attempted to take up the lesson. "You must—"

Leaping down, Anell delivered a swift but controlled slash to Birk's right shoulder.

All the others pulled back, except the two steadfast pups. Their gazes shifted from one stern face to another, searching for a cue before they dared move.

Anell snarled. "The cubs are not the only ones who must know their place."

"Across the sea west of Apple Coast," she continued, addressing Kalar and Sonsie but keeping a strict watch on Birk, "lay the wave-warded Isles. There Great Grian the Gold and Good Gealach the Silver, like firelight and snow afire, take their rest after lighting our days and nights."

"We know fire," Kalar said.

"But snow?" pursued Sonsie.

Birk pawed the grass. Anell raised her tail and let a rumbling growl escape from deep in her chest. She looked directly to Feela, who took up the lesson.

Feela moved closer to her charges, Anell to Birk. "You'll meet snow after you grow much bigger and have joined the hunt."

Hearing something about hunting, Kalar persisted, "What is snow?"

Feela cleared her throat and glanced at Anell, who nodded.

"When nights grow long and days short, the cold turns running water hard. We chase deer over clear water like flat rocks. Snow falls out of the sky in tiny, white clouds, growing in great piles, more than all the brown leaves scattered on the forest floor. On the high mountains it lives forever, even in summer—"

Sonsie squealed. "I have seen it! On three—"

"Silence," Anell cut in. "Today, you need know only that Wulf Run is home to many marvels . . . the bee filled apple groves for one."

Beag smiled. "Och, the bee-droning, honey-dripping cliffs." He licked his lips.

Akir growled, like thunder rumbling in the distance.

Birk, about to interrupt, instead shifted her weight, causing the entire pack to move. Anell laid her head over her withers, making certain to rest it squarely over the clotted bite.

The uneasy pack settled into a silence so hushed that Sonsie could hear the faint nicker of field mice as they scurried under the trailing azaleas. He tried to be patient, yet the mention of bees and apples pricked his memory. Losing control of his tongue, he blurted, "What about *Arasnababan* and *Arasnagafar*?"

Akir rushed upon his son. His hot breath burnt Sonsie's face. "Where did you hear such names?"

Kalar shuddered.

Well taught, Sonsie turned his belly to his sire's gleaming mouth. Eyes closed, Sonsie let his head fall back and presented his throat as well. He dared not breathe.

"Answer me!"

Sonsie opened one eye, then both, but said nothing.

Anell called. "Sonsie! Answer Akir."

"Only on the night wind," Sonsie managed to croak. "When you are on the hunt. When I hear voices."

Akir glared at Sonsie's green eyes. His hackles stiffened into a black ridge along his spine. "'Voices' you should not hear!" Akir barked. He spat and turned to his mate. "Finish this! Now!"

Anell called Sonsie and Kalar to stand before her.

Sonsie righted himself. He looked around. Not one silent wulf moved. Hanging his head, he made his way to Anell. Kalar came forward from the pack, careful not to touch Sonsie or show in any way that he knew him.

Anell waited until they stood before her. "Sonsie. Kalar. One of you has asked; both must hear. You both must do your best to be good hunters. That is all we ask. To learn the deeper names of our home you must master your lessons. Only then will you be worthy of knowing Covenant secrets.

"Sonsie. You heard, but not from your pack. You had a cricket lodged in your ear. Look at me, Sonsie! Good.

"Kalar, be not proud. Sonsie won't be punished for wanting to know before ripe-time.

"Sonsie, be not downhearted. Kalar won't be praised for wanting to hunt before ripe-time. Your actions gain praise or punishment."

She summoned the rest of the pack to surround the cubs. Karlon, Mundee, and Ro stood to Kalar's left; Birk and Beag came to Sonsie's right. Birk nudged Sonsie so that he knew she offered no comfort. Feela stood behind the two. Karlon and Birk forced the cubs to crouch before Anell. Akir stood apart—glaring, silent, motionless. Feela coughed just enough to get the cubs to raise their faces to Anell.

"*Aros-nam-ba'Bean*," she began, "Land of Lady Light, I say it only once, names the Faer Ones' beloved haven most often called Lisnafaer or High West. It stretches from the Wulf Jaw Mountains over which Grian rises each morning to the Guardian Mountains and high cliffs overlooking the West Sea. Then I name *Aros-nam-gla'Fear*, the ferlie, ever-green groves, Dwelling of Lord Green. I say this name once. Here roam the most splendid deer of all."

Kalar's ears perked. He began to rise. Karlon nipped his ear and threatened to clamp his muzzle in a bone-cracking grip. Kalar backed down but kept his ears pointed sharply at Anell.

She pondered Sonsie's muddled revelation of sacred names, not meant for wulf cubs to bandy about. She stared at him. Like an echo from a distant time she recalled hearing the warning about Alba's heirs. Her heart sank.

"Sonsie, if you must call names, use High West or Lisnafaer, being safer and just as true. So you will know when next the raven tribe pursues you, it means Garden of the Faer Ones." She turned to the east, her eyes searching for hidden dangers. "In these strange times Fortress of the Faer Ones the closer meaning."

Turning to Birk, Anell gave her a choice of presenting her belly or giving her spot to Feela. Birk backed away. Anell's eyes glinted, hinting a smile. "I am finished."

She sniffed at Birk's wound and then called Feela to come forward. Birk glowered in bitter silence.

Feela faced Kalar and Sonsie. "The Faers Ones, Solas and Dorcha, and their beast-cohorts have shared *Aros-nam-ba'Bean* and *Aros-nam-gla'Fear*—"

"Feela!" Anell cried.

Ro scratched her left ear as if every midgie in Lisnafaer had attacked. Mundee's muzzle twitched.

Feela lowered her head. She waited. With no further ire from Anell, or Akir, she looked up. "—have shared this blessed Covenant Land since the time of the first songs and High Faer One, Lady Light, walked side by side with Auld Green One, Lord Green."

Kalar's tail thumped Sonsie, warning him to keep still.

"As all know, wulves die without song, so too the Faer Ones without light, or at least the Solas-Faers. In the First Age, in the Crossing from There to Here, three stewards of the Green shared their most precious treasure. Wulves gave song, the Faers light, and the deer dance."

"What about cutters?" Kalar blurted. Sonsie stared at him.

Karlon spat. "Blades!"

"Like the strong and silent rocks crossing Melvalina," interrupted Anell, glaring at Kalar and Sonsie for emphasis, "that is what you all must be now. Time enough to learn of those who cut and those who mend and tend. Be silent. Rest. Then Akir will lead you on a hunt of your own."

Thirteen

TEACH A WULF TO HUNT, MAKE A RAVEN LAUGH

Cubs who stray off course find ravens—or worse.

Kalar and Sonsie came to detest the drawn-out naps in the bright, Grian-warmed days of late Vine Month when plumped blackberries and oozing grapes made the bears drunk. They could hear them roaring from the salmon runs in the wild, rushing burns. Kalar yearned to sink his teeth into just one bellowing bear.

The pack used their every wile to flush out the prey-companions clinging to whatever shadows they could find in summer's long light, but they always left the crestfallen brothers behind, despite Anell's promise. Making matters worse, the irksome ravens pestered them during their long wait for meat-shredded bones. Bumflebeak flew at their faces and pecked their noses. Knackerclaw and Grouser circled their heads, crying, "Save us some, Kalar! Caw! Caw! Not hungry, Sonsie? We'll take that bite." Then they'd fly off, cackling as they cleared the trees.

One day when the wind tore clouds to tatters, the ravens battled the gusts, forged ahead, wheeled in graceful arcs, their black wings glinting, and sliced the wind, rising and falling like dolphins in the sea. In ever-widening circles they made their way forward. Dancing the invisible waves, they called to one another. Dooleye spiraled down low enough so that Sonsie heard laughter sent in his direction. "Caw! Wulf leave-behind, ha, ha, ha, come hear secrets."

Sonsie ran after him, but Raven Lord shot toward the heavens riding a mighty updraft. Another "ha, ha, ha" sounded back to his pursuer.

Sonsie raced to keep up, trying to plant each paw firmly. He noticed every detail of the rocky ground he covered, paid attention to all the scents feeding his flaring nostrils, recalled all Beag and the others had taught him about the chase. Most of all, he strained to hear every word of the raucous crowd above, something about too many eyes in the forest, but that made no sense.

Later that night, after first lying on his left side then right, he finally stretched out on his belly and sang:

⋏ ⋏ ⋏

"Star light, star bright,
Merry Dancers gliding, Solas gaily weaving,
Not yet lamenting lack and loss.
Night dark, night stark,
Ebon barrows warding, Dorcha grimly watching,
As ever, dreaming doom and dread."

⋏ ⋏ ⋏

Kalar groaned. Night-black leaves of the nearby aspens quavered with the laughter of the roosting ravens. The ground-hugging pack looked at one another and shook their heads. "He's too young to know such things," Birk muttered.

In the morning light Sonsie asked questions about the song.

"Not now, Sonsie."

"It's nothing."

"You were dreaming."

Anell rested her head against Akir's. "Perhaps not too young, after all. You spoke true, Akir. Something crowds the woods."

"Then make them good hunters, Anell."

"Then let them chase the running, leaping prey and not a stick."

New Ivy Month brought fog, at times floating in hazy layers, and then pressing heavy and grey; the sky seemed to have fallen or sucked the earth into the clouds. No amount of shaking completely cleared their coats. Swollen water beads dropped from their whiskers. In the murk even familiar cries of their pack sounded strange, unsettling. Prey-companions escaped into banks of rolling mist, much more troublesome than any snow. The hungry pack snapped at one another or broke into fights that left scars.

When they wandered off alone, Kalar and Sonsie had trouble finding their way back to the assigned spot. Noise seeped through a sodden white wall that trapped them in a sightless world and insinuated unnamed creatures scurrying right under their noses. More than once they jerked and spun around to see if ravens had tweaked their tails.

Birk rebuked them. "Such brave hunters, afraid of your own paws cracking twigs. If you cannot see, you have noses and ears. Use them for once."

At night Sonsie became a fog-shrouded ghost. He insisted on inching right up to his brother to practice his latest howl. Kalar bit at the sound yet somehow always failed to sink his teeth into any flesh, let alone Sonsie's howling snout.

Kalar tried to ignore him. Yet often, awaiting the dawn, he couldn't turn his mind away from what Sonsie crooned in his ear.

"Alas and alack the strange ones:
Fell foe to Deer Lord,
Grim grief to Lord Green, Deer Friend,
Dark danger to Wulf Queen,
Bitter bane to Lady Light, Wulf Friend."

⋏ ⋏ ⋏

K alar protested, "Not again! Can you never be quiet? Let me sleep."
Sounding like Birk, he added, "Save your noise for when you chase the
fierce gnat, mighty hunter." He twisted his back to Sonsie, the unquiet.

⋏ ⋏ ⋏

"Why slash breathing, crying trees,
Cinder oak and pine,
Rip-wrack earth, stack stones?
Whence come cutter hordes,
Who know not the Change?"

⋏ ⋏ ⋏

K alar's teeth grated. In spite of himself he shivered and snarled. "Why
must you moan like the stricken mountain goat?"
Paying no attention, Sonsie just kept on.

⋏ ⋏ ⋏

"Beware sand-flame plagues.
Beware ice-wind scourges.
They hew and hack Faer Haven.
Who sends Terror Wulf?
Ice-North raiders, fierce, eating death!"

⋏ ⋏ ⋏

Against his better judgment Kalar turned toward his tormentor. "Where do you hear such lies?"

"Not lies, Kalar. I hear as you hear, I know you do. I just hear more—like the songs are inside my head, you know?"

"No!" Kalar huffed and scratched, then turned so that none of the adults could see his face. "If ever you shut your mouth for once and used your two good eyes, have you seen out here where we run—not inside your head." He edged closer to Sonsie. "A stag the color of Gealach? And do not sing about it if you have!"

Sonsie crept nearer and placed his muzzle on his forepaws that hugged the pine needles strewn all about. As many scents as stars above flooded his nostrils. He breathed deeply then answered, more slowly than his heart raced. "Not silver-white stag. Something else. Right after you got us mixed up with that ferlie beast with ram horns and black tongue."

"Me, too! Wait, what do you mean 'got us mixed up'? I didn't tell you to jump in the hole."

"You are my brother. After you fell, how could I not?"

"Never mind. I told you, we would never speak of that, that—wait! What 'something else'?"

"She is beautiful, Kalar!"

"Sonsie! What else?"

"Sometimes a wulf, a white wulf, fierce and bold, then something . . . something ferlie, two-legged, shining like Gealach, a long white mane. The same. But not. It gets all mixtie-maxtie in my head. I'm not sure."

92

"I'm sure." Kalar panted. "A mighty stag the color of Gealach when she is full and low. I know we seek deer-prey most of all. I will be proud one day to change my kill into wulf, yet . . ."

"Yet?" prompted Sonsie, now turning on his side and placing his paws on Kalar's ribs. He drew his head close to his brother's jaws.

"The beast calls me—I will snap your leg, Sonsie, if you tell any of the others—to follow him, like a hunt-companion, not a prey. Where he leads, I don't know. Am I awake or asleep when I see him? I never know. When I try to find him under Grian's light, nothing do I see or hear. Can he be true? With such a rack, like a walking tree?" Kalar moaned and then spat. "What if he's no more than one of your stupid songs?"

"Just as real in your asleep or awake head, brother, as the wulf I see clearly, as white as the snow that never melts on the Faer Ones' mountain fastness."

"Och! When have you ever been to their far retreat?"

"I have right here, inside my head, Enion and Edan and Marcus. Feela told me I saw true, Anvil, Fire, and Hammer. Sometimes I think I have really—"

Growling low, Kalar clamped his strong jaws over Sonsie's snout. Sonsie pulled his muzzle free. Kalar lunged. He pressed Sonsie to the ground. "No! No bad seeing. No bad doing. Not true! No such idle raven chatter. I won't." He lowered his voice to a bare whisper. "I won't see untrue things, no white stag, no dark hole filled with sounds and mad-making scents."

Light from the horizon shot through breaks in the clouds in golden streams.

Disregarding the beading blood about to run into his mouth, Sonsie replied, "Sleep-see it or not, you sneak away. I see you—then not see you, for true—with eyes awake, not turned inside my head in sleep. So 'mighty hunter,' when you meet it on the trail, follow. Or not. I mean to follow. I can't stop now that I . . . we . . . the wyrm and the apple. What songs does the Snow Wulf know? Where does the White Stag lead? Don't you want to find out, brother?"

Beag, returned early from an unsuccessful hunt, ended their dawn confidences. He barked. "Quiet! You two are worse than the nattering squirrels."

The rest of the pack straggled into camp. They circled again and again in their own sleeping dances and plopped to the ground. Sheltered by an ancient yew where the lower branches had taken root and sent up an outer trunk, Akir and Anell lay apart from the pack. Akir loved the long-lived wood, but Anell huddled close to her mate, avoiding any touch of the deadly sap.

Akir called out, "We will try again."

After a jaw-cracking yawn, he eyed the nearby trees before continuing. "Feela, see to Kalar and Sonsie. Time for first hunt, close by. See how they do. Only young and small prey-companions. We wait until Gealach goes to her rest and Grian first nibbles the dark. Best for the cubs." He sniffed the air, surveyed the entire compound, and dropped into deep sleep.

Later that night after Feela and Mundee told them the news, their first real hunt, Kalar and Sonsie ran in excited circles.

"What's this crazy swarm of pups' tails and dandelion foolishness?" Ro asked as she winked at Karlon.

"Settle down and stop wetting the grasses before and behind," Karlon added. He butted their back sides; they leapt and rolled on the ground.

⋏ ⋏ ⋏

The dawn of the young ones' first hunt found the wulves moving through a grey world, a trick of the earliest light and fog, perfect camouflage. Lifting mists revealed an Ivy Month full of color: some leaves had already turned red and burnt umber, tinged with gold. Red, green, and white marble rocks nestled in spiky scrub and tall grasses, still green but waving golden tassels, that pushed into the thick woodlands, cool and dark below, a rival to the rainbow above.

The adults laughed while herding the bouncy pups in the middle of their single file line toward a likely spot for a first hunt. The pups heard "use your noses and ears" so often that Kalar threatened to bite the next one who mentioned a nose. Sonsie told him to shut up. Birk swatted them both.

Karlon and Ro worked together to flush confused and scurrying game, but Kalar and Sonsie merely rammed into each other and tumbled like dried weeds. Infuriated, Kalar raced off on his own, only to career over a

94

slippery rock face and into a mud hole. Sonsie got a whiff of a young hare, but just as he narrowed the gap between them, he thought he heard an owl sounding suspiciously like a Faer One. He halted then stretched his head to peer into the treetops. The hare dashed on and leapt into the nearest burrow.

Down swooped what looked like a rat crossed with an owl. It had ribbed pointed ears and huge clawed, webbed wings. Proper feathers covered its body, but it trailed a long rat tail. Gleaming fangs under its piggy snout aimed for Sonsie's throat. Only Feela's and Karlon's intervention averted disaster. Dazed, the bogey-beast flapped and teetered before taking to the skies. Feela scolded Sonsie, telling him he should be glad that the pack paid more attention to their cubs than he did to his hunting. Sonsie's retort that the bogey could never carry a wulf aloft earned him one of Birk's sharpest swats and a rebuke that he was a morsel just begging to be changed. Beag agreed but pointed out, giving a nod to Feela, that the second dorcha assault on Sonsie, noisy and bothersome as he may seem, looked suspicious.

The two pups' next efforts repeated the comedy; they attacked each other or the wind or a leaf or a frog that leapt over their heads and into a nearby pond. At least a thousand insects swarmed into the air. All over trampled fields, under the thickets, and behind the rocks the unseen creatures' laughter magnified the irritating drone of the grasshoppers. Akir didn't laugh.

After their failed attempts to catch even a vole, not just one day, but several on end, Akir and the other best hunters thrust their flaring nostrils hard upon the young brothers' faces.

Now their patient teachers seemed deadly, all fangs and glaring eyes.

"Do you call yourselves wulves?" Akir roared. "Or are you quivering hares? My sons must be hunters, not empty bellies always waiting to be fed. I thought Sonsie the only faer-struck, useless one. Now I see Kalar blighted as well."

Beag frowned. "You can't blame the fog or the wet grass or anything else."

"Singing and dreaming catch no prey," Birk warned.

Anell intervened before Akir could cast more terror upon the cowering young wulves. "They are right, my sons. All living things hunt hungry, yet all around you the prey-mates almost fall into your mouths."

Not to be denied, Akir tongue-lashed his sons once more. "You have only laziness to blame for your poor showing. You won't die if you don't eat tomorrow. Hunger makes diligent hunters. You have a debt and duty to all."

Sad-eyed Kalar and Sonsie joined in the usual midmorning nap but avoided the rest of the pack and took care to lie fifty feet apart, their heads heavy upon their paws. Through sighs, each claimed he had not been a wretch like his brother and vowed a better showing at the next hunt.

By late afternoon clouds of midgies stirred the pack. With snapping jaws and flailing tails they fended off the buzzing pests. The ruckus drew the attention of Dooleye, in flight with his raven tribe, hunting for wulves to harass. Seeing mighty Akir hard pressed by a swarm of teensy insects delighted Raven Lord. Uttering a triumphant cry, he swooped upon the maddened pack, leading his raven cohorts. They snatched mouthfuls of wulf tail.

Karlon, Mundee, Ro, and even Beag bit at their new assailants, who flew to the beech limbs shading the wulves. To make matters worse, they dropped the hair on their heads—and laughed.

Knackerclaw taunted, "Better things for wulves to chase than their tails and brutal midgies, caw, caw."

Dooleye strutted right up to Akir. He raised his beak in imitation of a wulf howling but merely coughed as if clearing his throat of a cricket. He tilted his head and stared at Akir with one black eye before he spoke. "The forest harbors many secrets, high wulf. Ravens see all, more than you, wulf sire. Look to your sons."

Kalar, infected by the same agitation of his elders, crept up to Sonsie whose eyes stayed closed to the warm light. At the rustling in the grass behind him Sonsie's ears perked. His head jerked about. "Well, Kalar?"

Miffed that Sonsie had so easily detected his stealth, Kalar barked. "Birk is right. You sing too much, hunt too little."

"I hunt what I know is there because I listen and follow to the scent."

"Listen? Yes. But hunt? No. Just wait and wait! Bad enough. . . ." He paused for a response.

Sonsie yawned.

"Why must you always wail such odd songs?"

"And why must you run after every leaf and croaking tree frog?"

"'Croaking tree frog!'" Kalar bared his teeth and tried out several of Beag's fiercest expressions.

Sonsie grinned.

This putdown tickled the ravens. The beech trees exploded into a black cloud of raucous laughter.

Kalar kept on, "You howl, not for prey, not for warning, not for any wulf-doing at all. Those sounds that you spill out upon the air feel." He lunged at invisible flies. "They feel." He pawed the ground and shook himself from his wet nose to the tip of his tail. "Like . . ."

"Like something the Faer Ones would sing?" Sonsie gazed at his brother.

"Yes!" Kalar's jaws clamped shut, but unable to remain silent, he asked, "Why? Why the Faer Ones? They're not part of our hunt or the Change. Their screeches have nothing to do with us. Leave them alone, Sonsie."

"No, Kalar. No. We can't leave them alone—"

"You! You can't. I have no use for them or their gabble. Stick to your own kind. He would not haunt me—but for you—always seeking what you should not, you daftie, faer-brained fool."

Sonsie leaned down. After long silence he gazed up at Kalar. "Just stop running around like a midgie-mad ptarmigan and listen"

With no attack from Kalar, Sonsie hurried to continue. "Hear our own songs come floating back to us on the spice-scented air. Mundee and Feela say wulves, our wulf keepers, taught the Faer Ones to sing. I say Faer Ones know more, auld lore. Wulves sing our story alone, a shining stream, yet shallow, not like the river, deep and clear where the salmon play. I must know the deep story of Aros-nam-ba'Bean, like the mighty Ferlie-Bricht that flows to Lac Morna, dearly beloved."

Kalar yelped at the sounding of the auld names of their land.

Dooleye clicked his thick black curved beak. All the ravens stopped grooming.

Kalar glared. "Sonsie! You are not a keeper! You are a silly cub who can barely catch a mouse."

"I don't want to catch a mouse. I will hunt to eat, to feed kin, but, och, this biting in my heart." He stared off beyond the clouds. "It gnaws like the hunger when first we tasted our dam, yet never was I full. I ache to join the Faer Ones in full throat and throw their—no, our songs aloft on the night skies. I want to bind all together. From the then-before to the then-now to the then-after. Not only wulf songs, Kalar, something more. I know not. Sometimes my head hurts so. I wish I could meet Auld Alba. Feela says he was the first and finest makar ever."

"Sonsie, are you tick-bit? Feela is just a nursemaid who blathers; I can't bear her. She won't ever make us great hunters."

"Feela always does her part." Sonsie turned in a circle once and stared at the sky before he continued. "She feeds us, and more, you know. She hunts right along with the rest. She watches over Karlon, Mundee, and Ro as the pack goes in for the kill. I hear them after a hunt."

Again Sonsie turned in a circle. His tail thumped the ground. "Yes, Feela sings, a lot, I know, yet only about what all wulves must know, even you."

The hair along Sonsie's spine stood on end. He raised his tail and turned to face Kalar directly. "If you listened more and ran less, you would be a better hunter, Kalar."

Kalar growled. Imitating his more powerful elders, he stared fiercely into Sonsie's eyes. He flashed wet fangs at their unexpected color, neither young cub blue nor the reassuring amber of full-fledged hunters—something betwixt. Icy prickles made Kalar's hide creep.

Sonsie refused to flinch. The silence lengthened; even the crickets had stopped chirping. Neither withdrew his gaze.

A screech like a bone breaking sounded from a nearby tree. "Be wary, young wulf, for surely you have different souls. Who is to say which spirit masters, the hunter's or the singer's?"

Kalar growled and leapt at the blackened limbs. "I will be the best hunter of Aros-nam-ba'Bean—"

"Och! One teaches two; how-do-you-do? Two say the name; now each fair game—"

"Shut up, Dooleye, black-feathered cuckoo!" Kalar snarled and lunged. "Even better than Anell and Beag, I will out leap the mountain goat, outrace King Stag." His boast ended in a strangled cry.

"You have said it, young wulf, black as my tail."

Kalar turned, like one being dragged against his will. After long pause, he confessed, "I must hurry, Sonsie. I must hurry. I have a place to go. I know not where."

He stared defiantly at the horizon.

Pondering his brother, Sonsie turned his head this way and that. He made himself small before Kalar then nuzzled his head. "Perhaps, Kalar, when you find that place, I will be the one to tell you its story."

Kalar stood, utterly still, wrestling against an invisible leash.

Dooleye cocked his head. "Big, bad wulves beware, beware; tread not the path to dire despair."

Fourteen

Kalar Strays

Faer Ones change skins, change shapes.

"They're no better than ravens' fodder." Birk smirked. "Make Kalar and Sonsie go back to cubs' games. Let's see if that satisfies Sky-Wulf."

"Have a caution, Birk," Akir said. "I don't like calling out black-winged pests or the wulf-star." He looked to the southern sky. "Auld Alba's heirs shall never be 'fodder' if I can help it. As to their punishment, I agree."

A subdued Anell nodded agreement.

Beag and Feela encouraged the junior wulves to help the disgraced pair. Every time they could escape Birk and Akir's sharp-eyed scowls, they trained with Karlon, Mundee, and Ro, who ran them in the nearby meadows until their tongues dragged.

Determined to prove them all wrong, Kalar challenged the elders, collecting many buffets and scars. He could steal the stick from Birk, yet his fur wasn't thick enough to fend off her taunts.

"Kalar, the clumsy," she called him. "Fat-pawed flea killer."

"Don't worry, Kalar," Feela said. "She calls Sonsie worse."

"If you don't want her scorn, earn her praise," Anell offered her fretful son.

The camp and the tedious lessons sickened him. He begged to go with the pack on another real hunt miles from the gathering site and almost wore himself to hide and bones that summer. Hungry all the time, he never forgot Birk's slur, "What a sad change that fine red deer is making to the likes of you!"

During season-shift in mid month of the Ivy, as the rest of the pack lay snoozing off a freshly caught feast, Kalar crawled to the edge of their campsite, away from Sonsie and the wary adults. He found a lush clump of golden bracken waving in the breeze. Disturbing a field mouse, he snuggled against the ferns, content to stretch out with his head upon his paws. His strained muscles relaxed. Peace washed over him, like the time at Anell's side only four months earlier in the dark, pungent den of his birth. He drifted off to sleep, carried on the sound of water flowing nearby, oblivious to an intruder.

A long-lived stag who knew invisible paths upon which to tread with no more sound than the all-seeing but silent rocks advanced on the outskirts of the gathering site. A warm breeze moved over the slumbering wulves, carrying their scent to him and not the reverse. They lay as if dead. He studied the pack, paying particular attention to the cubs, now in their late summer growth. His glistening nose sought their scent. His ears turned this way and that.

Mindful of the danger, stepping so that not one pebble or twig sounded an alarm to trigger his doom, he gazed first at Sonsie and then at his defiant brother. What he discerned rewarded his flirtation with peril. He smiled to the depths of his ancient brain at the strong and sleek bonnie wulves. A danger for sure.

He silently withdrew. Well, he mused, black one all alone, is that your soul creeping like morning fog across your slack lips, seeking sanctuary as you dream? Tangle with White One Who Crawls, would you?

⋀ ⋀ ⋀

From their perch high in a sap-oozing pine, two owls, one a tawny gold, one a silver-tinged white, kept their wide eyes focused on Kalar and his visitor. Iova-Rhu and Lanark-Kyle had returned to scout the wulves at Master Arklevent's request. Safely concealed, they observed this surprising violation of prime quarry safety.

Iova-Rhu tightened her grip on the gnarly branch. *What is he doing so close to them and in broad daylight?*

Lanark-Kyle turned his feathered head, ear tufts raised, to peer over his shoulder. *He must be wood wroth or mightily compelled beyond all sense to stray into the wulves' den.*

Nae, White Stag never strays. He stalks with purpose.

After the stag's departure, Lanark-Kyle signaled for Iova-Rhu to follow him away from the site. From high in the sky they trailed the Stag until night then lost him under cover of the trees.

▲ ▲ ▲

Only ravens and eagles know for certain the leagues strong-jawed wulves can travel. Resolved to show his prowess, Kalar slipped away from his wardens, just beginning to rouse from their prolonged naps. He peered into the night, a good time for hunting. His bright eyes set in his black face reflected the light of Gealach's full face. His heart pounded.

The shadows and the dark trails under the trees ate up the streams of light that managed to filter through the dense leaves. The fogs, so bothersome earlier in the month, had only partly lifted. An owl's call sounded miles away or right above him, Kalar couldn't be certain. He disliked the sounds, worse yet, the odors creeping from every bush, lurking behind every blackened tree. He tried but failed to recall the warnings his elders had given of the night swoopers and crawlers that haunted the air and skulked along vine-covered trails, those different Faer Ones whose names no wulf liked to utter.

He approached the scent of something alive but not good like deer carcass, even days dead, or beast droppings that told of all berries and grasses eaten and left behind. On his guard, he advanced until the stink of rotten duck eggs gagged him. Kalar snorted, trying to clear his snout. He heard a thumping and crashing or maybe a crushing. The scent got stronger; wrath filled the young wulf. His eyes watered. He bared wet fangs and snapped his ears forward. The thing shrieked; all night noises ceased.

In the befogged light he saw it. What? No such beast, if beast it was, had Kalar ever seen before. Not much taller than Kalar, it had a head, to be sure, yet not one that wulves would suffer to live. Stringy, matted hair partly covered a hideous, gaping mouth with broken, yellow teeth; above that a bulbous nose; and above that one, only one, red eye shaded by a great bony ridge that served as a brow right in the middle of the face—all that atop a fantastic body. One, only one arm, crooked and scabbed, ended in a hairy hand with long, curling nails. The arm sprouted from a hip—or chest—upon which sat that horror of a head. Coarse feathers covered this middle portion from which one powerful, scarred leg led to one massive foot with nails to match the hand's grisly claws.

Kalar snarled. Every hair of his ruff and all down his spine stood erect. Unseen birds lifted through the black leaves and cut the streaming light into shards. They flew in fitful circles, calling warnings to their mates. The malodorous air carried the scent of decomposing sick frogs. Kalar gagged even as saliva coursed to the ground. Blood pounded in his head. Shaking himself, he took heart and roared, fit to deafen full-faced Gealach above.

The gruesome creature lunged so fast that Kalar could not mistake its deadly intent. When a filthy hand reached for Kalar's throat, he leapt over it and somersaulted. He attempted to take the deformed creature from behind, but it moved too quickly for the young wulf. Again it charged, its slavering teeth aimed for Kalar's snout. He jumped and twisted around in midair. This time he landed with all four paws on the thing's back. The talons of its foot dug into the earth. It writhed enough to discharge hot, foul breath upwards into the night air. Noxious odor enveloped Kalar. He fought to keep focused on the horror, yet all he wanted to do was run as fast as his shaking legs could carry him.

Kalar now had to deal with its mouth and hand and foot, each equipped with its own deadly weapon. His back paws pinned the creature's scrabbling foot, but the rest of it proved too much for Kalar's failing strength. Its screeching mouth scraped across Kalar's flank as its squirming hand inched toward his belly. Kalar sank his teeth into the thing's ear. A deafening shriek bolted down Kalar's spine. The taste of its blood in his mouth made him retch.

That distraction gave Kalar's foe all it needed. The creature's malformed body twisted in sharp-jerked spasms. The nails of its hand and foot squeezed Kalar' heaving ribs. No eagle clutching the wretched hare aloft in the sky gripped its prey in a crueler vise. Kalar's fiery lungs burnt up his last breath. In a final, desperate effort he turned his jaws toward the thing's head.

On the verge of unconsciousness he heard some kind of crashing racket approaching. With his last shreds of sense, Kalar awaited some new horror. A lightning swift hoof bludgeoned the monster. It flew into the air. A mad hatred blazed through Kalar's stunned relief; he sprang toward his tormentor. Cut off in mid leap, he crashed into a white wall, a warm and breathing white wall, no spectral fog.

"Be still, young wulf!" Kalar stopped, dazed and quivering in renewed dread.

The mighty wall of white pivoted on four slender but powerful white legs. His slashing hooves charged the creature that arced into the air and tumbled over and over before crashing into a grandfather oak. Its screeches ended in a series of yelps and then a stomach-turning bleat.

Kalar gaped at the alluring vision come to life before his very eyes. The lordly stag, just as Kalar had dreamt him, white and magnificent, turned his fair head and looked so steadily at Kalar's eyes that, instead of leaping in renewed attack at a seeming challenge, Kalar stood in rigid attention. The pain of his torn heart matched the stabbing confusion in his head. What? Attack? Run? He shook in place, unable to clear his head.

"Go falling into many-tunneled dens unbidden, accepting the kiss of the light wyrm—expect surprises. Some nasty. Forbear, young one, from playing with a fachan. These woods be not for you, this night, black and shining wulf. Neither be I."

The stag looked west toward Gealach, well on her way to night's rest. "To reach my goal by dawn, I must away. To follow, your choice. A good hunter, such as yourself, should find his way home with ease." He paused to turn his gleaming eye upon Kalar's face, so close to the stag's head that Kalar could count the silvery lashes of his exquisite eyes. "Were I you," he whispered, "I would seek kind Feela to mend those wounds. Then display them to your sire."

Kalar had no stomach to remain lost in the wood with the threat of unwholesome beings like the fachan attacking out of the fog. He looked away from the terrifying thing that had attacked him to gaze back down the route to his Wulf Paw home south of Lac Alina. Then, turning his head slowly to stare at the wulves' most desired prey, a beast with the mightiest hooves and the grandest rack he had ever seen, he stood in awe. He put his tail between his legs, flattened his ears, and lowered his head, coming as close to a bow as the son of Akir could manage at a time when he desperately wanted to show courage.

The white vision silently began to move on. Kalar recalled his last words. "A good hunter, such as yourself . . ." He yearned to follow; after five paces, however, the pain in his sides made him gasp. Yes, Feela was just the wulf he longed to see. He shook off his fears and thought of home and food, only to discover a new ache, his empty stomach.

Holding his ears forward and his tail smartly erect, Kalar pivoted and ran until he fell over the high bank of the Wild Hare, a stream that zigzagged along the red sandstone rock bed. He tumbled in a furry ball, dirt showering upon his head, and slid down the bank into the still, cold water. No tiny golden fish nibbled at his toes; no trout swam out between his soaked paws.

He sat in a dark sulk, cursing the Wild Hare, Sonsie, even the harmless crickets whose chatter magnified a hundredfold now that they had such a comical tale to spread. He clambered out and shook so vigorously that a silvery rainbow blanketed him and then evaporated in the breeze. He groaned but made himself breathe evenly. The wrenching in his gut renewed his pain. Famished, Kalar knew he had long missed the gathering of the pack. He headed home, relieved that the fog had lifted. Angry now, he howled, barked, and howled again.

That signal gave Beag all he needed to find him. He answered Kalar in a gruff voice, sharp enough to make even fools cower. Heedless, tail wagging,

Kalar raced to where Beag stood, feet planted squarely in the path. He grabbed Kalar by his ruff, shook him with three sharp twists, and spat him out. "Come home, you treacherous mealy-mite, you. We returned loaded with prey-meat to find Sonsie, who for once had nothing to say, all alone. You did not return our calls. Anell sent me to track you down. Everyone has eaten, even Feela."

Kalar's heart sank. Everyone has eaten. Even Feela. Nothing for me. He didn't even notice my battle scars. Kalar slunk forward, head down but tail up.

Beag pounced on Kalar's behind and snarled in his ear, "Behave, and mind your ears and tail."

▲ ▲ ▲

Brought home, not triumphant from his battle, but disgraced, forced to lie off by himself, Kalar curled his tail on his hunger and sighed through the long hairs. He watched the pine shadows shorten. His belly roared like an avalanche.

A thump nearby caught his attention; he smelled deer. Raising his head, he saw Feela return to the outer circle of the napping pack. Sonsie peered, one-eyed, through his tail.

"Feela!" Anell hissed. "He'll never be ready for the wilds of winter if you baby him now that autumn is hard upon us."

"Food first, wounds next."

"Wounds? What wounds?"

"Kalar went without leave. He had an adventure, make no mistake, and lives to tell about it. If you see fit. He bears the marks of a fight and should be tended."

"Do so, Feela, and draw him out. Let me know if his tale is fit to share with Akir or best left a secret between you two, and probably Sonsie, who should have enough sense to keep his mouth shut."

Fifteen

The Last to Know

A wounded wulf must have brave heart.

Sonsie tried but could not keep still; inch by inch, first paws then belly, he edged forward. His nose twitched and his tongue ran wet. He nearly choked trying to keep silent in the browned sedges yet steal close enough to hear Kalar. He tasted the danger radiating from Kalar's matted fur, smelled the well-known Kalar, his den mate, and something new, the intoxicating sweetness of live deer and a sickening odor that had no name.

Feela lugged Kalar into the nearby stream, hauled him out, none too gently, and then licked his face and other torn places on his body. For all Sonsie's effort, he only heard "stag . . . white . . . good . . . bad beast . . . broken."

Sonsie's tail wagged with a life of its own.

Feela pivoted. "Sonsie! What are you doing here?"

"Is he hurt?" He turned to his woebegone brother. "Kalar, are you hurt? You smell bad. What do you mean 'broken'? Where were you? Can I go too?"

"No! Stay put where we tell you, Sonsie, as Kalar should have, and settle down, young wulf, or I'll toss you in the water as well." Feela's fierce eyes now glinted with curiosity. "He is free, though, to answer your questions."

Kalar glared at them. He shook his coat as if he were shaking off a swarm of flies. He opened a few of the deeper wounds which Feela promptly attended, despite his steady frown.

"Kalar, tell me or your sire. Sonsie, go back. Kalar does not need you here, all wriggling ears and braying mouth." She barked. "Go!"

Sonsie turned to leave, yet his determined gaze told them both that he'd crack this bone to the marrow.

▲ ▲ ▲

Akir watched Grian's climb over the mountains, bringing welcome warmth to the chilled morning. Air, filled with aromas of hazel and beech nuts, ruffled his thickening coat. The golden leaves of the aspen, a mass of flaming tongues, all laughed in the light. Akir didn't care that the dawn frosts had burnt off to usher in clear skies. He wanted a night of good hunting. He shook his head and inhaled. He smelled change coming in the waning days of Ivy Month.

The urgent need to turn his sons into hunters kept Akir awake, made him snappish. During the day, instead of resting, he considered the many paths to likely prey and tried to ignore the unsought warning from the sky. At night on the hunt he pondered when to take the cubs again and how far to lead them before their strength gave out or they made some pup blunder that cost the pack a meal, or worse. He scouted safe hiding places for when the pack pursued prey too dangerous for cubs. He liked the cover of wooded trails, now fragrant with fallen leaves, or the rock-strewn ways of the high grounds that abetted the stealthy wulf.

Prior to leaving for the evening hunt, Akir looked up and gazed on Gealach's face. Her silver light poured over him. He sniffed the air and caught the scent of stags' velvet hanging from bushes and trees all over Lisnafaer.

He turned to his mate. "The time for great hunts draws near."

Her eyes glistened. "Restless stags rattle and bellow in the forests. The time to move draws near. Back to the coast." Her nose touched his. "There I would make new den, Akir. We can hunt along the way."

"Hunt first. Grian retreats. Gealach advances. Soon they share the sky; then the world changes: longer nights, meager days, stags rut, snow comes— and hunger. Kalar and Sonsie must help bring down prey. I would test them again, soon. Then we will see to moving east. Or west."

Anell persisted. "I seek to keep our sons safe. Sky-Wulf sent a faerwulf to warn us."

Akir snapped. "Warning taken. What better guards than a wulf pack?"

Anell's fur rippled. "No! After Kalar's rash run-in with a creature way beyond his ken, aye, far beyond his power to fight, I will bear our next offspring within the embrace of the apples—and no place else!"

"Kalar! Did what?" Akir roared. His muzzle wrinkled so that his teeth flashed dangerously.

"Got into a fight. Not badly hurt. Just shaken. Nips and tears, mostly. Feela has tended him, but you must see to your son, Akir."

"See to my son? What did he fight, coming home alive with no prey to change? When? Was he attacked? Where—"

"He wandered off, no alone, not with Sonsie, when he was attacked. Why don't you let Kalar tell you himself? I know little more. Feela and Kalar, and now Sonsie, are in a state. Feela fussing, Kalar hiding his head, just after sneaking a look to make certain we noticed his scars, and Sonsie leaping all about begging for details that his stone-jawed brother seems ready to die before he tells."

Akir spun around and called Feela. "Send Kalar!"

Feela didn't have to push her ward to face Akir. White Stag's words, "Tell your sire," stayed with him. Before setting off on what seemed like the longest trek of his life, far worse than taking the ill-fated trail the previous night, he gulped and pawed the ground, raking his claws in the grasses, tearing them loose, digging his nails in the earth. His nerve gathered, he looked for the ravens. Gone! He swallowed twice, praying Sonsie would keep quiet.

Feela had warned him to present himself a humble and contrite wulf. "This is no time to tip your ears or raise your tail. Don't add to your woes, young wulf."

Kalar's lip nearly betrayed his annoyance with the one who nursed his wounds. Grudgingly, he granted that she had saved him from hunger and festering sores. He controlled his face. He loped forward but struggled. His pride chaffed at the expected humility of a tucked tail before Akir.

Sonsie attempted to follow, but Karlon butted him so hard in his side that he flew into the air before tumbling into Mundee and Ro, who promptly sat upon him.

"Stay put, you silly wulf," they hissed.

▲ ▲ ▲

Akir glowered at his son, masking his admiration of the young one's straightforward courage in confronting him. Then he recalled Kalar's recklessness. His scowl deepened.

He allowed Kalar to stand in gloomy silence.

"I am waiting, torn and tattered wulf with no prey-mate claimed, no Change offered to your pack."

"I went to hunt. I took a trail I knew."

Akir roared. "A trail you knew? So! And what did you find, son who would be hunter?"

Kalar shut his eyes. "Nothing. Not at first. I got lost."

"Lost?" Akir snorted. "Look at me." He used silence as a rod.

Kalar hung his head. His whole body sagged.

At long last Akir spoke. "The rocks just leapt from the ground to tear your—what do you mean 'not at first'? What?"

"I don't know. The night . . . so strange, Gealach made everything in the forest different, the shadows not like the day. I liked them. Then this sick smell, so bad I choked."

He stopped, stared off into the air, and shuddered.

"Smells do not leave wounds, Kalar."

Akir paused to gaze upon the thickly shaded trail to the nearby woods. Dread chilled his blood. His ears felt ice coated. He allowed a trace of compassion to color his voice, a hint that he might tolerate Kalar continuing at his own pace.

"Kalar," he prompted. "Go on. What of your hunt?"

When he heard his disaster named a "hunt," the truth tumbled from Kalar's dry mouth.

"Awful. A broken beast. Bad. No Covenant prey-mate. All one! One eye, one arm, one forepaw, one leg, one hind paw, but all claws, fore and hind! Ack!" Kalar coughed and shook his head.

"Worse than its smell—its face and body! It came so fast. I don't know how. It struck like Dooleye at a field mouse with those claws—coming at me! I fought it. I tried to fight. It was strong. I never knew one paw, one foot so strong. The claws squeezed hard. I hate it!

"Then the grandest prey-mate, a stag, a real stag, all white, tossed the foul thing in the air with his great rack and kicked it with his sharp hooves. I saw it all, clear. Gealach's light fell all over us."

Kalar hesitated.

Akir saw the wonder of the event shining in his son's eyes, a sense of awe that slowly shifted to doubt. It pained Akir to see Kalar's eyes take on a new stricken look, as if doubt had opened his heart to disgrace. "Go on," he said.

"He sent me home. He told me 'tell your sire.'"

Exhausted, Kalar fell to the ground. He turned his belly to his leader, his sire, and awaited the worst.

Akir pondered his prostrate son and all he had heard. "He sent you to tell me. Why do I hear your tale from Anell who hears it from Feela—and Sonsie—before I do?"

Iced misery flooded Kalar's innards. "He sent me to Feela first. The cuts and blood . . ."

Akir's withering stare froze Kalar's tongue. "Who is your sire, Kalar?"

"You."

"You fought this sick-shaped creature?"

Kalar shook his head in affirmation.

"And you came home alive, without its meat. Good, my son. Get up."

Kalar rolled and turned. He forced his legs to raise him to his full height and stared into Akir's usually fierce eyes that beamed with surprising kindness and something else beyond Kalar's grasp.

His refusal to look away filled Akir's heart with unexpressed pleasure. "The dorcha creature is too rank for our tastes, Kalar. You should never have met one. The solas stag is too big—and deadly—for a near whelp like you to bring down. I like his counsel. I am glad he saved you. I like not that such beings waylay you. Know, my son, that the best hunters obey their teachers. You must do so on your next hunt. Go."

Kalar's heart raced. He repeated to himself, "On your next hunt."

Sixteen

Not the Last after All

Faer White One stalks all, knows all.

Arklevents's utter concentration warned Iova-Rhu and Lanark-Kyle that their report of Kalar's encounter bore unwelcome tidings. He rose slowly from his stone seat within the ever-spring meadow, seeming to struggle against his thoughts. Purple-tailed butterflies flittered about his head. His unfurling green and amber cape created the sensation of falling leaves, all intertwined with gold swirls and knots shaped as running wulves and leaping deer.

At length he said, "I will speak to Lord Phelan."

Iova-Rhu's brows rose, but she loathed to seek Lanark-Kyle's gaze.

"Ye are free to depart. Say no more of this matter . . . Rosslyn-Tir excepted. Guard your tongues near all bogey, no matter their connection; forget not the far-seeing eye of the raven."

He reached forward and placed his hands on their shoulders in a surprisingly tender grasp. "Go with my blessings," he added. "Think not to decrease your vigilance."

He turned smartly in the opposite direction and, barely nodding at Lightning-Eater, marched up the thickly canopied trail from the inner ring of oak and stone. It led to a second, grander stone ring within the guardian oaks that encircled a grassy knoll, companion to the circular meadow. Two huge rocks camouflaged an entrance into the mound.

Approaching a barely discernible fissure between the two stones, Arklevent clapped his hands sharply. Through a momentary gap he entered a space filled with the aroma of moist soil and spiced oak moss. A maze of passageways studded with luminous crystals led high, low, or straight ahead. Each pathway bore a color that indicated a destination. He took the amber path directly before him. Minutes later he approached two guards standing before a rectangular stone entryway. Massed crystals lined the uprights under a lintel that bore the likeness of a horse in full gallop. With flowing mane and taut, well-defined muscles, it seemed alive. He acknowledged the guards' salute. The dark green leaf patterns of their liveries stirred in the crystals' glow.

Master Arklevent's appearance at Lord Phelan's quarters prompted the sentries' immediate announcement of the hunt master's guest. Arklevent stood within the open portal of the antechamber. From an interior room Phelan's voice boomed a welcome. He appeared wearing a lightweight but sturdy silk shirt, embroidered weskit and breeches, and riding boots, still sporting chains of silver bells as befit a horseman. The hunt master always accompanied Lady Light on the Grand Trooping Rades the Lords of Light so delight in, but should the Dorcha grow troublesome, he had to be ready to lead far different troops at a moment's notice.

The season of gay jaunts had passed into the precarious time when Dorcha increased their unrest. The autumn equinox loomed. Soon the lost balance of day and night would usher in the dark New Year. As commander of the Night Hunt Aloft, Phelan controlled unruly Dorcha, the living and those long dead to this world. These ghostly sky-raiders swarmed whenever the Auld Year and the New Year broke asunder.

Phelan smiled as they clasped each other's hands. Arklevent drew strength from Phelan's forthright grey-green eyes. He warmed to his smile and his strong, disciplined touch.

"My dear friend," Phelan began, "to what do I owe this most welcome pleasure, a personal greeting from master guardian of the Green, and at this time of the year when Great Grian and Good Gealach share the sky in equal measure and dole out their light in even handfuls down to the last grain?"

He put his arm around Arklevent and drew him within a circular room that suited Phelan well. Like its owner, it reflected a readiness for any need. Tack and arms hung upon the walls. Books, papers, maps, and paraphernalia of the hunt covered the tables.

Phelan led him to a pair of stone seats before a massive hearth lit with glowing crystals. On the mantle jewel encrusted goblets flashed color around the room. Two squires brought towels and two silver bowls of spring water, one warmed and scented, one iced, and set them on the nearby table. At their heels two others followed with goblets and two flagons of wine, one honeyed rose-hip and apple, one blackberry. Arklevent gathered his thoughts while washing his hands. Phelan, in turn, perused his friend's face then poured the wine.

Once they were alone, Arklevent confided in his friend. "I have just conferred with two of our most trustworthy Guardians. They keep watch on Auld Alba's far-descended pack, especially the two new cubs of Sky-Wulf fame."

Phelan whistled softly but said nothing.

Arklevent nodded. "By the Light, my friend, they are not the only source of my disquiet this day."

"And what brings about this 'disquiet'?" prompted Phelan.

"Lord Green stalks this pack, and the cubs, Kalar and Sonsie by name, to the point of foolishness."

Phelan's back stiffened. "He stalks? In what guise, pray tell."

"The Stag, all white with full silver crown."

"White Stag . . . stalks the wulves?" Phelan's eyes widened. "How long?"

"It seems. . . ." Arklevent paused to draw a fortifying breath. "Ever since Akir called them from the whelping den."

"Ah, he reverses the usual order of the hunt. Given Sky-Wulf's warning, not surprising. Something I will keep tucked under my cap, not cause for alarm, unless . . . Master of the Green withholds something." Phelan placed his cupped hands upon his lips. His brows lifted, inviting a response.

"Aye, Phelan, I will unshackle my fettered thoughts. Last night, Kalar ran afoul a fachan! Just as dorcha-death had him in its grasp, his Lordship appeared. Whether it be the influence of Gealach in her glory or some other cause, he saved the young wulf."

"I would call this a most advantageous intervention, at least for . . . Kalar, you say?"

Arklevent nodded. "Kalar, yes."

The intensity of Arklevent's eyes highlighted his frown. He leaned closer. "I ask you this, protector of Lady Light and all her secrets, what make you of this: the wayward wulf, the grisly fachan, and his Lordship—all under the same light on the same path—at this time of the year? I suspect this confluence. Wyrd, so I name it!"

Before answering, Lord Phelan inclined his head toward his friend. He paused to sip from his goblet, gazing over the rim at Arklevent's troubled face.

"We serve the Light, seen and unseen, high and low; servants all: two-legged and four—even the White One Who Crawls, bearer of the cryptic warning. That Auld Green One, the wyrm's companion, roams abroad as King Stag—and saves an errant wulf in whom he has some interest—is his affair, not ours."

Master Arklevent sipped his yet untouched wine. His drawn face revealed the distress in his heart. "High wulf Akir grinds his chops whenever his pack meets with Faer Ones, Solas or Dorcha. Just when Anell draws Akir and their pack back to the Apple Coast, the son he prizes the most blunders into both! Of a certainly, Akir knows of the fracas."

"And what of the other, Sonsie, you named him?"

"Sonsie is the apple of his dam's eye. Auld Alba and all" He shared a knowing look with Phelan. "Already he seems destined to take after his ancient sire. Akir grows impatient with him."

Arklevent frowned. "This event, so surprising—not Sonsie lost on the trail or dream-tracking a faer song on the wind—but the one destined, by the Light, to be the hunter. He was attacked, and saved, not by accident, I vow!"

Phelan shook his head in agreement. "The woods harbor many an intrigue. Who knows better than you, Arklevent?" Phelan peered at his companion's troubled face. "Come now, my friend. What troubles your heart?"

Master Arklevent punched his right fist into his left palm again and again. The sickening pain of self-doubt wrestled with his faint hope that he had not waited too long to speak. "You do nae understand. Earlier, they disturbed the ram-horned wyrm, lurking under Wisdom-Shield!"

Master Phelan bolted upright.

"He made contact with them both, or so the ghillie dhu reported to my Greenguard. As nothing seemed to come of it, I hoarded this knowledge, I confess, hoping against hope the ghillie dhu erred."

Arklevent continued, his throat tight, his eyes imploring. "None of the pack, or the ravens I hope, knows of the first encounter. In light of Kalar's more recent mishap. . . ." He arose, silent but alert.

Nodding, Phelan stood and then strode from one passageway to the next, the silver tinkling bells the only sound. At each portal Phelan waved his hand bearing a grand silver ring whereon stags and wulves chased one another through knots of holly and oak leaf. Having secured all, he rubbed his temples before speaking. "Och! More evidence that the warning, coming from the heavens to the depths of the earth and finally to Alba's heir—did it come in the nick of time or, indeed, *cause* these curious events?

"The nexus of Sky-Wulf, Faerwald, and White Stag is obvious—but a fachan? Two brushes with wyrd, the second well-nigh fatal. Will Sonsie make a third?"

Arklevent drained his goblet. "That is not the least of it; Lightning-Eater passes the name of Wisdom-Shield and hints of burning cats."

Phelan's paling blue skin emphasized the wulf figures on his face. "The meeting of the cubs with Lord Green's Otherworld companion explains White Stag's intervention. That they escaped alive suggests they have passed some occult test the wyrm's ancient brain devised without their knowing it. Some purpose beyond our ken unfolds." He shook his head as if to clear his thoughts.

Arklevent drew a deep breath before speaking. "The fachan's attack comes on top of reports of cutter soldiers, no mere pioneers, on the march. Thanks be to the Light they have not breached the Wulf Jaw."

Phelan's eyes narrowed. "To hear of burning cats—I fear some dread verting of the Covenant."

Arklevent nodded. "Aye. I had thought the Greenguard more than equal to eliminating any trace of traps that misguided cutters set in their winter hunger. A trap here and there seems tame to what may come. I fear the young wulves are destined for something deadlier than cutter traps. I lose sleep asking who—or what—verts the Dorcha, who do not burn cats."

Looking deeply into Arklevent's eyes, Phelan rested his hand on Arklevent's shoulder. "Go, good friend. I shall tell Lord Arthgallo and leave it to him to inform Lady Light. More than one it takes to keep her secrets or Lord Green's. And commend your Guardians for the care they show to Auld Alba's long-distant kin. We shall help Anell and Akir safeguard these foolhardy young wulves."

⋏ ⋏ ⋏

Once Arthgallo, Lady Light's high counselor, heard of Kalar and Sonsie's encounters, troubling to so many, could he dare not tell her? Aged wisdom, not in its dotage, may withstand the powerful allure of her luminous azure face framed by bejeweled, snow white tresses. It may disregard ravishing beauty in one so like a living emerald in a gown that shimmered with all the colors of the summer glen in Grian's boldest light. Thus, the auld counselor remained unperturbed when her green eyes flashed at his unwelcome tidings.

She harped upon one note. "Apparently, in Lisnafaer simple ghillie dhus know more than their Queen!"

She paced between the living trees in her sky-lit chamber. "My wulf cubs, mixing with the wyrm, uninvited? And his Lordship? White Stag! And a fachan? By the Light, Gealach must have been at her fullest!"

At each sharp turn she cast ominous glares at Arthgallo and named the ghillie dhu once more for good measure but made no mention of the cats—or Sky-Wulf.

Though his right hand tugged at a silver cuff button on his embroidered left sleeve, Lord Arthgallo did not quail. Rather, she piqued his curiosity when not anxious concern but an enigmatic inner glow animated her face. He couldn't deny the challenge her green eyes directed at him when she hinted that she had known all or part of his story. He could see that she rather enjoyed calling forth a reaction from "one wise in the ways of the wyrm."

Chagrin did not choke him. Ah, so young, he mused. What is she hiding? No, her fairest of faces failed to touch him.

Her regal aura, however, glowing with all the splendor of heaven and earth, the essence of starlight shining through clear water, struck him to his heart's core. Ah, how dangerous.

Seventeen

Apples, Boars—and Cutters

All hunters are hunted.

When falling leaves muffled all the woodland trails and unpicked fruits burst their skins, the pack knew that long, dark nights would soon be upon them. Shifting winds carried the pungent scent of deer to delight their quivering noses, not so the detested wood smoke from the southeast. When the weather turned erratic, heightening all sensations, the pack snarled at every flying leaf. A sense of urgency made their hides itch, their tongues sharp, Anell's most of all.

The young brothers ran pell-mell into wind driven leaf piles. A hodgepodge of red, orange, gold, and purple leaves flew skyward before raining scents that made their brains just a little barmy. They chased and rolled and crashed into trees. Not yet allowed to join the hunt, they played with such rollicking fierceness Birk had to admit they might make something of themselves, if they ever took pack needs more seriously than leaves.

Not even Feela guessed each brother struggled with his own worries.

Every night, fearing he'd never get to hunt, Kalar strained to discover any hint of nearby prey-mates. He wanted to be the first to tell Akir, but remembered images of claws, teeth, and the star bright stag flashing in Gealach's light doomed him to failure. Though he tried, he never quite banished the visions—or his doubt. He suffered Sonsie's maddening devotion to the Faer Ones as a welcome distraction from reliving the horror.

Having much to prove, Sonsie played recklessly yet always cocked an ear for faer melodies. Convinced that Kalar held clues he sought for meeting a Faer One, Sonsie kept after him day and night to tell what happened before he came home so gloriously wounded.

First in his left ear, "Where did you go?"

Then scrambling to his right, just out of range of Kalar's teeth, "What did you see?"

They raced over logs, around moss-covered rocks, and down to the rippling water. Sonsie kept on, "Did you see any Faer Ones, Kalar? Tell me."

"Don't bother me, runt."

Leaping, Sonsie thudded on top of him. They hit the earth. From atop Kalar Sonsie huffed, "Take . . . that . . . back!"

Kalar flipped him over and bit at his throat.

Sonsie gasped, "Tell me!"

Of his misadventure that fateful night, no locked sea clam kept more silent than Kalar.

Sonsie persisted, "Tell me! Tell me!" until the brothers tumbled right into Birk, who smacked them flat.

"By Gealach's gleaming face, full when you lost your senses, Kalar, you must be daftie. You, too, Sonsie, to scare off every prey-mate from here to Mount Edan."

They inhaled great gulps of air. Their tongues lolled, hot and dripping, but looking up, neither answered Birk.

⋏ ⋏ ⋏

Most of the pack welcomed the young wulves' antics, anything rather than getting entangled in the high wulves' unending dispute, apples or boars? While Kalar and Sonsie busied themselves by tugging on a discarded deer hoof, the pack gathered in the shelter of a tumbled rock pile.

Akir argued that his sons grew quickly; they should move east, closer to the Boar Bristle Forest "where hunting is good."

Anell objected. Every leaf that fell brought a new reason to head southwest to the coast and the "friendly apples."

Akir insisted, "I like the boar hunt. How we will laugh to change the hard-tusked boar into wulf."

Anell turned up her nose. "Boar? They cost us more to take down than a mouthful of their fatty haunches are worth."

"It will be good for Kalar and Sonsie."

"No! The boar tusks kill even a strong jaw like you, my love. Take us west where heaps of oak and hazel nuts make the deer fat."

Akir dug in his paws. He glared, his ears leaning forward, his light brown fur bristling. "I go nowhere but east."

Anell pivoted and leapt to a massive granite slab atop the pile. Though trees obscured her view, she stared toward the sky blue waters of Lac Tara. "I make no den in the land of the boars."

"Anell!"

She refused to answer.

Beag advanced and risked Akir's wrath. "The Boar Bristle is good for the swift raid, but its chancy borders hide more than boar."

Akir snapped. "Can Beag fear the lynx or the bearded goat?"

The rest of the pack panted and bumped against one another but remained silent.

Akir paced, paws heavy and tail lashing the air.

Abandoning the standoff, Feela joined Anell at the rocks. They gazed toward the western coast. The breeze ruffled their golden fur, just beginning to lengthen and thicken. Their ginger markings blended well with the swirling leaves.

Anell indulged Feela's affectionate nudge. "Tell me," Feela said. "What?"

"The sea. I miss the sound and the scent of it. My heart ponders our young ones' safety."

"No hunt is easy or safe; you know that."

"That deep ache suffered by wulf dams renews its assault on my heart." Anell inhaled a short, sharp breath. "I know well the dangers to all our pack.

Three lost alive to the wilds last season, the two . . . cast out dead at this year's birthing." She broke into a low, mournful wail.

All eyes turned toward her. Alert to a new emotional undercurrent flowing from one pack member to another, the cubs ceased their play.

Anell turned to Feela and said, "Then Kalar and Sonsie came and gave me hope. The Apple Coast offers many safe dens; there is Wulf Ward, home of the great forest of Four Friends."

Feela nodded.

"And." Anell's voice grew soft. "Lady Light's apples."

"Aye." Her sister sighed. "The fifth great friend, strange and marvelous the apples of the Lady. And Alba."

Hush, now. Alba's name a bone in Akir's throat.

Feela jumped down and advanced toward Beag and Akir. Kalar and Sonsie tried to follow, but she stopped them. "Not for you, youngest wulves."

She paced evenly, tail tucked between her legs, ears back but eyes bright. Forcing herself to remain calm before them, she confronted Akir. "Dorcha pests worse than ticks live in the Boar Bristle, and don't forget the giant that lives just to the east, last of his tree-crashing ilk."

Not having lost the tip of her ear or nose, she continued, eager to speak her peace and move away from Akir's bared fangs. "'When seeking boar, beware the cutter blades that follow close behind,' so warned Auld Dunoon."

At Feela's calling upon the revered keeper's name, Akir blurted that he liked new places—only to have Anell laugh. "We've been away from home too long."

Several of the pack nodded.

He could disregard Feela as an overexcited nursemaid, but the weight of Anell, Dunoon, and most of the pack forced Akir to demand they wait until after the snow fell when they'd have better tracking.

The pack looked to Anell. She jumped down. After pointing out the falling leaves and the failing light, she argued for a new den, soon, before the ice-dark scorned their hunger.

Akir sniffed the leaf-scented air. He surveyed the pack. All but Birk huddled nearer to Anell. He paced back and forth, looking at his mate with each pass, and shook his head. He snorted. "Anell, you never make den until snow covers the leaves. What ails you?"

Anell bit the air. "We've got to go before the snow buries us and it's too late to move Kalar and Sonsie."

The two stood face to face. Beag and Feela withdrew. Birk sought to take Beag's place, but Anell's low snarl through glistening teeth turned her away.

"Too many Faer Ones on the coast," Akir said.

"Not true! In winter they stay fast in their golden mountains."

Beag and Feela shook their heads. The cubs chewed their paws.

⅄ ⅄ ⅄

As if the reluctant light recoiled from what the overlapping folds of land hid in festering gloom, autumn always came early to the glen claimed by the Scanlon brothers. Few penetrated the untended overgrowth of the converging forests that surrounded their dark-hearted place. It sat in a dank hollow, making it easy to disregard the Faer Ones' Greenlaw. That suited Freyen Scanlon just fine. He used some of his ramshackle outbuildings to store noxious plants, others to hold trapped beasts.

The wife of Freyen's brother Earm avoided all the sheds and, especially, the former stone milk house. Freyen had diverted its cold spring and turned the building into an indoor pit with an iron spit. What milk still gathered from the half-starved cow he used to lure cats to their doom. Earm's wife took to her bed for days with "brain-cramps," as she called them. Her nausea from head and spine spasms worsened with each burning of the cats. Earm welcomed her screams. They masked the outcry of the tortured beasts. When the flames grew high, scorching the roof beams, the cats' screeches filled the stone dungeon. The former milk house stank of burnt flesh and fur.

Household mousers were the first victims of the brothers' lust. Soon they and all their kittens had been cindered and cast on the dung heap. Next the brothers filched all their neighbors' cats for their grisly rites. Before long they were overrun with mice and rats so that, for a time, the brothers offered rats to the flames.

"Not enough cats and too many rats," Earm whined.

Freyen spat into the fire. "Find more cats. We need cats!"

Earm wrung his hands. "Rats'll have to do." He ducked too late to avoid Freyen's cuff to his head.

Freyen's tongue sucked his front teeth. His face contorted in brutish hunger. "We'll never wipe out the wulves without we conjure the Tail."

Eighteen

WULVES ON THE MOVE

Heavy is the heart of a wulf far from home.

Wedges of snow geese flew in and out of fast-scudding clouds. Wind gusts stirred the leaf piles into swirling, colored ribbons. Acorns and hazel nuts not grabbed by the squirrels dropped and bounced. The senior wulves paid them no mind but kept watch for deer, sure to be following the "pok-pok-pok" in their zeal to turn their nutty meat into fat against the oncoming winter. Hopeful that their next pounce would yield a plump squirrel or hare, Kalar and Sonsie invariably chased what their elders ignored.

Despite Anell's urging, Akir never left Wulf Paw Forest. One clear, cold night Anell looked up to the night sky and broke her silence. "Gealach's harvest light called all beasts to prepare for the long dark. We stayed." Her gaze shifted to the pack. "Our Kalar, attacked by a dorcha bogey, returned alive, thanks to White Stag." The junior wulves yipped in agreement.

Disregarding them, she continued. "We remained, despite the danger." Silence fell upon the watchful pack.

"Now, after light lasted as long as the dark and leaves fell, Grian retreats to the west, hoarding more light each day. Do we move? No."

Sensing the pack's support, Anell pressed on. "Frost creeps in with the dark. Soon Holly King dies. Hardships come." She barked. "Akir, we must move!"

Akir tested the air. He pointed his snout toward Boar Bristle Forest and howled, short and sharp. Turning to face Anell, he growled. "Hardships never hurt a wulf."

"Remember our dead, Akir. I do not bear life to see our whelps die. Go to the apples and risk a lone Solas or two. Go to the boars and expect Dorcha and Gealach knows what else. Go east and you go without me. Apple Coast calls me. Return us, heart's rest, to our auld home. I would give birth where we know it is safe."

ʌ ʌ ʌ

The next night the pack nudged each other and yipped. They raced in circles as their tails waved, fanning the excitement that flowed from wulf to wulf.

Sonsie looked to Mundee. "Why are we leaving?"

Kalar prodded Karlon. "Where are we going?"

In a hurry, Sonsie chased his tail. "Will we see Faer Ones there?"

"Will we find deer?" Kalar added. Eager yet calm, he stood before Karlon and Ro. The thoughtful expression upon his young face gave evidence of a new seriousness since his worrisome adventure.

The junior wulves answered in turn.

"We go where Akir leads because your dam is much loved."

"At the coast where deer sweets thrive we will find dancing red deer who call our Wulf Ward within the Forest of Four Friends by another name, Hart Haven."

"As to Faer Ones, you will find more than enough to suit even you, Sonsie."

All three laughed before Karlon added, "Now get moving, and don't make Feela give you the nose."

After hugging the eastern shores of Lac Lundi, Akir turned the pack south but stayed well within South Wulf Paw Forest. "Lac Ardra and Boar Bristle call to me," he claimed.

Anell cried, "No, go directly west to the coast."

The cubs tucked their tails and tried to make themselves invisible.

Akir recoiled. "Three bad choices that way. Apples! White Stag!" He wheezed. "And Faer Ones, caterwauling like . . ." He looked up at a tremendous cloud of red kites flying south. "a screaming flock of birds! What do we gain by going where they've trampled every sure path?"

"Deer!"

"Deer are easy to find far from Hart Haven, running amok, stag-mad! The auld, sick, and lame—most likely to make the Change. We go—"

Anell flashed him a piercing look that a lord knows only from his lady.

"to the coast."

▲ ▲ ▲

A singular forest creature, two-legged for certain yet no cutter, shadowed the pack he knew as long-descended from Auld Alba the apple thief. With a sturdy growth of antlers, he appeared more a beast, but not quite. His green hair fell in glossy ringlets to veil his bushy brows and eyes and shroud his shoulders. Around his horns and head sat a crown woven of shining green holly, sporting plump red berries, and red-tinged oak leaves. Holly clusters topped his staff of intermixed holly and oak. Leaves and splotches of mud covering his green garments allowed him to blend into the thickets and trees trailing roped vines.

When the pack took to the hunt, he withdrew, disappearing in the trees, but he always remained dangerously near, especially if the young ones waited alone. When the pack slept, he moved near. Lord Green, more ancient than Auld Alba and beyond the ken of Akir, feared neither discovery nor its aftermath. Greenlaw would prevail.

With both green hands he gripped his sturdy staff and banged it on the ground. The leaves trembled. They lifted in a swirl that advanced upon the sleeping wulves. They skimmed the wulves' closed eyes and caressed their ears. The sleeping pack dreamt of beasts with great curled tusks and fangs. In their sleep they turned on their sides and pawed the air, running from a mighty wulf with jaws capable of crushing rocks. Its huge teeth gleamed. The wulf was hungry. All dreamt of the wulf, but a huge cat much larger than the forest wildcat, snapping a long barbed tail, haunted only Sonsie's dreams.

During these last days of Ivy Month the weather turned blustery. Dark, broken clouds blotted the stars at night and Grian's waning light by day. The Lord headed west toward Hart Haven and Green Isle, home to sacred holly and oak groves. He needed to tend the free roaming deer. On his trek he kept a guarded watch for a white wulf that would track him though he flew on the wind or disappeared beneath the earth.

▲ ▲ ▲

The pack crested Deer Rack Mountain, heading down to Lac Tara. Gealach's face, more than half obscured, cast scant light over the slopes. Akir led them on debris-strewn trails through the timbers. They passed, flicker-flicker-flicker, between the silver trunks.

Owls observed their passing and called a farewell—or perhaps a warning to neighboring kin down slope. Their cries echoed from the rock faces. Not to be outdone, Akir raised a howl. One by one the pack joined in, Anell first, Beag and Birk next, adding their hearty voices. The rest completed the resonant group howl, each with a different pitch. Sonsie usually followed Kalar, but tonight they joined the chorus together.

Thus, all beasts knew that the lost pack of Auld Alba the apple thief were passers-through, not permanent intruders.

Halfway down to a valley yet green, Akir paused. Anell snarled, at first a low-throated grumble then a fevered grind. As apple picking time approached,

Anell's agitation increased. She had snapped at the other females, even Mundee and Feela, and now Akir. He shook his head. The elegant tawny mask above his cream snout curled in frustration. He reminded his mate that they were moving to the coast, after all.

"Not fast enough!"

Never satisfied with their pace, Anell often ran ahead of the pack, willing them onward to the abandoned den grounds on the coast.

Along the way, Kalar and Sonsie took instruction from their elders.

"At this time of the year watch for bears, Kalar." Beag winked. "They eat more than ravens before winter. You'd be a grand mouthful."

"How will we find prey on the move?" Sonsie wanted to know. "What if we miss them?"

"Water." Akir snapped. "Hungry wulves who live to carry on the Change always find food in the waters. Neala, the Ruler, is my favorite for—"

"Tara is just as good," Anell interrupted. "And we're far away from Neala and the Wulf Paw."

Despite the obvious need to hunt and eat, Anell always urged them to move on. None complained, but some grumbled, deep in their chests until Birk or Akir snarled through wet fangs. Their trek continued for several days under trees that moaned in the wind. "Terror Wulf's breath," the younger wulves cried.

One nightfall before a hunt, Mundee and Ro recalled snatches of a tale about an immense wulf. Mundee teased, "It's not the dark that eats the light. It's a wulf even blacker than you, Kalar."

Ro shook her jaws. "Aye, he's named Vilhjalmer, Terror Wulf. He's trapped in the Otherworld; he's so hungry he eats the light."

Kalar shuddered and shot a swift glance at Sonsie whose quivering ears stood upright. He rolled the strange name on his tongue, "Vill-mer, Vilh-jaer, 'Vil-hjal-mer,'" finally getting it right.

"Quiet, all of you!" Birk called.

Kalar's eyes opened wide. "He must be a very fierce wulf?"

A grunt was his only response.

"Tell us more," Sonsie urged.

"Hush, that's all Auld Dunoon kept." Ro hazarded a glance at Birk. "Wait till you're tail grows bigger."

"What if I can't?" Kalar insisted.

"Who is Dunoon?" Sonsie interrupted before Ro could answer.

No one wanted to rile Birk before a hunt. Mundee and Ro merely snarled—too late. Birk loomed over the junior wulves.

"Magpies are no good on a hunt. You'll stay behind to watch your brothers. And keep your mouths shut about bad wulves long gone."

That ended all questions until the next day when Karlon returned the lessons to everyday wulf lore. "We have more useful matters to discuss."

"Right." Beag nodded at Birk.

The whole pack seemed to pounce on that day's instruction, as if what each had to say were the last word in hunting.

"Keep vigilant against the airborne attack, Kalar—"

"Yes, you and Sonsie grow too heavy—"

"For even an eagle to carry—"

"But their talons, like cutter blades, leave nasty wounds."

Nineteen

The Game is On

When deer rut and wulves stalk, stay clear of high White Ones.

The days grew shorter. On the black night of new month of the Reed, three nights since Mundee and Ro's blundering confidences, Gealach never appeared. Despite his desire to please Anell, Akir made a stand on the north bank of Lac Tara. "To the coast I have taken you, heart's joy, but to cross into apple land. . . ." He cast a defiant gaze at his mate. "This season, I will not."

"Close enough."

⋏ ⋏ ⋏

Half way to Green Isle, Lord Green weighed the needs of the deer against the threat to Kalar and Sonsie. Turning from his intended destination—and safety—he pursued the pack. Browned oak leaves fell from his body. Under starlight, his antler shadows seemed elongated branches, emphasizing Deer Lord's likeness to a walking tree.

Ravens tailed him in flight. "What's this? What's this?" Knackerclaw called to Grouser.

"Has Holly King abandoned the care of his hinds for this ragtag bunch of fangs with tails?" Grouser cried back.

Dooleye swooped upon them. "Take to the trees, you careless chatterers, before we lose all chance of cracking this sweet nut."

The swirling ravens headed for the tops of a cluster of hazel and ancient oaks bordering Lord Green's path.

Once they settled, the chattering began in earnest.

"Not so ragtag."

"Plump and sassy."

"Good prey-pickings."

"Change into glossy feathers."

"No chasing ravens away in these fat days."

"Bones, bones, bones!" Dooleye spat. "What of the stalker who should be running with the deer but follows the wulves? Chew that morsel!"

Invisible in black trees, the ravens cackled, tormenting the night air. The beasts sheltered below wondered if they were clearing their throats after a successful day's bone-picking or plotting some mischief to drop upon their heads.

Lord Green drew nigh the trees. He merely smiled when the Raven Lord dropped from the treetops and landed on a gnarled hazel branch level with his head.

"I say, my Lord," Dooleye began, "could you be after fostering the young wulves, so eager you seem to scout them these many a night?"

"Say I, my Lord," Lord Green returned, "Dooleye—ever quick to the kernel."

He laughed and offered his hand as Dooleye's perch. "Has Raven Lord nocht better to do than disturb the care I take with my lands?"

"I say, my Lord, now that the branches sprout from your brow, have you abandoned your hinds? No succor for your wounded stags?"

Dooleye tilted his head. "All to follow Alba's lost pack. And the latest apples to fall from the womb of Alba's heir?"

Lord Green touched the tip of his holly-oak staff to his unmistakable antlers, stroked his beard, and shifted the pleased Dooleye to the staff.

"Say I, my Lord," he began cautiously, looking at his antagonist eye to eye, "ravens, even Raven Lords, who talk too much drop corn willy-nilly. Cracking your beak this way, my Lord, leaves a trail right to your enticing and unguarded behind!"

Lord Green's immense green hand swallowed the black body; he squeezed just hard enough to make Dooleye choke on what seemed his last breath. The hand loosened its grip.

"Keep to the trees and your scavenging, my friend. If I choose to escort the wulves from behind, thus safeguarding my herds, what I learn of their strength and resources is my business—not yours. Though you may pick many an auld bone, my Lord, you do not know all."

He let go.

Dooleye shot into the air. "So say you, my Lord."

▲ ▲ ▲

Sonsie and Kalar romped in the Ferlie Forest of Four. Light ricocheted from rustling colored leaves at their peak to reveal one vast temple of trees open to the sky. Ancient rowans nestled within the loving arms of the hazel and birch, all revered. Hallowed oaks protected them all. The Four guarded the fifth magical tree, the apple, found on the coast at Avalach Crossing. Tall swaying pines threaded throughout the Four. Needles and cones, toasted to a salty spice during the summer, mixed with the fallen leaves. Hazel nut and acorn clusters feasted the red deer. The Lady and Lord of Lisnafaer loved beyond measure the Ferlie Forests, ever changing, ever new. Here Kalar and Sonsie knew bliss for the first time.

During the first days on the north shore of Lac Tara, Birk and Mundee helped Anell scout a likely spot for her new den. She selected a long abandoned site near a shallow creek and began clearing a natural hollow in the sandstone.

Kalar and Sonsie pounced upon floating sticks, every once in awhile salvaging one to chew on. They produced no sweet marrow, but the chomping made their jaws feel good.

Anell's instincts for locating abundant prey-mates proved accurate. Each hunt returned more than enough to feed the pack, even Kalar and Sonsie, who ate like a wildfire. The pack buried bones against bleak days ahead yet played leisurely as the autumn winds tousled the growing hairs of their winter coats.

Whenever the pack howled, Sonsie's tail wagged joyfully; he raced to the top of the nearest rise to await a return howl from other packs. Not disappointed, he heard cries from the north and the east, but none from the south or any further west to the coastline.

Doubtful that no other packs had taken over their former hunting grounds, Akir cautioned his pack, "Where are the wulfkin who should be here? We must scout and mark our territory—and watch for cutters."

If allowed, the younger wulves raced after Birk and Beag to set the boundaries and scent-mark to their heart's content. Under Feela's guidance, Karlon, Mundee, and Ro joined Kalar and Sonsie in identifying the sounds of their new home.

When Kalar asked, "What's that?" they told him, "Seagulls. They like to carry tales of their adventures battling crabs on the sea's shore."

"And that?" Sonsie asked.

"Waves. Salted water crashes against the shore. You must be quick to gather the treasures they spill before the gulls snatch them." Beag sighed.

During all of Akir's waking hours he sought a faint, mysterious scent. Although rutting deer enticed them all, something else flirted with Akir's heightened senses. Not the gobs of browned bracken all over the forests. Not the scurrying pine martin or fox that ran riot throughout Akir's territory or far off wulf packs hunting in other sections of the vast woods. That it lived, he was certain. When he ran his tongue over his teeth, even after a successful hunt, he never remained at ease to let the Change proceed in well-earned leisure but jumped up and paced the camp.

Birk watched. "What troubles Akir?"

Beag sniffed. "Just being careful."

Anell checked Birk's curiosity. "He always frets this way when the nights lengthen and Gealach disappears. Soon her full, kind face will shine upon us. All will be well!"

▲ ▲ ▲

As Reed Month grew colder and darker, Lord Green stayed near the pack. Spiked antlers poked through his holly crown. Daylight dwindled, yet Gealach's face grew large, just as Anell had predicted. By mid month, Gealach had waxed to a shining perfection. Heavy with light, she hovered just over the horizon, shedding her bounty, transforming Lisnafaer below. The leaves, flame red by day, now appeared as raven feathers, edged in liquid silver. As if unable to quench his thirst, Lord Green drank her light.

Under the Hunter's Light the far-seeing eagles first spotted another singular beast, a she-wulf whose shape cast long, fluid shadows. Wherever she trod, silence followed. High above, the eagles had no care. They flew toward what could be a luminous specter for a closer look. They called to one another to watch the sport unfolding below. Overhearing them, the ravens soon spied an age-old drama, sure to result in an extraordinary feast. Ravens' eyes never deceived them; the grandest wulf that any in their long lives had ever seen stalked Holly King.

Gealach's face shimmered. Below, breaking cover from a mass of birch trees, the monarch white stag of Kalar's earlier mishap veered away from his surveillance of the hunting pack. He loped in the direction of the two bored and edgy young wulves, left to their own devices in camp. The substantial white wulf, not a misty shadow after all, matched him in majesty. Hunched low, she followed him through the high, tasseled grasses.

The wulf observed the tiniest shift of his rack held gallantly upright. She watched the play of muscles beneath the stag's shining white coat in a gaze so intense that she seemed to follow every breath in and out of his lungs, to pursue the ebb and flow of every drop of blood through his heart. She anticipated his intensions before he moved left or right. Pacing a discrete distance from each other, they reflected Gealach's light in a pearly glow upon their paths.

The stag's destination never wavered. He headed straight for Kalar and Sonsie. The wulf tried a new tactic. She ran ahead and circled back, now in place to confront the stag. Sure enough, out from the bend on the low ground burst a flash of white beneath a crown of silver antler. The wulf loosed a howl, raising the hackles on every beast within earshot. The stag barked and roared, hooves planted solidly in the ground. Undeterred, the wulf swelled then growled so deeply that every four-footed beast dashed away or dove into whatever cover it could find. The winged took to the air.

The two high White Ones stood not more than twenty-five feet apart, their gazes locking. Each roared as if challenging the most fearsome enemy known to its kind. The stag shook his head, mindful of the wulf's lethal jaws. The wulf, never losing sight of the deadly hooves, once again seemed to grow, her great mane flaring. She defied the one who crippled or killed with a thrust of his hooves or a slash of his mighty rack.

The wulf's constant growl reverberated from nearby rocks. Her fangs, wet and terrible, flashed in the light. She lunged forward and back, left and right. The stag danced back and forward then right and left, mirroring the wulf's movements, all the while lowering then raising his rack. He always kept the branched horns positioned precisely to assault the wulf at her weakest spot. Instead of attacking, he pivoted, leapt over nearby rocks, and raced toward the never-fail Stag Spring. The wulf countered with a straightforward lunge, missing her quarry but continuing in determined pursuit. Upon nearing the hawthorn-clustered spring, the stag veered west toward Green Isle, his holly and oak sanctuary. The wulf, not to be denied, took the opposite direction toward Queen's Mound. She arrived at the spring between two massive stone triliths just seconds before the stag.

They confronted each other in a standstill, the stag positioned under Kernunn's Gate, Gateway to Green Isle, the wulf under an equally impressive Keriwynn's Gate that guarded the entrance to Queen's Mound, covered in birch and rowan. They both breathed heavily. The waters of Stag Spring flowed sweet and pure. The wulf's red tongue hung from her mouth.

The stag tried to avoid watching that mouth and to focus on her eyes, green as spring grass in full daylight. In mere seconds their heart beats measured an eternity. Her ragged growl turned into laughter and the laughter into sly challenge. "I am pleased my Lord has taken so much care with my wulves. Accept my thanks for good deeds tendered in the past. Go in peace, but go far."

"That my timely arrival saved your wulves merely shows the brothers would be better served under my protection, especially if bogey-beasts frequent their paths. I think I shall take these wulves for my own, Lady Wulf, blithe and bonny though you be."

"Take? My wulves? No, King Stag. Think better to guard your hinds. Steal two of Anell and Akir's cubs? If the high wulves did not take you down, I surely would."

He pawed the earth. "Harvest time ends. Gealach now shines for the hunter. Soon she shall see her face reflected on crystal blankets of snow. If you think to take back your wulves, make your move tonight." Hot breath snorted from his flared nostrils. His bellows shook the limbs of the rowans.

Heavenly light magnified the whiteness of the wulf whose comely face twisted into a terrifying grimace. She matched each of the stag's bellows with an equally fearsome roar.

His hooves continued to rake the ground. She initiated a circling maneuver, mirrored by the stag. At best, their dance risked critical maiming—at worst, death. His horns lunged at the wulf. She spun and leapt, aiming her bared fangs to slash a haunch or catch a delicate leg in her powerful jaws. Back and forth, round and round they thrust and parried until each claimed a successful strike. Their hot, red blood seeping through their white, torn coats smoked in the air. Though excited with their gory success, they suffered profound shock.

Caught in the murderous struggle, more grievous now that they had drawn blood, they remained equally loath to inflict additional wounds, as if somehow they had found their perfect mate. Panting, they broke apart. Again they stared deeply within each other's eyes, her day green to his night.

The stag's hot breath blew over the wulf's face. "What say you to one wulf for each of us?"

The wulf's nostrils flared. "Which one?"

"Let them decide."

"How?"

The stag closed and slowly opened his royal green eyes. "The Cavern Perilous."

The hair on the wulf's back shot up. "How dare that with ones so young?"

"How not dare with what we know?"

The two remained fixed in place, still quivering with the heat of their struggle. Except for their deeply drawn breaths, neither made a sound. Their locked eyes never lost intensity.

The wulf broke the silence. "Ravens' gossip, nothing more."

"Your wulves dig up auld bones, in this world and the Other, cause Sky-Wulf to call Faerwald who sings auld songs in his deep lair. Deep must answer to Deep."

"Who shall lead them?"

"Sing the song, Lady Wulf. Sonsie will follow."

The wulf's head tipped back. When the stag heard her wail, he knew he had won a moot victory.

At last she answered, "Bait the trail, King Stag. Kalar will follow."

"Are we agreed, my sweet and deadly love?"

She lowered her head and stared at him eye to eye. "Agreed, my love, bittersweet and lethal."

Twenty

DEEP INTO WILDER TIME

When the veil between worlds is thin, keep your cubs home.

"There! Hear it? A strange wulf." Akir halted the pack out hunting late one night near the dangerous end of Reed Month. They waited, expecting a response from somewhere in the vast wooded hills. None came.

Again, the call rose, clear and pure, like a high mountain stream.

Karlon fidgeted. "Where is it?"

"Behind us, closer to the camp than to us, I'd say," Beag answered.

"Yes. It calls us to join it," Anell added.

Birk grunted. "Join it? Us? Are you daft?"

"Not Anell, just that lone wulf," Akir snapped. "Daft to betray itself— after Grian takes to her den in the west." He waited. "No pack answers its call."

Beag turned to Akir. "Go on or back?"

"We hid the cubs well. They'll clamp their jaws tight. Go on."

▲ ▲ ▲

B ack at camp within a leaf-strewn crook of a gully, Kalar and Sonsie strained through perked ears to identify the elusive sounds blowing their way on the cold breeze. Kalar made out "come" and "wulf" but little else. Each time Sonsie's tail thumped the ground, leaves flew in the air. His mouth watered all over Kalar's paws.

"Sonsie!" he huffed. "Stop slabbering!"

"Quiet, Kalar! I'm trying to hear."

"A strange wulf calls us to come." Kalar wrinkled his nose at this insult to his intelligence. "How stone dead stupid!"

"Stupid? Maybe. But why does she—"

"She? What makes you—"

"Quiet! Listen. She sings of some ferlie secret."

⋀ ⋀ ⋀

"Come wee wulf, come and play,
Way down the little derry-do, up the rocky hillock.
Ah, what treasures, yours to find, deep within the hiding hole?
Solas, Dorcha—or much worse?
Ancient tunes oft hide a curse.
Come bold wulf, come and run,
Behind the bristly tricksy-tree, through the tumbly torrents.
Ah, what faer songs, yours to hear, just beyond the crinkle-crack?
Solas, Dorcha—or much worse?
Ancient tunes oft hide a curse.
Come brave wulf, come and leap,
Over the grackly springle-sprat, past the weepy willow run.
Ah, what secrets, yours to learn, just across the flaming stream?
Solas, Dorcha—or much worse?
Ancient tunes oft hide a curse."

⋀ ⋀ ⋀

Kalar snorted. "Drivel and falderal mixed up with Faer Ones and a 'curse' on top. Forget this folly!"

"Folly asks no questions, seeks no answers. You hunt your prey, Kalar, I mine."

"Don't go. The pack brings prey. Wait!"

"Not all hunger alike. The Change means more than filling our bellies. If I find the hiding hole in the gringle-grak, I'll hear those songs."

Sonsie turned to call.

Kalar pounced on his head, smothering his mouth. Sonsie's howl died in a strangled gurgle. They tumbled over and over, biting and snarling, sharp teeth seeking a firm grip in each brother's fur.

Their wulf-whirl careened into a tall, rugged leaf-covered figure. A holly and mottled oak leaf crown did little to hide the monarch antlers rising through his curly green hair. Two huge green hands reached down and pulled Sonsie and Kalar apart.

"What ho, my bonnie wulves, having a bit of a tossup, are we? Ye could do better this night! So thin the veil, the worlds merge; here be there, there be here."

He shook them, their legs all a-dangle, then, keeping a firm grip on their ruffs, set them on the ground. "If ye laddies would calm down, we may talk and walk a ways. I have much to show you, Kalar, and you also, Sonsie. Aye, names—and hearts—I know. Ah, would not Kalar love to sink his teeth into that bonnie shining stag he blundered into not so long ago. As to Sonsie, your heart desires to find your own song whispered, mayhap, by the Merry Dancers of the night, glowing so brightly now that Gealach has gone dark for the New Year. Follow me, laddies. Follow me!"

In the embracing dark, the wulves searched in vain for Gealach, but the green and blue northern skylights blazed across the heavens.

"I know a place, laddie, where these same Merry Dancers make crystal walls sing," Lord Green confided to Sonsie, who stood transfixed by the light show.

Kalar sneezed. "Just what my brother needs, another wild raven chase."

"Presume to know what your brother needs? Rather task yourself to find your great need. Should not the hunter know his prey, Kalar?"

He loosened his grip and stood, freeing them to take his measure. They looked up to the towering green creature, neither plant nor beast nor Solas-Faer, but all combined, yet strangely agreeable. They smelled no danger but puffed their chests and raised their hackles anyhow.

The stalwart fellow belched a deep belly laugh that shook all the holly covering his body.

"What say ye two?" he coaxed them. "Here ye stand, smack at the height of Wilder Time when endings swallow beginnings and beginnings spew endings. Come, greet the New Year, much the wiser for the adventure; be there and back before any elders return."

Sonsie barked. "Come, Kalar. I'm going. You can't let me have this hunt all to myself!"

Kalar looked from one to the other. Sonsie's tail thrashed. Lord Green merely folded his arms across his chest, cocked one bushy brow, and grinned.

"Sonsie, someday I'll bite off that tail of yours and give it to Dooleye to wipe his beak."

Kalar turned to the holly-covered tempter. "How far?"

"Oh, just down the trail a bit and over a ridge or two, not far, not far. Follow me." He turned sharply and headed south.

The brothers took one look at each other and followed, both their tails held high. They journeyed along Lac Tara until they approached the mouth of River Tara.

Lord Green inhaled deeply. As his broad chest expanded, the holly rustled. "Before long Mother Grian will be rising from her slumber."

He quickened his pace. Kalar and Sonsie trotted by his side.

Kalar leaned into Sonsie. "I still don't trust him."

"You'd trust him fine if those antlers sat upon White Stag."

Their guide halted at the river bank. "Look upon Harts Hold. This spot suits high leapers, as well as ye whose great paws and strong legs make ye fine swimmers. Just take that dandy channel there. Swim, young wulves."

The current that swirled around a jumble of granite islands in the dark water reflected the northern lights, creating a glamour that obscured their guide's true shape as he jumped from rock to rock. One moment he appeared wholly stag, the next a fantastical, two-legged deer, then an upright Lord Green sprouting horns. Once ashore, he jogged easily toward the southwest. "Come on," he cried.

Eager to keep up, Kalar and Sonsie dove in. Kalar so enjoyed the swim that Sonsie reached the shore first. Having crossed River Tara without incident, they shook with all their might. Feeling clean and whole, Kalar cooed soft throaty noises before following Sonsie. Later, at his brother's side he laughed. "Wipe that stupid grin off your face, Sonsie."

They continued south at a brisk pace before stopping at another swiftly flowing river.

"Were Anell to find out," Lord Green said, "she would envy her whelps. Before ye flows the fabled River Avalach. We follow it west to the cliffs that shoulder the sea."

Kalar looked up. "How far?"

"Just a little ways. Not far, not far."

And so they tagged along, heedless of any peril, to follow their noses from one exciting new scent to another. At length, their thirst led them to drink. The water, like liquid flame in the dawn light, made the wulves leap. Their guide merely laughed. The cold, wet splashes had not burnt their paws. Chagrined, they lapped the golden waters before crossing and following the southern shore.

Cries of gulls and scent of strange water startled them. They halted, inhaled exotic sea breezes, and tilted their heads quizzically at their mystifying guide.

"Salt?"

"Sea. Listen. Now at land's end, hear how lovely Avalach tumbles over the rocks into the foaming sea. Should ye live through this chancy year, young wulves, ye may come to know well this river and the apples beyond. Mind the rocks, wulf.

"The falling water offers the swiftest descent from cliff's top to the sea—a way best left to the slippery salmon, wulf."

They followed his silent lead to the shore, carefully picking their way down the rocky outcrops that bordered the waterfall on the seaward face of the cliff. They stopped on the rocky flats leading to a gently rounded cove. Water without end lapped the shingled beach.

Their guide peered west. "The tide is out. Good. The sea abandons treasures—if ye know where to look. I suspect ye may find many a marvel over yonder a ways."

He gestured with his great holly-oak staff; the red and green holly capping the top rustled.

Kalar blinked. "Where did he pull that tree from?"

They looked in the direction of the extended staff. A churning burn flowed from a peculiar pile of rocks. To Kalar they looked like teeth. He growled and bared his own.

"Here I bid ye farewell, little hunters. Let us see what ye both may find." As swiftly as he had appeared hours before, he vanished in the dawn light.

Kalar looked to the rocks ahead then back to the space so recently vacated by their baffling companion. Harried by the questions that invaded his teeming brain, he turned to Sonsie. "What I wouldn't give to hear one of your cursed songs now. What of those rocks ahead? Don't they look like the jaw of a bear?"

"If a bear, it's long dead. Come on."

They waded up the burn whose singing waters created waking dreams. Dawn light sparkled in the dew drops caught in webs strung between waving grasses among the stones that edged the shore. The burn's foaming ripples, filled with light, resembled miniature water-borne clouds that clustered around their legs before being swept away. They stopped before jaggy rocks that chewed limp-leaved tendrils, a sight that repelled yet fascinated them.

Sonsie wrinkled his nose and stared. "Kalar! They're so dark green. They shine black like the trees at midnight, just like you."

"We didn't come all this way to talk about my fur. What about that tangle of leaves?"

They stepped nearer and sniffed.

"Not sure. Those curling vines could hide a face. See, a mouth and two eyes, there." Sonsie pointed his nose toward the wall. "A jaw—with teeth—but whose face?"

An aroma of wild raspberry and honeysuckle drew them forward. When they found themselves within inches of the face's bearded mouth, they lapped water as cold as flowing ice. Although frigid over their tongues and throats, it heated their bellies.

Hoping to clear their sight, they shook their heads. Kalar barked a sharp challenge that Sonsie joined. After getting no response, they saw not a mouth but an opening in the hillside.

Avoiding the sharpest rocks, Kalar crept inside. Sonsie followed.

No past training prepared them for their discovery. They had breached the narrow opening to a three chambered cave. Light filtered through myriad fissures in the rocks, reflected from the inner burn, and danced within the chamber like Gealach shining on wind-rippled ponds.

Alert to the slightest hint of danger, they followed the noisy stream, eventually coming upon the source of the roar that increased the nearer they got. A waterfall separated the first chamber from the second, itself huge enough to shelter several packs at need. From a ledge in front of them a liquid wall crashed to a foaming basin. Heady fumes from some unknown source enveloped them. Struggling for clarity in the murky grotto air, they turned their ears to catch any hint of danger. They found none.

"No more of that one-eyed stink from the forest," a relieved Kalar shared with Sonsie. "But what smells so sweet?"

"Feela always says to trust your nose. What does it tell you?"

"Something good. Just beyond that flowing honey." Kalar's snout indicated the wall of water that glowed golden from some light within. He leapt through the cascade.

He found himself in the second chamber lit by a fire that flowed beneath the translucent floor. Seconds later, a dripping Sonsie landed at his side.

Bolts of vivid colored light streamed from the crevasses running deep in the living rock. Vapours seeped from fissures in the floor. From far in the distance they heard crashing waves. The brothers stood momentarily confused.

Sonsie's ears turned to focus on the elusive sound. "Is that singing?"

"No, birds calling!"

"No! Singing!"

Kalar shot his brother a withering look. All the eerie songs that Sonsie called down from the night played again in Kalar's head. He could no longer tell sleeping from waking. "These weird sounds follow you, Sonsie."

Sonsie blinked once, twice, only to see winged beasts, some white, some black swirling in flight, whether angered or elated he could not resolve. A white wulf chased a white stag.

"Stop!" he cried into the vision.

"Sonsie! Come back!" Kalar stepped forward and barked.

Sonsie blinked again. His trip between the worlds and back returned him to Kalar's side within the moist chamber walls and the unidentified voices.

Kalar bared his teeth and growled deep within his panting chest. "Sonsie! You went away! Where?"

"I don't know," Sonsie answered and then his sweet voice lifted a song like a light.

ᐱ ᐱ ᐱ

". . . come and play
Down the little derry-do,
Up the rocky hillock.
What treasures, yours to find, deep within the hiding hole?"

ᐱ ᐱ ᐱ

Kalar stared at the rippled floor. When his head stopped beating, he said they should follow the voices. Sonsie agreed. Soon they came to a curved opening of a tunnel. The water reflected flickering light from the sporadic, glowing crystals that studded the portal. The highlighted opening revealed a long channel running to the back of the cave.

Sitting beside the warm water, they soaked their paws and stretched the webbing between the toes. Contented sighs turned into yawns. They curled around each other, their tails covering their noses, and fell into a deep sleep.

▲ ▲ ▲

With his paws flailing at invisible targets, Kalar jerked awake. He sniffed the air and noticed the honey scent, grown stronger. He danced a startled little jig. *Danger?*

Sonsie jumped upright. His tongue tasted the sweet air. *No danger.*

Kalar tried to imitate Akir's fiercest voice, but merely croaked. "Follow the voices. No prey here."

"Prey!" Sonsie yelped. "Treasure enough for me. Come on."

Following the channel, they came to a larger room with rock steps that led to an even higher chamber. They climbed to the opening and peered within. The light filtering through cracks seemed somehow different after their slumber. Dust motes flickered in its beams. All manner of creatures seemed to live on the walls: leaping deer with brave racks held high, ravens grounded and in flight, bear and salmon, wildcat, lynx, and mountain goat, and yes, wulfkind.

Sonsie was the first to pick out the tall, slender beings, unfamiliar though pleasing to the eye. "Two-legged, they must be Faer Ones." His tail wagged.

On the wall nearest him he saw some crouching creatures with two legs, but not Faer Ones. They looked like weak bears without the heavy hide. Some kind of long, pointed horns grew out of their front paws.

"Look, Kalar. What?"

"Only a keeper knows all the beasts . . . and others."

Sonsie studied the painted walls. "Do you see the not-right thing over there?"

Turning toward the image Sonsie indicated, Kalar spied the horror that had attacked him on the trail. Around it other not-right shapes crawled on the walls. Kalar's heart pounded and his belly tightened. He growled.

Sonsie came to his brother's side. Shoulder to shoulder they wheeled around in the immense cavern of painted creatures. The fitful light played tricks with their eyes.

"I think these strange beasts do not live," Sonsie ventured with as much hope as he could summon.

"I doubt they live, but I doubt my eyes even more. Look again, more sharp this time. What do you see?"

They turned slowly in place, but this time Sonsie reversed his position. His head pushed against Kalar's haunch; his rump pressed firmly against Kalar's head. Thus, heads to tails, the brothers surveyed their spine-chilling surroundings.

"So many and so mixtie-maxtie. The light does not stay still like Grian by day or Gealach at night. Shadows wave over the others, the still ones, see?" Sonsie gulped.

Kalar stared. "No! Yes, yes! Our shadows, like a wulf both coming and going."

"Stop!" Sonsie warned. "Something else!"

Kalar locked his paws in place, every muscle tense. He breathed heavily.

Sonsie endured the same alert tension, straining to see whatever had teased his sight.

Before they could settle the question of what, if anything, lurked in the depths of the cave or crept across the walls, they detected the fragrance that had greeted them in the outer chambers. Their dilated nostrils sensed additional flavorings: one a woody musk, the other a spicy wulf-tang, pleasing to their noses.

Kalar and Sonsie examined the walls all around them, hoping to spy eyes that would betray whatever else prowled in the hidden recesses of the cave.

"Kalar," Sonsie whispered. "I think I see some cat-like bogey-beast, bigger than any lynx or stripe-tailed wildcat in Feela's tales. Look at those teeth and ears! It can't be from Lisnafaer. It glows! No—just the eyes! Do you see it? Is it alive?"

"No! No cat, Sonsie," Kalar answered from a place low in his throat. "I see a wulf, fit companion for giant Lone Grumli. He must be alive; his eyes glow, too, but no matter. He's trapped. Thick vines cover his legs and back."

"Does yours move?"

"No. Yours?"

"No. Kalar, turn around. I want you to see my cat."

"You turn, too; see my wulf."

The exchange made, each brother searched for the other's sighting. Sonsie set free his held breath. "Well, do you see the cat?"

"No. You the wulf?"

"No."

Each turned his head over his shoulder and exclaimed, "See, right there!" But when they turned their faces forward, the vision faded from view.

"Where did it go?" they asked together.

"Care not." A new voice called from the shadows behind them.

Slanted eyes that reflected the sporadic light of the chamber slowly drew near. A voice urged, "Time to leave this place, wulf Kalar, wulf Sonsie. Ye have gathered treasure enough. Now the Others come to this place and pass into the world. Once again, the world wanders into Wilder Time."

The brothers barked. "What treasure?"

"Quiet," the voice hissed. "We must hurry. Soon they shall be upon us."

From the gloom behind them advanced the grumble of a jabbering horde. By the time their fetid odors reached them, the voice had materialized a body, a wulf body, determined to get them out of the inner chamber.

"Go!" the wulf urged.

Kalar froze. "Too many, too many."

He heard sickening sounds like the dream screeches he had heard on nights when his elders left him alone with Sonsie. Until he came to this place, he had never been awake when hearing such dreadful cries.

The wulf nipped at their hind legs. "Flit! Flit, young wulves!"

Kalar and Sonsie spun around; their hackles stiffened in terror. All their senses muddled, they ran, only to tumble down the stone steps.

The wulf swooped upon them and herded them down a black, curving passageway. In the dark they could not see it, but the wulf sounded familiar, especially to Sonsie.

"What songs . . . may ye hear . . . just beyond the . . . gringle-grak," he sang in breathless gulps.

"Not now!" Kalar snapped at Sonsie.

"The *crinkle-crack*, Solas, Dorcha—or much worse?" their drover sang back. "Right now, the Dorcha your only worry. Their Grand Rade Night, this! Move along!"

Shrieks, mumbled laughter, and hoots acted as lightning to the brothers' skittering paws.

Sonsie and Kalar stared wildly about.

"What if the walls burst?"

"What if those creatures from the walls attack?"

"Halt!" the wulf cried. It blocked their passage from the black tunnel.

The wulf flattened them. "Down! Stay down! Ye may see well enough as the Dorcha pass."

Wide-eyed, they peered from the dark. Over the glowing floor crossed such shapes, such sounds few wulves had ever witnessed up close, so how could the brothers hope to pretend the passing horde was a mere nightmare? Almost against their wills they began to growl, their mouths dripping in disgust and fear.

A second shock assaulted them; two powerful hands reached for Kalar and Sonsie's muzzles and clamped them shut.

"Silence!" a new voice rumbled, seeming to reverberate within their skulls. A figure with two leaf-covered legs crouched between the brothers; his bulging arms embraced the wulves' manes. He smelled of the deep woods. In the flaming floor's glow Sonsie knew him, the baffling, living thing clad in holly!

Before the huddled four trudged an array of misshapen creatures—a jumble of long, draggling arms; gnarled, clawed hands; flying or tangled hair; flapping bellies; and huge-headed grotesque creatures, followed by some hobblers missing a leg. Of those that wore clothes, many sported red jackets, some red caps. Most had two eyes, some had one, all red and glaring, terrible eyes made for the dark, eyes that hated the light. As the mob neared the radiant floor, they ground their balled fists into blackened sockets. Most dreadful of all, they gnashed green and broken teeth.

Their shrieks rose, swelled, then tumbled from the vaulted ceiling upon the ears of the hapless wulves and their protectors. Like a mercy when Great Grian lights the day after brutish mountain storms pass, the chamber cleared, leaving only their stink behind. The rabble penetrated the waterfall. Horrific screeches burst forth.

Kalar and Sonsie strained every muscle to break free from their captor's mighty grip.

"Be still!" he snarled. "Ye wulf whelps sought to prove yourselves great hunters. Obey the first law of the hunt. Silence! If your hearts prove true, ye shall see."

"As shall we," the wulf added. For the first time, in the intermittent light the brothers noticed its color, pure white.

"Trust the Lord of the Green. The nastiest come before Wilder Time ends. Be still. Be silent."

After the ground-hugging swarm exited the outer chamber, their cries dwindled to a grumbling murmur. Soon the air quivered as when thousands of bats take flight. Only they saw no bats. Beings neither alive nor dead but something atween flew past the mouth of the tunnel.

Sonsie gaped. "They wear their bones outside their bodies!"

The wulf and Holly King pulled back, giving Sonsie and Kalar open view. They gawked, shook their heads, and swatted their noses, trying to clear away invisible threads, as if myriad web-spitting spiders had crawled all over their bodies. Sonsie wanted to sneeze, but one glance at the white wulf and her green companion stifled that urge.

Kalar and Sonsie stared at one another. Free! They stood their ground.

After the space before them cleared, the wulf advanced. "Akir trained ye well. That first batch of tricksters who leave their slime upon the ground may do mischief, gross or grim, but the flying Host deals death. They kill cutter beasts—and wulf cubs—with their lethal bolts."

She turned to Holly King. "Lord Green, did these wulves stand the test?"

He looked around and winced, feeling the walls closing in upon his body. "Let us depart and speak of these matters under the starlit sky, having the wide world of air to breathe."

Not soon enough for their liking, Kalar and Sonsie dashed across the glowing floor and leapt the wall of water. Their throbbing ears echoing every rapid thump of their hearts, they exited the cave. Gealach the Silver yet hid her face this Eve of the New Year, but the stars blazed through a break in the clouds, lighting the vine-covered entrance—just as Lord Green emerged. Twin faces shone in the light before merging clouds cast a pall.

Agonized wailing drew all eyes heavenward. High above, the flying Host had gathered all the dorcha horde into their midst. A mighty band of fleshless bones, their skulls glowing red from within cadaverous sockets, rode upon skeletal horses with eye sockets aflame as well. The Host's lashing whips drove what appeared to be swarms of locusts or scuttling crabs. At the vanguard flew the mightiest of the flying Host, huge creatures, some winged, all spike-scaled. The very air conspired to abet their flight—until they abruptly arced back upon themselves.

Alight with all the glory of the cloud-obscured stars, grim Lord Phelan and the solas troops flashed into view as if Great Grian and Good Gealach themselves had parted the black veil between the worlds. Wielding Wulfstorm, ablaze like a comet in the night sky, Phelan commanded the Light Warriors, who rode glittering faer steeds. They brandished their own flaming swords, thus confounding the Dorcha's headlong charge.

Panting, Sonsie and Kalar halted. Their hackles bristled. They looked to the white wulf and Lord Green.

The Dorcha shrieked; their burning throats reeked smoke.

The Solas split ranks at the dorcha column's tail. Lord Phelan led the right flank forward.

Building in volume and intensity, a new sound blared. Sonsie thought a huge pack of wulves howled from within the dead of night. He began to shake, as did Kalar, but Sonsie raised his head to answer.

A green hand clamped around his jaws.

"Foolish, great-hearted Sonsie. Be still!" Lord Green breathed low into his ear. "Do not interfere or betray our location. Pipes you hear, massed, airborne pipers, as yet invisible. Wait!"

The skirling pipes drew closer, grew louder. When the crescendo climaxed, the entire troop of Solas-Faers burst into song. Sonsie's heart leapt to his throat. Kalar's jaw dropped.

At once visible, hundreds of aerial pipers marched alongside mounted, singing Faer Ones, a glory to behold. Their blended voices, rumbling bass to soaring soprano, neither quailed before the pipes nor drowned them out. As the Solas surrounded the dorcha flanks, their perfect harmony worked powerful magic.

Waiting until the Solas closed ranks at the dorcha head, Lord Phelan raised his crystal sword inlaid with starsilver. The music amplified Wulfstorm's blazing light. Its beams streaked to similar swords the solas troops held aloft. Light spoke to light.

Phelan ordered the riders to pivot. All horses wheeled in unison, forcing the Dorcha to reverse direction. Relentless Solas enclosed the Host trapped at the rear. Phelan compelled the ragged-voiced Dorcha to sing with the Solas. Sonsie's clamped mouth squelched any answering song.

Tearing winds blew the night riders, obscured by lowering clouds, toward the coast.

Kalar looked from the heavens to Sonsie and growled.

"It is safe," Lord Green said. He released Sonsie.

"My night's journey nears its end." He gazed upon the wulf. "I must away to those in my care," he added wistfully, "before dawn."

The white wulf's shining eyes sought his. *Well, my Lord?*

He stood and nodded. *Both be smart and willing with proven courage.*

He scrutinized Kalar and Sonsie. *They must survive the High West winter. After Light's Return, I—or one like me—will come to choose.*

She shook her head back and forth. *Their visions have done the choosing, my Lord.* Her luminous gaze settled upon her confederate in the night's venture.

I agree. Let us see who lives to greet us in the spring.

After bowing toward her, he addressed the brothers. "Hearken to me, ye two. Cutters encroach upon the mountains; the Green needs all in Lisnafaer to be chary. Take the swiftest trail home. Master all wily Akir's lessons."

He touched his staff to their brows. "This night will be as a drifting dream by the time ye reach home. Learn all ye are able through the bitter trials of winter."

He reached down and caressed their faces. "Farewell, Kalar the Hunter. Farewell, Sonsie the Seeker. Good hunting."

Facing the wulf, he embraced her with his voice, not offering to touch her.

"Farewell, White One. Blessed be to all your cares and concerns. Grant me and mine the same as lean days and long nights fall upon us."

He turned from them. In twenty paces he had disappeared although his woodsy scent lingered, a potent reminder of his presence.

After cautioning Sonsie and Kalar to keep silent, the wulf raised a fierce cry. Sonsie felt the rocks tremble under his paws.

"I have cleared a path, young wulf brothers. I shall lead ye a little ways yonder. Then draw upon your own powers to rejoin Akir's pack. Come."

She took them on a different trail that avoided the steep way they had descended. They ran like grass on fire until they came to Harts Hold where they halted to determine the best crossing place. Dawn had not yet glimmered over the horizon, so the deep, menacing water and the far bank remained black. Roiling clouds did their best to swallow the earth. The few visible stars battled the gloom just to stay aflame.

"There." She gestured. "See the rocks? Follow me."

They plunged into the icy water and swam as if all the water kelpies unleashed this night in Lisnafaer had congregated with the sole purpose of skinning them alive. Upon reaching the other side and shaking dry, the white wulf forced them to hunker down behind her.

The brothers looked around, confused. She ignored their imploring faces and gave clear and clipped instructions for returning home. Each stretch and turn seemed visible before them. Nevertheless, they remained dazed.

"Beware the Host," she cautioned, "who travel abroad unhindered as the New Year begins—"

"But it was first light when we slipped through the leafy mouth!" Kalar insisted.

"Yes, how long have we—" began Sonsie, only to be interrupted by his brother.

"What have you done with the night?" Kalar demanded, goading Sonsie to exclaim, "Yes, how long have we been gone?"

"No time at all and more than ye know. Ye slept, did ye not? The passing of the Dorcha in the Wilder Time heralds the New Year. Make your way home, young hunter, young seeker. Stop for neither sound nor song, Sonsie. Tarry not over tooth-pleasing prey, Kalar. I hope to see ye both again before your fates become clear. Go now. Outrun the raven. Farewell."

She butted their rumps sharply but refrained from using her glistening fangs.

Twenty-One

Faer is as Faer Does

After Wilder Time beware Gealach's three mad nights.

D awn of the New Year in the month of the Birch discovered Kalar and Sonsie's racing to outrun their dread: what if they failed to beat their pack back to the gathering site?

"Faster," they called to each other.

But the pack had turned south before the brothers ended their flirtation with Wilder Time. A successful hunt across the burn called Big Fox had filled their bellies, boosting their courage. All the way back they snarled, "Back Off!" at the unknown wulf they knew prowled near their territory. Hearing no response and finding no new scent, the pack believed it had gone. Relief filled their hearts, only to fade when the two leave-behinds failed to answer their calls.

From Feela to Akir, wulf blood ran cold. They outraced the truant brothers. At a stand of five birches a half mile from camp Anell and Akir raised an urgent cry; they expected a swift response from the young ones. Nothing. Dismay overwhelmed the pack's spirit.

"I understand Kalar being cranky and not answering, but never Sonsie," Anell said.

"Something's wrong."

Akir urged them on. "They better explain themselves, or I'll skin them with my own teeth."

The anticipated happy sharing of food and tales from the hunt turned into a frantic search all over the campsite. Karlon, Mundee, and Ro found their young brothers' trail and ran in glad pursuit. Then Karlon detected a foreign scent, partly beast, mostly not, yet pleasing to his quivering nose; he yelped, excited. Seconds later, Akir and Beag inhaled deeply. They frowned and shook their heads at each other. Questions with no answers followed. Why had the two-legged walking tree with antlered head come near the campsite? Had the cubs gone with him?

Before they could agree on how to find the errant wulves, Kalar and Sonsie crashed into the very spot between the two gullies they had left, they no longer knew how long ago. The pack turned as one to stare wide-eyed in their direction.

Unable to stop their headlong flight, Kalar and Sonsie slid to an abrupt stop. Their front paws dug into the ground, resulting in somersaults that deposited them in a tangled heap. They covered their heads with useless paws. Their parched tongues dragged on the ground.

Sonsie gasped, "How can this . . . be worse . . . than—"

"Shut up!" Kalar hissed.

"No! Speak, Sonsie. Stand. Both of you," Akir said. "Look at me! Go on, Sonsie. 'Worse than' what?"

Sonsie stood and scratched behind one ear, then the other, coughed, and wagged his tail.

Akir glowered. Sonsie's tail drooped.

"Sonsie, I'm waiting. You're always so eager to sing! Explain yourself."

The flash of Akir's eyes and the dangerous snarl creasing his muzzle alerted both miscreants that someone must say something, soon.

Sonsie got out, "We wanted a hunt of our own, but we only saw terrible things in the night and got lost—" before Kalar interrupted him.

"Right. No good hunting for us," finished Kalar. He lowered his head.

Sonsie shrank. "We should have stayed home."

Kalar's tail thumped Sonsie. *Quiet.*

Birk pushed Kalar. "And just how did the little lost wulves who never obey their elders find their way home?"

Sonsie sagged, as if he had swallowed a rock. Kalar breathed heavily. He swatted and nudged Sonsie aside, only to leave himself in clear view.

Birk's question alarmed the pack.

"A fair question, Kalar," Anell said. "All want to know. Now!"

Kalar debated. *Turn my belly up or stand here and tell the whole—*

"Kalar!" Anell said. "'Whole' what?" She searched her son's shocked face. *Yes, Kalar, I hear your thoughts.*

Kalar gave up. "A wulf we don't know helped us find our way home." He immediately shot Sonsie a look that threatened his very life.

"Follow a strange wulf?" Beag said. "Do you two know how close you came to death?"

They looked at each other and shuddered.

"Aye, the thorn in the paw, my sons," Akir said. His cream and tawny head turned slightly. "Beag knows the peril of mixing with a strange wulf."

He came before his sons. "What else?"

"Nothing, sire," the brothers answered together.

Akir surveyed the assembled pack, all their ears pointing toward him. He signaled them to back off and moved closer to his wayward sons. Even though they had grown large enough to be mistaken for yearlings, he dwarfed them. Akir searched their faces. He made no mention of Sonsie's green eyes.

Looking down, he merely said, "Well, at least you have not lied to me. At most you keep secrets. Not smart, not now. Did you go with Holly King?"

"You know him?" Sonsie blurted.

"Know him? All who earn the right to pass freely in the forests know Lord Green though he changes from season to season, Holly King to Oak King. Do you know him?"

"He came by the camp," Kalar said. His usually eager face turned guarded.

"He said we should know our tasks." Sonsie started to wag his tail but stopped.

"And a hunter should know his prey," Kalar added. He wagged his tail as if he had delivered the last word in hunting.

"And he'd show us if we followed . . . just a little way," Sonsie continued. In spite of himself he yawned, fit to break his jaw.

Kalar's yawn matched Sonsie's.

Akir's whiskers twitched. "And . . . what if you two are *his* prey?"

Their heads hung to the ground.

Anell took pity on them. "They are tired, Akir. Let them sleep. We must, too. They came home unharmed; perhaps they learned something to their benefit—and ours. Lord Green, whatever his guise, never has been our enemy. His scent leaves but doesn't return."

Akir pondered his beloved's appeal. "Have it your way, Anell, but I warned you—intruders swarm this land." His gaze turned to the others. "I will pursue this matter as I would King Stag—and any strange wulf in my territory."

The pack took their rest. This time the tender-hearted Feela left no meat for Kalar or Sonsie.

⋏ ⋏ ⋏

The entire pack prepared for the winter about to rush from the snow-capped mountains and swallow the hills covered in purple heather. While they could still hunt with ease, they ran the distracted rutting deer whose barks filled the forests. Anell ate her fill, gaining strength for mating. All seemed well, yet suspicion gnawed at Akir like a canker sore. He chewed the few scraps of detail drawn from the brothers about their time with Lord Green.

At twilight of an unseasonably temperate day in mid Birch Month winds from every quarter of the High West swirled over the pack. Grian's light had all but disappeared, but Gealach's full face cast wavering shadows of trees that swayed in the gusts. All lay asleep except the high wulves. Akir could not settle his mind and gave Anell no peace. Curled beside her he confided, "My heart tells me, when the horned walking tree chooses between wulves and deer, he always sides with the deer. If Lord Green, be he Holly or Oak, is the threat Sky-Wulf fears, I am to blame that Holly King led Kalar and Sonsie astray."

Akir stood and extended his sharp curved claws. His angry howl scattered nearby beasts, even the ravens, and awoke the pack who raised their heads, awaiting call to action. He paced the camp, Anell close beside him. Convinced that the ravens had flown east to find some untended carcass to strip, Akir decided. "Anell, see to the pack. Set Birk on Kalar and Sonsie."

Heading south, he traced the remnant of his sons' scent left behind on their return from wherever they had gone with Lord Green. Clouds rolled across the sky. Gealach's face flashed like lightning strikes in the dark. Not far from home, he found the three scents merged. Anger exploded in Akir's chest, quickening his pace. By the eastern shore of Lac Tara the odor grew so strong that Akir raced flat-out. Each mile increased his fury.

By the time he reached River Tara, snow began to fall. As the flakes landed on his red tongue, they burst into tiny spouts of steam. Confused, he looked up to Gealach. He knew the keepers told tales of her light's power, but he had dismissed them as drivel. How snow? The night air felt like a return to summer solstice when Holly King ushered in the waning year. Akir shook, attempting to dispel visions of the Lord abducting his sons. He gathered himself to plunge into the clear, chill water and then reared back, as if he had struck an invisible wall.

▲ ▲ ▲

That same night the pack deferred hunting. But as soon as Grian's light broke over the Deer Rack Mountains, they drove Kalar and Sonsie through countless games of tag, snag the tail, leap the log, and jag the leg. At the end of a very long day, way after the golden light faded, they practiced creeping on their bellies and, hardest of all for Kalar, just standing still and listening. He yearned for a swift run. He wished Akir would return and take him to hunt. Sonsie gladly spent hours listening. He craved sounds, the more the better.

Under Gealach's unblemished full light on the second night of Akir's absence, the hungry pack hunted. They left Feela to watch Kalar and Sonsie. Birk refused to stay behind. Akir did not return.

⅄ ⅄ ⅄

On River Tara a swan coracle glided out from a swirling snow cloud. Bathed in Gealach's silver light, Lady Light stood in the center of this seeming apparition. Not Holly King, but as good as, Akir longed to leap, to crash his wrath upon her. Adding insult to this sore sight, she wore a white wulf hide cloak flowing from a wulf mask that crowned her head. Under the veil of falling snow her white hair, indistinguishable from the thick fur, seemed alight with fire, momentarily blinding Akir. His rage and awe combined to nearly strangle the born hunter. When his vision cleared, the sight of her constrained him like a thousand iron traps from a cutter forge.

Her coracle floated to shore, directly before Akir. Spasms of conflicting emotion shook his body. It came to him now that he heard song, increasing his confusion. Was the swan boat, in truth, a swan, singing upon the snow-drinking waters, or was the Lady truly a wulf? He almost looked around to make certain Sonsie had not followed him, had not conjured this creature with his incessant singing. He dared not take his eyes from hers, true wulf and green as summer grasses. *Like Sonsie's.* He focused on the wulf skin she wore. *Whose?* His own coat rippled.

As she came to a firm stop, not five feet from his jaws, he knew no swan sang but Lady Light herself. In wulf voice, alluring and hazardous. She seemed to drink Gealach's light and turn it to song. The cold light froze his heart. *Makar . . . Sonsie. . . .*

⅄ ⅄ ⅄

The second day after Akir began his quest, Grian's beams warmed the Deer Rack Mountains. His youngest sons stood surrounded by leaf piles that just matched Feela's flecked coat gleaming in the autumn light. Kalar hesitated in identifying the howl of a hungry wildcat over by the Little Fox. Beag prompted, "Don't let the scent of these leaves distract you. You are more than a tail at the end of a big nose. You must be ready to hunt."

Anell called Akir to come home. He did not.

⅄ ⅄ ⅄

Lady Light's song ended in a curious little growl that belied her smile. "Greetings, good wulf. Join me." She shook her head. "But no. My poor swan upon the water offers so little space to stand, should Akir dare to make the leap. That grassy bank, though, affords me ample room. I shall come ashore to you who love the land. Aye, master wulf?"

Akir started, annoyed that the Lady, who should use faer voice understood by all wulves, used wulf voice. He couldn't overlook her insinuation that he feared the water. He bared his teeth and pointed his ears forward. Ignoring the wulf head, he concentrated on her eyes, his pupils expanding dangerously. Offering no response—and assuredly not leaping aboard her swan coracle—he intensified his scrutiny of her face. He searched for the minutest hint of fear or treachery, expecting both.

She stood right before him as if she were Anell. Her deep green eyes held him in thrall, yet his chest rumbled like an approaching storm. He fought to maintain his swiftly crumbling posture of dominance.

"Wulf!" Against all good sense, she dropped to her knees, thus bringing her face and the head of the wulf she wore level with his face. The force of her will assaulted him. And yet another surprise, she held out her slender blue arm, bare but tattooed with intricate knots, and offered it to his eager mouth.

He pulled back. "What trick is this?"

"Take. Eat. Crack the bone, wulf. Suck the marrow."

Snarling, Akir ran his tongue over his lips and fangs. He sniffed no sickness. Her faereyes, now green as mountain pine, invited no death, unlike the deer at their end.

Her gaze, neither sick nor mad nor resigned to a fate controlled by an enemy's power, taunted Akir. He clamped his jaws over her sky blue forearm. Any movement on her part would prove fatal. His tongue felt her blood flowing through her veins.

"Love bite?" she teased.

He increased the pressure on her arm, his teeth hesitating within a gnat's eyelash of breaking the skin.

She refused to flinch. Their rapid heartbeats synchronized. Her head bowed.

Not to be fooled, he scowled, suspecting her sign of submission. Disturbed yet captivated, Akir found himself staring into the eyes of the wulf atop her head, unfathomable eyes—in shape so like Anell's.

He heard a voice calling from a distance, also within his head. "*Truce, master wulf?*"

Releasing her arm, he replied, "I have no great need to crack your bones."

She raised her head; a faint smile betrayed her sense of victory. "Good!" She held her open palm before his mouth. "My hand, gallant wulf."

With one swish of his tongue he tasted his adversary, first the salt of her blood and tears. Save for the water lapping against the shore, no rustling grasses, no calling birds, no chatter of the beasts hidden under browned, snow covered bracken distracted Akir. Myriad sensations filled his brain: salt lick in summer; wind of a High West morning; fresh pinesap; mint in spring rain. He closed his eyes, risky he well knew, and savored the intimacy she granted him. He sensed no buried malignancy of any sort, no concealed poison, not any his keen senses could detect, and yet, a well of sorrow—and a secret. *A trap?*

Lady Light lifted her wulf-washed palm and placed it on his forehead between his closed eyes. Likewise with eyes shut, Queen of the Faer Ones to high wulf of the lost pack of Auld Alba, she willed Akir to hear her: *Our Green faces death, wulf. No mere winter of long, death-dealing nights before happy dawn. A storm advances from the time yet to be from the time long past. We gather our friends. If friend you cannae abide, be not our enemy. All who will perish to stave off the Dark and to save the Light, I know not. This I do: two rare gifts, a singer and a fighter, you have to offer of your free will, "Akir."*

When the wulf-clad, wulf-speaking Faer One named him, he trembled. His eyes snapped open to find the tips of their noses nearly touching. He pulled back, breaking their silent communion.

"Akir, allow them to choose," she said, her gaze imploring him.

He bit at the falling snow. "How easily you ask me to sacrifice my sons."

Now in faer voice she said, "Not so easy."

She stood. Her long white hair and the wulf fur that draped her shoulders trailed behind her, nearly enveloping her gown, the deep green of mistletoe so prominent in the oak boughs overhead. She took a long awaited breath, brushed snow from her pale blue face, and sighed. "Akir is not the only forest dweller to make sacrifice, to break your heart for the sake of the Green."

Akir raised his guard hairs into a full mane, now covered in snow. "Before I or my sons choose, I must know: are you, who speak both wulf and faer to my face, true to the Light in all your guises? Or merely seeming-friend to wulves and deer as you skulk through the forest?"

Ignoring his slur, she answered simply, "A friend, tried and true, of the Light, the source of all that is Green. A foe to Akir I am not."

"You are not *my* friend, Lady, who wears the wulf as second skin. Do you kill my kind to parade your power? You and your consort stalk me and mine, steal my sons away from me and Anell . . . who still grieves her losses." He found it difficult to breathe.

"Believe what you will. He whom you seek is not yours, High Wulf Akir, to hunt. His time comes as surely as the shortest day, longest night of the year. Return to Anell. Guard your pack. Know that Lord Green does no ill to your sons or any green life that seeks the Light."

"And you, Lady, who shadows my pack unbidden?" He nodded, his gaze triumphant.

"Your bitterness, brave wulf, helps neither the Faer Ones nor your sons."

"Stay away from my sons. Stay away from Sonsie."

"I have no choice. No choice. But Akir . . ."

Her tender smile could not hide her deeper sorrow. Her eyes reflected Gealach's silver light, compelling his whole attention. "I would not harm them, Akir; know that in your heart. They have a powerful wyrd. Hinder not their destiny."

Akir fought to break free of Lady Light's gaze. He felt lost in fields of summer grasses glazed with ice. Struggling to lift his head, as though an avalanche had buried him, he howled, calling on Grian to aid him.

▲ ▲ ▲

The gloaming crept across the land on the third night since Akir had left. An owl haunted the stand of five birches, alerting a mate of food nearby. "What's that, Sonsie?" Birk asked. "Don't let mist fool you. You are more than a mouth under two big eyes. You must be ready to hunt."

Akir did not return.

▲ ▲ ▲

Looking down upon the clash of wills between Akir and Lady Light, Grian smiled on the beleaguered wulf. Daylight burst upon the snowy land and turned Tara's water gold. Lady Light bowed to a greater power come to claim her time to shine.

Melancholy deepened Akir's howl. Using the glimmer of hope Grian's warming light gave him, Akir cautiously addressed Lady Light. "I see no good if my sons mix in your affairs, Lady."

She held her pale blue palms before him. "I am the Good of all that is Green, so, too, the Lord you seek. As to your sons, teach them well to serve the Green, as you have done since coming into your power. Lord Green and I love the trees, the deer, *and* the wulves equally well, love all the beasts and the wide green earth. We three—wulves, deer, and Faer Ones—honor Greenlaw: life and death, change and life. Know this: Akir belongs to the ancient Greenlaw Covenant."

Akir acknowledged this truth. "A matter of pride to all wulves, Lady."

From Lady Light's faergreen eyes great pain and a glimmer of hope shone forth. "Surely you know, wise hunter," she whispered, "past bliss makes no sure guard against the morrow's doom. We have all lost those we love to natural change. Alas, we know not what the coming of the cutter hordes, who be not faer friends, threaten for Lisnafaer. And something worse, I fear."

Hot spittle flew from Akir's mouth. "No, Lady Light makes no warrants!" Bristling, he growled. "Faer Ones' riddles. Name this 'worse.'"

"I dare not, lest in the naming I conjure it. Neither would Sky-Wulf."

"Yet you dare seek my sons for some unnamed darkness to come. Perhaps cutters distrust Faer Ones for good reason. They threaten not wulves! You go too far, Lady."

"I fear you go not far enough, wulf. Would Akir deny Sky-Wulf's warning?"

The anger boiling in Akir's heart turned his ears hot. His nose grew dull and dry. He coughed, trying to wet his parched tongue. "Och! I will think upon Greenlaw and my sons."

He turned and raced toward an oak grove; snow flew up from each of his pounding paws. Her last sight of him was the waving of his black-tinged gold tail disappearing into the forest.

"Help me, Akir!"

Lady Light called to one already gone. Pensive, she stood on the banks of River Tara, oblivious of the swan. She remained motionless so long that the snow, despite Grian's return to the sky, mantled her in a third layer of white.

Twenty-Two

HE WHO HUNTS MUST ALSO TEACH

Obey Greenlaw: hunt, teach, thrive.

Like a wulf gone mad, Akir raced home, Sky-Wulf's warning and his sons on his mind, yet no matter how fast he ran, the vision of Lady Light's green eyes pursued him. They sent a chill down his spine.

Once home, he couldn't explain being absent for three nights and missing a hunt. He insisted he'd been gone only one night. Anell and Birk shook their heads, agreeing for once. Beag held his tongue. When Akir spared many a rutting stag's life, the shocked pack passed low grumbles back and forth.

Kalar and Sonsie bore the brunt of Akir's qualms. He scrutinized his sons' every move, making them skittish. Not even avoiding him or resorting to sly stratagems worked. Kalar, who heard the stags' thrashing pursuit of fragrant hinds to snag for their own, tried to dash beyond the borders of the training ground. Akir ran him down. At seven months old he had no hope of challenging his sire, even if he could get Sonsie's help. Far away from Akir as he could get, Sonsie chased Faer Ones' songs.

On a cold but unquiet night in the last days of Birch Month Gealach had disappeared. Kalar drew attention to the echoes of barking stags coming from any number of glens, an easy run for good hunters. He complained of hunger and urged Anell and Akir to let him hunt with the pack. Having detected hints of song on the night air, Sonsie joined his efforts. Birk and Beag howled, letting Akir know they wanted to go, too. All the rest joined in, Anell last but keenest. Kalar winked at Sonsie.

Unwilling to risk a bloody revolt, Akir howled, topping them all. The urge to hunt raced from the tips of his ears all the way down his spine to the tip of his waving tail. Kalar and Sonsie marveled at how he seemed to have swelled in size. At this sign of a hunt all the pack mobbed one another then happily ran circles in a controlled frenzy. The eager young brothers felt certain they'd follow with them alongside Karlon, Mundee, and Ro, but just as the pack warmed up for the hunt, fog rolled in.

Akir yelped a sharp "halt!"

He advanced on his youngest sons. He glared down at them, seeming to Kalar to be just as huge as the long-fanged wulf of the cavern walls. "Unready hunters die! The ravens would love that. Your pack needs good hunters, not dead cubs. If you can't obey, you'll be dead to our eyes, dead to our ears, dead to our hearts. Soon you'll feed ravens, who never care what they eat, just so it's dead. Be here when I return."

Akir turned and led the pack out into the fog-bound night.

▲ ▲ ▲

Kalar stomped to a nearby clump of bracken, brown and limp, and settled his hind quarters into the faded grasses. Sonsie joined him. He butted Kalar, toppling him over, and then lay down with his head resting on Kalar's side. "Very clever, Kalar."

Kalar merely grunted.

They tried to sleep, but the fog amplified every sound. Kalar was certain he heard the clacking of deer to the south, opposite of the direction the pack had taken. The clacking and some sort of braying got closer. Their jangled nerves made their thickening fur ripple in fits of excitement. They agreed to venture forth, just a little ways, to find whatever made this garbled noise, like laughing and singing from badly smashed mouths. They made their way through dripping undergrowth and over curving roots that snaked their way across the woodland trails. The clacking got louder. Almost before it was too late to avoid revealing their presence Kalar drew a deep sniff of something certainly not deer, not beast at all, more like rotted fruit. The cubs halted. Three creatures staggered in their direction.

He pressed into Sonsie. *Danger.*

Sonsie gulped. *What?*

They dropped to their bellies. Fog wrapped the birch trees and all the undergrowth in a thick blanket. The wulves strained to sense what capered directly before them.

Three bogey-beasts! Nothing covered their hunched backs and bowed legs except for hides tied around their scrawny necks and sunken waists. As they pranced, the pelts flapped over protruding hipbones. Each bogey gripped earthen jugs from which they took long draughts that spilled over their crooked teeth and down their chins. In their other hand each wielded long wooden sticks that they smacked against their comrades' sticks, the jugs, and each other. They laughed and stumbled, the more so with each swig they took.

Dumbstruck, Kalar and Sonsie shook their heads. They had been told that bears got tipsy on too much honey, but these weren't bears, and the pungent stuff they drank didn't smell like honey. Not daring to move but pointing their ears forward, the wulves resorted to silence.

Between guffaws, the bogies jabbered: two cutters, a dark hollow, east, Black Woods, something about Dorcha of the Gloomy Deeps. The cutters wanted cats, something to do with gold apples. They brewed firejuice. The bogies could have all they wanted, just take traps into the west or bring back gold apples. One bogey said he liked the way it made him happy. Another lamented the firemoan head. They grunted, drained their jugs, and laughed again.

"Gold apples!" They guffawed and rolled on the ground.

"Traps!" Cackling, they grasped their knees and spewed their drink.

"As if we'd touch iron jaws!" croaked one between snorts.

The revolted cubs, unable to shake the image of the deer leg caught in the trap the pack had brought home, shimmied backwards until they had cleared the scrub. Relieved to hear the bogies stumbling away from them in the fog, they bolted for home camp.

⋏ ⋏ ⋏

An hour after the birds began their morning calls, the pack crested the ridge about a mile from where the sleepless cubs waited. They could smell the familiar scents of Beag and Anell . . . and Akir! Wary, the young wulves watched them draw closer. True, they waited just as Akir had told them to, but what about the tipsy bogies and the cutters—and the gloomy Dorcha?

Carrying deer home to share, the glad pack bounced as they ran. Mundee dropped a hide-covered chunk at their feet. The cubs pulled into themselves, their posture defensive.

Karlon limped forward. "What? No Thanks?"

Oh!" Kalar and Sonsie said and hung their heads. "Thanks."

Birk nudged forward. "Is that all? Food for you, so hungry and eager to hunt. And you hang your heads like brainless slugs?"

Eager to know what they had to say for themselves, Anell maneuvered Birk away from the cubs. "What is it, my sons?"

Sonsie poked Kalar. "Tell them, Kalar."

Kalar locked his jaws.

With narrowed eyes Feela studied them. "What, Sonsie?"

Sonsie shook his white coat, imitating Akir, making himself larger. Out poured the story of the drunken bogies and the cutters who wanted treasure and cats and tried to sneak traps into their mountains.

The pack stood, panting but otherwise silent. They looked to Akir. He stared at Kalar and Sonsie who forced their gaze in his direction. But Akir saw only Lady Light's green eyes, heard only "Our Green faces death, wulf . . . and something worse, I fear."

He kept his unseeing gaze upon them so long that Sonsie nearly fainted. Akir broke his silence. "Good work, my sons. I am pleased that you keep no secrets from your pack."

Kalar and Sonsie grinned at each other.

The older wulves nudged one another. A crisis had passed.

Turning to the rest of the pack Akir declared, "We ate. We live. Karlon was brave. He will heal. Kalar and Sonsie obeyed their sire. Feed them. We must rest and think."

▲ ▲ ▲

L ater that afternoon, clouds raced across the darkening sky while the wind whipped leaves and thistledown in wide spirals. The waters of Big Fox drew all the pack for a drink. The senior wulves agreed—the bogies were cutter-sick, but long on their way. The pack could do nothing about cutters far away in a dark hollow. And how could they harm their pack? Especially now that they knew to look for traps, not funny as the sick bogies seemed to think. No, now that winter approached, they must find deer and teach Kalar and Sonsie.

The topic of deer hit the cubs' raw nerves. Why did the pack seem to think the deer smarter and swifter and braver than wulves? Sonsie piped up to say the deer could only roar and snort; they couldn't even sing. When Ro countered that they could dance, Kalar spat out a mouthful of cold water. "Och! Dance? Let me run one down; he won't dance. I'll change him to a wulf who outruns the eagle."

Ro stifled a laugh, her grey-masked eyes betraying mirth despite her attempt at sternness.

"You must show more respect," Anell said. "Look at Karlon. Before the kill, the hind delivered a nasty blow to his ribs."

Karlon looked up. "They're just as fast as we are, maybe faster."

Beag told the cubs if they wanted to claim a clever, nimble deer they must learn to call their fated prey-mate, often the sick and the lame or the elder ones. "That's how you do trees and deer good. Take down a great stag and you'll do yourself and your pack great good."

When Sonsie heard "call" his ears perked, but before he could do anything, Kalar objected to Beag's curious notion of being good to trees.

"Why be good to something I can't eat? Trees are deer food," Kalar scoffed.

As if the effort vexed him, Akir shook his head. "Anell!"

He huffed as he paced between the lichen-covered rocks and the greying sedge at water's edge. The rest of the pack scratched and stretched lazily but eyed one another, then Akir and Anell, waiting.

"Do you love the trees, Kalar?" Anell began.

"I never think about trees—only the chance to sink my teeth into a fat boar."

Birk sneered. "Fat boar! The likes of you?"

Anell ignored Akir's sister. "And you, Sonsie? Do you love the trees?"

"I like to hear the trees but don't always know what they say." Sonsie's tail thumped happily.

Kalar's nose curled in a sneer. "That's just the ravens."

"I see," Anell said in a tone too sweet for her keen glare. "It seems naughty wulves who sneak away with Holly King on midnight frolics waste a chance to learn."

She paced directly to them, halting within an inch of their downcast faces. "Look at me! Soon we no longer feed you. Hunger stalks all wulves all our lives, even you two."

The late afternoon wind drove away the clouds. Grian beamed light but little warmth. Her sudden appearance, now low in the west, cast a weave of shadows, many small ones that disappeared within one immense shadow. They reappeared off to either side of the steadily advancing shadow with pointed ears. Kalar and Sonsie ignored the flitting of Dooleye's flock, but the shade that heralded Akir's approach prompted a cold, sick knotting in their guts.

Bumflebeak called, "You're in trouble, now, young wulves! Caw! Caw!"

Playing deaf to his taunt, Sonsie and Kalar called upon all their courage to face their sire.

Though more intimidating than his shadow, the reality of Akir surprised them. Their severe taskmaster became teacher. In dignified calm he said, "To be the swiftest prey-companions, wulves dare not grow fat and slow. Change what you eat into wulf, good and strong, but eat only enough to stay alive, not all prey you see. Live with the hunger that pursues all beasts. One day you'll be thankful to eat grubs and worms—"

"Not me!" Kalar interrupted. "Never!"

"A grub?" Sonsie spat.

Akir gave both a swift swat.

"You think big paws and howling jaws make good hunters. Cubs who don't learn to hunt must join the ravens and use their claws to dig beetles from dead trees."

Mundee and Ro nodded in agreement. Birk looked smug. Akir let them know he needed no help. Karlon and Beag inched closer to Anell and Feela, the four of them keeping their faces stone still.

Led by Bumflebeak and Grouser, the ravens shrieked merrily, lightning strikes to the rebuked wulves. Kalar leapt; his jaws snapped in a futile effort to snatch even one of the pests.

Akir would have none of it. "You want to play with the scunner ravens? I can release you, Kalar. Follow the maggot-loving scavengers, and you'll be hungry sooner, longer."

Holding his body rigid, Sonsie swallowed bitter saliva just to keep it from overflowing his tightly closed lips.

Akir turned to the trees that hid the troublesome snoops.

"Fly, nebby gnats! Tell your Lord that I know how to catch rash ravens whose meat is far tastier than grubs and whose feathers clear my throat."

A storm of flapping wings and raucous cries filled the air. As he flew aloft, Knackerclaw answered, "I will give him your compliment, sire of two unruly sons."

Akir turned to Kalar and Sonsie. "Always know where these rackety bone pickers gather. Watch and listen. Learn more from ravens than they do from you."

He waited until the ravens disappeared from view. "You saw the cutter-sick bogies. Heard their talk of traps. Greenlaw condemns traps. Greenlaw names two-legged trappers outlaws. Understand your part in the lawful hunt.

Know you one true thing: deer eat the Green. The time of the desperate dark kills them."

The nodding pack drew his attention. He took a deep breath, moving his head up and down as if to clear a cloud of midgies from before his eyes. Kalar and Sonsie shifted and stretched. With a face turned savage, Feela glared at them. Shocked, they dared not yawn.

When Akir continued, the brothers found themselves straining to hear. "Wulves make fast the Balance Green: Life. Death. Change. Lord Green, Lady Light, and the Faer Ones look to wulves and deer to safeguard the Green. We give our lives to do so. So be it! Though all beasts hunger, even the ant and the beetle, none should die of wasting death. No Change, no honor. We die and live by the hunt."

Akir held his sons' rapt attention.

"Aye, trees are deer food, Kalar. Having too many deer kills the trees. Cull the deer, save the trees. Save the trees, shelter the beasts. Waste no tears on lost deer. Victorious stags mate with hinds who escape our jaws. They give birth to hardy, ever swifter young. Strong deer make stronger wulves.

"No one cries 'save the wulf!'" Akir barked, sounding like an exploding rock. After his anger subsided into a self-satisfied grunt, he continued. "Too often the stalwart deer strikes us down." He glared at his sons, as if they had become allies of the offending deer.

Anell's sigh, followed by his quick glance her way, changed his tone. "Not the tree-felling beaver or skittering hare, not any deer we cull from the prey-herds are so easy to catch as wayward cubs might think. If you want to live— and eat—you must hunt. Be swift and as quick-witted as Ro, Mundee, and Karlon. I do not ask that you rival Anell or me, or even Beag and Birk."

Beag attempted to give Birk a comradely nudge, but she trotted away in a huff. Anell bared her teeth and snarled, all the while herding Birk back to the circle.

Akir waited for silence. He fixed his gaze upon his sons. "So tell me. What were you doing with Holly King?"

"We don't know," Kalar said. He whacked his brother with his tail. Sonsie gulped but said nothing.

The ravens, having circled back to land in the topmost branches of the nearby trees, took up the call, "'Don't know,' 'don't know,' 'don't know!'"

"And that worries me," Akir said.

"'Worries me,' 'worries me,'" the ravens croaked.

Twenty-Three

DARK DAYS, DARK DEEDS

Shortest day, longest night: Holly King dies. Long live Oak King.

In Lisnafaer's forests light dwindled, seeping through grudging grey clouds; snows depressed the halest pine branches. Between storms, the pack drove Kalar and Sonsie to sharpen their hunting skills. By the winter solstice in the month of the red-berried Rowan, hunger gnawed at Akir's cranky bones. His nostrils flared; he set his face into the wind, attempting to catch the slightest scent on the iced mountain breezes. He longed to sink his teeth in the neck of a fine red deer at the end of a flat-out chase.

He searched the heavens. "Kalar! Sonsie! See Gealach's face, almost full? She shines when needed most. Do you see anyone you know? A Faer One? A wulf?"

The jittery young wulves looked at each other and shook their heads. "No, sire."

Anell came to his side and looked up. She laid her head over his abundant ruff and whispered in his ear, "How wide and full the sky. Even Gealach can't hide the stars."

"Soon?"

"Yes, soon." Anell smiled to herself.

Their sons watched as she nuzzled her mate; they sensed some mystery connected their sire and dam. Anell's warm tongue played affectionately with the tip of Akir's nose. He touched his tongue to hers. Their breaths froze in the air. The pure night air tasted like mountain springs at first thaw. It carried the fragrance of pine, but no scent from Anell called Akir to mate, nothing to burn away the images of the wulf-clad Faer One.

Akir's gaze took in the great arc of the solstice sky. "Holly King dies this night."

"Long live Oak King!"

"Long live Lord Green!" Anell completed the oath familiar to all forest dwellers.

Sonsie and Kalar starred at one another in disbelief.

Sonsie gulped. "I feel a little sick in my chest."

"Best keep our eyes open for this Oak King."

Snapping and biting, Akir urged all the pack to hunt. Only remarkable good fortune allowed them to find prey unaware and theirs for the taking. The vole and the hare nestled in tunnels buried beneath snows upon snow. The beavers lazed under frozen mud and wattle. Not so the wulves who ran the deer. Whatever the season, day and night, these hunt-companions lived under the open heavens. What secrets wulves and deer did not know, the ravens did.

⅄ ⅄ ⅄

Fat Earm Scanlon hurried along the twisting path to Scanlon Hollow. Even on this blustery winter day sweat beaded upon his furrowed forehead and dropped in round globes from his notched nose, a correction from his brother Freyen. In a jagger-scarred and filthy hand Earm gripped the sack of blood-roots he had traded the lumbering bogies for Freyen's home brew. He had thrown in the sack a bloodsucker bat, wangled from the bogies for an extra jug of whisky. He counted on Freyen to be pleased; an adder would have been better but impossible to get in winter. The other hand, no cleaner, wielded his kebbie like a weapon to whack bushes and thump the snow covered rocky ground. He looked up at the pewter sky. The closer he got to home the more difficult to tell if the sun had set. The long nights and short days of January all seemed as one in Scanlon Hollow. And he was late.

He emerged from the thicketed trees that surrounded Freyen's blotchy white-washed house. First one dog then another began to bark. A lone candle shone from the common room window. Earm bypassed the house; his wife and daughter could wait, not Freyen. The half starved dogs continued their frantic barking. Earm hurried to the shed, Freyen's laboratory where he turned deadly plants and animals into toxic concoctions.

The door stood ajar. Earm drew a deep breath and sucked in his gut, but a voice from within deflated his attempt at bravado.

"That *you* . . . Earm? I've been expecting *you. You* know I don't like to be kept waiting."

Earm's gnarled walking stick pushed open the door. He held the squirming bag before him. Bowing and sniffling, he entered the candle lit shed, as cold inside as out. Flickering shadows distorted the shapes of the bound plants that hung from the rafters. Freyen's shadow loomed like a giant scarecrow. He turned a dirk in his long-fingered hands. At each twist its blade flashed in the candlelight.

"Yes, yes, brother. I'm back with the bloodroots and, and a treat on top!"

"Looked for you well afore this. Agnesia useless, you not here. Blamed that accursed head of hers again." Freyen inspected the tip of his dirk. He drew a drop of blood. "That daughter of yours is off somewhere, curse her."

He stropped the dirk upon his leather apron, taking one swipe for each word. "Look . . . around . . . Earm." He stabbed the nearest workbench as if he were killing spiders. "Notice anything?"

Using his stick as a pointer, Earm scanned the rectangular space: the littered tables backed against the three solid walls; the crocks stuffed with weeds and dried plants, useless or noxious, he never knew which; the overburdened shelves stacked with animal cadavers; the cobwebs clustered with dead flies; the cages under the tables housing the trapped cats. . . .

Earm's bowels flushed icy cold. He dropped the stick. No cats. Not a one. The cages open. Mounds of cat turds the only evidence of once captive cats.

Earm's fat body shook. He looked wildly about the shed, the walls closing in on him. What if his wife or daughter had set them free? He uttered what passed for a laugh in Scanlon Hollow. "Is this? Is this a joke, brother? Where are the cats?"

Freyen's eyes hardened in his pinched face. "Burnt. All useless. No Scrag Tail."

Earm's ashen face regained some color. He held up the sack. "I brought back a bat. Found under a rock. Maybe it will work—"

Freyen dashed the muddy sack from Earm's hand. It fell upon the straw-strewn ground. From within came an angry squawking. Earm jumped back. "Take care, brother! Don't let it out!"

"No, Earm, it's not a bat I need. You know what I need. Cats! Not mewling and puking house cats, but wildcats."

Freyen's mouth puckered into a grin, but his narrowed eyes remained hard. He moved swiftly, catching Earm off guard, pinning his arm to the nearest table top in a vice grip. He plunged his dirk into his captive's arm just below the elbow."

Earm clamped his free fist to his mouth and bit down.

Freyen's laugh sounded like a rusty hinge. "Just look, brother. I jammed it in so hard; it got stuck in the bone. Do you know how hard it is to pull a knife out of bone?"

Earm's eyes beseeched his tormentor.

"You are going to deal with your women, aren't you?—unless you want me to?"

Striving to avoid fainting, Earm nodded, first yes then no then just hung his head.

"And you are going to get me some wildcats, aren't you?"

⋏ ⋏ ⋏

The month of the Alder heaped more snow upon the sky-high hunting grounds as brittle boughs clattered in the wind. The wulves plowed through drifts, Beag and Akir in the front, the others following. Balls of ice clung to their bellies. In these bleak days scrawny prey or none, usually bought with exhaustion, made a bitter diet that melted the flesh from their bones.

Daily tidings, passed between wulves by way of scent marking and twilight howling, told Akir that one, maybe two other packs shared the northern ranges of Wulf Ward, beyond Big Fox, beyond Lac Neala into Red Deer Forest. Perhaps two other packs hunted to the southeast in Raven Wood and Wulf Paw Forest. Far fewer than he had expected to find.

Allowed to follow the pack to observe, Sonsie and Kalar struggled to keep up and yowled dolefully when they lagged behind with only their paws to suck.

The others shrugged. "Keep up."

"Beware of the sharp-eyed Dorcha," Birk chided.

"Yes," Karlon continued, "they carry slug-boned cubs—"

"and bad cutter cubs—" Beag interrupted Karlon with a sly grin.

"into the spider pits of Mount Ansgar, the Warrior—" Mundee broke in.

"or worse, Mount Cadman, the Fighter," Ro finished with a wink at her sister.

Kalar and Sonsie shuddered, stealing knowing looks at each other, but pretended they were shaking off snow.

Their legs dragged snow as they hastened to carry on. A determined Kalar confided in Sonsie. "When my eyes close in sleep and Lisnafaer goes away, I see Dorcha, like before. When my eyes open, they are gone. Are they only in my head?"

"No, Kalar. I hear them all the time, awake or asleep, and see them, too, with my sleep eyes inside. I try not to. Birk must be right. They crawl and fly everywhere. I do not like what I hear. Listen." He let out a rumbling howl from deep in his chest then some screeches that sounded like an irate ferret. None of the pack paid him any mind. He ran to catch up to Kalar.

In the mountains, the snow fell steadily. Foot by foot, it deepened, a blanket that pulled sound from the air. Each snow created the land anew. The mists from the western isles rolled inland from the coast, froze, and crashed into the fury of the nightly blizzards. The wulves' senses grew keener. They heard small beasts tunneling. Smoke from cutter fires drifted from the far eastern banks of River Fawert between Mount Marcus and Barra where the wild cherry trees swayed. Sometimes the wind shifted from the south, carrying a scent of burnt flesh. The pack tried to get Kalar and Sonsie to ignore it and concentrate on the hunt, but they grumbled.

"How close is the fire?" Sonsie asked.

"The run of many days and nights from here," Beag said.

"I saw no lightning. How can fire burn on snow?"

Birk snarled. "We warned you of the hacking, burning cutters!"

"Cutters? But how could cutter fires be so close?" Sonsie persisted. "I thought the Faer Ones protected Lisnafaer."

He stretched and searched the heavens. "Are the cutters Dorcha?"

"Och! No! Scary though they be, Dorcha don't burn trees—or beasts."

Kalar turned his head from side to side and wrinkled his nose. "I thought the tree killers far away or just a Feela-tale to keep us from running away."

Feela acknowledged Anell's wry smile. "Like Sonsie, like Kalar! We're doomed."

Kalar let out a growl. "Who burns beasts?"

Anell glared at Birk then turned to her sons. "Quiet, both of you! Cutter smoke can't keep you from feeling prey-mates scurrying beneath the snow. Pay attention."

"Or are you not hungry?"Akir added.

"Smoke doesn't make you deaf." Birk sneered. "Listen to the hare moving through the white tunnel."

Even though Kalar and Sonsie promised to do better, ominous sounds or fleeting visions of marching Dorcha haunted them. Sonsie couldn't help himself. He broke into a coarse howl, sounding like any number of beasts being skinned alive. That earned him a good wallop. Sometimes he yearned for the blindness of the warm whelping den where he heard only his dam's heartbeat.

With no loss of biting cold Alder Month blew into Willow. Need pressed the pack. The minutest tremor or flickering movement arrested the entire pack who directed lethal stares near and far, their nostrils quivering. They turned their ears toward the slightest breeze. At twilight Akir's blood raced. His urgent cries roused the pack to hunt. He made them shake the snow from their backs and chase him. Each nip and growl, each perfectly timed sideswipe maneuvered them into a team that could wheel and turn with the precision of the golden eagle on high. He tolerated nothing less than their total effort, even from eight month old Kalar and Sonsie. Whenever they fell behind in the heat of the chase, their longing for a share from the first stripping of a felled deer kept them going. More often their reward was some gaunt hares flushed from a snow-bound warren. Even when successful, the pack labored, protruding ribs heaving, for each mouthful. They heartily thanked their prey-brothers for making the Change. When they failed, they endured yet another night of flesh-wasting hunger.

Night swallowed day; the heavens sagged in endless gloom. Gealach wandered, lost behind lowering clouds. Through the driving ice storms Grian's face shed little light or warmth. Pelting ice needles aggravated swarms of Dorcha who vexed unwary creatures. The wulves nestled together under the pine boughs, awaiting a better time to hunt.

Sonsie tried to ignore the beat of wings, not raven or owl or eagle, no prey bird he knew.

He turned in circles and fell to the ground. He struggled to close his ears, but the wind made every swaying bough cry and magnified jabbering laughter only he seemed to hear. A pine cone poked his ribs. Furious, he bit the cone and growled.

The irate adults taunted, "You'll never be a hunter—you never listen and never shut up."

They had not eaten much more than the dwindling supply of vole and hares, barely enough to stay alive. The next night the pack scouted for deer west of Lac Lundi, paying no heed to the wretched weather as their fur repelled the worst that harrying storms visited upon them. Once again, the running hunt proved disappointing.

Having returned to camp before dawn, the disgruntled pack put Karlon and Ro in charge of settling the cubs.

"Save your strength and stop looking about for mischief," Ro said.

"Yes, Grian is still resting and so should you two. Now!" Karlon said. "Kalar! Be still!"

Ro added, "Gealach has gone to her bower, asleep for the day. Take heed, Sonsie, no singing."

Groggy but jumpy, Kalar threatened to rise. Karlon smacked him flat. Ro's throat rumbled as she threw her head over Sonsie. "It's the dregs before dawn. The dorcha horde from the Black Woods of Tara-Ardra clamber about, making trouble. So bury your worrisome noses under those fine tails and don't be calling the night swoopers from Mount Dreich the Dismal on our backs. The ravens are woe enough."

Always snappish after a poor hunt, Beag growled. "Silence, the bunch of you, or you won't need dorcha bogies to keep you quiet!"

The entire pack shifted into well-earned sleep, content to let the snow cover their winter grown coats.

⋏ ⋏ ⋏

Earm Scanlon ran his scarred thumbs up the boney ridge of his wife's spine into the base of her skull. Intermittent moans seeped from her pinched mouth.

Earm reached for a phial of amber liquid and shook it. Camphorated spicy sweet vapours wafted toward the stricken woman. Offering it to her he said, "Take another sip of your remedy, my dear. Freyen's elixir will set you right."

Her thin white hand grabbed at the glass container. She drank it down and licked the rim.

Pulling her frayed shawl tightly around her depressed shoulders, she sighed and whispered, "Yes, yes, but keep on. My head hurts so."

"That's right. Now just close your eyes. Think about something else, love. Like the mountains of home. You like them, right?"

"Mmmmm."

"Right. I'd think your people would know all about the wild beasts that roam the hills and glens, protecting the gold apples, and all."

He laughed, sounding like a drunken mouse. "Faeries' tales for children, but still. . . . Where would your people look for wildcats . . . should they want to find some? And wulves?"

Twenty-Four

WULVES CAN'T EAT THE LIGHT

If you live to greet Oak King, the worst has passed.

By the end of Alder, a month after the winter solstice, a hidden wonder tantalized the famished pack, adding to their mounting tension. They felt it down their spines. They sniffed it on the air. A strange gnawing delight simmered within the heart, not the belly. A bad case of nerves alerted Kalar and Sonsie to this different but strangely familiar presence. Kalar searched hollow trees and discarded cache sites. Sonsie sensed singing in a voice that gave him shivers; he wanted to laugh; he wanted to hide.

Then one frozen day, in answer to the call of increased light, deep within the wulves' feral brains images of uncoiling fronds beneath layers of decayed bracken stirred the pack. They turned their muzzles skyward, nostrils flared and ears taut. Hunger-honed senses detected something almost as auld as Grian's light, yet new! They breathed in the essence of oak. The walking tree with antlers! A prickle of hope teased the pack's hearts. Akir whooped and nipped at their feet. The entire pack ran in boisterous play. They crested a rise, broke from the cover of pine, and stopped. Their teardrop shaped manes rose in unison. First Akir, next Anell and Beag, Feela and Birk, then all the others howled. Their voices became richer, as if each had just swallowed that sweetest part of the ham with the pocket of dark blood.

Just after Grian settled into the mists that enfolded the western isles, Akir detected a red deer herd sheltered somewhere north, near enough to promise full bellies, finally a reward for all their determined efforts to find food. He gathered the pack. "My guess? They eat willow scrub over the next ridge, probably near Lac Tara or Neala. That puts them within Hart Haven. All must go, Sonsie and Kalar, too."

"If only they don't—" Birk attempted to add.

Akir glared. "Silence!"

They sought the herd for several nights, finding no deer but signs that another pack had moved on, perhaps weeks ago. Hunger drove them on. After a brief shift of the wind, their luck changed. Deer! Akir eased them into a jaunt along the banks of Lac Tara. In the dark, they slunk along the Little Fox toward the deer encampment. Again the wind shifted. Southwesterly ocean breezes crossed Lac Tara and dropped snow on frozen Little Fox. Not wanting to alert the herd on the downwind, Akir moved them east toward Raven Wood. Silent and resolute, they moved under a clacking canopy of ice-covered branches. They turned north around Big Fox, moving toward Hart Haven and checking for scent markings, not only of deer, but any other presence, be it beast or cutter or Dorcha.

The first flickering of tree-topping light flashed rainbows from iced boughs over the snow as if the Merry Dancers had descended from the sky. Some force was making itself felt in the High West. Soon dawn inched over the snow, moving in streaks toward the coast. As spasms tormented the pack's empty bellies, the hearts of even the youngest were made lighter; they tasted and smelled a new light.

Akir sniffed and grunted. "Wulves can't eat the light."

Soon they spied tracks left by black grouse, hares, best of all, red deer. The dawn breeze carried scents from the south. Akir led them to approach their quarry upwind.

"Grian will be our ally," he confided.

In the early calm the deer breathed easily, exhaling little white puffs. They nestled in a dell flanked by low lying granite outcroppings, twisted trees, and scrub, just the sort of cover Akir loved. The pack approached the deer from the northeast. The wind whistled over the reclining herd's backs into the wulves' faces. Kalar's mouth watered at the sweet aroma. Mundee and Ro pressed against the brothers to keep them utterly silent, especially Sonsie.

Akir studied the deer huddled on the shore of the Big Fox where they had pawed away enough ice to get water. He intended to drive them away from the rising light to the frozen center and let the ice aid them in a kill.

Grian had nearly risen. Akir signaled; the pack divided. Akir and Beag on the west and Anell and Birk on the east crept up rock steps on each side of the herd to take the high ground. Kalar and Sonsie brought up the rear of the divided pack, fronted by Ro on the west flank and Mundee on the east. Upwind, Karlon blocked the narrow space between a tumble of stone and dead trees to the north. Anell and Birk hid behind waving yellow grasses that braved the snow drifting off nearby rocks. Never losing sight of their prey, Akir and Beag sought the cover of lichen-encrusted boulders.

The deer's shadows crept toward Ro and Sonsie. Sonsie shook, like that time in the cave when the Dorcha had passed within inches of his hidden nose. Just as shadow and substance merged, the deer started, heads twitching, muscles flexing, but still not running. Anell dug her nails into the hard ground, her attention riveted on the herd. Birk moved forward, searching for a deer eye to catch in her treacherous gaze.

Seemingly sightless, the entire herd faced Karlon. Maybe meddlesome ravens gave first sign of the wulves' presence, maybe a hare blundered into the teeth of death, but for certain, the wind shifted. The deer breathed unmistakable wulf scent coming from the west. Akir and Beag crept from hiding. Seven yards from the surrounded deer the wulves waited, poised to strike.

Every heart beat faster, yet pursuer and pursued seemed turned to stone. At last a battle-scarred stag flinched. Though big and gallant, he was well past his prime. That one twitch spooked the herd and sealed his fate. Each member of Akir's pack targeted him. They began the fatal running of the crazed herd.

The stag's lunge did not head as expected, but directly east. Grian's full face flashed upon his blinded eyes. Beag moved in from behind to harass his legs. Anell attacked in a frontal assault. Both took care to avoid his perilous hooves. He leaned into his run, dropping his great antlers low to the ground. Others in the pack selected secondary targets from a third of the herd that ran with the aged stag and kept them in sight.

They chased him for nearly a mile over snowy, rock-strewn ground. Karlon, Mundee, and Kalar raced to join the fray. Ro and Sonsie stretched to close the space between them. Birk and Akir drew alongside the gasping beast. His reeky breath grated up his throat. Anell spun around to bear down upon the stag from his front. She ripped one of the stag's shoulders. Birk took his haunch. The snow turned crimson. Akir leapt and clamped lethal jaws over his face; his antler-heavy head thrashed up and down, sideways, and again up. Akir hung on and ripped off the stag's mask. Blood gushed from the gaping head. Down they crashed.

The strongest wulves gutted the carcass. Taking turns, they gorged themselves, gulping hot flesh and crushing bones to suck the marrow. Their bellies swelled and nearly brushed the ground. Several dragged severed pieces of carcass to a cache site.

On the trek back to their camp, they celebrated their prey-mate and honored him for making the Change. Dead, he was deer; reborn, wulf.

Kalar and Sonsie grinned at one another.

"Our first good hunt, Sonsie."

"Our first earned Change, Kalar."

With each drop of his blood that they licked from their chops, they gave thanks for the Change and their full bellies in these ragged days of winter.

Twenty-Five

Wulfsbane Tree

Hunters hunt. Keepers hold. Makars fly.

Gealach never showed her face on the dark night of new Willow Month. Night-swooping Dorcha, searching for hapless creatures to carry aloft, eager to add their victims' shrieks to their own screeches, flew through a green and purple aurora that streamed across the black sky. Its reflection from the glittering snow intensified the Dorcha's torment.

The pack returned early from a failed hunt. Under the Merry Dancers' glow Akir and Anell snuggled against one another, their tails spread over their feet and muzzles. The earth trembled. Akir peered over the bodies of the sleeping pack. Again the earth rumbled, vibrating his ribs. Anell stirred and yawned.

Both howled. The entire pack, alerted to a felt but invisible presence, joined in. Sonsie cocked his ears and turned his head. Kalar sniffed the air. They looked about, wary of some new marvel.

Sonsie fidgeted and made squeaking noises like chattering spring squirrels. He called. "What? What? Flee? No? Yes? What?"

In their bones all the other wulves felt the unhurried, inexorable movement. Feela crept forward. Anell let her pass. She came to rest beside Sonsie.

His short, hot breaths crossed her muzzle. "Flee? Chase? What?"

"Sonsie," she crooned, "It must have happened!"

"What?"

"The Green returns."

"Green what?"

"Who! We hunt his domain. He's moving."

Sonsie shuddered. "When?"

Feela hummed. Sonsie's breaths deepened into a calmed rhythm. In response, she laid her head across his neck.

Kalar watched them then barked. When they ignored him, he coughed and snarled at Akir, at the air in general. His hackles started to rise.

Disregarding Sonsie, Akir stared down Kalar.

"When?" Sonsie urged Feela.

"In the month of the Alder's last days, Willow's first." Feela began a tale of mystery and magic. "Winter: Grian and Gealach vanish in blizzards. White Lisnafaer lies barren. Lady Light, her long white tresses flying in the wind, weeps. Faer Ones mourn."

Lost in reverie, Feela paused.

Anell snapped at her to continue. Ancient urges wrinkled her brow and curled her lips. She sought the eyes of her mate.

Feela told of storms battering Wulf Run during Willow Month, of winter defending its domain, biting more cruelly than even in the longest, darkest nights of Rowan Month. "Dorcha bite and prick, curdle milk, steal cutter cubs, sink sharp teeth and nails into waylaid cutter flesh, and worse, pester wulves on the hunt. The wights who live in death swarm in the dregs of the long-dark."

Her harsh voice turned gentle. "Fear not and be glad. Three great lights: the Lady, Grian, and Gealach dance unbowed by the storms' fury. In Willow Month behold a mystery! Their three-fold power summons the Light out of darkness! Faer Ones rejoice. Green returns. Ice and snow bite no more. Now streams rush; salmon leap. The Lord and Lady—"

"Feela!" Anell barked.

Feela focused on Lord Green. As she sang, something ferlie that Sonsie and Kalar had vaguely sensed grew in strength, pinching their entrails, and flashed before their inner eye. It walked. Like the bear, but no claws. Not beast, yet tall and powerful, clad in mistletoe and wilted holly. In her song all came clear: a vision of newly opened, bright green oak leaves and mossy bark strips that covered flesh the color young oak boughs. A cluster of mistletoe topped his holly-oak staff entwined with oak leaves.

He and Holly King shared curiously similar faces. This one's green hair curled around a crown of white-berried mistletoe and fell over his massive shoulders. He had antlers, too, just like his holly-covered twin.

Under Feela's raised head, Kalar and Sonsie stared at each other. "Long live Oak King!" they cried.

Kalar turned to Akir. "Is he wulf friend or deer friend?"

"Is he friend like Holly King?" Sonsie began. "Will he come to take—" He clamped his jaws.

Both brothers trembled, attempting to rid themselves of this intruder in their heads.

Akir let go a brief roar.

After the entire pack gathered round, all howled. Sonsie's heart raced. Kalar peered into the darkness. He sought whatever caused his paws to knead the earth, as if he were fixing to outrace King Stag. The black night vied with the fading Merry Dancers for control of the skies.

Sonsie turned, chasing his tail round and round. Before Birk could reach him, Feela gave him a mighty head-butt. He crashed to the ground. She pinned him with her forepaws. Akir flashed Feela an approving look.

A veil lifted within Sonsie's mind. "Feela! Are you a keeper?"

She lowered her muzzle to his ear, covering his mouth with her winter-grown mane.

"All wulves know the keepings of the Great Dance, the Coming of Light and such."

Sonsie squirmed. "I didn't know the Great Dance."

"Well now you do." She rolled him over, pinning his back against the ground. "I hold the keepings of our days on the Apple Coast and hunts in Wulf Paw. The bits and pieces from others who tell their story alone in the dead of night I keep, but the far Auld Story, well, that's more Dunoon's territory."

Kalar growled. He detested strange sights in his head, eyes open or closed. Soon Karlon, Mundee, and Ro squirmed as if beetles nipped their bellies.

"But Feela!" Sonsie persisted.

"Silence, Sonsie!" she warned. Her body, fur bristling, thudded against him.

Birk inserted her nose into the tangle of agitated younger wulves.

Kalar looked from Birk to Sonsie and Feela who rolled back and forth on the ground.

Just as Anell and Akir bore down on them all, Beag having decided to stay well away from this squabble, a hundred pricks rippled over Sonsie's body.

He shook free from Feela's embrace. His first wail lifted the hackles of every pack mate, even Akir's. As if transported or dreaming awake, Sonsie sang the images swirling within his brain out to the night on the wings of his new-found voice.

⋏ ⋏ ⋏

"Each night, haroo, hoorae
   Gealach, sweet Silver-Light, pure and bright,
   Calls starlight from the black depths of night,
   Draws light from the vasty dark sae cold.
   Ferlie the lights of the Ladies sae auld.
Each dawn, haroo, hoorae
   Silv'ry Sister-Light, lovely the sight,
   Sings to Grian, Fire-Light, hot and bright,
   Sends light Mother-Light spins into gold.
   Ferlie the lights of the Ladies sae auld.
Each day, haroo, hoorae
   Great Grian, our Gold-Mother, splendid might,
   Makes sweet Change, breathes golden life from light,
   Sings hallowed story, each day retold.
   Ferlie the lights of the Ladies sae auld.

All day, haroo, hoorae
    Great Grian, our Gold-Mother, meet and right,
    Bathes Lisnafaer with her love-light,
    Frees Lisnafaer from death's leasehold.
    Ferlie the lights of the Ladies sae auld.
Night and day, haroo, hoorae
    Light grows. Love grows. Life grows.
    So Love is: giving and taking, dying and living.
    Queen Grian, Blessed Mother-Light, calls the children:
    Beasts in caves and dens and lairs,
    Lord Green lost in burrow grim,
    Deep down under wulfways.
    Doleful Lady Light, seeks her Lord,
    With his arm strong and staff firm.
    Mother-Light sends love, sweet and warm,
    Dries her tears, lights her way.
    Love-Light shines.
    Light laughs into Green.
    So Love is: calling and seeking, returning and blessing
    Lisnafaer."

Kalar bared his teeth, raised his ears, snarled. Standing before Sonsie's face, he watched the eerie light in his brother's eyes fade. Unsure if Sonsie's soul had returned from a far-flung journey between worlds, Kalar grunted and huffed but did not move.

The two brothers stared at each other.

"So!" they said in unison.

The pack stood stone still until Feela could endure the silence no longer. "How does Sonsie know Sky-Wulf's song?"

Birk heard that. She fumed. "Akir, you must do something with Sonsie! He has no right to sing Star-Wulf's song."

From Akir's side Anell shot back, "Not now! I heard no lies. Leave him." Her mouth grinned death.

Akir ignored Birk. *Right or not, Anell, Sonsie sang for all to hear.*

Birk's tail hung low, and yet her grunt trailed into a whining snarl. Anell streaked into a run. Akir watched her make three circuits around the pack, driving them into a tight huddle, a silenced Birk caught in the middle. Anell landed hard at his side.

He knew the signs well. Before long, Anell would be in heat. He had to bide his time. He merely said, "Rest. Soon we hunt."

▲ ▲ ▲

After his outburst, Sonsie squirmed, trying to settle his jangled nerves. Unable to sleep or keep still, he looked for a space to call his own. He felt neither cold nor tired, quite the opposite. He panted, his hot tongue dripping.

Turning round and round, he moved in a line that took him far away from his mates. He plopped to the ground and pressed his spine against a massive granite stone. Its cold seeped into his body. He looked at the sky, black, clear, and brimming with stars. The colder his body grew, the clearer he could see. Feela had told him to watch the stars, but he had only tried to listen. Tonight he seemed to live outside his body, every sensation magnified.

One star over to the southwest drew his gaze. A shape materialized, a wulf, huge and powerful. Star-clouds swirled over its back.

Sonsie's mind raced. Akir had asked him about a wulf in the sky. Why? But that night Gealach showed her full face. Tonight she is hiding. She does every time a new tree month begins. Why? They expect me to know this. Why? They never make any sense. Grian sleeps and Gealach is lost. Who is this Sky-Wulf? How fast does it run up there in the night? Do the Lords of

Light know this wulf who comes out when Gealach hides? Where does she go? Does it hunt Gealach?

The eye of the wulf flared. It enthralled him. It beckoned him. Sonsie's heart beat faster.

The wulf came closer, closer.

A cry of fear and hope escaped Sonsie's jaws. What songs it must know. I could join him if I just leap high enough.

The wulf called. Sonsie soared up, out to the stars, yet his body, a white fur body shining in the starlight, lay still against the stone. Soaring Sonsie looked back to sleeping Sonsie and detected a glowing string of light connecting them. The glory of the firmament filled his heart with joy.

His ears tingled. If I can reach the wulf-star, I will learn where all songs come from.

He looked for the wulf's eye. There! Yes! "Tell me! Tell me," he cried.

Aiming for the wulf's glittering eye, Sonsie ascended, his legs stretched for a sprint. At the zenith of a high luminous arc he began a slow descent.

Losing sight of the eye, he plummeted. The dark closed in, worse than that time in the cave. He thrashed, fighting to catch one glimpse of the eye. "There!"

It blinked. He tumbled over and over, righted himself, and hovered. "Where am I?"

Having lost sight of the silver thread's earthbound end, he searched for the bright star to the north, Wulfguard according to Feela, and discovered a grove of mighty trees. He drifted ever closer to this sky-wood. Something collared with spiked iron, hanging from a tree upon iron chains, something familiar. Furred with pointed snouts. Long, furred tails. Wulves? Wulves!

Sonsie reared back. The silver cord had grown quite dim but remained intact. He tried to scream, but his dried throat closed. He floated before the gruesome wulves.

He could not make his gaze turn away. Very bad. Wulves so grand should run the green earth and change the finest red deer. Even now, dead, dead, dead . . . so, so, yes, like Akir, strong and. . . .

He recalled Anell's pride in her mate, her voice warm like flowing honey. "Don't you want to be braw, like your sire?"

Aching darkness filled his heart. The urge to cough up sick grasses overcame him, but the far-flying Sonsie could not, and the sleeping Sonsie had turned to stone far, far away. He wanted to free the hanged wulves, cover them with rocks, lament their deaths, sing all their great deeds, name all the grand beasts they had changed into fine, strong wulf.

"Give me your names. I would sing you to my pack. I would remember you to the Faer Ones who like to gather names of all the beasts. I was told so by one who knows. I would be such a one. Help me."

He paused, searching for any sign of life, foolish though he knew his hope to be. In the cold night he looked to all the glowing stars and sought the might of their radiance.

"Help me. Feed me. Send me your light," he begged. "I would sing to name and honor these braw kith and kin."

The eye of the wulf blazed. Neighboring stars glowed with extraordinary brightness.

His voice filled with starlight, Sonsie sang.

⁂

"Hear me, brothers. Hear me, sisters.
Awaken. Cast off cruel slumber.
Breathe mountain air, clear and sweet,
Drink melted snow, pure and cold,
Sing to dancing deer.
Run green glens and rejoice."

⁂

A great light-wind streamed from the head of Sky-Wulf to the hanging tree. One wulf stirred then wound upon her chain. Her eyes drank in the light. Unable to speak at first, she struggled to gaze upon her mates. They, too, twisted cruelly, but their efforts rewarded Sonsie's song. The wulf to the right of the first one opened his eyes; they shone, intelligent and grieving. Soon all the hanging wulves regained their sight. The she-wulf maintained eye contact with the one to her right. Some inscrutable intelligence passed between them. Turning, she looked upon Sonsie; then her jaw moved.

"Young mortal wulf with slender hold upon life," her rasping voice replied to his appeal. The strangled wulf coughed. "A long ways you come. More than you know. You waken us. To agony—auld and new. And yet I thank you. For releasing my voice. Alas, silenced most bitterly . . . by this cutter iron."

She paused to seek the eye of her nearest companion: as before, their souls' correspondence remained a mystery. After several coughs, she resumed.

"Brash wulf, would you hear from the lost?"

Sonsie shook his head. "Neither brash nor brave, high wulf, but one lost as well. Yes."

"So be it."

Her voice grew less harsh with use. "No high wulf I, but Adair, wulf singer. You must ask Krika, our high wulf, to name the rest."

Sonsie strove to keep his own voice calm and clear. "Krika, I grieve for your pain. I call upon you to tell me your names."

The entire pack turned to face Sonsie. Krika growled as if a raven claw had lodged in his throat. At last sound issued from his dry lips. "Beside me hangs. . . ."

He fell silent. His tail rose. His forepaw stretched. He could not touch the wulf to his right. He seemed to choke. His eyes expressed an emotion too deep for Sonsie to read.

"Beside me Ellrin, high wulf, life-mate. Mark you, our fame. Ask Adair."

He twisted to his left. "Beyond Adair see Flintry, the fierce, Balfron, the bold, Garve, the great, Skiak, the sly. Nigg, the noisy—a good singer but keeper and makar beyond his power."

He stopped. His chest heaved. His throat rumbled. "Take heed. More than singing makes a keeper . . . more than knowing creates a makar. Ask Adair."

He turned to Ellrin. His sigh, drawn from another time and space, pierced Sonsie's heart.

Adair resumed, "My brother Krika gave what you asked, bold wulf. Our pack fears not your knowing our names; what worse fate than hanging on Wulfsbane Tree, deed most unkind, from cutter leash not slack?

"We fell in Wulf Wars, after the Great Crossing, after the Ice-North raiders and . . . Vilhjalmer attacked. Beware their return!"

The spectral wulf's voice grew faint. Sky-borne Sonsie noticed a new light entering the heavens, Grian rising from her nightly slumbers. The hanging wulves faded.

"Forget us not, Far-Seeker," Krika sighed.

Ellrin called. "Come back, brave wulf, to free us."

"Wait! Wait!" Sonsie cried. "How? Who did this to you?"

Adair whispered, "Ask the Faer . . . Light Kee . . . Who Know . . ."

Then they were gone, as if no Grian-warmed day had ever known the tread of their hard-nailed paws upon the green earth, as if no gallows-grim night had ever witnessed slaughter most terrible of such fine wulves.

Twenty-Six

HAUNTED HUNTING GROUNDS

Secrets make heavy the heart of the hunter.

Something pounded on Sonsie's ribs. He began to fall. Repeated blows compressed his chest, causing his lungs to burn. The silver cord drew him so violently to the earth that his rock-backed body shook. A sour sickness rose up his throat and coated his dripping tongue. Up came all that he had last eaten. He struggled to breathe, seeming to wander, lost in endless tunnels far beneath the earth.

From a distance—up or down, in or out unknown—a voice called. "Sonsie! Sonsie! Wake up. Time to hunt. We're leaving."

Thrashing to break free, Sonsie pushed his paws against invisible boulders. "Sonsie, wake up. They call us to hunt."

Sonsie opened his eyes. There stood Kalar; smirking pity pulled his lips into a disdainful grin. "You make us look bad. Come on!"

Sonsie muttered to himself.

Kalar shook off Sonsie's garbled ramblings. "Time to hunt!" He looked to the east but saw no glowing cobalt line to suggest the dawn. "Come on, Sonsie!"

Sonsie labored to follow Kalar to the pack, now roused from their dreams of fragrant green fields and plump prey-mates.

Akir and Anell frisked and affectionately nipped at each other. The powdered snow flew in the crisp air. The pack joined the high wulves' capers; all laughed and barked. Akir paused briefly, led them in a raucous howl, and then ran them until their breaths smoked. Beag found a remnant deer hoof to toss back and forth on the run. Kalar shadowed whoever had the prize, nearly swiping it from Karlon's mouth, but overshot his target so that Ro stole the dropped hoof before Kalar could turn and capture it. Furious, he barked, but Mundee flew over him and jeered, "You have to be quicker than that, laggard wulf," only to crash into Sonsie, sending them both tumbling in the snow. Kalar laughed.

Mundee's tremendous wallop to the still muddled Sonsie cleared his head. No longer dragging himself through the drifts, he sprang to his feet and cried, "Sky-Wulf! Adair!"

Taking a quick look around, he raced to Kalar and yelled, "Stop—jumping—on—me!"

This set the entire pack to running around the young brothers, all except Akir. Now that they were warmed and ready to begin their search for well-hidden prey, he forced a brief pause.

He turned to Kalar. "The hunt makes feast or famine for even the tiniest punkie and ant. Make this hunt a blessing, not a curse."

Kalar wagged his tail.

"All wulves hunt," Akir continued, casting his sternest gaze on Sonsie, who met his gaze then bowed his head, "even you, my son who calls out strange names. Look at me, Sonsie!"

Sonsie shook his raised head and then fastened his sight on the tip of his sire's nose.

"What did you say?"

"When?"

"Just now. You called a wulf. Who?"

"I don't know, sire." Sonsie's belly turned sour. He coughed, choking on bile. His blood ran hot, but he shook like one chilled by the ague. Fighting nausea, he forced himself to stand firm and look upon his sire's dreadful face.

"You named wulves, one revered above all, and one, a long lost singer slain in the Wulf Wars . . . and kin." Akir nearly choked on a lament long stifled. "And you 'don't know'?"

He looked upon his miserable son and saw no deceit, just bewilderment. He sought the eyes of his mate who looked on with tender concern, but she held her tongue. Akir forbade that she ever mention his ancestors lost to the Wars. He blamed Alba.

Akir's gaze returned to Sonsie. "My son, you must do your duty to the pack or die. New life will come. You must be ready, like Mundee, Karlon, and Ro before you." He sighed, seeming to struggle with an invisible opponent. "You are brave in your own way," Akir continued. "Let not far off songs make you forget your true calling. You are wulf. No matter the prey-mates, the hunt is your life. We need to fatten our bones, especially Anell's. Songs do not feed the pack."

He searched Sonsie's face, saw how his son's luminous eyes, now clearer, were tinged with a glimmer of hope. Akir's heart ached. "Ah, Sonsie, what will become of you?"

Sonsie focused on his sire's many sharp teeth.

Akir placed his head over Sonsie's and forced him to kneel. "You did well, Sonsie. You survived. You must do more."

Akir stood tall. "Kalar!"

When the brothers stood side by side, Akir resumed command of the pack. "The hunt is no playtime for pups, who, smitten by Gealach's glow, risk their pack's lives. You will hunt when called. You will protect the good Green. Leave bogey-beasts and songs to the ravens. Do you hear me, Kalar?"

"Yes, sire." His tail wagged rapidly.

"Do you hear me, Sonsie?"

"Yes, sire." He stood perfectly still. Not even the blonde hairs of his ears moved.

Wide-eyed, the cubs listened to their elders' debate. Birk objected to taking them. Akir agreed they might slow the hunt and cause problems near Anell's breeding time. Their hearts sank. But Feela called them equal to full-grown yearlings. Beag nodded. Feela argued a successful hunt depended upon them all. Anell pounced. "As the cubs follow, they can alert us to danger from the rear."

Akir hesitated. Anell drew close to him. "Think what you, their sire, can teach them."

⅄ ⅄ ⅄

Each evening the brothers followed the pack. Sonsie tried to focus on the trail and forget the Wulfsbane Tree. Kalar declared himself the valiant rearguard, only to bump into his often distracted brother. He bit Sonsie's tail.

The hungry pack crept upon a covey of sleeping rock ptarmigans that never took flight and flushed a husk of mountain hare, at least two discovered by the trailing brothers, but lucky finds of voles and weasels barely filled them. Yearning for a chomp on a boar haunch, Akir sought Anell at the head of the column. His breath caressed her. "Fat boar, Anell, how sweet to change in these lean days!"

She remained firm. "Now late in Willow south is good. Go east when Kalar and Sonsie can tend the new cubs. Go to your sons; show them the ways of the trail."

Pressing on, Akir searched the skies just as a flock of ravens hastened toward Lac Tara.

He turned the pack in their direction, following the scavengers to Tara's eastern banks; even Anell was happy that he did. There they discovered the remains of a recently felled hairy kyloe, red balls of ice hanging from its shaggy hide. At first they shied at the unexpected, two-footed tracks approaching and leaving the site, but hunger overcame caution. They easily dispersed the angry ravens and began the glad task of changing the kyloe to wulf.

In the days that followed Sonsie resisted sleep, becoming even groggier on the trail. Kalar attempted to prowl day and night, but Birk chided his foolishness. In secret Sonsie confided his misgivings about running into their former guide to the horrific cave. Kalar puffed his chest, ready to declare his fierce response if he met him again, but when Akir appeared at their tails in a shower of snow, they hung their heads. At their approach to Harts Hold, they flashed each other knowing looks. Akir observed. His jaws tightened.

Anell wanted to cross River Avalach and explore the Guardian Mountains, but Akir tried to lead them east, along River Tara through the Great Woods of Lisnafaer to the Black Woods of Tara-Ardra.

"True, the Black Woods shelter many a prey-companion," she conceded.

"We have no good luck in those woods," Birk interrupted.

Akir shot his sister a baleful look and huffed. Anell watched.

"Don't the Dorcha—" Sonsie piped.

"Shush!" Birk snapped. "No one seeks your advice."

He persisted. "But I've heard—"

"Nothing we haven't!" Beag's stern voice contradicted his smiling eyes. "Just wind through the tree bones."

He looked to Anell and shook his head. *Don't let Akir get lost in a fog of dorcha sightings.*

Before Akir could answer, Anell resumed her argument. "The Black Woods keep Dorcha and beasts well-hidden, taking all our strength to make them break cover. Great effort, little change, empty bellies. We'd fare better in the Guardians. Prey-mates abound without the nuisance of the tangled woods and all they hide. Hunters love prey not shelter. Come Akir."

Feela ventured a suggestion. "I recall many a fine ram and ewe roam the Guardians."

Birk's mouth drooled. "Ah, I'd like to change one of those rock leapers into wulf! Come brother, we can go to the Black Woods later."

Anell winked at Feela.

Birk searched the sky. "Gealach shows her full face this night, a good light for the mountains. Wait for summer before attempting the Woods of Tara-Ardra."

Akir stared at the unlikely trio of allies, then at Beag, nodding in agreement. The pack crossed River Avalach.

🠗 🠗 🠗

River Avalach! With eyes, ears, and noses at full alert, Kalar and Sonsie tried to take in every possible sensation of their surroundings, ever fearful that some ferlie creature would steal them away. Sonsie clamped his teeth on the topic of the Wulfsbane Tree. His efforts to convince himself he had dreamt of Adair and the rest faltered whenever he alone, it seemed, saw the starry Sky-Wulf shining each night. He shivered and hinted as much to Kalar, who scoffed at the mere idea of some wulf living in the sky. Even so, Sonsie reminded him of those beasts in the dreadful cave. "Something is prowling above us, Kalar. High up. Or in that Otherworld. It yowls. What . . . I don't know. I don't like it."

"Not know? You? I thought you knew every ferlie song in Lisnafaer."

"This is no song, Kalar!"

Twenty-Seven

In the Spring a Wulf's Fancy Turns

Hunt, eat, change: make new wulf. Mate: make new wulf.

As Gealach waxed to a low hanging fullness, Anell and Feela celebrated coming to the foothills of the Guardians. They sang praises for mountain ranges that fold into one another and cradle rosy mists glowing in Grian's evening light; pines, green and blue, weaving between leafless trees on the mountain sides; crags above the tree line, home to soaring golden eagles; and giant icicles hanging from huge outcrops of granite, melting into water that foams over rocks and cuts gullies down the mountains. They thanked Grian for smiling so that all wulves had water, no matter how cold the air, and for loving the Guardians that protected all beasts.

Birk shook her head, muttering about Alba's curse and no wonder Sonsie was a singing fool, but the sisters' robust cries roused them all. They gave thanks for nights filled with prey-mates just waiting to be changed into swift-running, loud-howling wulves who love Lisnafaer as much as any deer who dances under Grian's and Gealach's beaming faces.

Akir welcomed the pleasure Anell found in these mountains. He looked longingly at his mate, sure that they'd get back to the new den site in good time.

Feela often took Karlon and sometimes Mundee or Ro to scout likely spots with good cover and water to rest between hunts. When she reported seeing new prints, two-legged, but not Faer Ones or bear or any beasts she knew, Sonsie shivered. He recalled the mumbling he heard in the withered bracken or tangled thickets that haunted his nights when the frozen rocks seemed to croak to one another.

"Something is hungry out there, Kalar," Sonsie confided. "They're angry that Lord Green is coming. They hate the light. They want to eat it."

Karlon glared. "If I get any hungrier, I'll eat it, too."

▲ ▲ ▲

Willow Month waned. Gealach began her monthly hiding game. Anell snapped, happy to see Feela depart, happier if the other females went with her. She often snarled at Birk. In one short row, more loud than vicious, she forced a bewildered Karlon and Beag to keep their distance. She took the lead on hunts, moving them ever closer to the apples. Her hunting prowess led them in the direction of distressed bleating and the scent of blood and sweat-soaked fleece. They discovered a grandfather ram with enormous horns. It struggled upon an outcrop of a rock face that climbed to the height of the eldest oaks in the Forest of Four or Five. Their luck held in finding him separated from his herd and their formidable guards. The pack crept round the foot of the rocks. Sonsie and Kalar halted, their jaws agape.

The ram lurched up and forward but fell back, his front hooves skittering on the iced granite surfaces. A crevice held one of his back legs so firmly that he had cut it to the bone in attempting his escape. Bright blood spurted from the trapped leg, but even in his agony he remained a splendid, sturdy mouflon. A white underbelly and huge spot upon his back highlighted his rich brown woolly coat. Heart-shaped horns curved around his ears to reach his white nose. Each pain-filled bawl enlarged his amber eyes, exposing red-veined white.

Sonsie stood beside Kalar. "See, it looks just like the wyrm you fell upon in his den!"

"Don't be daft. That's no wyrm. It's just those horns. We must change it!"

"No! Kalar!" Sonsie bounded up a series of rocks to the trapped ram whose wild gaze locked with his. Sonsie missed his mark and shot through a curved horn. As Sonsie landed, one of the ram's free hooves slashed him. He turned to the ram, only to have the rest of the pack scramble over him. Several gripped the stricken beast in their crushing jaws. The force of their assault catapulted ram and all earthward where, released from its struggles, the ram ceased to feel pain. As the pack sorted itself out, Sonsie found himself gripping the ram's ear in his blood-filled mouth.

Akir told his stunned son, "You have helped to take a prey-mate's life, your first. You must give thanks for its blood."

Sonsie retched. "I meant to release him."

"The ram's life is exchanged for yours—a wulf! But I see by that cut on your haunch that it gave as good as it got—a good lesson."

Akir looked to Kalar, who had done his part to assure the kill and now waited to take his share of the feast. "At your time to eat, Kalar, you must thank this king ram for its life. Now back away!"

Enacting an ancient blood ritual, Akir and Anell then Beag and Birk tore at the belly of the ram to gulp smoking chunks of liver and intestines. Next Karlon, Mundee, and Ro, then Feela joined in. They ripped hide from flesh, flesh from bone, relieved they had no need to carry food home to their ravenous young.

Kalar and Sonsie crouched in the nearby grasses, withered browns and new green shoots, splattered in ram's blood. They swished their tails and fastened their gaze upon each gulp that their elders took. Their mouths drooled. They could not help it. The aroma of rapidly disappearing flesh, the crunch of bones, the growls or delighted moans of the feeding pack, and at least a hundred other sensations united the pack in a natural sacrament. Sonsie ran his tongue over his lips.

At long last Feela invited the hungry brothers to devour the remains, just enough left for them. Kalar leapt and began to gnaw with relish. Try as he might, though, Sonsie could not go forward. With his mouth yet tasting the ram's blood and his head throbbing, he turned instead and curled upon himself.

Carrying a bit of bone in his mouth, Kalar returned to his side to gloat, but Sonsie told him to shut his mouth and enjoy his meal. "Go away."

That afternoon the pack succumbed to a delicious languor. All except Sonsie. His brain swarmed with songs of uncanny beasts and images of lairs and wyrms, caves and bogies, and hanged wulves. The dozing pack enjoyed the silence, until Sonsie's belly-growls erupted as if the giant Lone Grumli were smashing rocks against his skull.

Kalar reached out with his back legs and kicked him. "Eat some snow, Sonsie!"

Feela chuckled. "That's the price he pays. Remember this Sonsie," she said between yawns, "the next time you seek . . . strange sights . . . and sounds."

ᐧ ᐧ ᐧ

Anell fretted. This night, entirely dark except for Grian's far-distant children glimmering in the heavens, Gealach gave the last of her light to Grian. So began the new Month of the Ash. Finally those first hints of the mating season, the need to secure the den for the new cubs, urges that had been pricking at Anell since the New Year, swelled to a ripe desire. Anell's heart thumped then raced as it pumped fevered blood. She shook herself, trying to loosen her knotted muscles and clear her head. What about the pack, leery of Sonsie and his songs, what about Kalar and Sonsie, so much power and passion—but something else? The tussle between Feela and Sonsie—what did he suspect? What of new cubs?

She ached. Now a hunger more intense than the mere taste for deer overtook her body. She yearned for Akir and the joining. So far she had managed to keep the other females away from her mate. She paced, sniffing the air. Birk's scent. Birk—eager to take over, a new high wulf? Never!

She heard Feela call Kalar and Sonsie. How keep Feela safe yet one more season? Seek Akir; make new life! When new cubs come, what of dreaming Sonsie, daring Kalar? They must please Akir!

She lifted her head to the heavens. Now the nights, so black, black, deadly cold and black.

She crooned, "'Silver-Light, pure and bright, calls starlight from the black depths of night.'" Cold. Cold and dark. Still it snows. They must survive! Hunt-meat-life! New life must come—Apples!

She turned. She called, "Akir!"

⅄ ⅄ ⅄

Akir, increasingly watchful as the tree months passed, felt his muscles tighten down his spine, across his chest, between his eyes and ears, in his loins. Each year the same; they needed no keeper to remind him. The hotter his blood the more knotted his muscles—a tension that filled his brain with a kind of sweet madness. Only Anell's heat cooled his burning blood. He growled at nothing, at everything. So far baring his alarming fangs and releasing a few calculated snarls had kept Beag and Karlon well away.

He barked at a low-swooping owl. Lead the hunt. Train my sons. Contend with the sisters, faithful Feela, biting Birk. Fend off Lady Light. Protect Kalar and Sonsie from Lord Green. Find prey in snow. Will wind never cease howling, driving the snow? Dark of the Ash now upon us. When will Light laugh into Green? Cold. Cold and dark. Still it snows. We must survive. Hunt-meat-life! New life must come—Boar!

He turned. He called, "Anell!"

⅄ ⅄ ⅄

They ran together from the banks of the small pond, over the flowing creek, and around the rocks, some standing, some fallen, on ground

210

awaiting a flowering meadow come summer. Snow-covered pines guarded the clearing. Anell's and Akir's wet noses flashed black against the snow; their tails waved high, scattering the sprays of snow their paws cast behind them in arcs. They gulped in the cold, pine-scented air that caught at the backs of their hot throats before it filled their lungs.

They pulled to a stop under an overhanging boulder. Their steaming breaths cast clouds out into the winter air. Their gazes met. Lisnafaer and all its creatures disappeared. Only Anell and Akir—blood pumping, hearts knowing at last Anell's time had come. They laughed, satisfied that they were truly mated, summer, fall, winter, and soon, glorious spring. When their breathing quieted, making absolute the stillness known only in winter, Anell rested her head on Akir's withers. Waiting as long as he could stand, he shook himself, thus freeing Anell from her reverie.

Anell nuzzled her mate's nose and, ah, the delight, nipped his shoulder. She raced away but beckoned him. He caught up to her and turned them both in one powerful push. He loped at her side. They stopped their romp within the sheltering masses of giant firs, heather, and rhododendrons. Whatever else may happen on the slopes of the Guardians, they would quicken new life under as favorable conditions as possible, now when Good Gealach had emptied her silver bowl into the sea for Great Grian to sip at dawn.

All that Akir cared about was devouring one scent, Anell's. More urgent than the craving to hunt King Stag was his desire to mate with his lady.

The pack paused from their travels within the shelter of the lush evergreens at the borders of the apples, venturing out to hunt at need. All the Guardian forests, streams, and lakes teemed with prey-mates, much to Akir's satisfaction. With persistence even a poor hunter could feed. He made no objection when, once again, Anell called for a new den. She had led them south, and his fond heart followed. He nuzzled his mate. "So be it. Soon we will greet the spring cubs."

They gathered their strength to secure the boundaries of this new territory. Fierce howls and the ability to back them up in fleeting skirmishes with the few wulves they found made the southern border of the Guardian Mountains a home to Akir's family. He had expected to find more packs and those more ready to defend their territory. One departing wulf called back to acknowledge the arrival of the pack long-awaited to reclaim the Apple Coast. She seemed to hint that they had been saving the space for Anell's safe passage. Thriving prey-mates in other parts of the Guardians to which they went meant all would be well.

"What does she mean?" Akir wanted to know.

"Nothing," Anell said. "We have a new den to find."

Anell and Feela began searching immediately. They found just the spot near a waterfall, an abandoned corrie at the south eastern foot of the Wulf Tongue Pass, a treacherous route that twisted between sky-scraping ridges to the coast. Any misstep along the narrow pass where storms had eroded the sides sent careless travelers crashing down upon jumbled rocks. Even the deer and wulves paced it single file.

All through Hawthorn Month the pack settled in their new home in the foothills of Wulf Tongue and gladly explored its many hummocks and hollows. Several intersecting trails, now mapped within Akir's mind, identified the best possible spots to find newly awakening, always hunting prey-mates. They played in spring rains before hunting and slept satisfied after. Little matted tufts hung from their full bellies.

Kalar and Sonsie asked, "When do we scout Wulf Tongue Pass?"

Feela answered, "Soon."

The ravens of Raven Wood often flew by, dipping low to the ground whenever they spied any of Akir's pack. They had been pestering them for more leavings than any wanted to share, especially Anell. While the pack laughed at their antics and jibes, their aerial tag got on Anell's nerves, now that she had felt the first stirrings of new life. Jealous of her den site, she snarled, her eyes grim.

She lost sleep keeping watch for the uninvited faerwulf and his unsought warning from Sky-Wulf. What of the new litter? Would he mar their birth with new words of woe?

Twenty-Eight

LADY LIGHT'S QUEST

In spring keep watch. Faer Ones Troop the Green.

Akir rousted the entire pack for a scouting trip.
"You, too, Anell. The youngsters chase their tails. New Green beckons. A good run will make our rough coats gleam." He winked. "Give the ravens some trouble."

His black lips curled high over wet teeth; he huffed a wulfish chuckle. "A laugh at Dooleye's tribe—a jolly bonus to a jaunt under blue skies. Move along."

⋏ ⋏ ⋏

They broke from the pine cover into a glade. Across the open field they spied a series of cone-shaped knolls as tall as aspens that led to a conical mound of rippling moss-covered earth. It dwarfed all the others. A path wound in and out of the overlapping knolls.

Just as the pack was about to cross the field, the perfume of almond, honey, apple blossom, and mountain rose filled the air even though shredded blankets of snow still hugged the slopes of Wulf Tongue Pass and the adjoining mountains. Akir growled warning. Then, as if the stars rejoiced, sweet melody showered the Green. The wulves' tails fanned the warm air.

A cavalcade of mounted Faer Ones appeared from behind the mound and circled the hillocks, moving in and out of sight. In the breeze their capes waved while the high-flying banners snapped, appearing to top the conical peaks. The entourage's apparel, decorated with bright blooming spring flowers, sported a hundred shades of green from lettuces and grasses, pines and firs, dandelion stems and peas, mints and mosses, to kelp and sweet potato vine. They seemed a wind-blown meadow. The knotted starsilver trim on the Faer Ones' regalia and their gallant steeds' silver hooves flashed in the light.

The bright-eyed wulves recognized Lady Light, leading the Grand Trooping Rade on her white steed, and Lanark-Kyle and Iova-Rhu riding with the Greenguard. All the rest remained a mystery—from the lords of court and the adepts of light, music, and horse to the other Greenguard in all their colorful variety. All the ladies, even Iova-Rhu, wore flowing jeweled gowns that draped over their mounts. Elaborate feather and fern crowns adorned their heads. The males wore cockaded bonnets with long green ribbons; silver bells jingled at the ankles and tips of their boots. Live birds and butterflies fluttered upon the capes of all except Lady Light.

Soon the procession of merry singers drew near enough for the entranced wulves to hear clearly the verses sent back and forth between two choirs, one on the right flank, one on the left:

▲ ▲ ▲

"Oh ye of radiant face, who shines aloft,
Return your smile; send forth your beams this day
To warm the still-chilled Lisnafaer once more,
And we will spend our days in thankful play."
    "The Green Lord languished in the earth sae dark.
He carried wounds sae bloody, all knew the fear

That he'd been vanquished, he'd nae more leave
The biting dungeon, deep down, dark, and drear."
"Our Lady Light mourned all the winter long
And called upon her friends to aid her quest,
Adread to think that she'd see him nae more.
Sure they must find the Lord she loves the best."
  "Dear Mother-Light, pause now with your faer friends;
  Melt ice-bound streams; call forth the grasses green.
  Ride with us all across these lands once more
  And dance at mid day as our Shining Queen."
"The foxes and the wulves bark out their calls;
The salmon in their streams leap in the air.
All beasts rejoice to see your face once more;
And we ride forth to greet our Queen sae fair."
  "Our Trooping Rade winds through the hills in hope
  To see the long sought blessing of your might.
  Thus we implore you, bless our Lady's Quest—"
Lady Light: "Call forth Lord Green to life and light!"
All: "Queen Mother dear embraces Lady Light;
Their light and love calls forth the Lord sae brave.
Our Green Lord withers underground nae more;
He foils the bitter plot, escapes the gruesome grave."
Lady Light: "Rejoice! Rejoice! Lord Green comes once more!"
All: "He joins Our Lady Light in dance and song.
Our Mother-Light sends forth her precious beams
To bless this lovely land all summer long."

▲ ▲ ▲

Akir stood his ground and kept his pack in check.
Kalar's eyes widened. For the first time he felt the full impact of faer-song. His ears stood up. Oh, to run with these? That smell so? Cutters? No?

Unlike Sonsie, Kalar had no images to call forth, knew no secret trails that such beings haunted. He yelped, calling for play. His tail flailed so that Sonsie feared it would fly off. Sonsie strained to hear every note that lingered on the mountain breezes. He nudged his brother and growled for him to settle down.

That nudge set Kalar afire. He dashed forward and barked the closest to a laugh that any wulf can manage. The Faer Ones fanned out in a semi-circle at the edge of the glade. He skidded to a halt right before the Lady on the cloud white horse. Down he fell, opening his belly to the skies, and laid back his head. His throat was hers to do with as she chose.

The wulves gasped. Akir grumbled as if he were half stifling an earth-quake. The Faer Ones sat their gallant steeds in silence. All but one.

Lady Light's laughter sent misery—and delight—rippling over Kalar's body. "Now is not the time to grind your back into the earth," she said. "Oak Month heralds summer and Mother-Light calls forth the Grand Rade. We seek Lord Green."

She motioned for her most trusted courtiers to come forward. Lords Phelan and Arthgallo took their place to her right and Lady Patha and Master Arklevent to her left. She addressed Kalar.

"Stand and show your face, young wulf."

Kalar rolled over. He felt his paws touch the earth, heard his companions panting. He stood and faced his interrogator, the elegant Lady covered in shimmering green that matched the color of her eyes.

Seeing only the Lady, Kalar blinked, trying to comprehend the image before him. Seated upon the great horse whose tail whipped like whitecaps in a gale, she seemed the essence of summer bursting forth from beneath retreating snow on mountain meadows. A starsilver crown, like icicles shin-ing in the light, encircled her long white tresses. Wild flowers on ivy trailed from her shoulders to drape across the silver inlaid saddle and the horse's glistening white haunches. The horse, too, was caparisoned in starsilver in-tertwined in green silk, columbines, and bluebells. A white peafowl perched upon the Lady's shoulder, its tail feathers falling down her back to fan the saddle.

When the Lady laughed, the bird unfurled a great feathered arc. The horse pawed the ground and snorted. "Hush, Starbold. Be still and mind your manners. Fantoosh, your tail surpasses the glory of dawn, but your claws!" Both mount and bird relaxed into alert quiet.

"Kalar, know that we see and accept your gesture. Your heart, gallant and full, shows nothing amiss. Such prodigious paws suggest one who will make a fine hunter, such as we need for the deer to remain hardy.

"I'd say you have run near a year upon the Lord's Green. Time enough, my impetuous wulf, to claim your calling. Come see us when Gealach's face shines full on the anniversary of your birth. Look for us under any fine grassy mound, or within the enchanted conical hills, or if you dare, within the halls of the mountains." She laughed again. The happy agitation of her body provoked the peafowl and steed to answer in a flurry of white feathers and tail.

"We shall continue our quest, for 'tis the season of love and new life. Our blessings to you and your kin. Guard well your dam, young wulf."

She looked to Akir. "High wulf, see to it. Your numbers dwindle. When the snows melt and those called cutters drink the heady wine of the open air, they turn skittish. They should be like wulves who always sleep under open skies. Not snow, rain, fog, or hail daunts wulves with their ice-safe fur; wulves do not burn forests to keep warm."

Akir glared, his claws gripping the spring grass. "I don't need a Faer One who addresses a whelp before his sire." He grimaced. His teeth gleamed. "Who fails to name those called forward to greet a high wulf and his pack—to tell *me* what to 'see to.'"

Akir paused to lock his gaze with hers. He lowered his head to the slightest degree but intensified their eye contact. "Lady of the strange green eyes, I see you have exchanged a peafowl for wulf." He sniffed. "At least this one lives." His red tongue curled over his dripping fangs before swiping his black lips. "If cutters burn forests, *you*, Lady, have more than trooping the Green to attend to."

At this provocation Lord Phelan broke ranks to urge his steed forward. Blaze's nose inched just ahead of Starbold's. Anell, Beag, and Birk advanced to either side of Akir. Feeling as if an eagle had clawed his heart, Sonsie whimpered; he looked from his glaring pack to the Faer Ones.

Lady Light motioned for all to halt. Fantoosh's white tail arced into a feather-laced fan.

Her claws bit through the Lady's spun gold and green silk shawl into her pale blue shoulder. She neither winced nor moaned in the slightest degree. Her gaze held everyone captive in anxious silence.

With a nod so low that her hair fell forward and mingled with Starbold's mane, Lady Light acknowledged Akir. Her head rose. Her sad eyes belied her delicate laughter. "You have spoken truth, Akir. I ask your pardon, sire of two sons of lofty lineage who make their way under the eye of the wulf-star."

Anell shuddered and drew closer to Akir.

The Lady's serene face reflected her formal demeanor. "Anell and Akir, I name to ye Lord Phelan, hunt master; Lord Arthgallo, high counselor; Master of the Green Arklevent; and Lady Patha, trusted healer."

Upon hearing their names called, each courtier nodded.

Staring at the hunt master, Akir inhaled deeply. His throat constricted. The scent, never to be forgotten—the warning, a pall upon his heart.

Forestalling any act on Akir's part, the Lady extended her pale blue, jeweled hand. "Akir, ye and your pack share the same cares as I and the Faer Ones. Accept my thanks for your reminder. Blessed be."

Turning, her gaze fell upon the young faerblack wulf. She wagged her finger. "And watch where you run, Kalar, soon to be a grand wulf. Stopping will not be so easy."

Her mirthful chuckle showered the onlookers; caught up in the spirit of her jest, the entire Troop joined her. Butterflies danced around their heads. Before turning Starbold, she beckoned to the troubled faerwhite wulf who struggled to obey his sire's commands even as his heart's desire called him to rebel.

"Sonsie," she cooed, "call back your soul from your eyes. Under Gealach's full face in Oak Month come visit us in our mountain retreat. Tell me of your travels. We shall sing and celebrate your birth date."

Then she waved a command. The company redressed the double line and sang heartily as they wound to the west in the direction of Wulf Tongue Pass.

Anell pondered this encounter then turned to her maturing pups. She called them to her side.

"Well, Kalar, who tries my patience at every turn, you have met the Lady face to face, a ferlie image, beware. And Sonsie, you now have a song, fresh-found, to add to your lore. Should you. . . ." She broke off, sending her mate a quizzical look that he swallowed in silence.

Sonsie moved forward. He gave three sharp yips.

"Aye, eager Sonsie, who troubles my heart each time you chase song upon the breeze, you could cry *that* song aloft for many ages to come, for did not the Faer Ones name the wulf?"

Akir, followed by Beag, signaled their retreat, but Kalar and Sonsie huddled together, unmoving, even after the Rade of the gaily flying pennants had long disappeared. They asked each other if they had met this Lady with the strangely familiar eyes before.

The entire pack milled around; they sniffed and muttered to one another, hesitant to leave this enchanted spot. Under cover of this distraction, Kalar and Sonsie bolted down the trail the Faer Ones had taken. Karlon and Ro ran around the huge conical mound. At last, Akir challenged the afterimage that teased his sight. All the males howled and grumbled. The females, led by Anell, began their return to the den ground.

At that moment, a small band of cutters broke from a cleft in the rocks to the east. Upon sighting the pack, they took cover behind the tumbled stones of an abandoned shelter from days long gone when those now known as cutters were welcome to cross Lisnafaer on their way to the sea. A tall bearded one clad in a leather jerkin and woven breeches pulled at the long stick with a shining end the shape of a serpent's head. He stretched a string that hummed upon release. The first missile, like a flying viper, struck Anell through the ribs. "Thwang, thwang," two other sticks with the sharp, biting heads pierced her side, low, under the ribs. She sprang and twisted in the air. Another cutter shot her belly. Anell crashed to the ground.

Birk forced Mundee to the right, away from Anell to a nearby mound covered with thick shrubs. Feela turned Ro to the left. She careened into her flank just as they reached the edge of a rock-strewn gulley. Down they tumbled then scrambled to their feet. Birk and Mundee peered from the bushes, Feela and Ro from the gulley rim. After giving Ro and Mundee the harshest warning to stay put, Feela and Birk sprinted to help Akir, Beag, and Karlon, who had pivoted in wrath at the first assault. They attacked the bunker of fallen stones.

Twenty-Nine

WULF FRENZY, WULF JOY

Wulves must hunt, cutters kill.

M aking their way to Wulf Tongue Pass, the trooping Faer Ones followed the curving glen around islands of sky-reflecting waters, surrounded by crimson rhododendrons in full bloom. Their glossy leaves shone
in the morning light. The entire troop sang of the glistening sea, of the waves'
call that floated on salt air and flirted with the gulls skimming the shore. Their
light adepts laughed, eager to reach the pass and begin the climb through
Grian's gold light. By now her beams fell aslant the mountains, spreading rainbows like violets, ripe for plucking. The light weavers claimed they gathered
the best bows atop Wulf Tongue and down the trail leading to the western sea.

"Ah, spring, how delicious!" all assured one another.

They came upon a haphazard clump of felled trees. Leafless birch limbs,
snapped and frayed, covered hacked pines, their sap long dried, their stiff
needles brown. Lord Arthgallo marveled that cutters had dared to enter so far
into Lisnafaer, let alone desecrate trees.

Tears brimmed Lady Light's eyes.

Before she could speak, a spiking pain drove out the sorrow that weighed
down her heart. Gasping, she clutched her breast, pitched forward, but caught

herself on Starbold's mane. Her mare's head jerked upward. Starbold shrieked. Fantoosh's tail unfurled.

Lord Phelan, riding beside Lady Light, reached over to calm Starbold. Attending Guardians who rushed to aid the Lady and take Fantoosh found no wounds. Even so, nausea washed over her in waves. "The wulves," she moaned. Once her head cleared, she wheeled Starbold in a half turn and commanded the troop to return to the glade where they had encountered Akir's pack.

⋏ ⋏ ⋏

When Kalar and Sonsie heard their pack's furious cries, they raced back to find Anell's riddled body. The adults had already swarmed the stones where the cutter bowmen huddled. Mundee called from the scrub-covered mound, Ro from the rocky gulley. Defying commands to keep safe or face the pack's wrath for disobeying, the two junior females dashed to their younger brothers.

"Here! Follow us! Birk said so." They led Kalar and Sonsie to shelter on the mound where they held the shocked brothers between them.

Kalar and Sonsie howled. "No run? No hunt? No Change! No honor!"

Mundee and Ro agreed.

Kalar and Sonsie struggled. "We must help!"

"No!" Ro snapped. "You two stay here or Birk will rip out your tongues and tails!"

Ro signaled Mundee. "We go."

"Take us!" Kalar and Sonsie cried.

"No!" Mundee's eyes threatened death.

A cutter shriek pierced the wulf snarls. "Father, wulves, wulves! Father! Wulves!" one wailed.

All three cutters drew their dirks. The blades flashed before turning scarlet. Despite their wounds, the wulves pressed their attack against the cutter interlopers. Added to their foul odor now came the reek of fear, like a dead toad under a wet rock. The wulves lunged. Two of the cutters, a redhead with soiled trousers and one with a belly that jiggled over his belt, tried to make a break for it, leaving the younger one behind. Akir and Beag focused on the redhead. His stench drove them wild. Birk and Karlon dashed after the other one. Feela leapt the barricade and pounced on fat belly's son.

Both runaway cutters attempted a return to the fallen wall. They tore at each other but came to grief on the waist high stones. The redhead managed to get an arm and leg over. In his terror, fat belly, failing to heave his gut clear of the wall, straddled it like a squealing hog. The wulves tore at their kicking boots. Forced to turn, the cutters faced raging wulf jaws. With dirks drawn they slashed wildly, clipping Birk on the snout. Blood gushed upon her tongue. In renewed frenzy she spat it out. Blades rose and fell, cut left and right, maiming each wulf, turning their fur crimson.

Scorning the blades as nothing compared to lethal deer spikes and hooves, the bloody wulves pressed on. Karlon twisted to attack. He snapped the fat cutter's arm. The "crack!" boomed on his teeth. Feela crushed the younger cutter's thigh. The cutters flung their torn arms over their faces. Only their bloody dirks and leather clothes saved them.

ᐧ ᐧ ᐧ

With Lord Phelan at her side Lady Light led the Solas-Faers back down the trail by which they had so recently departed. The staffs of their gay banners, now turned to deadly lances, streamed battle flags. The Troop thundered toward the mêlée. They divided to surround the combatants, cutting off Mundee and Ro from the chaos before they could clear the brambles.

Lord Phelan and Master Arklevent leaned low and grasped Akir. Swift-riding horse adepts grabbed Beag, Birk, Karlon, and Feela. They tossed the slashed but blessedly alive wulves near Anell's body where Lady Light, her eyes wild and dangerous, already attended Akir's stricken mate. They landed on their paws and shook themselves out of a temporary shock. Lady Light's dreadful eyes held them in place.

Mundee and Ro gathered their younger brothers and scurried to their wailing mates. In the center of the chorused misery lay Anell's arrow-pierced body. The wretched young ones joined the adults' howls. The pack's keening drew Lady Light's pain out through the pores of her skin, now a paler blue than her throbbing veins. Her emerald eyes turned such a deep green, true faerblack, that they seemed smoldering coals. Her parted lips disclosed teeth clenched against a baleful scream. Kalar and Sonsie shook. Anguish and terror competed, nearly stopping their hearts.

Taking advantage of this distraction, the cutters retreated towards their encampment to the east across River Lavina. They lurched, supporting one another, alternately groaning and filling the air with hateful maledictions.

The Lady's severe face compelled the pack to draw close, momentarily halting their lamentations. After making eye contact with each of them, she stopped at Akir. Holding his gaze, she led the galvanized wulves and the troop in a combined cry, pouring their hearts' grief upon the turbulent air.

When the swelling of their voices climaxed, she silenced the Solas-Faers. She continued in an eldritch wail that sounded like the bawls of the marching Dorcha-Faers—only worse—on the night when the veil between worlds is thinnest.

Now riderless, Starbold wheeled round, defying the wind's increased force. Swaying trees moaned. The horses joined the wulves in piercing screams. Stones burst. Rocks split. No Faer Ones joined the angry chorus. They called upon all their skills to remain seated upon their rearing mounts.

Phelan maneuvered Blaze to Starbold's side. He grabbed the white mane. One rider and two high-spirited horses fought madness until the hunt master willed Starbold and Blaze to heed his command. They could raise thrashing hooves to the air and add their cries to the Lady's, but they would remain faithful to those they served and their duty to Greenlaw.

Lady Light's call reached to the stars. The wulves' hackles rose—and still they howled. The riders of the Grand Rade encircled them. Sheer force of will, wed to the deep bond between Faer Ones and their horses, kept the troop utterly still but ready to act. Whatever danger threatened, they would protect their Queen and the wulves.

The wild notes fled upon rushing wind. Mortal enemies frozen in a blood-soaked tableau: three bleeding and broken cutters, icy dread flushing their bowels, and nine wulves gripped in hatred so intense the world seemed to vanish before their eyes. Black clouds, pressing upon their heads, ate the light.

Lord Arthgallo's warning shattered the silence that had shrouded them. "Dorcha! My Lady! Oh, doleful day!"

"Dorcha! Dorcha!" The cry rippled through all the company.

A roiling storm swirled over their heads as if a giant had tossed slag from Mount Edan's fiery entrails. The maimed cutters bolted. Not even the one whose belly jiggled in his flight survived the onslaught. In the conflagration of flaming ice and sleeting smoke the wulves panted as fast as their hearts raced. Revulsion gagged them; saliva poured upon the ground. The assault harmed no grasses, yet the blackened imprint of the three cutters' bodies remained. Their leather clothes and boots vanished along with their bones, even their heads. Only a few scattered teeth and charred bone fragments fused into melted buckles, brooches, or blades gave the only other evidence of their trespass into Lisnafaer.

The acid aftertaste of the dorcha scourge coated the wulves' tongues. They sneezed in rapid convulsions but failed to cleanse the scent of flesh vaporized by the Dorcha's wrath. Kalar stood four-square. He curled his big paws into the ground, the nails biting the grass. Sonsie dug his head into Kalar's side. His head rose and fell with each breath Kalar took.

The wind's fury lessened, yet the boughs of all surrounding trees swayed as if reaching for the departed apparitions, so swift was their passing. Eager to be away, Lady Light's troops gathered the cutters' arrowheads and blades, any slightest scrap that remained of their evaporated bodies, all to be carried and tossed into Mount Edan's fires. Phelan led Starbold to the Lady's side in hopes of restoring tranquility to their troubled spirits.

Thus united, she and Starbold stood in perfect stillness. Only the whipping of the Lady's hair and the lashing of Starbold's mane and tail in the wind proved they had not been turned to stone, visible now that the dark of the terrible dorcha storm had passed. Tears fell from Starbold's eyes. Lady Light, gripped by visions played out on some interior landscape, stared ahead, seeing nothing of the external world.

Lord Phelan wasted no effort to reach her whom he could neither hinder nor help but approached Anell. Loathing the grim indignity of her bearing those bloody arrows, he nearly choked. "Pernicious betrayal!" escaped his clamped teeth.

"My Lord shall know of it," Lady Light answered. Her blue hand caressed Starbold's neck.

Phelan dared to look her way. "We must depart!"

"We must give succor to these wulves, our cousins in need," she countered.

The dorcha attack had left the stunned pack unable to attend Anell. Their muscles twitched, held in check by wills honed in desperate hunts. As their racing hearts calmed, their ragged breaths eased. The pack awaited their leader's command.

Akir's intense gaze shifted from the Lady to Phelan.

Despite the peril, Phelan looked directly at Akir's eyes, waited, then bowed.

Akir exhaled a long-held breath.

Phelan crouched before Anell. He gently upheld her limp head, placed the slack tongue within her jaws, and began to close them.

"Still breathing!" he cried. "Still alive!"

All the Faer Ones gasped.

Lady Light's aching throat released a glad cry.

The wulves gathered behind Akir, who loomed over Lord Phelan. At her mate's approach, Anell's eyes within the peaked black mask opened, her pain evident.

Phelan kissed her brow. He whispered, "Be brave Anell, my darling. We shall help you."

Though eager to extract the arrows, he sought permission to further violate her living body. "Truly, Akir, her life depends upon faer hands, not wulf jaws, to withdraw the biting heads of the serpent-headed arrows."

Akir nodded consent. To prevent her from biting Phelan he tenderly clamped his jaws over Anell's. One by one, Phelan extracted the ugly missiles. Akir growled but held Anell fast. The puckering flesh at the open wounds and the spurting blood proved that she yet lived. Akir licked Anell's face while the rest of the pack hovered around them. Dark blood matted her golden hair. Removing her shawl, Lady Light covered Anell's quaking body.

Phelan broke each bloody shaft in disgust but saved the pieces to be carried along with her body to the closest help.

Fingering the star-silver buttons on his cuff, Lord Arthgallo broke the silence of the Faer Ones, gathered at a discrete distance. "First woe then joy." He shook his head. "Beware a counterstroke."

One of the Lady's court turned to their minstrel. "Perhaps some music, Elphinlark?"

He stopped wringing his hands and nodded. "I know just the trooping song to help us leave behind the wreckage and ruin of this day."

A music adept cautioned, "No, Elphinlark, a soothing song. Sing it now." He doffed his bonnet, bowed, then crooned,

🔺 🔺 🔺

"Soft, soft, fret nae more.
Let the Ladies of the Sky
Shine on you healing light. . . ."

🔺 🔺 🔺

Lady Patha, kneeling beside the Lady, took over Anell's care. The Guardians went to the other wounded wulves, leaving Akir to Lord Phelan. Before attending the high wulf, Phelan shared his heart's misgivings with Lanark-Kyle who stood guard a short distance away from the volatile pack. "Something pernicious works its way in the Green, and this pack is in the thick of it, I fear." Lanark-Kyle nodded, his mouth locked in a tight grimace.

🔺 🔺 🔺

Akir followed Lady Patha's slightest move in dressing all of Anell's wounds; despite her gentle touch, he never ceased growling.

Lady Light sighed. "Akir, I beg you. Remain calm. We shall save your good mate. And see how the Greenguard care for your wounded comrades? Your wounds must be tended as well."

Her words soothed Akir's disturbed spirit. Taking their cue, Lord Phelan, followed closely by Lanark-Kyle, came to Akir. Holding their breaths, they eased their knees to the ground, paused, and offered to mend his torn hide. The ever-dangerous wulf snarled, but taking a begrudging sniff and casting another glance at his beloved, Akir finally agreed.

The Lady signaled her minstrel to continue.

ᛣ ᛣ ᛣ

"Hush, hush, doubt nae more.
Let the Faer Ones sing
Away your cares and woes.
Sweet, sweet, sigh nae more.
Let Faer hands banish pain,
Heal all your weeping wounds."

ᛣ ᛣ ᛣ

After all dressings had been tied, the Queen beckoned the troop to her side. "The wulves?"

Lady Patha wiped a last bit of healing unguent from her hands. "Their physical ills, my Lady, concern me not."

She gazed at Lady Light's clenched fists twisting a hank of her white hair. "And yet. . . ?"

"Patha, we dare not tarry. What about travel?"

"As to that, these stout-hearted hunter wulves may travel," Lanark-Kyle replied.

"Albeit with hearts more tender than tough for the nonce," Lady Patha hastened to add. She frowned. "We must carry Anell, my Lady, but best that we all move—sooner than later—considering the, emm, mad assault. What were they doing out in daylight?"

Lady Light's confidante looked deeply within her sovereign's heart where boiling blood raged against cold, sick shock. Patha gasped.

Showing nothing of her turmoil, Lady Light turned to her other counselors who had gathered nearby. The adepts of horse and light as well as master of the Greenguard reported that the mounted troop waited upon the wulves and Lady Light's will. The Lightguard affirmed that after the passage of the Dorcha-Faers the light had returned to its pure state, as befit the beginning of summer. Even so, many feared that Lady Light's quest to find Lord Green, marred by such baleful shocks, cast shadows on the new Oak Month. None dared to mention his name before the Lady. She solicited suggestions. Lord Arthgallo urged preparing defense should unlawful Dorcha renew their assault. Never shy of displaying his valor, he thrust aside the folds of his embossed cape and brandished his crystal dirk. Light flashed between his fingers.

Lady Light viewed the skies. "Arthgallo, we seek other illumination."

She motioned for him to sheath his weapon. "That which we witnessed shall be debated, later, in safety. The attack, unlawful I grant, and unsought, shall be addressed. All whom *I* summoned—but *one*—even now secure the forest."

Master Arklevent's scraggly brows twitched. "'But *one*'?"

She lifted her arms in a gesture of embrace. "We must tend to these wulves. And find Lord Green."

She looked about as if hope could summon her heart's desire. "Other counsel?"

Hunt Master Phelan's eyes narrowed. "My Lady, if a wild hunt flies unleashed, I and my people must be ready to ride."

Nodding, Lady Light said, "Anell first, Lord Phelan. Anell looks to Akir. Speak to him. He knows you—if there be not love, there is respect—at least for the truth you spoke."

Akir agreed to depart but answered Phelan's assurances that all would be well with a sullen growl and a curt "sweet scent, empty belly."

Not a few of the troop, their hearts heavy, scowled. All heads turned to Lady Light.

After the Queen of the Faer Ones remounted Starbold, she rallied the troubled Solas-Faers. "Hazard and harm cancel not duty. Our first belongs to Akir and Anell. We shall move Anell and her family to succor."

She surveyed their faces, still clouded but determined to answer her call. "By the Light, I see your anxious hearts in your eyes, dear ones. Anell. Dorcha. Lord Green. Cares come in threes to make full our days and long our nights."

She raised her hand in salute; her jewels flashed. "Dorcha-Faers abroad this season, this day, in this light? Cutters and Dorcha, crossing paths this far within the heart of Lisnafaer! Kith and kin of Light, I vow we shall know why."

Turning Starbold in a full circle to survey the entire company, she spoke her will. "We shall divide. The Low Road, swiftest route to assure Anell's recovery. The High Road, Wulf Tongue Pass, surest route to find Our Lord who brings back the Green."

Thirty

Parting of the Ways

Faer Ones' hidden trails: watch and learn.

The wulves' noses twitched. They smelled blood—their own, caked in matted fur. As one, all heads turned toward a new scent coming from the site of the cutter attack. None could mistake the harbinger of the white-haired Faer One: mint in spring rain; a High West meadow, newly bloomed; fresh pinesap; and a summer salt lick overlaid with the scent of tears, bitter, not sweet.

Alone and carrying Anell's wounds in her heart, Lady Light raised her head, regal in restrained pain. Well aware of being deprived the counsel of Lords Arthgallo and Phelan, she rode her white mare straight at the wulves and pondered the sight of the wulves' torn coats bound in gaily colored banners. Were the time less dire, she would laugh to see sturdy wulves thus bedecked.

She closed her emerald eyes. Alas, their bloodied fur. How to deal with Akir?

She rallied. "Bonnie wulves, take heart. We go to help and health on the edge of Faers Weald." Leaning low upon Starbold's mane, she whispered to Anell, "Ah, dear one, we go to the apples. They must be blooming now."

Lady Light turned to Akir. "High wulf, I beseech you. Bury auld grievances. Join us in moving your dearest mate to the apple keepers, great healers and our friends. Be assured, by taking the Low Road, swiftest and most sheltered route, we keep Anell safe. Bring along Feela and Sonsie.

"Those best suited to protect Kalar and the rest of your pack shall escort them up the High Road. Some wyrd is unfolding. Help us. Hinder not your friends. I swear, neither I nor any of my kind intends harm to any of your kind."

She restrained an urge to nudge Starbold into action. "Akir, will you help me?"

They stared into each other's eyes. Two images clouded Akir's vision: Anell's face and Lady Light wearing the wulf head, its snow white pelt draping her blue shoulders. Their eyes, he mused, so alike, clear and true. He licked his parched lips. The supreme hunter measured the Lady to the very depth of her soul.

His curled lips revealed fangs eager for revenge. "Why should I?"

"High wulf Akir's worthy mate lies wounded, clinging to life. Put aside your distrust for once and help us save her life, a joy much coveted by all."

He stiffened, allowing not one whisker to twitch. In the silence Lady Light's heart boomed, proof enough she had one. He nodded. Anell could have her way at last. He cared only that she lived. She'd bear new pups in some hidden, safe green, even if it be amongst the apples.

Repercussions from the deadly dorcha assault continued to harass the travelers. The fair breezes of early morn turned sullen. The pure light that had cast glory upon the Grand Rade faded, leeched from the sky. Intermittent rays struggled to pierce the fleeting gaps in the tumbling black clouds that pressed ever lower upon the mountains.

All the wulves nipped at flies vexing their eyes, ears, even trying to crawl up their flaring snouts, but Sonsie and Kalar suffered the worst.

Cranky and lethargic, the pack joined in a low, droning lament. The Faer Ones urged them to quicken their pace, but the wulves resisted being herded. At every lichen-encrusted rock or turn in the trail, Kalar threatened to bolt from the group, only to face Birk whose irritating nips grew into bites. Sonsie insisted on howling his own song.

The Lady's high counselor winced. Arthgallo inclined his head to the hunt master and whispered, "What if the precocious yearling calls forth another mad flight of the Dorcha?"

Lord Phelan shrugged. "Though I see a trace of stardust in his faergreen eyes, he is hardly the cause of the first. His heart harkens to his wounded dam. Leave him be, Lord Arthgallo."

The heavy air broke into throbbing gusts that punched the tree tops and scattered the dead leaves left behind after the snow's retreat. Soon roaring winds from the north brought a numbing chill. Branches just coming into bud groaned under invisible weight. Gloom shrouded the wayfarers. The wulves' hackles stiffened. His fangs bared, Kalar broke from the pack to issue a grumbling challenge. Akir fought his way back to awareness of his world from the depths of his soul-deadening fear for Anell. He joined Kalar in a fierce growl. Sonsie added his voice, high and clear, grief upon wrath. All joined in full chorus, their woe changed to warning; they would crunch bones: deer, wild kyloe—even Dorcha—just to slake their rage.

Churning clouds, bruised purple-black and sickly green, crushed the natural light. Below, a grimy murk ate pale flashes striving to break through. The jewels in the Lords' sword hilts gleamed in the glow of the Guardians' brandished crystals; even so, palpable darkness assailed the Lords of Light.

The wulves' rhythmic keening set a cadence to which they and the horses trotted, but whenever the wulves planted their claws in the earth and howled, more defiantly each time, all progress halted. The riders' knees cleaved to heaving ribs of spooked horses. Sweat poured from their necks and flanks. The Guardians leaned forward to whisper in their ears, caress their strained faces. They ran long, slender fingers around their ever-turning ears and through their silky manes.

Hearing her pack's howls, Anell thrashed in her hammock strung between Iova-Rhu and Lanark-Kyle's horses. Her groans hurt her mates more than any bodily wounds. Their howls grew shrill.

Lady Light acted. "Phelan! Patha! I will not have the wulves verted to blood lust. It will kill Anell. Combine your talents. Succor our cousins in pain."

Lady Patha hummed a calming song, as if a thousand bees were calling for drowsy afternoon naps. Lord Phelan dismounted and, removing his tunic, walked between the howling wulves. Upon his blue body wulves leapt, seeming to fly in azure skies. Astonished at the wonder of these markings on his blue flesh, Akir's pack sensed a comrade. They obeyed his call to keep moving, but their rant continued.

Phelan walked beside Akir, never attempting to touch the grief-stricken high wulf, but he spoke his mind. "Akir, you are Covenant-pledged to obey Greenlaw and protect the Green. As are all Faer Ones, your allies. Count me your brother, Akir. Grant your Lady Anell respite."

Akir's growls subsided into a mute despair. The pack's sad silence followed.

Phelan remounted Blaze.

Alert wulves and wary Faer Ones exited a trail lined with rowan trees. Brown-tipped decay marred the five-petal ivory blossoms in full bloom. The Guardians nodded to one another, their brows knotted. Lady Light urged her party forward to the base of a grand mound. Ripples of mossy earth rose to its towering peak like waves upon a shore. Spiraling to the top in clusters, white stones, seemingly jumbled, protruded through trailing ivy.

The Queen of the Faer Ones called out, "Wulf Anell. Wulf Akir. Wulves of the lost pack of Auld Alba, now found. We must deliver Anell to proper shelter.

"Map Keeper Thornheart, hand of the outland, shall guide those who climb Wulf Tongue to the sky and on to the Apple Coast. Keep vigilant for signs of Lord Green." She paused. A sigh escaped, betraying a heart too full.

She willed herself to sit arrow straight. "Stay alert for miscreant Dorcha and dangers—dangers I pray stalk us not on the inland route beneath the mountains. Although we part, we remain united. Hold fast the Light that abides in each of our hearts. All shall be well."

Her voice, sweet to Sonsie's ear, flowed in his blood. He looked up at her as she sat upon Starbold of the flowing white mane and tail, taking the splendor of the Lady's silver-clasped white tresses, her sky-blue throat, and her depthless emerald eyes matched by her spring green gown into his heart like a magical seed in fertile ground.

She smiled. "Ye shall not quail or fail your duty. I command ye, hold fast to your course. Go with Great Grian the Gold's love smiling upon ye. Cherish her light, against which no darkness might prevail.

"If ye see Lord Green, salute him on my behalf. Blessed be."

"Blessed be," called back those heading around the mound to the north-west and the High Road. Kalar and the departing wulves, as well as those remaining behind, barked mutual farewells, but none had the will to howl.

Even Sonsie confided to Feela, "Too sharp."

They joined those who ascended the mound and circled to the east, falling in behind Akir, who closely followed Anell. Lady Light led the troop with Lady Patha and Lord Phelan riding closest to the four wulves. The court minstrel carried a subdued Fantoosh whose tail nearly swept the ground.

Not to be fooled by ivy and moss, Sonsie alerted Feela to a path that ran from one stone heap to the next.

"Shush, Sonsie! Watch and listen."

They came to a spot on the eastern quadrant of the conical mound centered exactly between tip and base. Sonsie stared at the ivy-covered stones and yelped. "Feela! Look! It's a—"

"Hush!"

Lady Light pulled ahead, positioning Starbold directly before this tumble of white stone and curling ivy. None failed to see a face, not even the other wulves.

"Phelan, keep them back!"

She held up her fisted left hand, pointing her ring, emblazoned with oak and holly, wulf and deer, toward the face. "Aros-nam-ba'Bean."

The stones parted, leaving a gaping maw in the side of the mound. Out leapt a shaggy canine, easily the size of a young bull, its color a green so dark it appeared black.

"Find Him!"

The hound raised its head toward the wind, tasting the air. Without a sound, it glided away on its huge paws.

Lady Light beckoned Lord Phelan.

He herded the group within. "Quickly!"

The last Guardian cleared the threshold. The stones rumbled closed. In the dark they awaited Light Master Lady Ula's awakening of the light that she carried with her. Sonsie recalled the eve of the New Year. Images of the Dorcha from that night, jumbled with those of this day, plagued him.

Lady Ula waved a glowing crystal. Underground Lisnafaer came alive, born anew on the silver-veined and jewel-encrusted painted walls. His fearful memories banished, Sonsie sighed and focused on unfamiliar but sweet aromas, delicate and complex, like a breeze after dawn showers.

"All here? All well?" Lord Phelan called.

"Yes. Yes," everyone agreed.

"The Low Road beckons," Lady Light said. "Map Keeper Brighteye, hand of the inland, lend us your hand."

Thirty-One

HIGH ROAD BOGIES

Hunt in stealth. Dorcha roam the night.

Mounted Faer Ones and heart-weary wulves climbed the High Road as Grian began her obscured descent toward her bower in the west. Teeth-grating grit made it difficult to breathe. Undaunted, the Guardians lifted their crystals higher. Red-orange-blue light, riding on brilliant white, flashed to push back the untimely dusk. Countless hidden and harried beasts scuttled high and low. From deep within the forest recesses chattering added to the teeming unrest. An unnamed sound, not mere rustling leaves, insinuated itself in the ears of the wulves and horses. As they tried to find its source, their hides crept. The Faer Ones said "there, there" and patted their horses' heads. No one reached down to comfort the wulves.

Aloft, a screeching, like beasts caught in mill wheels, resounded from one cloud bank to another. Lowering skies proved no barrier to the cackles, hisses, and hoots, punctuated by some other sound, like sharp, grinding teeth. Minute by minute a faint scent of some feral dung heap grew stronger. Kalar shook his head. The wulves sneezed and rubbed their snouts. The Faer Ones gasped and covered their faces with silk handkerchiefs. Sky-borne hooves thundered toward them. The very air had become a highway for dorcha marauders, unleashed out of time, out of season. Birk and Beag choked through growls.

Mundee called to Kalar, "Something bad up above the trees, nasty voices, but I can't . . . if only Sonsie—"

"Quiet!" Kalar snapped.

Ro risked a question. "Kalar, do you hear other voices, down here, near the trail?"

▲ ▲ ▲

About a half mile from the trail a bogey crouched behind a hodge-podge of rotted trees. Within their fungi-coated trunks beetles and grubs burrowed frantically into the squashy wood or balled themselves into little pills to avoid long bogey nails that scrabbled for snacks. A panting companion joined him. Their bulbous noses sported black bristles. Warts like freckles covered their dark, wrinkled faces. Their grunts thrust spittle through crooked, gaped teeth.

The grating cackle of one of these lowly shambling Dorcha pierced through the din of a troubled forest. "Well? Where's she, then?"

From within the rustling dark a voice answered, "Under the storm o' the hunt." The bogey snagged a beetle, crunched and sucked its body, then spat its carcass. It caught in a cobweb strung between two fronds of fiddlehead bracken.

"Out racin' her vulves, then?" the first voice continued.

"Nah, too many come a-clatterin', court and all." The spitter paused to scratch the festering head of a tick dug into his neck. "Sparks flyin' from their silver hooves, curse them. I been trackin' them ever since that ear-splittin' screech loosed the dead!"

The first speaker grunted. "Unh! The Big Rade, then. Them's got this itch to scratch for bein' seen, unh?"

"Some as do, some as don't. She's gone Low, takin' some o' her ilk down under, don't yer know? Vulves, too."

"Did she find Himself?"

"Nah, Oak's late this season. Now the rest searchin' out the likes o' ye, spyin' all yer nasty tricks." The voice cut off in a spasm of hoarse laughter.

"In the murk?" the other voice whined. "When the likes o' us knock into bric-a-brac at every bush and barrow?"

"What murk? Them with light galore in pockets and pokes—shush . . . caution now. A mob's upon us. More vulves, too."

"Told yer there'd be vulves!"

"Shhhh!" A gnarled hand attached to that voice buffeted the head of the half-crouching bogey to its left.

"If it weren't for them and their cursed vulves," he hissed, "I'd crack yer neb for yer, by the Tail."

The bogies lumbered forward on their balled fists and back feet, hopping frog-like. They found a thick, upright tree to squat behind and steal a peek at the passing troop. As the light of the Faer Ones' flaring crystals struck their eyes, they winced and pulled back behind the tree.

"One low pass o' the night swoopers cuts that light," the bogey tracker hissed. "Not bein' Dorcha, them needs light for seein' or bein' seen." He searched the sky for High Dorcha.

"She unleash the Harrow Host on purpose?"

"Paugh! How? She don't command Dorcha nah more."

▲ ▲ ▲

The air cooled long before true nightfall. Sounds, similar to the crunching of beetle backs crisped on hot rock, followed the wulves and their companions. Wind buffeted the tree tops and laid low the wayside undergrowth. Squawking ravens ceased their flight to huddle on nearby branches. Unconcerned with the deadly currents swirling over their heads, owls sent an early call to cats to begin their nightly hunts. The faer troop pulled their cloaks more tightly about their shoulders and bent into the wind.

Lord Arthgallo inquired of Master Arklevent how soon the trail would rise above the timberline. Kalar's ears perked. He heard the Master of the Green reply, "Blink of an eye as the ravens fly." Kalar's snout wrinkled.

Arklevent added, "For those who tread the winding trail of the Wulf Tongue, Great Grian may have departed ere we clear the trees. Too bad, the view of the Western Isles has no equal in all Lisnafaer."

Kalar breathed easier; he welcomed the dark. When Arklevent proclaimed that he always gave thanks for the Light, even in the dark, Kalar scoffed. The Faer Ones were no hunters. He yearned to be quit of their tedious company. Even so, Arklevent's notion of Great Grian "never failing since she sang the world into being" caught his attention. He thought of Sonsie, hunter of song. The remembered feel of Sonsie at his side in the cave eased the lingering tightness in his chest. He tossed his head back and forth, up and down, sniffing the swirling air.

Against the assault of unwholesome scents, his pack's howls thickened to guttural drones. He joined their chorus. Arthgallo signaled all the Solas-Faers to close ranks around the wulves, but Kalar defied every attempt to drive him into their center. He positioned himself at the rear of the pack.

When Arklevent surveyed their agitation, he softened the gaze of his weather-wise eyes. He reached out to them. "Troubled hunter wulves, be not dismayed. Though it seems Grian sleeps and Gealach hides her face, tempting Dorcha to suck dry the very stars, know this—they shine far above Lisnafaer where no Dorcha ever flies. Just so, light shines within the deepest mountain halls of the Solas-Faers. We have nothing to fear from clouds that answer only to wind, not Dorcha!"

Arklevent's brave words about wind and clouds rang hollow to Kalar. He scented a creature he shuddered to meet again—and no White Stag in sight this time. His heart raced. He maneuvered himself between two of the horses. Under his bristling fur swift-flowing blood swelled his muscles, prepared to fight or flee.

Clever and curious, the bogey trackers edged closer to the High Road to follow the Faer Ones and wulves. They maintained a parallel course at a distance safe enough to bolt and scramble up the trees if need be. Absorbed in their dilemma—how to spy without being spied—they blundered upon a fachan.

Its large single eye, hidden within yellow blossoms on green-leaved willow branches, saw them first. "Ya, yin now," it croaked. "Ya, yous gaberlunzies, what're two bog-faces doin' tramplin' about in my patch o' the woods?"

The two bogies threw their arms about each other and halted, stone still. "D'ye see him, then?" voiced one.

"Nuff, wiff," the other struggled to reply, "yer hairy arms, unh, stranglin'm'face. Ge'offme!"

A voice within the willows warned, "Shut yer mouths or ye'll draw them slabberin' vulves down on all our heads."

They jumped apart and crawled slantways toward the voice.

"Grasphand?"

"And what if not, Grungegrind? Such a rack-a-rack bogies make! I been hearin' ye, ye and Pricklewort both, since before bats been born!" He paused to rub his back against a willow trunk. "Flyin' furry frogs! A wonder ye haven't pulled entire court off their Rade, bad cess ridin' with vulves."

Grungegrind and Pricklewort hunkered down at the fachan's foot and looked up with all the caution of a pair of worms under the shadow of a hungry raven. "Watch them claws on his hand," Pricklewort whispered. To their singular host they offered gap-toothed grins.

Panting, Grungegrind asked, "What o' the day, Grasph—"

Pricklewort reached over to shut his companion's mouth.

The fachan shrugged. "I been mindin' the trail, scoutin' comin's and goin's, ye might say."

Through Pricklewort's fingers Grungegrind volunteered, "Dunderdug! Between host above and court, drat them, below, we been makin' our way through a scramble o' beasts."

Grasphand's enormous eye blinked. Shredded deer pelts hung from his shoulder and hip. He fingered a dangling hoof with the one hand growing from the bony ridge of his chest.

"Ya, now, my bug-a-boo pets, have ye kept yer noses too close to ground to tell me where deer be? I can see vulf tribe slinkin' into yon court for meself."

Pricklewort blurted, "All the herd's in hidin'. We been hopin' to catch up the addled deer, seein' how it's their master's big day to shine."

"So!" The fachan sucked air over his pointed teeth then muttered to himself, "Nah herds and the court leadin' the Rade to welcome him back. This time o' year them horned leapers can't wait to mob Deer Lord, call him Oak or Stag." He spat. "Or what ye will. Find deer, find their prancin' Lord."

His eye focused on the two groveling bogey-beasts. "I been meanin' to catch a dawdlin' herd along the trail, pick off one o' them tender fawns havin' no sense. Them as got one leg use it less, nah more, know what I mean?"

The bogies stared at each other, their mouths clamped shut rather than risk offending a fachan.

He loomed over them. "Why aren't ye turnin' in yer two tiny heads how High Dorcha linger late for the season, fly early for the night? Strange doin's."

Grungegrind rubbed his nose. "What would Dorcha be chasin', then? What with court all out and about and Himself on the rise?" He tucked his skinny legs under his bottom.

The fachan peered down at him, never blinking. The coarse tuft on the top of his head stood upright like cock feathers. "And ye with the extra eye and all! They be houndin' prey other than deer or long horned kyloe, sure ye know that."

He sucked in another great gulp of air. "So hungry they be. Burn yer cat, nah need to skin it."

His laugh sent shivers up the bogies' backs.

⋏ ⋏ ⋏

B eag doubled back to the last place he had heard Kalar and followed him a quarter mile off the trail. He found the yearling's attention focused on the tangled undergrowth. A hundred layers of leaf and vine couldn't hide the scent of fachan. Kalar's nostrils flared. Tense yet eager to prove he could take down the one-legged horror without the help of the stag, he strained to find his prey.

Beag nudged the over-excited yearling. "Leave it"

Kalar snapped; his bared fangs ripped out a tuft of Beag's grey, black-flecked ruff.

Beag flipped Kalar on his side and clamped his jaws around Kalar's throat. Hot breath burnt their throats. Beag's larger, stronger body appeared to smother Kalar. When Kalar's legs flailed, his paws caught in Beag's fur. Beag waited.

Coming to his senses, Kalar went limp, exposing his belly to his captor.

Beag released him. "You are too old to play the fool. Be thankful I'm no grisly fachan or Birk. We have no Feela to soothe your wounds. Get up."

Kalar obeyed but his tail drooped. He gagged on bile, spat, and kept his head down, a chastened wulf who walked meekly beside his unsought mentor. They rejoined the troop and began to climb the rocks leading back to Wulf Tongue Pass.

▲ ▲ ▲

Neither horse nor wulf liked the eerie calls piercing the dirty purple clouds. Working his way with the rest of the pack members, Kalar said, "What's that cry? It hurts my head."

"That's no eagle, loon, or raven," Mundee added. "It hunts, but what?"

The solas horses snorted, swung their heads up, and tugged at their reins.

Kalar broke rank as if his tussle with Beag had never happened. He raced ahead only to turn, plant his paws, and confront the troop. "What is it?"

Beag and Birk eyed one another and then the Faer Ones.

Master Arklevent stroked his chin. "I suppose educating the yearling in dorcha lore causes no harm."

He addressed Kalar. "A wild hunt, all members on their own, out for themselves alone. They may look like a pack, Kalar, but they are not. We have seen them swoop low on cutter battlefields where wulves go to change the dead or dying horse to an honorable end."

"That's true, Kalar," Beag added. The grey wulf shuddered. "Their mounts' eyes glow, sick and sad."

Birk took over. "Some ride on dead bones—"

"But no Change, that's what Feela says," Ro interrupted.

Lord Arthgallo signaled Master Arklevent to attend to the wulves teaching keeper lore.

Birk nipped Ro in her nearest ear. "Ride on dead bones," Birk resumed. "You hear beasts in pain. They run before the Dorcha Host who need no carcass-horses, the never-changed, to fly upon the night air. Keepers say they seek cutters, but not their bodies." Her close set eyes narrowed. "We know not if cutters make Change."

Beag snorted and spat. "Never forget, their foul bones fly only by command of their dorcha masters. The eyes of masters and mounts send forth a glow like lighted swamp gasses. We ask, what feeds that fire?"

The yearling's own eyes grew large. The juniors yelped as their tails swished. Beag growled a warning.

Birk scrutinized the Faer Ones, saw the Guardians look back and forth, the grips on their reins tightening. "Enough!" she snapped.

$$\blacktriangle \ \blacktriangle \ \blacktriangle$$

Amongst themselves, the Faer Ones debated the shocking events they had witnessed with their own unbelieving eyes. The Guardians were glad to have Arklevent with them. All wished that Lord Phelan were leading the Faerguard of the Night Hunt Aloft but agreed that the Lady and the wounded dam needed him more. To their voiced forebodings Lord Arthgallo stiffened his always straight back. Some wondered if the Dorcha, so helpful to hearth and home, neglected their nightly duties and asked what brought them out in the light of day.

"I'm thinking the lure of cutter blood, perhaps tasted not for the first time, has verted them," Arthgallo answered.

Arklevent recoiled. "You go too far, Arthgallo. All Faer Ones, Solas and Dorcha alike, uphold lawful Change, may Great Grian always shine."

Raising his voice, Arthgallo replied, "Indeed! I can hear them scoffing at the Lady's ill-advised command, even as they hastened to do her bidding."

Master Arklevent shook his head. "Presume not that Lady Light initiated their coming," he cautioned. "That she flew upon her powerful keening is sure; that the Dorcha-Faer answered *her* summons is not. I say look for the verting within the cutters' camps."

All the Guardians nodded in agreement.

Birk howled, ending their discussion. Her angry eyes peered through half closed slits. She curled her nose to reveal fangs and the tip of her tongue. Having gained their attention, she asked, "How soon to the height? How soon to the apples?"

Map Keeper Thornheart smiled and bowed his head. "Not long, my friend."

Birk grunted. "Good. These wounds, endured by wulf alone, begin to vex."

Thirty-Two

Low Road Wonders

To venture underground: a matter of life and death.

Lord Phelan and Map Keeper Brighteye led the Queen's party. Lady Light and Lady Patha rode just behind them with all the remaining Faer Ones following. Even though Lanark-Kyle and Iova-Rhu kept a steady watch on Anell, the wulves' noses pressed the hammock in which she lay. Their descent wound around the many-sided basalt columns that united the floor and the roof of the cavern. Holding their crystals high, the Faer Ones lit up the deep brown and ocher cave walls, some with figures depicting faer or beast life. Sonsie looked closely to see if they moved. When they came to a swift stream moving toward their destination, they turned the horses to follow along its banks. The minstrel made catchy lighthearted tunes out of the notes that lifted from the running water.

Lady Light and Patha, as they had so often since childhood, rode close enough for their horses' hindquarters to touch. The Lady leaned toward Patha and rested her head on her friend's shoulder. A few locks of the Lady's snowy hair escaped the clasp of her starsilver circlet. "After we tend Anell and the other wounded," she confided, "we must discover what caused this verted event."

In hushed voice, Lady Patha asked, "My Queen, did you not call them?"

The Lady sat upright and stared at the keeper of her secrets. "Patha! Auld friend, think you so? Nae, never would I cause such strange verting of our quest to greet Lord Green!" She paused, giving her friend a knowing smile. "I own sending the promising warrior wulf on the High Road, in hopes. . . . But the Dorcha!" She shook her head. "Nae."

"Forgive me, dear one, but you uttered a fearsome cry and, well, gave every appearance of issuing the fearsome command. And they did follow hard upon."

"True, I acted—solely on behalf of a treacherously attacked wulf dam, obviously near her time to deliver. Violated on our sacred lands. I called Lord Green with whom I had anticipated happy reunion. Alas for our ruined Rade." She bowed her head a moment before continuing. "We shall discuss the unknown call—not mine!—once we put cares for Anell and her loved ones to rest."

Lady Light shivered and pulled her shawl tighter. "Ah yes, Anell." Upon learning from Iova-Rhu that Anell had so far tolerated the journey, the Lady ordered Lord Phelan to pick up the pace.

She stroked her brow. Thoughts of Anell's youngest sons, now parted by her command, churned within her. *The brothers have caught the eye of Sky-Wulf. Light Wyrm knows, or suspects, something. They have a powerful wyrd. What part do they play in these strange events?*

Quick on the uptake, Patha said, "They remain determined, fearful yet fierce for a quest."

Startled, the faer Queen faced her companion. *Of course, you read my thoughts.* She smiled.

Nodding, Patha removed one of her scarves; streaks of blue and white blended into grass green, as if a fair High West sky over a lush meadow draped her shoulders. She handed it to her friend who wound it around her throat. Having bought time to consider her words, Patha said, "They need training, more than any wulf tribe may teach them."

Patha reached over and adjusted the scarf to cover Lady Light's shoulder and then placed her hand lightly on the Lady's arm. Their horses maintained a steady pace. Patha leaned her head near the Lady's ear. "The little faerwhite singer with the sweet face and long tipped snout, ah, those eyes, so sad with his soul shining forth, would come to your side this instant or at the last soul's crossing, even if it meant the death of him. The faerblack midnight wanderer with the mighty paws shall never be happy unless he is on the hunt, yet I sense he is for the Otherworld. Aye, uncanny, both of them. More I know not."

"Aye, Patha. My thanks to you."

▲ ▲ ▲

Anell's escorts continued to follow the stream, pausing only for the wulves and the horses to drink. At each stop the Guardians checked the wounds of each suffering wulf. Akir defied any comforting touch until Lord Phelan reminded him that he had to stay strong for Anell's sake. Iova-Rhu used the last of her healing ointments on Anell. Lanark-Kyle and Barras-Garve emptied their vials on Akir and Feela, both of whom had stressed their wounds in the often steep descent. Sonsie hung his head, asking himself why he had done nothing to help his pack fend off the cruel cutters. He tried to sing, but images of the dorcha attack froze his throat; each time he tried to sing he only produced squeaks. Akir grumbled. "Shut up, Sonsie."

Trudge, trudge, on he plodded, until at last Sonsie became so fascinated with all the drawings on the cave walls that he lagged behind. Feela nudged him, discouraging any delay. Still, she couldn't stop him from asking, "Who? What?" every few yards.

Barras-Garve laughed. He chewed on some honey-soaked spearmint and suggested that if Sonsie just moved along perhaps their minstrel would lead them in song. Better yet, if he kept quiet, maybe he would learn something useful. Sonsie smiled.

Elphinlark needed no other cue. He began singing an ear-pleasing ballad about true love lasting through many a trial and trouble. His clear voice set some of the crystal outcroppings to ringing. When he shifted to a spirited number about a frog and a hare in a jumping contest, all the Faer Ones joined in. The wulves noticed their continued descent but felt no alarm as this jolly song lasted until overhead they saw vast roots trailing down to the clear, flowing waters.

"Ah," Lady Light sighed. "Apple roots!"

She dismounted and approached the stricken wulf. "Anell, my dear, overhead the apples bloom. We approach the sea. Be brave! Hold on to your precious life. Save it to run under the fruited apples. Mother Grian longs to smile upon you again."

⋏ ⋏ ⋏

Sonsie fidgeted; he could not help it. He longed to see the mysterious apples and sniff the sea again, but he heard his name.

"Sonsie . . . Sonsie, Sonsie."

He was sure; he felt compelled to answer.

"What?"

Feela barked. "Not that again."

Akir growled. "Clamp your teeth shut! No more questions."

"But—"

"No 'but.' Move along!"

"Ssonssie!"

Miserable, he felt his heart thump. Didn't they hear it?

When the group passed an opening in the wall to their right, he heard his name again.

"Sssonsssie!"

He paused at the opening that cast a soft glow upon the wider chamber through which they were passing.

After bidding the others to wait, Lady Light rode toward Sonsie. She cautioned him to wait. He looked up at her and then to Feela and his sire. The Lady stifled all objections from the wulves with a wave of her hand. Akir's glare came to nothing; he turned tail to his son. Feela followed Akir's lead but looked back as they left Sonsie behind.

Lady Light said, "Go on, Sonsie! Answer the call," then offered no further encouragement.

He had to cross the stream that fed the apple roots. Every hair in his ears quivered. As if he were scouting hidden prey, he stepped toward the glimmering light to answer the repeated call of his name. A long-buried but familiar scent teased him. If only he could remember.

Splashing as he went, he followed an offshoot of the major stream into a much narrower tunnel. A will stronger than his own drew him on.

All sensations blended into one: the radiance; the cold, gurgling water that accentuated the call of his name, "Ssssonsssie"; a sweet, oily-musky scent on the heavy tunnel air; and the occasional trailing apple root that brushed against his head, tickling his wet nose.

He swallowed. "What?"

From within a glowing mist shrouded in darkness a voice answered, "Come to me."

Sonsie entered a circular chamber with a ceiling high enough to allow him to leap nine feet off the cave floor—if he wanted to. He did not. At the center coiled a former acquaintance with ram horns crowning his triangular head.

Light Wyrm leaned forward. "Do you know me, young wulf?"

Sonsie jumped. "You!" He felt himself being drawn into the wyrm's gaze.

"Do you know me?"

Sonsie shivered. From that night when Kalar had tumbled into his den, Sonsie remembered the black-tongued wyrm who gleamed in Gealach's light. Here, another one? No. The same, the huge bright white wyrm, erect and grinning, five yards from the tip of his nose. Sonsie nodded. "You are the white one who rescued us."

"And you?" He leaned closer. "The little bard, yes?"

Sonsie waved his tail. "I like to hear the Faer Ones sing. I like to sing their songs."

"Yesss." Light Wyrm's black tongue flicked, testing the air. The wyrm drew closer; his tongue waved before Sonsie's face. "Drinking the blood of my far kin, I see. Have you changed the ram, broken and bleeding, into yourself, young wulf? Do you know me?"

Sonsie stared. Their eyes locked. The ferlie beast raised his semi-coiled body to a height of five feet. Sonsie's head tilted up to follow the wyrm's gaze.

Looking down on Sonsie, he said, "Breathe, Sonsie. Do you know me?"

"Sha . . ." Sonsie attempted to draw back but could not.

"Yes? Go on." Still looking down on Sonsie, the wyrm tightened his white-scaled body.

"Sharp Sighted One!" Sonsie gasped.

"Ah, Sonsie minds well what the night breezes teach." The wyrm contracted into a tighter coil. "A little deeper, methinks. Let us see if you can sing a little song with me."

Sonsie looked around at the wet walls; the water streamed down, heightening the colors: gold and red, black and white. He turned his ears toward the larger passageway, hoping to hear Feela or even Akir. He recalled the image of his dam, suspended between two faer horses. A moan escaped his throat, his sorrowful heart unable to contain his grief.

Light Wyrm said, "I know you yearn to rejoin your friends, most of all Anell, brave and beautiful." His head hovered a foot above Sonsie's. "Still . . . we meet not by chance."

The wyrm's gentle, rhythmic swaying captivated Sonsie.

"You stand on a threshold, soon to be adult. A wulf does not always meet his wyrd on the chase for red deer, Sonsie. Let us see what we shall see. I sing then you sing.

"What a wet nose you have. . . ."

Sonsie thought and guessed, "The better to track you, track you, track you."

The tip of the wyrm's tail appeared from behind his head, stopping between his ram horns. It moved barely three inches side to side. "Good. What white teeth you have. . . ."

Sonsie grinned. "The better to change you, change you, change you."

The wyrm's head lowered as his tail rose. The tip swung leisurely, moving forward in a slow but sure pace. "Good. What a red tongue you have. . . ."

Sonsie swallowed, feeling his own tongue, but focused on the wyrm's tail, enthralled. "The better to taste you, taste you, taste you," he whispered.

"Good. What big ears you have. . . ."

In ever-slowing pulses, the tip of the wyrm's tail waved back and forth between his horns, Sonsie drifted into a waking dream. "The better to hear you, hear you, hear you."

"Good. What bright eyes you have. . . ."

Sonsie could not take his gaze from the tip of the wyrm's tail moving in time to his heart beats. Light Wyrm's slit eyes, black ovals, loomed large. Sonsie's field of vision shifted so that the wyrm's tail faded from Sonsie's consciousness. Sonsie hissed, "The better to see you, see you, see you."

Sonsie had no will to move. His waking dream continued. He heard a voice from far away or deep within, two voices. "I cause you to see what looms up front. . . ."

Sonsie answered, "For to make you forget what lurks behind."

The wyrm's eyes closed. "Excellent, Sonsie! Best yet." His tail crept forward down his head and came to rest between his wet fangs. It swayed in the same slow rhythm. He seemed to sing. "A little deeper, now."

The sound of his voice slid down Sonsie's spine. "I live over and over. . . ."

In rapid succession the two white beasts completed their litany.

Sonsie said, "I live here and there."

The wyrm's head, eyes still closed, moved so close that his nose came to rest an inch from Sonsie's. He breathed in Sonsie's scent. In casting out his serpent breath upon the faerwhite wulf he said, "I hunt the world's vermin, high and low. . . ."

"I hunt cutter souls, for greed, for gold." Sonsie's voice imitated the wyrm's.

The wyrm opened his eyes. "I live on the fumes of burning flesh. . . ."

Sonsie gulped. He struggled to pull away, but he could not break the grip of Light Wyrm's gaze.

"A little deeper, Sonsie. Whatever you say or say not, I shall take you back to Herself and your dear ones. I live on the fumes of burning flesh. . . ."

"I live on the shrieks of kith and kin."

"Good. My whiskers wave. . . ."

"My claws scratch."

"My humped back hides. . . ."

"The scorpion's lash."

"For I am. . . ."

"Scrag Tail!"

Light Wyrm reared upon a tail now coiled tightly under his body. "So be it! Sonsie, Bane of the Unclean."

Thirty-Three

KALAR MAKES A DETOUR

Both Solas and Dorcha have hounds.

Kalar followed Beag and Birk with the remainder of the tail-dragging pack up the winding Wulf Tongue Pass. He ignored Lord Arthgallo at the lead and the other Faer Ones, easy to do. But not Master Arklevent who rode Rowanberry in the rearguard position hard upon Kalar's rump. Kalar wagged his tail in defense, but each swish drew the aromas of the dapple grey horse and Arklevent's deep forest's tang to his quivering nose. The flickering embers of his irritation threatened to flame into genuine interest. Kalar growled and focused on the rock-strewn trail.

Over or around tumbled rocks their climb took them higher. When they passed through the Forest of Four, the air cleared. Hardy pines and flowering rhododendrons wove between hazel, oak, rowan, and birch. Grian's descent to her western bower sent slanting rays that lighted the narrowing trail ahead. It snaked in switchbacks that threatened death over the steep sides for any careless misstep. Kalar decided not to attempt a break from the troop.

At each turn, great rock faces, looming to the left and right, swallowed the trail ahead. The Faer Ones whispered encouraging words to their mounts and sang ancient songs much favored by horses. Had the mission not been so urgent, they may have dismounted, happy to feel their horses' warm breaths upon the back of their necks.

The Green, so alive and juicy, conspired to entice the wulves to stray. New, succulent fern lined rock-edged burns. Water sparkled in the light and foamed over the rocks. Bees feasted on wild flowers like land-strewn rainbows. Birk tried her best to make the younger wulves keep their gaze upon the trail, but they tired of viewing paw prints of the mate who trod ahead. They sneaked looks left and right.

Karlon's grey-tinged black shoulder nudged Mundee's. "Could this be the same land that the Dorcha fouled with their killing attack?"

Mundee raised her black and brown head. "Maybe Dorcha don't like to fly this high."

From behind the wulves Master Arklevent observed, "The Dorcha fly anywhere in the dark. They do not favor flying into the light when it falls from the sky."

The party neared the timberline; above, sharp-edged rock jutted through thinning scrub. A shrill, barely audible whistle carried on the wind. Kalar's ears perked. To a second series of three trills he shook his head, sniffed, and pawed his ears. Again and again, a third time. He looked all around. Birk also had heard something but barked at them all to keep moving. Beag agreed. So did the Faer Ones.

⋏ ⋏ ⋏

Several miles away down slope within the cover of the pine boughs, a tall, green-leafed figure whistled. A crown of white-berried mistletoe and bright oak leaves, some red, some green with newly fledged acorns, sat his head at a saucy angle. The remains of some wilted holly sprigs dangled from his verdant hair. A weave of mistletoe bound the hair that flowed down his back, much like the Faer Ones' horses decked for a Grand Rade. Tendrils from his crown twined around a pair of antler buds five times the size of the acorns.

A third time the leaf-clad figure called with three short trills. From the north came three booming bays. Lord Green smiled, broke from the cover of the fir trees, and clapped his hands. He cupped them around his mouth and called, "Kuu! Kuu!"

The answering three howls echoed and reechoed. Then ground thunder rumbled closer.

Lord Green turned north. Just ahead, over a mass of low boulders leapt a huge, shaggy black-green canine with immense paws and luminous eyes. His tongue hung from wet, black lips; his long curled tail waved back and forth. The stag-treemale stretched out his arms to the advancing great hound. Upon meeting, the beast rose on his hind legs and rested his paws on Lord Green's broad shoulders. They jigged joyously, round and round, shaking the bright green oak leaves and strips of mossy bark. The beast licked Lord Green's face.

Through his laughter Lord Green cried, "Enough!" He gripped the hound's paws and made him stand foursquare. "And mind your tail! Who set you free, Kuu? Or did you sneak out when the Dorcha ran riot?"

"Herself! So eager to see you, my Lord. Hunting or hiding have you been?"

"Hiding?" Lord Green's eyes crinkled. "You found me! Now Kuu has better hunting, a yearling wulf, just about your shade. He's hereabouts on a gloomy trek over the Wulf Tongue."

"No happy to see you, Kuu? How do you Kuu?"

"You make my heart sing, good mound guard." He bowed with green arms outspread. "And, yes, glad I am to see you." Rising, he added, "Will you hunt before we curl into a wee nap?"

Kuu regarded his tail, thought it very fine, and then scratched his ear before answering. "This wulf? A name? A pack? A journey's end?"

Lord Green reached out and scratched Kuu's other ear. "Aye, Kalar, one of the two latest born from womb of Anell, sired by Akir, on the way home to the apples of Auld Alba the apple thief. Anell hovers near death. Akir the bold will be bitter."

Kuu's bright eyes studied his companion's face. "Danger? Dorcha?"

"All wide-ranging beasts expect danger."

Kuu's wet nose wrinkled. "Dorcha scent strong, my Lord. Strange goings-on."

"A darker day looms, methinks. Something stirs the Dorcha. Go! Sniff him out. If he passes the test of your worthy nose, bring him to me."

"Here or there, near or far?"

"All is one. Follow along to the apples. I shall find you, alone or with the yearling. Seek our auld friend Arklevent in the company of those who climb to the skies on the way to the sea."

"Why Kalar?"

Lord Green gripped his staff. "Kalar's trip to Cavern Perilous revealed his wyrd bound to Vilhjalmer."

The Queen's hound took off for Wulf Tongue Pass in a straight loping glide, along the way disrupting from their nests angry white-bottomed ptarmigans, their mottled wings flapping.

⋏ ⋏ ⋏

Seeing the summit just ahead, Lord Arthgallo turned to report that the most difficult part of their trek had nearly ended. With words of thanks to their horses, the Faer Ones urged them and the wulves to mind the trail, still dangerous, but soon to turn down to the coast. They paused at the top, their hearts gladdened to view the sea, flashing crimson and gold, and the teasing glimpses of the mist-covered isles to the west. Cries of gulls lifted in the same breezes that carried scarlet back-lit mists up and over Wulf Tongue.

The younger wulves pestered Beag and Birk with questions about the fabled apples. In answer, Lord Dewain, the music master himself, began a silly song about the reluctant maid who delayed her wedding each day by cooking yet one more apple dish for the nuptial feast. Neither Kalar nor the others could make snouts or tails about why the Faer Ones laughed. About this time they heard snatches of song seeming to arise from the earth itself. "Alas . . . love, where . . . you hide . . . amongst the . . . sae . . . and green?"

Mundee and Ro sniffed and turned their ears east and west. Birk nipped at their rumps. They had cleared several downward stretching switchbacks on the precipitous west side of the pass when thunder assailed their ears. The wulves turned as one toward the summit.

Master Arklevent spied Kuu, at first just his nose. Sure as violets follow spring rains, the shaggy hound burst over the top. He zoomed in the straightest line he could fashion out of the switchbacks. The steep banks that fell from the trail had no effect on their pursuer. Up and over, down and up came the midnight green beast. When he overtook the tightly assembled troop, he slowed to keep pace alongside Master Arklevent. Rowanberry snorted a greeting. The tips of Kuu's ears came well over Arklevent's knees. The Queen's hound nodded to the master of the Green but wasted no time. "Kalar?"

With raised brow Arklevent directed him to the young wulf. Arklevent turned, and watching Kuu approach Kalar, called to his pack mates. "Ye need not fear this loyal and brave near cousin, a great hunter—and friend to wulves."

Kalar had watched the hound approach Arklevent. Who was this beast that seemed so familiar with the Green master? Why should a great hunter and so-called friend to wulves call his name? Before Kalar could cough up this vexing hairball, Kuu stood by his side. Feeling crowded, Kalar bristled and bared his teeth, but keeping his head down, he glanced at his new companion—dark, shaggy, and huge. Seeing that their paws were nearly the same size, Kalar grinned.

The hound sniffed. "Kalar?"

Receiving only a guarded stare, he asked again. "Kalar?"

The two not-yet-friends, not-yet-foes sniffed each other, both their hackles raised.

"Maybe yes. Maybe no. Your name?"

Kuu stared down at the yearling wulf. "Known to my friends. Make this a lucky third. Kalar?"

"Aye," Kalar admitted. He squared his body before the larger beast. "I need no 'friends.' I have my pack."

Kuu flexed his long claws. His curled tail lashed out and back. "In dorcha days all need friends."

Kalar did not flinch, but his eyes grew large.

Kuu pressed the point. "What does Kalar, a trespasser in the Faer Ones' mountain halls, fear?"

Kalar refused the bait and quipped, "I fear Sonsie will never stop singing, and we will never get off this wyrm-backed mountain where the only good hunting belongs to the eagle."

"A hunter! Not a singer. Pity," Kuu added, as if to himself. "What would Kalar hunt?"

"Anything that puts food in my belly."

Kuu laughed. "I will walk this path, wider now, perhaps to the apples."

Kalar shrugged.

Kuu's silent patience prompted Kalar to open his heart to his new companion, a good listener at need. "I wonder how they're doing," Kalar mused aloud. "If our . . . how Feela is . . . and Sonsie. Will Sonsie have a new song when . . .?"

Kuu's tail snapped. "Songs and Faer Ones—have one, have the other."

"Like songs and Sonsie—never fail," Kalar agreed. "Still, I wouldn't mind hearing one about what he sees on the Low Road."

"Plenty. Call me Kuu."

⅄ ⅄ ⅄

Gold Grian continued to the Western Isles. The High Road party pressed on down the western side of the Wulf Tongue Pass. Meadows adorned with alpine flowers came into view between the crags. Mountain sorrel and dwarf willow grew thick beside the splashing rocky burns. The wulves longed to chase the ptarmigan, their feathers now beginning to turn from winter white to summer mottled brown. Arklevent promised them food aplenty when they rejoined the rest of their pack at the coast where the fishing was always good and their hosts were generous. With no urging, the wulves picked up their pace.

Beag huffed. "We need to run."

When they cleared the woods, Ladies Kundry and Keelin, horse adepts, agreed they could risk a brief run to the apples. While they loped along, they again heard bits and pieces of song.

The Faer Ones took up singing a haunting melody upon which hung the wind-battered words, "The wild . . . on . . . so blithe . . . brings . . . one . . . to cheer. . . ."

Kuu added his own triple bay that echoed from the surrounding hillsides, effectively drowning out several words. None of the wulves knew if the song lamented or celebrated something wild. They shook their heads and sniffed the air.

"The words turn all mixtie-maxtie," Kalar said. "Sonsie would know."

"Don't be too sure. You never know with Faer Ones," Karlon answered.

Birk coughed and spat. "As to them, Akir is right. The less we have to do with their ilk the better."

Beag challenged her. "If they save Anell, I'm all for them."

⋏ ⋏ ⋏

By late afternoon of the baleful day, one that had started so fine and gay, they stopped about ten furlongs from the shore. Arthgallo and Arklevent blew their silver horns. A similar call rose from somewhere on the shoreline.

"Ah, that must be Barras-Garve." Brodie-Gare grinned. "I recognize his lip. Good thing his horn is not a boiled sweetie. He'd have it sliding down his throat before he could blow one note."

A troubled sky with roiling thunderheads sickened into a gangrenous hue, casting a pall on the happy reunion. Piercing cackles filled the air, followed by the mournful baying of hounds, all dead black. In the wake of their sky-borne passage light seemed to drain from the sky; the hounds' fiery red eyes flashed in the gloom. Kuu bristled and let loose three tremendous bays. Confusion fell upon the company. The faer horses reared. Their forelegs beat the air, their silver hooves flashing in the intermittent light. Beag and Birk led the wulves in frenzied howls.

Having found Master Arklevent, Kuu clawed his leg. "Get to the apples. Find Lady Light. Go!"

Kuu turned sharply and raced to Kalar, now gripped in the pack's wail of protest against the intruders. He pressed into the wulves and cut Kalar from their midst. Taking a terrible chance, he faced him, staring directly into Kalar's wild eyes. His will prevailed. Kalar had no choice but to hear Kuu's urgent appeal.

"Dorcha seek Oak King! Help! Ye must come!"

Kalar followed without thinking. Straight as the raven flies they raced in the direction of the baying hounds, ignoring the switchbacks. Kalar closely pursued Kuu. They bounded over rocky ridges, down gullies, up steep slopes, scattering any beasts that got in their way. Paws pounding, they zigzagged through rowan and hazel, oak and birch.

Countless birds, driven into alarmed flight by the dorcha assault, had just begun to settle on their perches when Kuu and Kalar streaked beneath them. The watchful and the wise called out, "Seek Him at the Circle of Nine."

Kuu yelped "thanks," quickened his pace, and urged Kalar to keep up. The early evening sky, no longer unnaturally dark, was merely dusky on the eastern slopes. Although their fully alert senses failed to detect any Dorcha, Kuu spat at the foul stench that remained from their passing. He stopped to test the air, panting heavily, like any beast who had run a difficult course, but pain stabbed Kalar's heaving sides. This merciful pause in their breakneck run allowed the yearling to gulp air which his starving lungs devoured. He struggled not to cough or utter one word of complaint yet snarled at the thought that Lord Green should be the target of a second dorcha attack. He couldn't forget the sight of the blackened ground. Fury gave him strength.

From that part of the Four Friends' Forest where the hazel predominated, they heard the cries of mad dogs.

"Dorcha!" both yelped. Through dense, fetid air they ran toward sound coming from a gloom-shot whirlwind.

Kuu called to Kalar, "Elders Grove Pool. Hurry!"

They followed the blackening vortex, the gagging stink, and the yowls that each minute increased their menace.

▲ ▲ ▲

Map Keeper Thornheart turned to the wulves left behind who trekked the last leg of the High Road. "Not far, not hard," he urged. The Faer Ones' horses welcomed the more gently sloping switchbacks that looped between shorter ridges than had been their lot at the summit. Beag and Birk, however, forced the wulves to stop. They demanded assurances that they were not being maneuvered into a cutter trap. All the wulves agreed.

Rosslyn-Tir adjusted his bonnet to a jaunty tilt, smiled, and winked. "Call your mates on the shore."

Before Beag or Birk could respond, Karlon, Mundee, and Ro broke into a defiant howl wrapped around an undertone of appeal.

A sweet, pure wulf howl lifted in the air.

Their tails wagged. "Sonsie!"

He called them home to a place he had never been before. They woofed happy return cries. Ro asked if Sonsie had found any apples. Sonsie cried back asking if they couldn't smell the blossoms.

"Wait till you see! Where's Kalar?"

"Gone. Dorcha! Is it safe?" asked Mundee.

"Yes! Kalar? Where's Kalar?"

The three keen-eyed younger wulves turned to face their elders. The Faer Ones looked back and forth, eager to be gone but reluctant to make the first move. Arklevent argued that only fools goaded troubled wulves, especially a shocked pack, sundered from mates hard upon the bloody attack and forced to travel a dangerous road.

Beag chastised the three junior wulves for not asking about their wounded dam. Birk warned they'd find Anell helpless and in the hands of Auld Alba knew who, or worse—dead. Remembering Anell's great goodness, Ro and the others hung their heads.

"Go?" Mundee implored.

"Go!" Beag barked.

The entire company galloped through the widely scattered pines and hardwoods and leapt foaming waterfalls that fed deep pools before falling again over mossy rocks. Their final pathway, lined with white birches, was wide enough to allow two horses abreast; a wulf could have squeezed in if one had wanted to trust the faer horses' hooves. They did not. All pressed forward in one final effort.

A stiff breeze buffeted thick coastal fog, breaking off gossamer wisps that allowed-teasing peeks of delicate pink and white flowers, massed like fluffed clouds. The fog and the blossoms merged so that the wulves couldn't distinguish between blossoms and the sea spray rolling into a backlit, fiery fog.

They came down to the shore of a large bay. Waves of sea foam crashed over well-rounded stones that gave way to sand. Looking west over the wave caps of a much larger body of water, they saw on the far horizon a series of turquoise and cobalt islands floating in the mist. Orange blazed from behind the island hills.

Sonsie raced toward them. "Look! Look up!" he cried. He bounced like a new pup on his first trip beyond the nursing den. "Up! Up! Apple trees!"

The Faer Ones laughed and followed his orders as did the rest of the wulves. Everywhere, on the cliff's edge and on terraces that spiraled down the mountain side, apple blossoms festooned the branches. Enough of the fog had lifted for the wulves to see a golden halo caressing shiny green mistletoe and millions of blooms. Their scent upon the sea air made them all giddy.

"Come," Lord Arthgallo urged, "we must find the rest of the party and Lady Anell."

"Right!" Beag barked.

"Right!" Birk agreed.

Thirty-Four

Songs to Sing, Tales to Tell

With two-legged faer friends trust your nose.

Kuu and Kalar slowed their pace in pursuit of sounds that led to mortal danger. Kuu warned Kalar, "Be warrior. No Change today." Kuu's fierce eyes stiffened Kalar's nerve.

Hunched low, they moved toward a great circle of elder bushes, just budding. Soon their sweet fragrance would fill this glen. Today, a nauseous odor, riding upon vicious growls, came from within the elder grove, perhaps at the pool itself. Calling upon inborn stealth, they poked their heads through the tender green leaves.

Between the elders and the nine hazel trees surrounding Elders Grove Pool a grand stag fought three snarling black mastiffs with blood red eyes and ears. The stag radiated a silver-gold aura, as if Grian and Gealach had embraced in the gloaming. Velvet covered new antlers, hardly the magnificent rack they would become—if he lived. So far, his thrashing hooves held off his attackers. He roared, though he called no hinds or threatened no rival stags. White Stag braved the attack alone.

The dogs filled the air with such intense dreariness that the sound of their cries and the stench of their rank breaths seemed to issue from a void equal to any dark, bogle-haunted pit in one of the Dorcha Mountains. While the stag's glow conspired to hasten his doom, it gave his would-be rescuers a focal point for their counterattack.

Kuu and Kalar rejoiced that the stag still lived. "Leave the center one to the stag," Kuu ordered. "Take the left, the right for me." His three horrific bays drowned the mastiffs' snarls. Kalar roared so that the hazel trees swayed. Together they leapt into the fray.

Kalar charged, grazing the center dog's tail just before veering left toward the flank of one who growled through dripping fangs. He sank his teeth into the creature's neck and ripped with all his might, only to come away with a mouthful of bristly fur and enough blood to burn his tongue.

Distracted from his main quarry, the howling dog now turned its wrath upon Kalar, who scrunched down tightly, prelude to a leap in any necessary direction. The black dog glowered, drooling spittle that scorched the grass.

Unfazed, Kalar attacked his opponent's side then leapt, twisting in mid-air, to thud down upon the beast's back. They toppled over. Closing his jaws on the underside of the dog's throat, he tore a mouthful of flesh. The beast turned so that its great claws raked Kalar. Its fangs gripped Kalar's shoulder, forcing him to the ground.

Kalar wrenched himself from his enemy's bite. He flipped over, clamped his jaws on the creature's underbelly, and pulled. Entrails fell upon Kalar. Blood, hot and foul, washed over him. The beast died with Kalar as its bier. He wriggled free of his odious load, gasped, and fainted.

Kuu had already engaged the other assailant as promised, leaving the third to the stag's formidable hooves. Both fought gallantly, Kuu prevailing with an assault marked more by passion than precision. He crushed every bone he could trap in his mighty hound jaws. At last he snapped the backbone of the black beast; it collapsed on the blood-soaked ground.

Kuu drew air deeply into his aching lungs. He turned to witness the stag deliver a flurry of kicks that broke all the ribs on the right side of the third combatant. From the beast's last howl, Kuu knew that the stag had punctured its heart.

At each death of the dorcha dogs, the air brightened. The stag shook his body, spraying sweat and blood, not only his enemy's. Kuu looked for Kalar. He limped to his fallen comrade and licked his face. Upon coming to his senses, Kalar disgorged a foul mass of black blood and hair. He crawled to Elder's Grove Pool. His eyes implored the stag. At his nod, Kalar drank his fill.

"That should give you wisdom, brave wulf, as well as cleanse your soul. Do you know me, Kalar?"

Kalar shook his head. Clear, pure water sprayed out into the twilight. Little rainbows rose and fell. Before him stood not a stag but a robust, two-legged being, all green, except for the mistletoe's white berries and a last few red oak leaves, not yet turned their summer color, adorning his green hair and beard.

Lord Green knelt down and cupped his hands to withdraw the cold water. Kuu advanced and rubbed his head against the Lord's leg. He reached down and caressed Kuu's head. "My thanks, brave one, loyal one." Turning, he added, "And also Kalar who proved worthy. Any wulf may hunt. Rarest of rare is the true warrior. When Akir's cares for Anell end, I must tell him. Here, let me wash your wounds in this healing water."

Overwhelmed, Kalar offered no resistance. With each pass of Lord Green's hands he breathed easier.

Evening fast approached, bringing welcomed breezes that carried away the foul odor of the vanquished dorcha dogs. Lord Green suggested he drink again, a mighty gulp. "It will do more than slake thirst. It will fill your belly and succor any manner of bodily hurt. When ready, follow Kuu to your friends."

Kalar stared at his nurse, remembering Feela and the many times she had taken care of his wounds, so often the result of his own recklessness. He hung his head. He ached to see his pack once more.

"Drink, Kalar," Kuu said. "Then I will take us on a short cut to the apples."

Lord Green smiled. "We shall meet again, Warrior Wulf, pure of will, brave of heart.

"Though not beholden, as is Kuu, you saved my life. Accept my thanks. When your brother's tale you hear, remember: each champion has his own wyrd, his own path made light . . . or dark by the choice he makes." His smile turned rueful. "The Green and all who live by the Light may one day be in your debt. And Sonsie's as well."

His face clouded. "Be kind to your brother—as he shall be to you, no doubt."

▲ ▲ ▲

K uu led their departure. Kalar attempted to look back at the mysterious being who had washed his wounds and offered words of praise, as welcome to him as the water he drank, but Oak King had disappeared into the forest. Kuu pressed on at breakneck speed.

No matter the obstacle, Kuu held fast to his southwest course. Kalar thought back to all the endless chases with his elders and laughed. When Kuu pulled up short and sniffed, Kalar nearly shot past him. Kuu's ears turned back and forth. Kalar imitated his battle-tested friend, not knowing what Kuu sought. He signaled Kalar to follow, hunkered down, and entered what appeared to be the hole of some underground den.

Kalar balked. "Not again."

"Short way to apples. Don't lose my tail," his guide warned.

They crawled, bellies dragging, for so long that a biting hunger gripped Kalar. Lost in his yearning for a fresh, juicy deer haunch or a fat hare at least, he nearly crawled under Kuu, who stood within the entrance to a much larger tunnel and shook himself. Glad to walk as a proper wulf, Kalar followed. This tunnel overflowed with unmistakable scents: his pack, some wounded, one very badly; Faer Ones; horses, making Kalar's mouth water; a sweet underground stream that flowed from the mountains; and salt, the sea. They had picked up the trail of those who carried Anell.

Eager to keep on, Kalar barked.

He and Kuu locked gazes.

Their hearts agreed, they raced side by side toward a hazy light at the end of the Low Road. They burst from the depths of the earth and found themselves enveloped by a low-hanging cloud that filled the cave mouth. From somewhere in the mist they heard Birk bullying Mundee and Ro. Kalar nearly laughed. Instead he nudged Kuu forward, so eager was he to rejoin his mates, even Birk.

"Beag!" Kalar called. "Birk, Karlon, Mundee, Ro! Where are you?"

On the shore below, the pack broke into a joyous howl. Kalar and Kuu sped forward, following their noses along the final path that the travelers, first of the Low Road and then High, had taken to the fog-bound coastal sanctuary of the apple groves.

Just before the last bend in the trail, Kuu blocked Kalar's way. Kuu turned his gaze toward the sounds on the shore; then he howled: once, twice, thrice! Even though every hair on his spine bristled, Kalar stood firm.

Kuu's gaze shifted to his awestruck companion. "My work is done . . . for now." With one ear cocked toward the shore, Kuu continued. "Try minding Sonsie's songs a wee bit more, Kalar. A wulf never knows, perchance learn a secret of an auld friend needful to know . . . should he cross your path again."

The huge hound ran straight for a mass of rocks, sprang, and disappeared.

All the wulves on the shore called to Kalar. Now free to choose his own path, he heaved a contented sigh and ran to the pack, all huddled together. They nuzzled and licked him, completely ignoring his absence and failure to seek any permission at all. He looked to Birk to see if she gave any sign that she would make him pay. She didn't.

When Sonsie careened into their midst, all his fears evaporated.

"Kalar! Kalar!" Sonsie yelped, beside himself in a kind of ecstasy. "Come see the apples!" He bounced and pawed the air, much to the amusement of the Greenguards.

Birk chastised the fond brother. "Sonsie, settle yourself! Don't be leading your brother astray, once again!"

Kalar gave him a huge wink. Sonsie managed to keep his paws on the ground even if he had lost complete control of his tail. Lord Phelan, who had followed close behind the young singer, interrupted. "Sonsie, while we take ye all to the good auld woman and the good auld man, tell Kalar about your journey." He addressed Kalar's mates. "Your family awaits ye."

Phelan rode back to the end of the weary travelers, pausing to greet each wulf by name. "Beag. Birk. Karlon. Mundee. Ro. Anell is still in this world. We attend her with our best healers." His open-faced, compassionate gaze and good news reassured them.

Upon encountering the troop, Phelan crossed his arms over his heart and bowed his head to Ladies Kundry and Keelin, Rosslyn-Tir, and all the rest of the Faer Ones on up to Lord Arthgallo and Master Arklevent. By this time all the Faer Ones' gay costumes, bereft of bird and butterfly, off in forlorn search for Lord Green, had wilted like sad dust-coated fields. Yet Phelan found reason for joy. "I thank the Light for your safe return. We had the shorter and *nearly* uneventful journey. Our care was to bring Anell to safe haven."

He turned to Master Arklevent. "Tell me of your passage as we hurry along. We'll leave Sonsie to inform Kalar of his encounter as he chooses. No doubt Kalar will have much to tell his brother." Phelan leaned closer. "Any sighting of Him?"

⩔ ⩔ ⩔

Wagging his tail, Sonsie frisked about Kalar. He led his brother between the tall white birches that lined the coastal road. Hundreds of daffodils, salmon, yellow, and white, covered the banks that sloped down to the road. Soon they came to a rapidly flowing burn that fed a clear pool surrounded by ivy and purple iris. The cold water cooled their tongues.

Though eager to share his tale of the trek under the mountains, Sonsie shook his head and waited. Kalar drank like one cast upon the desert where, Feela warned, they send bad wulves, lazy hunters who do not mind their elders.

"So, Sonsie." Kalar paused to lick his dripping lips. "Anell? Is she still . . . ?"

"Alive? Yes!" He turned once in a tight circle, his tail wagging. "The Faer Ones who carried her along the trail took her inside the mountain where the auld ones live. More, I don't know."

"What do you know?"

Sonsie took him to a birch grove with soft grasses at their roots. He circled round and round then plopped on the ground, inviting Kalar to do the same before he answered.

"I know that I have seen the Faer Ones, Lady Light Herself . . . and more. We passed by walls alive with strange creatures. They glowed on the walls when the Faer Ones held up rock stars in their hands. They carry day into night! I wanted to know the names of all I saw, but we always hurried on. They fretted for Anell. Akir shadowed her like a hawk on a hare. I was the youngest, Kalar. No one wanted to talk to me, to name the beasts on the walls. Until. . . ."

"Until?"

"Until I saw him again, the one from the pit you fell into."

"The wyrm with the big horns? Did it give you a song, Sonsie?"

"Not really, not a true song, more a riddle."

Kalar got up, shook his coat and tail, bared his teeth, and growled. "Och! How many more ferlie beasts, always pouncing, high and low?"

He lay down on the other side of Sonsie. "Some use riddles to show how clever they are. Like Birk. Did you know the answer?"

Sonsie shook his head. "He sang and waited; then I sang back. Before I knew it, I named 'Scrag Tail.' He smiled and answered, 'So be it.'" Sonsie licked his paw. "Then he called me 'Bane of the Unclean,' like another riddle, my name."

Kalar grunted. "Nothing more, no 'true' song, Sonsie?"

"Yes, but not from the wyrm. And you? What happened to you on the High Road?"

"Never mind, what about the song?"

Sonsie huffed. "I thought you hated my songs."

Kalar hunched his back. "Not 'hate' . . . they just bother me like midgies in my ears. When we came down the mountain, I kept hearing little dragonfly wings of song. Kuu told me to pay attention. I'd learn something useful—"

"Kuu?"

"The hound with a big mouth. What song? Who sang it?"

"Lady Light. She's looking for someone. Listen:

'Alas, my love, wherefore you hide, amongst the boughs sae bonny and green?

A sad, long time I call your name, the sorrow sae deep, sae bitter keen!

I search sweet flowering hawthorn groves. Alas, your face I cannae see.

Wild hawk on wing sae bonny blithe brings nae one word to comfort me.

Let doomster ravens never find my ane true love—slain on night sae dire!

Oh cruelest stroke, Terror's worst by far, sae fierce our foes to set the Green afire.

And tho you lie in burrow deep, we cling to hope. Your ferlie friend most kind

Rebukes fell deed, renews your life. Come. Leave bleak death behind.

Remember us in your time of trial, we who mourn your grievous pain.

Remember the deer, the wulf, and the one who yearns to greet you once again.'"

$$\blacktriangle \; \blacktriangle \; \blacktriangle$$

Kalar jumped up, his tail waving. "Yes, Sonsie! Yes! We heard snatches on the mountain.

"All the Faer Ones broke into soft, sad howls. Kuu asked me if I knew him, but I never heard all the words. He hinted. You know how Feela hints about some feint we must learn before Birk or Akir . . . well, hinted that the song names some hidden danger, but what name?"

"Och!" Sonsie stood. He faced Kalar. "Like the big-horned wyrm tricked me into naming some—I know not what—but I think I saw it once. That terrible night, you know?"

"The big cave with the beasts on the walls!"

"Aye, my beast . . . with its own secret."

Kalar's eyes opened wide. "I saw a beast you did not." He groaned. "Why would Lady Light want to find a giant wulf fit for Lone Grumli? What do they want, Sonsie? If you're so clever, hunting faer song instead of kyloe or deer, don't their songs tell you?"

"Not yet, but it's not just songs." Sonsie's ears twitched. "I saw braw beasts, cohorts from all over Lisnafaer, also dread ferlie beasts, like before on the walls; they gave me shivers."

Kalar's eyes glared. He grumbled but let Sonsie continue.

Sonsie licked his lips. "Faer Ones drew the beasts of Lisnafaer on the walls of their dens. Feela said some come from the Otherworld. High Faer Ones, she said, carry all these beasts on their sky-blue bodies just like on the walls. I don't know, but the ones I saw on the Low Road have eyes that live, but they don't breathe. I think they want to. When we passed them, Elphinlark sang words I didn't understand to keep them on the walls. Faer Ones' songs hold secrets." Sonsie paused and closed his eyes, seeming to be lost in the memory.

Kalar smacked his brother. "Sonsie!"

The bemused wulf jerked and shook his head. Opening his eyes, Sonsie continued as if nothing had happened. "And power to make us do things—just like the horned tree who walks on two legs and the white wulf. And Light Wyrm."

"Och!" Kalar scowled. "The one Kuu took me to. He kept talking about a 'wyrd,' not 'bane,' a 'wyrd.'" He turned to Sonsie. "What of the 'auld woman' and the 'auld man'? Did you see them?"

"Aye!" Sonsie romped all around Kalar.

By now dusk had settled into a calm, clear night. Fireflies, their tails ablaze, mirrored the starry sky. An equal number of the tiniest beasts hummed and cricked in the lush grasses. Gulls lifted into the sea breeze to hunt insects now that the crabs had burrowed into the sand. High tide roared into the shore.

"Aye," Sonsie repeated as he plopped down beside an exasperated Kalar.

Kalar's tail waved to and fro. His hackles remained raised. He snapped, "Well?"

"They do not live outside like wulves, but they must spend much time out under Grian's face. They smell like the air. From the end of the trail under Wulf Tongue you can go in to where they live, like a cave, but different. Feela and Akir didn't want to go into a place had the scent of cutter. That's what they are, Kalar. Cutters! Just . . . different.

"Akir followed Anell underground. His mouth watered, but the good fighter who masters the Dorcha, you remember Lord Phelan, promised him, 'All will be well, stout wulf. Good hands tend your mate. None will harm your good Anell. Come see for yourself. Give her courage, Akir.' So our sire went. Feela took me around on the land high above the water.

"The 'auld woman'—Lady Light calls her granniejean—came to us before Feela took me away to the land's end. She held out her hands, still and straight; down she sank with half her legs against the ground, still holding her hands for Feela and me to sniff and taste. We did.

"Her hands, the taste, the scent—all good! I could smell all the beasts her hands had touched, but no fear. No fear in granniejean, no fear from the beasts. The bones show under the skin, not blue, Kalar, but I like her hands.

"She kept her eyes down until she asked me if she could seek mine. I didn't know what to answer, so Feela said, 'Go ahead, Sonsie,' so I let her. Not so bad. Her eyes are green like Lady Light's. Then she stroked my head. She ran her hand over my ruff and called me 'Good Sonsie.' It felt like a touch from Feela's and Anell's tongue. She made my tail happy. Feela nudged her, and she made Feela happy. Soon she hurried away. 'To see to your good dam, Anell,' she said.

"All the way under Wulf Tongue the Guardians kept talking about granniejean and grandiegavin, the 'auld man.' He must be granniejean's mate. When she went, he came. They met and joined hands, and he leaned down to touch their heads together.

"When he came to me I smelled earth and nuts and smoke—oh no, not burning trees! In his mouth something burnt; it looked like a stick with a pinecone at the end. He sucked on it like we do a bone; smoke came out of his mouth. It smelled like cherries.

"He held out his hand, white like granniejean's, for me to smell and taste. I could scent her on him and all the rest. His hands, great big, and his feet great big, covered with sand and grasses. He stands tall and broad. But he's gentle, like granniejean. When I lifted my paw, he wrapped his hand around as gentle as Feela when she licks a wound.

"'Soon we can have a good visit, Sonsie,' he told me,' He knows my name. So does granniejean. Then he said, 'I must go to stand by Akir as he guards your dam. Go get some water. We will feed you, have no fear. Worry not, young wulf. We will save Anell.' And then he went back inside, under the mountain top."

Sonsie's bright eyes opened wide; his tail waved. "Come on. I'll show you."

Thirty-Five

Anell Advises her Sons

Faer Ones are Lords of Light, not life.

Sonsie led Kalar along a path filled with familiar scent of the pack. Upon hearing their welcoming cries, the brothers dashed forward, happy that in a world grown strange they had their mates to count on. They arrived at twilight. The wulves romped around them so much that Beag called for all to settle down. He took Kalar and Sonsie to a pile of pike, newly caught and left for their use. Grandie Gavin had already taken away an untouched previous offering.

Kalar sniffed the fish. No matter how hungry the clash with the dorcha dogs had left him, his jaws remained clamped. Beag came to him. "You must earn your red deer, but the pike and brown trout fairly leap from the streams hereabouts. Eat your fill, Kalar."

"No, not now, Beag. Are the others . . . Akir and . . . ?

"Then drink. Whew! Clear your tongue of whatever last befouled it. After rest, we'll see about Anell. Akir and Feela are with her."

Upon their arrival at the apple keepers' home, Akir and Feela refused to let Anell enter their dwelling. She rested on a great flat rock outside. For the stricken wulf's comfort, Lady Light had spread her own green and gold shawl and the cloaks of the other Faer Ones. Red-leafed lettuce, endive, and various herbs for the kitchen garden lined the walkway that encircled the rock. Beeswax candle lanterns cast a soft glow. Anell's nurses counted on loving care and restorative aromas of wild pansy and rose scent mingled with that of the apples to give her relief.

All that afternoon and evening Jean had worked to keep Anell's soul and body knit together. She stitched her nasty wounds and brought down her initial fever. She and Gavin never doubted her full recovery and eagerly anticipated the birth of the new cubs.

Then a spiking fever returned. Anell's nose grew dry and hot; her swelling tongue turned grey. Her still beautiful fur responded to loving hands, but the flesh beneath began to stiffen. She could no longer move her tail or ears.

Jean stroked Anell's head and face. "Anell, my beauty, Anell, my darling girl, hear my voice. Stay with us."

Gavin's strong hands worked her muscles first toward then away from her heart. He caught Akir's gaze and assured him they were doing all they could to save Anell.

Jean opened a stone crock and extracted honey with a silver spoon. "Open, my darling." After coating Anell's tongue, she stroked her throat until she swallowed. Gavin and Lanark-Kyle repositioned Anell to ease her breathing.

Jean turned to Iova-Rhu at her side. "Hold her head, just so."

Iova-Rhu tipped Anell's head so that Jean could pour an apple seed elixir down Anell's throat. She coughed in weak spurts. Feela and Akir paced around the rock table. They crossed back and forth, scrutinizing every movement of these ones who looked like cutters but acted like Solas. Fierce-eyed Akir and Feela watched for any flicker of movement that threatened Anell, ready to crush these two or the Faer Ones, even if it meant their own death.

Lanark-Kyle stepped in close to Jean. "I fear more at work here than mere arrow wounds."

"Aye, my friend, we have washed them many times over. At first, after her blood ran pure, they closed cleanly, but now she languishes. We have no water from the Healing Well of Lac Morna—we were waiting for Lord Green." She frowned. "Gavin, we must try the wildstones Aden-Cree gave us."

Gavin opened a pouch hanging from a braided cord around his neck, removed the innards of a white deer, and put them in Jean's palm. When he clasped his warm hands around hers, they blessed the stones. Jean placed them, one by one, on Anell's wounds.

All bowed their heads, except the wulves whose hot breaths enveloped the now shivering Anell.

Jean gasped. "The stones, they've turned the color of an angry bruise, the poison they draw, most rare and long vanquished. I had thought. Look!"

She poured the remaining elixir on Anell's wounds. "They fester beyond the power of the stones."

Akir growled through bared teeth.

"I mean no harm, high wulf. I speak you no lies, mate of worthy Anell. Her wounds have taken a turn for the worse. So, alas, has she."

Iova-Rhu uttered the dread word, "poison!"

"Far worse. Scrag!" Jean whispered.

Akir snarled.

Jean turned to Lanark-Kyle. "Take over! Don't touch the stones! Gavin, see to the wulves."

Gavin relinquished his hold on Anell to Lanark-Kyle. He approached Akir and Feela. Their ears pointed back; their wild eyes flashed. He fell to his knees, landing face-to-face with Anell's fuming mate and sister.

"Cousins, we have many cures, all that the good Green can provide. You brought her to this refuge of the blessed apples. Stay calm. Breathe peace and hope into this space."

He smiled. His voice turned tender. "After the delivery of the new cubs, we mean for Lady Anell to run the hunt once more. We will do all that—

"Gavin, she calls!" Jean cried.

He turned toward his wife. Akir and Feela rose, their paws upon the table, crowding in to see Anell more closely.

"Call Kalar and Sonsie. They are dead!"

"Who?" Akir and Feela cried.

"The unborn cubs. Call my youngest. Now."

🝰 🝰 🝰

Looking from the window of Jean and Gavin's great room that faced the star-lit western sea, Aden-Cree and three other Guardians kept watch on the wulves. Denied access to Anell, the pack had curled into a fretful slumber under the first glimmering of stars, perfect to light a hunt. The sweet fragrance of apple blossoms, borne on the night breeze, caressed them as first one wulf then another rose, stretched, and fell back into place.

Inside, candles burning in sconces cast a welcomed glow. A running stream surfaced in the great room, ran a rock-strewn channel, and continued outdoors through a small stone archway. Blooming water lilies, floating between the rocks, carried the green within to the apple keepers' home. To enhance the murmur of the stream the music adepts coaxed sweet melody from their flute and harp while Elphinlark stood ready to bring any ancient song to bear that would aid their counsels. He hummed along, waving his hand to the beat. "No situation is so dark that a song fails to help," he said to his distracted comrades.

Facing the window, Lady Light sat upon a stone bench before a huge crystal-lit hearth that opened to the great room and the kitchen. Forming a circle, open enough to admit the welcome observations of the rest of her court, Lord Phelan and Lady Patha stood at her right, Lord Arthgallo and Master Arklevent to her left.

Lady Light sighed. "I never called the Dorcha." She sat motionless. Except for the pulse throbbing in her lovely throat, she might have been a statue of sky-blue topaz.

Nodding, Patha affirmed the Lady's truth. "We must look elsewhere to unlock the dorcha riddle."

Lady Light addressed Arklevent. "They came on top of the cutter assault. Why? But Lord Green does not. Why?" She twisted her ring, fingering the wulf and deer running through oak and holly. "Gone our long-awaited glad reunion."

"That is not precisely accurate, my Lady." Arklevent's smile offered hope. "He must linger close at hand. Witness the calling of Kuu, whom my Lady released in quest of his Lordship."

"Aye," Arthgallo avowed. "Kuu came and spirited away young Kalar, who has returned to our company alone. I recommend finding answers in your hound, Madam."

Phelan bowed to Lady Light, showing his respect in the face of painful questions. "Why summon Kalar? And why offer no word of greeting or comfort for our Lady?"

Lord Arthgallo coughed. "More to the point, how is it strangers creep far within the borders of Lisnafaer and attack wulves? Who were they?"

"Aye, would faer friends strike down a wulf?" Arklevent shook his head. "A direct descendant of Auld Alba? Never! These strangers must—"

Lanark-Kyle burst into the room. "Pardon upon pardon, I beg ye all. Lady Anell takes a turn for the worse. She calls for Kalar and Sonsie. We fear a still birth—if she lives. Jean and Iova-Rhu suspect scrag venom! Consider Akir's wrath should our worst fear come to pass."

Lady Light rose. She willed herself to remain calm, making her face all the more beautiful for the suppressed pain that shone forth from her tear-glistened eyes. "Phelan, see to Akir and Feela. They must neither do harm nor suffer any. Arklevent, go to their awaiting kin. Bring back Kalar and Sonsie—"

"Arklevent," Patha interrupted. "Expect them to have, em, wandered."

As Lord Phelan bolted out to the garden, Lady Light turned to Master Arklevent. "Carry no fear to the young; merely invoke the duty they owe their dam. Trust their training for the rest."

He signaled for his Greenguards to follow.

Taking Patha's hand, Lady Light resumed her simple makeshift throne. Her head sank, spilling her silken white hair over their clasped hands onto the polished stone floor.

All music ceased.

▲ ▲ ▲

Aden-Cree and three other Guards worked their way through the restless wulves. "Have ye seen Kalar and Sonsie?" they asked, only to meet with puzzled faces. None of the wulves, including a chagrined Birk, knew just where they were—or when they had last seen the mischievous yearlings.

▲ ▲ ▲

For an hour Sonsie had tried his best to sleep. He squeezed his eyes shut, but the lure of the apples proved too much for him.

"Kalar," he breathed low in his brother's ear. *Kalar . . . keep quiet, follow me.*

Also unable to sleep, Kalar allowed Sonsie to draw him to the far edge of the pack. They crept silently. None of the other wulves called after them even though, with every inch he advanced, Kalar expected Birk to bark their names.

Just as they got to the black canopy of the apple boughs that blocked out the stars and the blossoms' perfume had nearly overwhelmed them, they heard someone bothering their pack, asking questions about them.

▲ ▲ ▲

Master Arklevent quickly surveyed the many cleverly designed rock terraces, perfect nooks for hiding wayward wulves. Off to his left he heard the unmistakable sound of fur slipping through bent grasses that complained of wulf bellies crushing their new green shoots. Turning toward the nearest of the apple groves, he spied the tips of two wulf tails disappearing in the undergrowth.

He yelled, "That's far enough!"

⋀ ⋀ ⋀

Kalar's heart skipped a beat. *Arklevent!* But both brothers jumped, violating all their repeated vows never to leap before they knew what they faced.

"You two!" His voice thundered in smart imitation of their sire.

Kalar and Sonsie whirled around, their breaths caught in their throats, to face Master Arklevent.

"In need, Anell calls for ye. Recall the duty ye owe to the one who gave ye life. Your sire expects ye to be brave, hunter Kalar, singer Sonsie." The compassion that shone in Arklevent's eyes reassured them.

To his simple "Come!" they tucked their tails, lowered their eyes, and followed at his heels. He led them within the walled terraces into a mixed world of succulent greens, lush roses, and low-bending, blossoming apple boughs.

As soon as they saw Akir and Feela standing between Phelan and Lanark-Kyle, the overjoyed brothers ran forward. Their sire, strangely motionless, uttered a harsh growl. They halted, hearts racing. Feela appeared woeful. Equally frozen. Closer scrutiny revealed that they both bore a leash, slight but potent, suggesting silk or silver. In truth, these slender cords of light, the making of which the faer world kept secret, flowed into radiant nets that covered their bodies. The distraught wulves had wrestled the light, but it held firm.

"Come here!" Akir barked. "Anell calls. Hurry."

His eyes, fierce as gale-whipped lightning bolts, warned them away even as he urged them forward.

"But gently," Feela cautioned. Her sorrowful eyes glistened. "Be light-footed as the deer, silent as the trout in the shimmering burn."

Kalar and Sonsie came forward. At first they got a whiff of apples and honey. Then they detected something bitter, noxious. Their snouts curled. Anell seemed to be looking off in the distance, as if searching the horizon for telltale movement of deer. When their hot breaths crossed her face, the first they had ever known, she turned her attention to her last-born.

"My sons, come nearer. Let me see you, both so dear to me."

They crept so close that their noses almost touched Anell's. And yet they held back. Her labored breaths frightened them as much as the fading light in her eyes.

"My sons, nothing Green ever dies. The Change . . . if lost . . . may be found. If not here then there. I cherish your good hearts, strong and brave."

She paused for a long while. Feela reminded Kalar and Sonsie to breathe. They watched the ones called Grannie Jean and Grandie Gavin touch Anell, call to her, attempt to force some liquid down her throat. They wanted desperately to make them stop, to make their dam leap up and lick their faces, as in the young days in the safe den with her warmth and milk and all was well with no ferlie creatures crossing their paths. Akir and Feela strained against their glowing tethers, made all the brighter for the force they exerted against them.

Desperate, Sonsie felt as though he were hovering, watching from above, yet he could hear Anell's heart beating, dull thuds too far apart, hear her breath seeping out and her gasps, coming in an ever-slowing rhythm. He saw Jean and Gavin hold glowing round rocks in their hands and pass them over her body.

Kalar and Sonsie paid no attention to Phelan and Arklevent who concentrated on the wulves' light leashes or to the others who called to Anell, imploring her to stay in this world, to help them usher in the summer when surely the Green Lord would dance with Lady Light and celebrate her full recovery. "Stay darling Anell," they pleaded.

The yearlings only heard, "My sons!" Anell called in the barest whisper. "Feela and I . . . nourished your hearts. They will give you strength when hope seems lost. Be patient. Like Beag. What you seek or need will appear.

Be severe. Like Birk. Outlive winter and hunger. Above all, be smart like your sire. Use all Akir taught you to serve the pack . . . the Light . . . the Green."

Her eyes closed. "Akir!"

At Anell's last breath a precious light disappeared behind an invisible veil, leaving three sets of disparate beings: wulf, faerie, and human—all united in grief.

Thirty-Six

Auld Friends and New Mysteries

When Lord Green appears look for better days.

The long night seeped into a reluctant morning. Lady Light, her court, and the two apple keepers joined Akir and all his pack around the remains of their beloved Anell. The stunned allies, heads bowed, seemed lifeless as well. No birds sang to greet Great Grian the Gold. Not one sound, neither of cricket, nor field mouse, nor reckless hare in uncoiling fern disturbed the misted morn—until Grian's light first touched Anell's body.

Lady Light raised her hands in blessing. She sang a wordless lament. The simple linen cloak she had borrowed from Jean to cover herself in respect to Anell parted to reveal her green, bejeweled gown. It cast rainbows that danced in bright contrast to the sorrow in her voice. All in attendance joined in—except Akir. Though released from restraint, now that the essence of Anell had departed, he refused to move, to speak, to acknowledge this world.

As if to comfort the grieving, Grian enveloped them in light. As her warmth dispersed the morning vapours, the mourners' voices faded into a profound silence.

The need to act goaded Lady Light. "Dear friends, we must confer on the next, best action." She paused, her voice strengthened by sheer force of will. "Rest assured honored wulves: Akir, Feela, Beag, Birk, Karlon, Mundee, Ro, Kalar, and Sonsie."

She turned and beckoned the Faer Ones to join Jean and Gavin in facing Anell's body. She called her music adepts: Elphinlark, Lord Dewain, and Lady Mavelle. "We count upon a song for Anell that shall last until Great Gold Grian and Good Silver Gealach drain their coffers of the last grains of precious light."

Her arms reached out as if to embrace the entire company. "I vow we shall celebrate Anell's life at her final Change."

"And so shall I, my Lady," a booming voice added. Lord Green appeared. All the Faer Ones cried, "My Lord!" Their faces beamed.

At Oak King's every step blossoms brightened under glistening dew drops; all grasses and every leaf flushed with renewed vitality. Resplendent in a gold-embossed green cape, he stood before the Queen. His luxuriant green hair, no longer bound in dying holly sprigs, sported robust oak leaf garlands that trailed upon the ground.

All but Lady Light and the wulves bowed their heads.

Keeping a discrete distance, the wulves tested the air for yet one more sudden menace or wonder. Detecting no threat, they sat upon their haunches to await the next move. Kalar and Sonsie shook their heads, as if trying to banish haunting images of Lord Green's other guises.

He reached forward to Lady Light, his right palm upright. She responded with her right palm, blue sky touching green earth.

"Thus are the Green and the Light united and upheld," he said.

"Thus are our hopes and fears intertwined," she answered. Her slender blue fingers slid between his substantial green.

"Blessed be the Light. Blessed be the Green," they said in unison.

"My Lord arrives hard upon our shock and sorrow. We missed you on a happier day." She did not smile to ease her reproach.

"My Lady, as with all green things, I come when the time is ripe. Like my deer and your wulves that seem to travel according to their own singular whims, they lead and follow one another, fulfilling a larger purpose—all good."

Her face clouded. "I beg to differ, my Lord. Covenant Cohorts respect our ancient laws but not those Dorcha who have violated the Order of the Light. Something verted has befallen the Green. Cutters using scrag-poisoned arrows trespass the borders of Lisnafaer! Dorcha-Faers fly—unbidden—in daylight!"

"Unbidden by Lady Light." His tender voice did not soften his stern eyes. "One culprit may answer for both crimes."

"Ah, quite true!" She searched her companions' faces. "The night has been long, indeed. Some of ye more weary than others, but all, heart-sore, grieve as one."

She extended her arms in a wide embrace. "Let us break for whatever is needful to refresh mind and body. As Grian climbs to her throne on high, perhaps we shall feel a loosening of the dark cords binding our hearts and spirits. Reconvene at Auld Alba's tree. May we count upon Akir and your pack to join us, if not in good will, at least harboring none ill?"

Akir's eyes flashed a smoldering rage. By the time his gaze rested upon Lady Light, mute despair had dampened the fires of his wrath.

Lord Green stepped forward. "High wulf, blame not the Faer Ones. Your Lady lies dead at the hands of interlopers, driven desperate by some odious agency, not Faer, at least not Solas, and certainly none who stand before you. The wulf and the deer remain steadfast prey-mates. We honor ye for your part in preserving Greenlaw. Others in shadow, deadly as the poison that killed your revered mate, dare all, it seems, to destroy the Balance Green."

Not offering to bend his knee, Lord Green stood before Akir. He did, however, hold his holly-oak staff in one hand and extend the other before the wulf's mouth. All in attendance held their breaths.

Akir's howl raised all the wulves' hackles.

Lord Green took care to avoid looking at Akir; instead his gaze sought Kalar's—and held it. Kalar's throat constricted, his answering cry stifled. Lady Light rested one hand on Sonsie's white snout and stilled his voice. Karlon, Mundee, and Ro found that the Greenguards in attendance had silently slipped to their sides. Lanark-Kyle, Rosslyn-Tir, Barras-Garve, and Brodie-Gare laid their hands upon the wulves' heads, the two cousins on either side of Ro, thus quelling her anxious urge to laugh. Iova-Rhu comforted Feela, the miserable. Master Arklevent knelt between Beag and Birk. He offered his throat, a gesture so appreciated that they accepted this submission of his life into their keeping as proof that he meant them no harm.

The pack respected Akir's solitary protest.

The Faer Ones held firm, gazes fastened upon this wounded wulf and his pack.

Jean and Gavin embraced, weeping anew for Anell. Like a balm, their tears calmed Akir's raging soul.

He ceased his rant. "Promise me Anell will be no raven fodder!"

"Scorn not the ravens, valiant Akir," Lord Green urged. "They know more than those who tread the earth and never take to the skies. They pass unseen at midnight and snatch valuable tidbits from the dark. Would it be so bad for Anell to fly?"

"Each leap Anell took carried my heart with it . . . and brought it back. You name the apple thief's tree. Anell loved the apples. Not I. But I loved Anell. Bury her at the roots of her far kin's tree. Change her into what she loved—not into a flock of carrion-pecking ravens!"

He spat. "No matter how far or high they fly or what morsels of gossip fall from their scavenger beaks."

Lady Light declared, "Akir, we shall do you one better. Neither raven nor any verted creature shall touch her! We shall change Anell—whole and pure. We must!"

⋏ ⋏ ⋏

The knocking at the front door ricocheted around Agnesia's brain making it impossible for her to ignore the light that streaked through the gaps in the shuttered bedroom window. Each rap felt like a kick to the back of her head right at that tender spot where her skull met her spine.

She waited to see if anyone else would answer the door. The pounding continued. Thinking go away! she said, "I'm coming." She sat up. The floor lurched. From her temples the pain wove a tight band across her forehead. She staggered to the dresser to brace herself and checked her reflection in the mirror. Dull eyes looked out from dark hollows moldering within a field of pinched skin. She caught up straying wisps of gingery hair into her dust cap and tucked her dingy cream muslin blouse into her waistband.

"Coming, coming," she called, making her way down the stairs, one hand feeling the wall, the other shading her eyes against any rebel light that had penetrated the closed shutters.

The door boomed like thunder. Her shaking hands pulled back the double bolts Freyen had insisted on. Making certain to put her booted foot against the bottom of the oak plank, she cracked the seal by three inches. A vertical bolt of light struck her. She winced. "Yes?"

A voice outside the house screeched, "Where are they, Agnesia Scanlon? You must know."

"Who?" Agnesia's white-knuckled hands gripped the door. Her forehead pressed against the hard wood.

"Who? Why my husband and boy, that's who, last seen at MacGillroy's pub with that Earm of yours and that no account trapper who'd sell his grannie if he could skin her."

A stout arm broke through the narrow opening. A woman from the nearby village of Malginnie confronted her reluctant hostess. Agnesia gestured out the door. "They went trapping up to the northwest."

A thick finger pointed in Agnesia's face. "That Earm of yours and his scoundrel brother filled Harry's head full of 'gold for the plucking and riches beyond counting'—that's what he said, all for the sake of a few cats brought home dead or alive, 'alive best'—that's what he said."

She shook the skirt of her dirty apron at Agnesia and then dug her fists into her hips. "Dragged our young Randall up with him well over a month ago, to 'check old traps'—that's what he said. Expected them home first of May, no sign, no word. What's all this about wildcats and gold? Don't look to me like you been lolling in gold."

Agnesia pressed her fingertips into her temples. "Why Rose MacGivins, I have no idea where your husband and son could be, seen neither hide nor hair of them. Earm's been gone and collecting specials, herbs and such, for Freyen's apothecary trade. I'd advise you to keep Harry and Randall away from MacGillroy's."

Agnesia pushed her assailant back outside. "Go. Go before Freyen comes."

She slammed the door with a resounding thud. Leaning her back against it, she gasped ragged breaths. Hoping to find a dose of Freyen's remedy, she made her way to the kitchen muttering "gold . . . wildcats?"

Thirty-Seven

Gathering of Allies

If ravens speak truth, take care.

When Great Grian shone directly overhead, light showered the High West. Sweet apple blossom air flowed cool and inviting within the shade of the groves. As viewed by the eagle or hawk on high, the trees, not planted in rows like the cutter orchards, formed intricate knots, circles upon circles in the same patterns used to decorate almost everything that the Faer Ones wore or created.

At the heart of the apple maze stood a hundred-branched tree Auld Alba had claimed as his own ages ago. Clustered blossoms nearly hid the globes of mistletoe growing from its shining limbs. The wulves awaited their hosts under its shade that cast a woven circle around them. The rustling leaves accentuated the pack's restless pacing, all but Kalar and Sonsie. They stood like stone statues, peering intently toward the apple keeper's garden where Anell lay.

First Sonsie's, then Kalar's tail beat the ground. The pack turned in unison and joined the yearlings. Lady Light, hand in hand with Lord Green, led a solemn procession of the Lady's entire court, the Greenguard who could be spared from guarding Anell's body, the apple keepers. And a stranger. Sonsie shook his head and pawed his eyes. They were all two-legged, different yet alike somehow: Lady Light, sky-blue, wearing apple blossoms over green like new grass, her mane a white cloud and green stars; Lord Green, ferlie oak and holly treemale with horns, wearing a gold-embossed green cape; the apple keepers, pale, not blue, not green, white cloud manes, one holding roses. All green-eyed. Sonsie's ears tipped forward.

The Lady's party paused six feet from the pack then parted, the court on the Lady and Lord's right, the Greenguard and three humans to the left. Sonsie nudged Kalar and pointed his snout at the two-legged stranger who smelled of fire. All the pack except Sonsie and Kalar edged back.

Sonsie took one step forward, focusing all his attention on the male of dangerous scent. His knotted rose gold hair hung down his chest like a tail. He wore a flaxen shirt tucked into plaid pants. The shirt's rolled sleeves exposed muscled arms, a ruddy hue, not pale like the skin of the two beside him. His long, darkened fingers stretched out and then made huge fists that seemed eager to grasp something.

Sonsie leaned against Kalar. *Kin to granniejean and grandiegavin?*

Kalar gritted his teeth. *A cutter?*

Just as Lord Green stepped forward, a dense, flickering cloud circled overhead.

The Greenguard moved closer to Lady Light.

A multitude of flapping black wings shred the light and descended. Dooleye and his crew, Grouser and Knackerclaw right behind their leader, perched on the uppermost branches of Auld Alba's tree, their ebony feathers shining through the apple blossoms. Their cries competed with the wulves' yelps as they raced around the tree.

Lord Green brandished his staff. His dark green oak leaves rustled. His cape waved, its gold, knotted circular trim flashing in the light. Breathing heavily, the pack bunched together and stopped, but then Grouser threw down a taunt that Karlon attempted to answer. The Lord's thundering voice halted all turmoil. "I invited the ravens, my eyes and ears in the hinterlands. Lord Dooleye promises courtly manners—I see ye Grouser," he said, pointing to the unruly bird. "—as long as he and his are treated with equal civility."

He lowered his staff. "Wulves and ravens make peace long enough to pick the bones of my deer; grant me the favor of stifling these growls and screeches. Listen to what I and my other friends have to say this sad and sorry day. Now be still!" He bowed to Lady Light.

⋏ ⋏ ⋏

Flashing emeralds adorned the Lady's flowing white hair. Her green sleeveless overdress covered a cream chemise, borrowed from Jean, who had embroidered new green apple leaves and white-pink petals upon its sleeves and skirt. Their patterns duplicated the interlaced boughs overhead. When the breeze stirred the living leaves and blossoms filtering Grian's light, Lady Light became one with the apple tree.

Though her countenance remained stern, her eyes smiled. She gestured to the entire group. "Give me your thoughts at this perilous time."

Lord Arthgallo pulled a silk handkerchief from the sleeve of his moss green waistcoat and cleared his throat. He bowed to all, including the wulves and the ravens. "My Lady and all who love the Green, this we know: Wulf Jaw no longer stands as our sure defense. Lisnafaer has been invaded, the day of the Lady's Quest verted to mayhem and murder."

He stopped to mop his brow. "Strangers breach the boundaries of our garden fortress to slay our cousin-kin Anell."

A harsh voice near Jean added, "Look for others!"

"Ah," Lord Green said, "allow me to introduce Jean and Gavin's lad Andrew who goes where even the ravens may not. All manner of folk have need of a good smith."

The Faer Ones smiled at this simple term used for one well known for his special services on their behalf. Andrew bowed to all, going so far as to dip his knee to Akir, a gesture not lost on the keen-eyed wulf.

Andrew's eyes narrowed. "Hard-hacking soldiers from the south, the red-jacketed invaders of lands beyond the Covenant, have verted the tribal fathers. They force their kith and kin from ancestral lands. Even now they slash and burn; they make roads to bring wheeled treachery to the very feet of the Wulf Jaw Mountains. I fear they will drive the homeless into Lisnafaer then follow with their engines. They don't need hunger and desperation to make Lisnafaer seem a paradise for the taking."

The wulves stirred. "Who could treat pack mates this way?" Mundee asked.

Ro gulped. "What of our kin . . . and the Green?"

Karlon's hackles bristled. "Aye, if they do this to their own, what about us?"

Sonsie and Kalar remained silent but alert.

"I can vouch for what Andrew says," Lord Green said. "I have been far afield searching for answers to many a troubling question. Otherwise, my Lady, I would have joined you much sooner."

Sonsie's tail batted Kalar.

"Perhaps this explains the trespass and the murder, but not the poison," Lord Arthgallo said.

"Forget not the larger question." Lady Light pointed skyward. "Did those who called the Dorcha . . . conjure the Fell One? How else the poison? When day seems as night to the high-riding horde and ancient venom kills esteemed Anell, all order of Lisnafaer and the world at large, the very Balance Green, may fall to a tragic verting we must prevent!"

She paced back and forth.

Lord Phelan strode forward; he stopped at the base of the tree, awaiting the moment when Lady Light might pause before him.

"Lord Phelan?"

"My Queen, the Night Hunt Aloft fared well at the New Year, as you know. Yet something goes amiss, some other darkness, one, I fear, emanating from the bleak cutter heart."

"True," Master Arklevent spoke up. "We hear murmurings from people of the Green Way. Homes, cut from the living timber, abandoned. Vile fences intact, but gardens left to rot, whole villages empty, forests burnt. Those driven helter-skelter from their homes and, as yet, unable to penetrate the Wulf Jaw push north and south to the sea, there to live off kelp and fish."

All the Faer Ones and their friends shuddered.

"Some terrible hunger must compel them," Lord Arthgallo declared, "but why destroy all that sustains life?" He waved his handkerchief as if to dispel some swarming evil.

Aden-Cree joined the discussion. She wore a tartan sash fastened with a starsilver brooch; entwined running deer circled its rim. "I frequent the Border Lands. Desperate, starving wayfarers forget the auld Green. True, those Dorcha who uphold cleanliness, honest labor, and order drive back most weary cutters who wander into Lisnafaer. However, someone harvests others, so the rumors say, those mean in spirit, cutter and Dorcha alike, at a hidden fortress of some kind."

Dooleye cried, "Caw! Caw!" The entire flock burst into shrieks. Some lifted off to fly around the tree before setting down. Satisfied he had everyone's attention, Raven Lord added, "Look, if you have eyes, deep in the forest beyond the Black Woods of Tara-Ardra."

Akir's ears perked. Boars! He glared but remained silent.

"Agnesia!" Andrew blurted.

"Not Agnesia!" Grandie Gavin ground his teeth. "That gutless husband Earm and his villain brother Freyen!"

Arklevent looked to his Greenguard. "Aden-Cree?"

"All I hear thus far from scattered mutterings is that within Lisnafaer grows a craving not even food and life-giving waters may quench." Shaking her head, she added, "Somewhere east of Apple Coast, west of Wulf Jaw. I had delayed reporting these rumors until after the happy reunion . . . of our Lady and Lord." She tugged at her sash. "And then Anell. . . ."

Lord Green raised his staff and threw his voice to the top of the tree. "Lord Dooleye, Anell lies dead, a dire murder. Ravens knew her as a valiant hunter whose leavings filled your cohorts' bellies—and yours as well! We have no time for your coy tidbits. Speak to clearer purpose."

Shadow and light played tag as the entire flock lifted heavenward to circle the tree. As they flew, they called to one another before descending in a spiral. The boughs shook. Thousands of blossoms drifted to earth.

Grouser cried, "Look."

Knackerclaw called, "Seek."

Bumflebeak shrieked, "Ask."

Dooleye strutted back and forth. "Find."

Moving forward to stand beside Lord Green, Lady Light warned, "Dooleye! You shall not out fly all wulves!"

Lord Green roared, "Dreadful bone picker, speak now—or never shall Dooleye find rest on any tree, living or dead, on any green growth—spring, summer, fall, winter!"

All who heard this terrible oath gasped.

Sonsie frowned. "Ravens. Doomed to endless flight. Never to find rest— except on bones of the dead." He shuddered.

Akir grinned.

Dooleye turned his head toward the southeast. He measured out a tithing of what he knew. "Look where hooves and tusk battle wing and claw for sovereignty under the shadows of the Dorcha Mountains. Find those who would conjure the Fell One in fire and death. Burning cats and running rats. Ask Lone Grumli."

A chill shook Sonsie's spine.

"Caw! Caw! Grumli! Grumli! Grumli!" The chortling ravens lifted off and cried, "Beware the Hunger!"

"Good riddance!" Akir snapped. The defiant wulves howled, some in grief, others in anger, all feeling an insult. They raced after their airborne tormentors but soon got disoriented in the maze of apple trees. At last Lord Phelan and Master Arklevent raised a power chant to call them to their senses. Lady Light held her hands aloft. She called to Akir, to Beag and Birk, to Karlon, Mundee, and Ro, to Kalar and Sonsie. Following her strong, pure notes, Akir and his family returned to Alba's tree. Sonsie nearly outraced his elders. Kalar was not far behind.

After a semblance of calm had returned, Lady Light sought any final words of counsel.

Aden-Cree spoke first. "The mutterings grow upon each solstice."

"Aye," Iova-Rhu and Lanark-Kyle affirmed together.

"Each Transfer of the Green, Holly to Oak, Oak to Holly, intensifies the signs," Lanark-Kyle said.

Iova-Rhu squirmed, avoiding looking at Kalar and Sonsie. "We thought they pointed to, em, the wulves and deer."

"An assumption not without merit, my Guardians," Lady Light said. Her brow knit. "Auld Alba's lost pack returns to the apple fields. Yet that fails to explain. . . ." She glanced at Lord Green. "Explain the Dorcha—unbidden by myself or any of the Solas Court."

She sought each Faer One's eyes to confirm her spoken truth. Satisfied, she said, "Dorcha—stirred by some rogue will—bring not order but confusion and, alas, death! Perhaps worse! Vile verting!" She clenched her fists in a gesture of combat. "Strangers thus lost in darkness can never come to love the Green."

Her gaze returned to the tall, leaf-covered Lord. *You know how I long to ride Starbold across flower-strewn meadows or race with the wulves.* Stifling a sigh, she spoke. "With us now stands our Oak King, thank Great Grian and Good Gealach. Speak, I pray you, upon this matter."

His face troubled, Lord Green nodded. "Soon I face the Challenge, the Solstice Change, when danger and agony cohabit. Natural dark covers the Green."

His eyes sought Lady Light's. "We must stand against the verted dark, bred of a corrupt will, a will most foul. Dooleye confirmed it."

Color drained from the Lady's face so that it seemed nearly as pale as her hair.

Lord Green reached out to her. Their hands touched. She trembled. *Alas, my Love.*

His gaze embraced her. *What help but my wyrd, my Love?*

His gesture embraced the entire assembly. "My deer, your wulves, these good comrades who guard the apples, all your court have a part to play. If Raven Lord speaks truth, we must stop the return of the Fell One—before far worse is visited upon Lisnafaer."

Lady Light looked upon her love, drawing strength from his tender gaze, courage from its reminder of their sacrifices on behalf of Lisnafaer. With her green eyes half closed in unyielding resolve she ordered, "We go to Mount Edan. First we honor Anell. Next we tend to the Green. Come!"

Thirty-Eight

FARE THEE WELL

Wulves live. Wulves die. Wulves live on in makar song.

An honor guard composed of high Faer Ones escorted the bier that carried Anell's body. They covered their gay attire beneath stately cloaks turned inside out, revealing a rich, dark green, like oak leaves in the shade. With Akir's pack and the Greenguard they wound their way down the Pass of the Piper to the glens between the Guardian and Deer Rack Mountains of the west. They proceeded through the Wulf Paw Forest to the northeast.

"We must allow Anell to bid farewell to the mountains she loved so well," Lady Light told Akir. "I know she hunted all these hollows and rocky ledges."

Akir winced. "She hunts no more." If ever a rider drew too near, he growled.

Tails down, heads down, not stopping to vent their despair to the pine covered crags, Kalar and Sonsie traced the hoof prints of the mounted Greenguard.

All along the route, from one mountain peak to another, solitary pipers saluted Anell's passing. The pack took Akir's lead, keeping silent, all except

Sonsie whose melodic complaint underscored the pipes' solemn airs. Not even Kalar had the will to silence him.

▲ ▲ ▲

E yes well hidden in the forests' dark thickets remarked Anell's stately journey through the mountains that the Dorcha considered their possession at night. Dorcha-Faers squatted on the moist ground, their knees drawn up to their chins. Others perched in gnarled tree limbs. The pipers' music filled their knobby skulls and short-circuited signals that would have sent their cramped legs scampering, but their crooked mouths jabbered. The bogies near to running streams whispered to the water kelpies. Soon all water-dorcha knew the Solas-Faers were heading home with some great treasure. Maybe the crazed cutter in the dark hollow would send firejuice to find out more. Sporadic cackling broke out along the route.

They looked up through the breaks in the trees and chortled to see low cloud cover on the first night of Oak Month when Gealach never showed her face. Double dark sky meant good cover for double dark deeds. Come nightfall, the Solas-Faers, their pipers and dirges, and this strangest of all Grand Rades would be long gone. The bogies and kelpies gnashed their teeth.

▲ ▲ ▲

B y the time Anell's cortege came to a meadow leading to Faerswell Forest, they had heard the last of the pipers, but the field hummed with tiny beasts busy about their tasks—until the procession began to cross. Except for the nickering of the horses, the silence continued as they passed through the first outlying saplings and approached the oak forest, sentinels surely as ancient as the grains of sand at the western shores. Hidden within its depths lay blessed Lac Morna. When viewed from above, the central islands within its sky blue water portray the Lady's face, dearly beloved.

Lady Light called a halt and blew upon her silver horn. Soon three wedges of wild geese filled the sky. Each successive wave swooped down and landed ahead and to the left and right of the group. At a wave from their Queen they rose and accompanied her in three formations, their wings beating a solemn tattoo. They seemed to pull the downcast company on invisible strings. The geese called ahead; one by one oak-branched portals covered with curling vines opened to them concealed trails through the forest.

When they came to the shore of Lac Morna, all gazed upon *Faerspeed*, the Queen's own ship. Shining gold knot work, linking entwined beasts, decorated the white ship. A figurehead of Lady Light with similar beasts on her azure skin completed the bow. The wonder-wrought likeness of Lady Light appeared to breathe.

Faer Ones attempted to lead the bereft wulves on board, but the pack balked, preferring to swim.

Lord Phelan spoke truth to Akir. "You are wounded and Anell cannot swim."

Akir swallowed bile. He led the pack up the gangway.

▲ ▲ ▲

*F*aerspeed sped east on blue water so wed to the sky that the ship seemed to fly towards the mouth of the River Ferlie-Bricht, the bright wonder that shone with reflected light from Mount Edan. While the troubled wulves huddled under a taut white sail at the ship's bow, a somber Lady Light stared ahead, oblivious to the strands of stray hair battering her face.

Her companions searched the river banks for any hint of danger. They kept a friendly watch on Lord Green who had said, "I prefer my feet to tread the firm, green earth."

Through the thick foliage at the water's edge they caught occasional glimpses of him. Master Arklevent spied a huge, faerblack beast loping at his side. He caught Lady Patha's attention, nodded in the direction of the shore, and mouthed "Kuu."

Patha laughed, but her eyes did not smile. "Some larger purpose is being served, Arklevent."

Standing beside his Queen, Lord Phelan gripped the jeweled hilt of Wulfstorm and watched the skies for Dorcha. "They covet this sort of affair, Lady. To mark and mar!"

"Have no fear, Phelan. Look!" The Lady's swans had joined the wild geese; their powerful wings churned the air. The geese shrieked angry threats to any intruders. With the Lady's sky-borne guard leading the way *Faerspeed* slid into a concealed slip just as Lord Green and Kuu appeared at the dock.

ᐱ ᐱ ᐱ

Kalar and Sonsie watched Anell's pallbearers, accompanied by their pack, carry her ashore.

Sonsie turned to Kalar. "They're taking her into Edan."

"Not without us." He led Sonsie to catch up with Karlon and Mundee.

ᐱ ᐱ ᐱ

At Lord Green's command, Kuu restrained himself, keeping silent, yet his tail waved briskly as he loped to Kalar's side. Lord Green, magnificent in his robes of clustered oak leaves and bright green acorns, took his place at Lady Light's side. She put her hand in his. The slightest tip of her silver-crowned head was the only salute he received, or expected.

The wild geese settled upon a deep pool lying at the foot of a huge cairn of chiseled, glistening white granite, each block the size of a fully grown bear. The stones reflected upon its serene, golden waters. Light so played upon the boulders that one could scarcely distinguish natural from giant-crafted stone.

The silent geese awaited their final act in the solemn rite while overhead the mourning swans circled, their cries echoing from Mount Edan. The wulves answered with a dolorous howl. At last Lady Light added her voice in a shivering glissando. A heartbeat later, as promised, Lord Green joined in with deep, booming notes. He nodded to Kuu; the power of his answering cry made their hearts pound. Lady Light's emerald eyes called to the extended

Solas Court, including all the Greenguard, heretofore silently bearing Anell's body. They, too, lifted their sweet voices to a swelling chorus.

At the height of the crescendo Lady Light and Lord Green spoke two names, she "Kernunn" and he "Keriwynn."

The boulders slid apart, releasing a rush of wind that swept over the mourners. All fell silent except the swans. Queen Keriwynn and King Kernunn strode forward, their hands joined, leading the pallbearers and the pack within. The increasing pressure of his green hand upon hers was the only sign he gave at what cost he penetrated the underground vaults of Edan.

As soon as Anell's body crossed the threshold, the geese took to the air. Their piercing cries punctuated the swans' aching lament to gird Mount Edan with powerful magical wards. Eventually, the swans and geese glided down to land on the golden pool. Remaining ever vigilant but silent as the dew's breath, they alone did not enter the mountain.

▲ ▲ ▲

Rose MacGivins had given Agnesia Scanlon quite a scare. Not that she couldn't handle the likes of Rose. It was worry over the men that kept her awake at night, made her days a misery. Harry and Randall had never come home. She tried to find out what happened, but a terrible row broke out between the brothers. The noise nearly split her skull. Earm ran out of the house.

Freyen pressed one of his polished dirks against her lip. It hurt. "Just you shut that big mouth of yours, or I'll make it so big you can swallow a hog."

She sought refuge in bed. Hours passed. As was her habit, she talked to herself. "Just sit up; don't open your eyes. Forget that throbbing in your temples and the daggers lodged behind your eyes. Count to ten. Breathe. Don't throw up; you haven't eaten since Thursday.

"Put your bare feet down on the cold stone floor. Your blood'll pull the cold up your legs to your lungs. Breathe. To your heart, breathe. Up to your neck. Find that knot at the back of your head. Breathe.

"Listen for the sound of the men—are they day sounds or night sounds? Move only if you hear no sound.

"Grip the bed post. Pull yourself up—there! Don't open your eyes. Turn. Face the window. Take those four steps. One. Two. Keep your eyes shut! Three. Don't worry about the light; it can't hurt you if the curtains are shut. Four. Reach out; feel the muslin. There, see if the curtains cover the window."

Yes, yes.

"Now reach through and feel the glass. Is it cold?"

Cold!

"Press your forehead against the glass. Draw in the cold. Is it night? Squeeze your eyes tight; look for the red haze under your eyelids—light and blood, light and blood."

No blood—night!

"Open your eyes. Don't laugh. Don't think you are safe. Open the window. Cover your mouth. Deep breath, now. That's it. Can you smell it? Burning hair and flesh. Don't gag."

What's that?

"No, no, don't hear the shrieking! Don't scream—the men in the old milk house *doing it* will hear you.

"Turn around. Grab your shawl on the bed—"

No, no, close the window. Close the curtains—tight!

"Put on your shawl; find your daughter. Call her; call Jenelle."

No! Don't call her! Don't make a sound.

"Light the candle. Go find her. Pay no heed to the pounding in your head. Listen for the footsteps of the men. Be careful. Don't set your shawl afire."

Find Jenelle? Tell her to escape? Get help?

"No! Trust no one; hang on to her; keep your eye on her.

"Ignore the pain. Find Freyen's elixir."

⋏ ⋏ ⋏

Lord Arthgallo and Lady Ula, dressed in hunter green hooded cloaks with simple starsilver clasps, joined the procession to escort the bier well within the interior of Mount Edan. A company of the Lightguards, silent in the near dark, held up rose crystals to light their way. Akir and the pack, torn between their distrust of these forbidding surroundings and their desire to remain at Anell's side, moved forward, straining to detect any sign of danger, but try as they might, they neither sniffed nor heard anything amiss.

"Strange," Beag whispered to Birk, "no song for once."

"Be wary when Faer Ones fall silent and lead us not even Grian knows where." Akir growled.

And so they came to a circular, high-vaulted enclosure. Queen Keriwynn signed for Anell's bearers to place her on a flat raised stone in the center. All gathered round the bier. Lady Light stood at the head and Lord Green at the foot with Lord Arthgallo and Lady Ula on either side. Lady Light and Lord Green raised their beryl crystals, she white, he green. Directly, Lord Arthgallo and Lady Ula raised theirs, blue and yellow. White, green, blue, and yellow light of the four Guardian Crystals fused. A radiant star filled this inner chamber of the fire mountain. Its light flashed upon them all, but the rose glow provided by the light adepts shielded the sensitive eyes of the wulves who were drawn to a sweet, comforting sound emanating from the light.

Lady Patha joined the Faer Queen, one standing on either side of Anell's head. Still holding her crystal overhead, the Queen laid a hand on Anell's eyes. Patha placed garlands woven of holly, ivy, heather, and mistletoe around her head, taking care to lay the trailing streamers over her wounds. The Queen recalled Anell's capers in the forest, her long runs over field and rock-strewn uplands, her faithful service in the hunt, her part in the Change, essence of all life. She named the famous prey-mates Anell had changed into wulfkind, blessed her for the cubs she brought forth and the care she took to raise them, praised her as a good and true mate to Akir, and thanked her for the life she never got to bring to the light.

Bending low, she said, "I promise, you, Anell, your last living sons shall do great deeds."

Kalar's and Sonsie's ears shot up. All the pack looked to Akir whose silent glare at his youngest sons lowered their ears.

Then Lady Light and Lord Green, Lady Ula and Lord Arthgallo lowered their crystals so that north, south, east, and west touched in the center. Over the joined quadrants the Lightguards stepped forward and covered Anell's body with fragrant yew boughs.

The Faer Queen called to Akir. "It is time, good and faithful wulf."

His soul poured forth from his eyes.

She opened her well-guarded heart and drank in his pain. Never taking her eyes from his, she crooned:

▲ ▲ ▲

"Farewell, Anell.
We give Anell to Mother Earth.
Mount Edan's flames shall warm your bones,
Heat your blood.
Edan's forest roots shall draw your marrow to the skies.
Anell shall be changed."

▲ ▲ ▲

Lady Mavelle continued:

▲ ▲ ▲

"Farewell Anell.
Anell shall inhabit all that lives upon Lisnafaer.
Anell shall live in our hearts.
Anell shall live again,
As the forests give forth life,
As the mountains give forth spirit."

▲ ▲ ▲

L. N. Passmore

*L*ord Dewain sang next:

"Farewell, Anell.
Go beloved wulf,
Blessed High West wulf,
Great Alba's Heir,
Heartbeat of Akir, Great Kark's Heir,
High Mother of warrior and singer."

*S*onsie and Kalar stared at Akir who groaned in spite of his vow to spurn any recognition of these detested proceedings. The brothers looked at each other. *Kark and Alba, warrior and singer.*

Once again, the Faer Queen lifted her voice:

"Fare thee well, Anell,
Faer friend and pack mate.
Fare thee well, Anell,
Blessed be, child, mate, mother."

*T*he pack's courage nearly failed at this reminder of all they had lost in one lone wulf. Feela heaved a sigh. She would have died rather than to disgrace her sister with a voiced sob. She and the pack struggled together to give their lost companion her due honor.

All those gathered to honor the slain high wulf affirmed: "Blessed be, Anell."

The four crystal bearers expanded their circle. They paced around Anell's yew-draped body. The hovering star expanded. The bier rose high over their heads and burst into flames, becoming one with the star. It continued to rise until it disappeared into the great fiery heart of Mount Edan.

Sonsie could no longer contain himself. He called to the swans; he called to the spirit-bearing geese. Soon all, including King Kernunn, Lord of the Green, joined in a final elegy.

Kalar's heart raced. He barked a challenge to the molten rocks and flames that devoured Anell.

Thirty-Nine

Time to Pay the Piper

What is a wulf without a pack?

In their return to the outside world, the pack left the Lords of Light behind in what felt like the gloom of the deepest dorcha pit. They looked from one wall to another, but couldn't escape the afterimage of Anell's fiery change. No matter where they turned, even with eyes shut, they saw her burning body. Kalar and Sonsie trudged at the rear, but well beyond the glow of the Faer Ones' crystal lights. The young brothers' faerblack and faerwhite fur appeared grey, but their troubled hearts offered no such illusion of sameness.

Kalar cared only to leave Mount Edan and all its bitter memories behind. He stretched his head toward the surface and peered ahead, searching for a glimmer of light. If only he could breathe open air under true sky and run with the wind tugging at his fur.

When green scents floated on fresh air, Kalar cried out to the daylight "at last."

The sweet fragrance of the antlered treemale whose leaves rustled as he walked teased Kalar's quivering nose. He thought on his mad race with Kuu and their fight on behalf of the stag.

Sonsie stifled the lament that threatened to break free of his clenched jaws. He forced himself to listen to the Faer Ones' hushed talk. Among all the whispers, only Lady Light's voice registered. Every word she spoke seemed a melody to the singer's eager soul.

⋏ ⋏ ⋏

After all had boarded *Faerspeed*, Lady Light sang to her ship, urging all possible speed to the far shore. It landed before Birk could find the slightest infraction to bring to Akir's attention. The pack stirred. Just ahead of Birk, Feela nudged Akir, who roused himself to lead them. He leapt overboard in a great arc, followed by all, the last being Sonsie.

The former den in Wulf Paw Forest seemed a good place to go, yet Akir's heart ached for Anell. The ravens' cry, "Beware of the hunger," echoed in his memory. He coughed. Ravens know hunger? Miserable bone pickers—not Anell's! Hunger? Faer Ones know nothing of the hunger that stalks when the rumbling, snow-covered earth cries Oak King's return. Hunger? Anell—burnt by the Faer Ones in Edan.

The pack called their leader. Akir pawed the ground, lost to them. His heart filled with sand. The heaviness pressed him into the earth. Each year when the tree months changed from Alder to Willow, Anell's scent, robust and feral, sweet and pure for Akir, had drawn him to her. Longing for Anell swept over his body as fire over dry grasses. He wanted to run, run far from ravens and Faer Ones and cutters, to run with Anell, high wulf with high wulf, mates forever, to make the pack strong with new pups.

But the season of heat had passed.

⋏ ⋏ ⋏

Beag and Birk growled. Kalar and Sonsie watched Akir as Beag drew closer to their sire who struggled to breathe. Now that their dam had become one with Edan's fire, they worried.

Kalar's tail thumped Sonsie. *Will Beag or Birk challenge Akir?*

Sonsie pawed the ground. *Or Karlon? Young but bold.*

Never taking his gaze from Akir, Kalar dismissed that notion. *Karlon? No. Our sire will be high wulf . . . or Birk?*

Sonsie shuddered and shook his head. *For the pack, better Beag, a good hunter. But pack leader? Feela?*

Kalar snorted. *Never.*

They agreed. *It must be Akir.*

Akir dragged himself up. Kalar and Sonsie searched for any sign of weakness. They watched his every movement, the slightest nuance of his eyes. No prey-mate ever got closer scrutiny. Seeing nothing to encourage their hope, his youngest sons joined the pack, all heartsick, and straggled after him.

▲ ▲ ▲

About fifty yards beyond the shore in a rock-enclosed hollow, they found Lord Green with hound Kuu at his side waiting to welcome them. Neither made a sound; the scent told the wulves all they needed to know. There lay a freshly killed red deer, not aged or diseased or a slightly muscled calf, but a fine young stag, noble even in death.

Kalar's rumbling belly alerted him to a pain equal to his sorrow. He crawled forward, leaving a trail of crushed spring grasses. He nosed the body. The kill must have occurred moments before they came ashore. He looked to Kuu, the silent. Not daring to touch the deer, Kalar yelped to his elders, a lackluster wave of their tails their only answer.

"Ye must eat," Lord Green said. "Wulves, I give ye one of my own for your greater good. Full bellies make clear brains. Take. Eat. Be comforted."

Lady Light, who had joined her long-sought companion, nodded. "Yes. Take. Eat. Live. Ye have much to ponder. But first ye must change this grand red deer into life-loving wulves. Do not scorn this blood offering, I pray. It comes at high cost to your benefactor." She bowed to Lord Green. "We go now to Mount Enion. Grave matters demand attention. Akir, we welcome you and your pack."

Kalar and Sonsie's heads turned toward Lady Light. Their tails wagged as if they had found the trail to a fragrant deer wallow.

Akir maintained grim silence.

Lady Light regarded the faerblack and faerwhite brothers and then looked to their sire and bowed. "As Akir wishes. We shall wait long enough for ye to honor the deer's sacrifice."

Lord Green added, "Ye all might leave just the tiniest scraps for the ravens, your friends—will ye, nill ye."

"Kuu." Lady Light called her own hound to her side as she withdrew.

Lord Green offered his arm. "My Lady, Keriwynn."

"My Lord, Kernunn."

Kuu looked up. "When does Kalar—"

"Hush, Kuu," Lady Light interrupted.

The Lady of the Light and the Lord of the Green moved behind a marbled stone.

⋏ ⋏ ⋏

B reathing in the scent of the prime stag, their mouths watering, first Kalar and then Sonsie yelped. The pack's gnawing hunger called them out of their rough-coated doldrums. Left alone, they turned to Akir.

The rhythmic thuds of his heart broke the silence. They had lost the next generation and their sovereign breeding wulf. The pack had to survive; to survive they must eat. Life. Death. Change: the Covenant of Greenlaw with the Lady and the Lord. He shook the stupor from his bones. The unrelenting hunger, sharper than the one for Anell, returned like an antler spike to his gut. The urging of his body to take down the prey-companion after hearty chase across a glen determined his course. None had eaten since before the fatal attack. He gazed upon his pack; their dull eyes hurt him.

He sniffed the air. "We need the joy of a furious run, glad hearts pumping hot blood."

Before them lay the satisfaction of every wulf's hunger, ready to make change. Allowing himself one piercing cry, he fell upon the deer. Beag and Birk joined him. In an ancient rite sacred to all Covenant Companions, the rest of the pack finished changing the deer into wulf. They remembered the ravens but left not one drop of blood.

The Lady and Lord smiled.

▲ ▲ ▲

"Akir," Lord Phelan called. He dressed in the simplest traveling attire, his boots and cape decorated with figures of running wulves. Phelan pointed to the assembled Faer Ones. "We hasten to Faer Home in Enion. Ye all may come with us—if ye please. We dare not wait longer."

In no hurry, Akir stared at Phelan. "How shall I answer the one who carried the message that ruined my life?"

He kept Phelan hanging through several tortured breaths. "I will lead my pack where hunting is good. We go west to Wulf Paw . . . or Boar Bristle. We must run and hunt. We have had enough of Faer Ones who draw the cutters yet cannot save. . . . We go west."

▲ ▲ ▲

The pack moved as one to follow Akir, except for the two youngest. They felt drawn to some other place, where they knew not. Kalar took three paces toward his departing pack. He stopped, face forward. Sonsie never moved when Akir gave the order but turned to face Lady Light; his eyes betrayed longing and confusion.

Lord Green raised his staff. "Kalar. Come."

Pivoting, Kalar saw Lord Green, now almost completely covered in lush oak leaves.

"Kalar has an auld debt to pay, and I have not much time to find Lone Grumli before the solstice. You chose your wyrd when first straying from your obedience to your sire. Wulves who enter the auld den must pay the price for what they see. You have a task, a furious foe to face, rebel Kalar. I have seen your valor at Elder's Grove. Shall Kalar be a warrior?"

From off in the distance baying, one . . . two . . . three, came strong and clear, straight to Kalar's perked ears.

"Come, Kalar," Lord Green commanded.

Akir barked. "Kalar!"

Locking gazes with his sire, Kalar bared his teeth. Akir's snarl sounded like rocks cracking in an earthquake.

Feela barked, "Kalar!" She stood between Kalar and Akir. "Kalar!" she cried. "Don't!"

Birk leapt to stand at her brother's side.

Lady Light advanced. Like Phelan and the others, she wore a plain green riding outfit, her boots woven of white wulf hair, her own long white hair bound many times over. "Sonsie also has a debt to pay. You chose your wyrd the first time you stole one of our songs. Wulves who enter the auld den must pay the price for what they see. You have a task, a foul fiend to outfox, riddle-solver Sonsie. I have heard your songs under the eye of Sky-Wulf. Shall Sonsie be a singer?"

"Sonsie!" Akir growled.

Sonsie raised his head in Akir's direction. "Yes, sire." But he searched out the huddled pack.

"Feela," he cried. Anguish, threatening to extinguish his joy, nearly overwhelmed him.

Feela stood tall. "Follow your heart, Sonsie."

"Feela! You stupid cur," Birk rasped. She bit Feela deeply enough so that blood welled from the tear.

Never flinching, Feela said, "Go, Sonsie. Come back a makar. Sing me an auld song."

For once Sonsie uttered not one sound, and yet love poured from his soul and flowed to his faithful nursemaid. He turned and went to Lady Light's side.

Akir's anger came out in a howl like trees cracking in an avalanche.

Trembling, Kalar tore his gaze away from Akir. He forced himself to look in the direction of the voice that haunted all his strange adventures.

Closer stood Lord Green, the beginnings of a deer rack now clearly visible protruding from the foliage on his head. He waved his staff, beckoning the yearling wulf.

Kalar followed.

Lord Green and Lady Light called, "Akir" whereupon Lord Green added, "Your sons have chosen their wyrd. If they survive what faces them, you may acknowledge true champions of the Green."

In hopes of appealing to Akir's noble heritage Lady Light said, "Akir, heir of Kark, we would have you and your pack as allies in the dark storms and strife to come. We thank you for the training of these braw wulves. If they are to live and return, they have secrets to learn that only Faer Ones may teach. Your blessing bestowed would be a boon."

Akir looked to the heavens. But in Grian's full light Sky-Wulf was invisible—and silent. Receiving no help, Akir gave none.

The Lady and Lord turned and led Kalar and Sonsie in tight-jawed silence to the marbled stone, leaving Akir behind.

Akir's gaze followed his sons, the last born of Anell. "The Faer Ones have you in thrall. If you break away and come slinking back to your pack, prepare to fight."

Calendar

TREE MONTHS of LISNAFAER

1: **BIRCH (November)**
   The New Year Begins
2: **ROWAN (December)**
   Winter Solstice (Oak King initiates Waxing Year)
3: **ALDER (January)**
4: **WILLOW (February)**
5: **ASH (March)**
   Spring Equinox
6: **HAWTHORN (April)**
7: **OAK (May)**
8: **HOLLY (June)**
   Summer Solstice (Holly King initiates Waning Year)
9: **HAZEL (July)**
10: **VINE (August)**
11: **IVY (September)**
   Autumn Equinox
12: **REED (October)**
13: **ELDER**
   The Wilder Time, the last three days of October

October 31, New Year's Eve, also called Halloween

Glossary: Characters, Places, And Terms

CHARACTERS

Faer Ones. Supernatural beings, divided into the Dorcha Host and Solas Court.

Dorcha Host. Tend the Green in the dark, also called Dorcha-Faers, Faerdark, flying Host, Harrow Host, Host, and night swoopers & crawlers. Some shapeshift. They include:

> **bogey-beasts.** Also called bogles and bug-a-boos. Low level, mischievous Dorcha.
>
> **dorcha dogs**. Great black dogs with red eyes and ears.
>
> **fachans**. Often grumpy and always dangerous, having one eye, arm, hand, leg, and foot.
>
> **Grasphand**. A fachan.
>
> **Grungegrind**. A bogey-beast.
>
> **Pricklewort**. A bogey-beast.
>
> **water kelpies**. Appear as young horse or shaggy man, associated with water.
>
> **wights**. Grimmest of the flying Host who live in death.

Solas Court. Tend the Green in the light, also called Court, Faer Ones, Faers, Lords of Light, sky-kin, Solas, Solas-Faers. Some shape-shift. They include:

Lady Light. Queen/Lady of the Faer Ones and all who serve the Green. Consort to Lord Green, also called the Lady, Lady Light, and Queen of the Light. A supreme makar/shape-shifter. Horse is Starbold; bird is Fantoosh; ship is *Faerspeed*. See Wulf Queen.

Lord Green. King/Lord of the Green and Consort to Lady Light, also called Auld Green One, He that is nowhere and everywhere, Holly King, Oak King, and Our Lord who brings back the Green. A tri-therianthropic being: tree or treemale, deer, and Faer One who functions not unlike a God and changes shape/being according to season and need. See the Stag.

OTHER SOLAS-FAERS, FRIENDS, and UNCANNY BEASTS

Arklevent, Master. Guardian Master. Leads all the Guardians of the Green, also called Master of the Green. Horse is Rowanberry.

Arthgallo, Lord. Lady Light's High Counselor.

Brighteye. Map Keeper, also called Hand of the Inland.

Dewain, Lord. Music Adept.

Elphinlark. Minstrel.

Faerguard of the Night Hunt Aloft. Elite members of the Horseguard and Lightguard.

Faerwald. Dragon, chthonic being with the power to co-dwell in the Otherworld and in Lisnafaer's physical underworld. Companion of Lord Green and faer friend, also called Light Wyrm, Ram-Horned Wyrm, Sharp Sighted One, and White One Who Crawls.

ghillie dhu. Humble Solas-Faer who lives under guardian oak Wisdom-Shield.

Lone Grumli. Giant at Mount Barra, the Spear. A faer friend and last of giants.

Guardians. Faer Ones who tend the Green, both flora and fauna, also called Greenguard, forester(s). They include:

Aden-Cree (f.).

Barras-Garve (m.). Cousin to Brodie-Gare.

Brodie-Gare (m.). Cousin to Barras-Garve.

Iova-Rhu (f.).

Lanark-Kyle (m.).

Rosslyn-Tir (m.).

Keriwynn, Queen. See Lady Light.

Kernunn, King. See Lord Green,

Kundry and **Keelin, Ladies.** Horse Adepts who lead the Horseguard.

Kuu. Queen's hound, mound guard, and oft-time companion of Lord Green.

Light Wyrm. See Faerwald.

Mavelle, Lady. Music Adept.

Patha, Lady. Empath and healer who is Lady Light's oldest friend and confidante.

Phelan, Lord. Master of the Hunt, leads the Faerguard on Night Hunt Aloft. Horse is Blaze, Sword Wulfstorm.

Ula, Lady. Light Adept who leads the Lightguard.

Scrag Tail. Demon, also called Fell One, neither Dorcha nor Solas, of the cutter world from whom is extracted scrag venom.

The Stag. Also called Deer Lord, Deer Friend, King Stag, and White Stag. See Lord Green.

Thornheart. Map Keeper, also called Hand of the Outland.

Wulf Queen. Also called Lady Wulf, Wulf Friend. See Lady Light.

HUMANS

Andrew. Son of Jean and Gavin, light smith, special scout, and emissary for Faer Ones. A faer friend.

Agnesia. Daughter of Jean and Gavin, married to Earm Scanlon.

Grannie Jean. Apple keeper, known as good auld woman. A faer friend.
Grandie Gavin. Apple keeper, known as good auld man. A faer friend.
MacGivins, Harry. Cutter, dupe of Freyen Scanlon.
MacGivins, Randall. Cutter son of Harry MacGivins.
MacGivins, Rose. Wife of Harry MacGivins.
Scanlon, Earm. Cutter husband of Agnesia, younger brother of
  Freyen Scanlon.
Scanlon, Freyen. Cutter apothecary and practitioner of malevolent
  magic, neither Solas nor Dorcha, elder brother of Earm.

RAVENS

Bumflebeak.
Dooleye. Raven Lord.
Grouser.
Knackerclaw. Cousin to Dooleye.

SKY

Gealach. Moon, called Light of Night, Good Gealach, and Gealach
  the Silver.
Grian. Sun, called Light of Day, Great Grian, and Grian the Gold.
Ladies of the Sky. Stars.
Merry Dancers. Aurora borealis.
Sky-Wulf. Wulf-Star, a constellation in shape of a wulf.
Wulfguard. Polaris, the North Star.

TREES

Auld Alba's tree. Apple tree from which Auld Alba the apple thief
  stole apples. Most ancient and magical apple tree.
Lightning-Eater. Guardian oak in Faerswell Oaks.
Wisdom-Shield. Guardian oak, called Grand Warder.

Wulfsbane tree. Otherworldly gallows tree from which hang the bodies of a noble pack of wulves slaughtered in the Wulf Wars against the Ice-North raiders.

WULVES

Auld Alba the apple thief. First and greatest wulf makar, ancestor to Anell. See L.N. Passmore's website Moving Mountains www.lnpassmore.com for his story, "Alba the Apple Thief."
Auld Dunoon. Renowned keeper.
Gallows Wulves. Hang on Wulfsbane Tree. They include:
Adair (m.). Wulf-singer, son of Kark, brother to Krika.
Balfron, the bold (f.).
Ellrin (f.). High wulf, mate to Krika.
Flintry, the fierce (m.).
Garve, the great (f.).
Kark. Great warrior wulf, lost in the Wulf Wars, sire of Krika and Adair, ancestor of Akir.
Krika (m.). High wulf, son of Kark, mate to Ellrin.
Nigg, the noisy (m.).
Skiak, the sly (f.).
Lost Pack of Auld Alba the apple thief. Famed pack of Lisnafaer that defends the Balance Green. They include:
Akir (m.). High wulf, heir of Kark, mate of Anell.
Anell (f.). High wulf, heir of Auld Alba, mate of Akir.
Beag (m.). Second best hunter in the pack, solid and reasonable.
Birk (f.). Temperamental and bossy sister of Akir. A biter.
Feela (f.). Sensitive and discerning sister of Anell. Nursemaid to Kalar and Sonsie.
Kalar (m.). Latest born to Anell, brother to Sonsie. Earned the name Warrior Wulf. Royal Green or faerblack fur.
Karlon (m.). Brave but incautious brother of Mundee and Ro, two years older than Kalar and Sonsie.

Mundee (f.). Sharp-eyed sister of Karlon and Ro.

Ro (f.). Jovial sister of Karlon and Mundee.

Sonsie (m.). Latest born to Anell, brother to Kalar. Earned name Bane of the Unclean. Royal White or faerwhite fur. Is a faereye. See Faereye.

Terror Wulf. Called Vilhjalmer in the Ice-North, a Dire One.

PLACES

Apple Coast. Site of Avalach Crossing, also called apple land. Home of Grannie Jean and Grandie Gavin who tend the Faer Ones' apples.

Avalach Crossing. Center of Apple Coast, site of the Great Crossing.

Blessed Covenant Land. Lisnafaer.

Cavern Perilous. One of the Faer Ones' inner sanctuaries, Kalar and Sonsie's testing site.

Conical Mounds. Series of wonder-wrought peaked hills, the largest of which is an entrance to Faer One's underground realm.

Circle of Nine. Hazel trees that surround Elders Grove Pool.

Deer Retreat. Lord Green's name for Lisnafaer.

Elders Grove Pool. Site of battle with dorcha dogs.

Faer Haven. Lisnafaer.

Faer Home. Mount Enion.

Ferlie Forest of Four (or Five). Magical rowans, hazel, birch, and oaks (the Four Friends), the fifth being the apple trees at Avalach Crossing on the west coast.

Flower Dale. Favorite haunt of Faer Ones, especially in summer.

Gates of Song. State of mind allowing access to realm of song, magic, and makars.

Green Isle. Refuge for Lord Green and deer in Lac Neala, also called *Aros-nam-gla'Fear.*

Guardian Mountains. On west coast, protectors of Avalach Crossing, beloved by Anell and Feela, and site of Wulf Tongue Pass.

Hart Haven. Land within the Forest of Four Friends, beloved by deer. Wulves call this shared territory Wulf Ward.

Harts Hold. A crossing at juncture of River Tara with Lac Tara.

Healing Well. Located on island in Lac Morna.

High Road. Wulf Tongue Pass taken to Avalach Crossing.

High West. Lisanfaer.

Ice-North. Home of the raiders and Terror Wulf.

Keriwynn's Gate. Guards Queen's Mound, east of Stag Spring, Lac Neala, and Green Isle.

Kernunn's Gate. Guards entrance to Green Isle, west of Stag Spring and Queen's Mound.

Lisnafaer. Garden/fortress of the Faer Ones, the land under the Faer Ones' protection, all the Covenant Land from Wulf Jaw Mountains to the West Sea. Also called *Aros-na-ba'Bean*.

Low Road. Underground route below Wulf Tongue Pass taken to Avalach Crossing.

Malginnie. Small village near Scanlon Hollow.

Pass of the Piper. Way through Avalach Forests and Guardian Mountains.

Queen's Mound. Portal to the Faer Ones' inner realm and the Otherworld.

Scanlon Hollow. Home of the Scanlon brothers where the southern edge of Boar Bristle Forest converges with the Black Woods of Tara Ardra and Eagle Claw Forest.

Stag Spring. Never-fail spring between Keriwynn's and Kernunn's Gates.

Wulf Jaw Mountains. A series of seven mountains: Enion, Edan, and Marcus to the north, Solas-Faers' province; Barra, home of giant Lone Grumli; and Dreich, Cadman, and Ansgar to the south, Dorcha-Faers' province. Wulf Jaw separates Lisnafaer from the cutter lands to the east.

Wulf Run. Wulves' name for Lisnafaer.

Wulf Tongue Pass. Perilous route over Guardian Mountains to Avalach Crossing, favored by Light Adepts for collecting rainbows.

Wulf Ward. Land within the Forest of Four Friends, beloved by wulves. Deer call this shared territory Hart Haven.

TERMS

Aros-na-ba'Bean. Land of the White Lady.

Aros-nam-gla'Fear. Dwelling of the Green Lord.

Auld Ones. Ancient, revered, extraordinary wulves, initiators of new realities.

Balance Green. What the Covenant protects under Greenlaw to be preserved at all cost. Ultimate goal of all Covenant members. See Covenant of Greenlaw.

Change. Consuming and changing one life form into another. All Covenant members revere and give thanks for all those who sacrifice their lives to make the Change.

Covenant of Greenlaw. Compact between beasts, faer friends, and Faer Ones on behalf of the Green. Without Light is no Green. Without Green is no Life. See Balance Green.

Covenant Cohorts. All parties to the Covenant.

Crossing (from There to Here), also called Great Crossing when Faer Ones came into this time and space, creating Lisnafaer.

daffin. Playful or foolish behavior.

dark time. Deep winter, also time when Terror Wulf and Ice-North raiders held sway.

Dire Ones. Fearsome beasts, thought long-banished.

dorcha days. Hard times when the influence of the Dorcha darkens the day.

faerblack. Royal Green, darkest green.

faereye. Green, aka faergreen.

faerwhite. Royal White, color of Lady Light's hair that shines with Grian's and Gealach's light.

faer friends. Humans who are special friends of Faer Ones, also called people of the Green Way.

faerwulf. Faer One/wulf: one in both, both in one. The transmutation of one being into the other, an operation of a higher order than the temporary guise of a hide-changer.

ferlie. Wonder, marvel.

Ferlie-Bricht. Wonder bright or bright wonder, name of river.

Guardian Crystals. Four beryl crystals: white (Lady Light), green (Lord Green), blue (Arthgallo), yellow (Ula).

Grand Rade. Grand daylight procession of the Solas-Faers in OakMonth/May to find Lord Green.

Grand Rade Night. Eve of the New Year on the last night of Wilder Time, referred to in cutter world as Halloween.

Greenguard. The Guardians of the Green.

Greenlaw. Covenant law that protects the Balance Green, wherein all life is precious, no beast is killed for sport, and no Green is wasted. Preserved by the Noble Three, Stewards of the Green.

Horseguard. Faer Ones' cavalry.

hunt-companions. Hunters, the wulves.

keeper. Wulf name for historian, keeper of needful lore. May also include Faer Ones or humans.

Lady's Quest. Day when Lady Light leads the Grand Rade to greet Lord Green, also called Day of the Lady's Quest.

Lightguard. Faer Ones who gather, preserve, and use light.

Light of the Hunter. Hunter's Moon, Reed Month/Oct. 15, when Gealach's full face shines.

long-dark. Winter season before the return of light in Willow Month.

makar. One with the gift or power to create reality, including the power to transmute.

mixtie-maxtie. All jumbled up, crazy, mixed up.

never-changed. Beasts that die but are not changed into another life, like the corpse-horses of the Dorcha.

Night Hunt Aloft. Airborne hunt overseen by Lord Phelan and Faerguard so that the Wilder Time flight of the Dorcha does not vert into a wild hunt.

Otherworld. Another time and space, sometimes viewed as a spirit world, beyond but often congruent with the common physical world shared by beasts, Faer Ones, and humans.

people. Humans in general, not confined to "cutters."

Rade or **Trooping Rades**. Great and lively processions Lords of Light delight in, winding all through Lisnafaer.

prey-companions, prey-mates. Prey, partners to the Change.

queerie. Odd or strange.

scunner. Disgusting, loathsome, irritating.

slabber. Slobber.

vert. Turn or change from one's true or lawful nature.

Wilder Time. Elder Month (the last three days of October), the thirteenth month, when endings merge with beginnings and the unwary can become *bewildered*, culminating in eve of the New Year or Halloween.

Wild Hunt. Unlawful, uncontrolled flight of Dorcha, often wreaking havoc.

wildstones. Stones from the innards of a white deer, used to draw poison from wounds.

wood wroth. Excessively angry, mad. [see *Le Morte d'Arthur* Book XXI, Chap. IV]

wyrd. Fate, destiny.

Acknowledgements

First thanks go to the two wolves I adopted: Matsi of the Sawtooth Mountain, ID, wolf pack and Cherokee White Rose at Wolf Sanctum, Bakersville, NC. I got to meet and touch White Rose but, alas, Matsi had died by the time I made it to the Wolf Education & Research Center, Winchester, ID, final home of the Sawtooth pack. Getting to learn from Jeremy Heft, biologist and Sanctuary Director of WERC, and Liz Mahaffey, Director of Wolf Sanctum, inspired me. Other research visits included the Grizzly & Wolf Discovery Center in West Yellowstone, MT, and Wolf Park, Battleground, IN. Add to that the happy meetings with Rob Grudger, wildlife biologist and Wolf Education Program Director, Maggie Valley, NC, and his wolves. Again, I experienced the rare privilege of touching a wolf. All these wild and semi-wild wolves taught me a unique perspective on tolerance and respect. Many thanks to all the wolves' skilled and attentive caretakers.

Numerous published resources on wildlife and environment helped me create reality-based albeit fantasy wolves and their world. Especially noteworthy are Barry Lopez's *Of Wolves and Men* and the works of legendary Jim and Jamie Dutcher who lived with and documented the Sawtooth pack: *The Sawtooth Wolves* (with Richard Ballantine), *The Hidden Life of Wolves,* and *Living with Wolves*. Additional resources include Liz Bromford's, *The Complete Wolf*; Ken Long's, *Wolves: A Wildlife Handbook*; Leonard Lee Rue III's, *Wolves*; and Candace Savage's, *Wolves* and *The World of Wolves*.

Creating the milieu of Lisnafaer necessitated consulting other resources. Those of special help include: William Anderson's *Green Man: The Archetype of our Oneness with the Earth;* Katharine Briggs' *An Encyclopedia of Fairies;* Matt Cartmill's A *View to a Death in the Morning: Hunting and Nature through History; The Columcille Celtic Calendar;* Hugh Fife's *Warriors and Guardians: Native Highland Trees;* Jane Gifford's *The Wisdom of Trees: Mysteries, Magic, and Medicine;* Kim Long's *Wolves: A Wildlife Handbook;* Fitzroy Maclean's *Highlanders: A History of The Scottish Clans;* Ed. Beverly Moon's *An Encyclopedia of Archetypal Symbolism;* Paul Ramsay's *Lochs & Glens of Scotland;* and Kenny Taylor's *Scotland's Nature and Wildlife.*

Membership in the Arbor Day Society, Defenders of Wildlife, the Greater Cincinnati Friends of Jung, the National Park Association, and the Sierra Club helped immensely.

The Independence Inklings and the Southeastern Writers Association offered guidance and constructive criticism while the Covington Writers Group gave helpful publishing advice. Thank you.

John Patrick, John Patrick Illustrations, created the splendid cover art, and Matthew and Terry Patrick, Paradrome Press, provided invaluable technical expertise. Mike Wiseman (www.gwydian.com), webmaster/designer of my Moving Mountains website also created the map of Lisnafaer (see: www.lnpassmore.com). A special thanks to you all.

For help with the arcana of light I thank physicist/educator Ted Spickler, author of *Gaining Insight Through Tacit Knowledge.* Commander Mike Alverson, USN (Ret) former Navy Bandmaster and Director of Music, The Citadel, shared vital insight on music and song (Sonsie adores Mike Alverson).

Loyal friends sustained me, their insight always helpful. Thank you Chris and Ed, Rita and Mike, Joyce and Bob, Dana and Mike, Soledad and Barry, Carol and Stephen, Sally, Cathy, Linda, Karen, Keitha, Alvena, Brenda, Kamellia, Monica, Tom, Holly, Sandra, and Roberta.

Above all, to my husband, Dan. Sweet Love, through all the highs and lows, you always believed in me and my wolves. Thank you.

About the Author

As soon as she could walk, L. N. Passmore toddled into the sea. At age six she got lost in the woods, perfect for communing with tree spirits and departed ancestors. No wonder living in the Appalachians made forested mountains--filled with secret music and light—her muse. Beloved cats, dogs, and a Morgan-quarter horse became wise teachers.

L. N. has lived, worked, and traveled all over USA: from the Atlantic Coast to Alaska, the Navajo Nation in Arizona, and Appalachia--north and south, urban and rural; in the UK: from John o' Groats to Land's End. When first sighting the Highlands, she found a home new to her eyes but not her soul. Exploring Skye, Fingal's cave on Staffa, Mull, and Iona, where the veil between worlds is thin, awakened her Irish heritage and revealed the truth of Old Powers.

Other adventures include walking from the rim of the Grand Canyon down the Kaibab Trail to the Colorado River and back up the Bright Angel Trail, camping overnight in the Canyon; earning an open water SCUBA license; and taking an overnight horseback ride in the mountains of Medicine Bow National Forest, WY.

Visit her website Moving Mountains at www.lnpassmore.com to read more, including Tales from Appalachia and Tales from Lisnafaer. Read her "Mayhem with a Beer Chaser," and "How Bright Eye Became Sky-Wulf," in *Anthology 2016*, Covington Writers Group, available through amazon.com.

Praise for *Wayward Wulves Beware*

"What a great read, like *Watership Down* with fangs and claws. Who knew wolves lead such exciting lives? I recommend *Wayward Wulves Beware* as much for the richly detailed wolf lore as the thrilling hazards confronting Kalar and Sonsie."

Rick Robinson, author of *Writ of Mandamus,* Grand Prize Winner at the London Book Festival and *Manifest Destiny,* Best Fiction at the Paris and New York Book Festivals and honored as the 2010 Independent Book of the Year.

▲ ▲ ▲

"Any good story that moves us deeply carries a patterned way of increasing our consciousness. L.N. Passmore's engaging and instructive narrative, *Wayward Wulves Beware, Book I of the Eye of the Wulf Series,* imbeds us in a complex myth that includes animal, human and natural worlds. Its energy is palpable, because this intricate plot has the capacity to "move us" to a new way of understanding the interconnected webbing of all parts of the created order and the conflicts that arise when disharmony struggles to prevail. I came away from reading it with a new sense of the power of myth to shape consciousness itself through the presence of archetypal constants that shape our imaginations. What a journey the two young wulf brothers, Kalar and Sonsie take us on. I recommend this finely crafted novel to all who seek the mythic subplot behind our world's unfolding story."

Dennis Patrick Slattery, Ph.D., author of *Riting Myth, Mythic Writing* and *Bridge Work: Essays on Mythology, Literature and Psychology.*

᠕ ᠕ ᠕

"*Wayward Wulves Beware* has a timeless, folklore feel to it. I highly recommend it for fans of *Watership Down.*"
Dee Garretson, author of *Wolf Storm* and *Wolf Ridge.*

᠕ ᠕ ᠕

"Richly imagined, deftly written, Passmore's inventive tale *Wayward Wulves Beware* will provide hours of pleasurable reading and leave you wanting more."
Gillian Summers, author of *The Faire Folk Saga: The Fair Folk Trilogy and The Scions of Shadow Trilogy.*

Made in the USA
Columbia, SC
15 March 2018